P2
4

W9-AEV-925

1977

Research Center
Wisconsin Veterans Museum
30 West Mifflin Street
Madison, Wisconsin 53703
Ph: (608) 267-1790

DISCARDED

Kramer's War

Also by Derek Robinson
Goshawk Squadron
Rotten with Honour

Derek Robinson

Kramer's War

THE VIKING PRESS   NEW YORK

For Alan and Jan

Copyright © Derek Robinson, 1977

All rights reserved

First published in 1977 by The Viking Press
625 Madison Avenue, New York, N.Y. 10022

Published simultaneously in Canada by
The Macmillan Company of Canada Limited

LIBRARY OF CONGRESS CATALOGING IN PUBLICATION DATA
Robinson, Derek, 1932 (Apr. 12)—
   Kramer's war.
   I. Title.
PZ4.R6617Kr3 [PR6068.01954]   823'.9'14   76-51776
ISBN 0-670-41516-2

Printed in the United States of America

Set in Videocomp Times Roman

Acknowledgment is made to United Artists Music Publishing Group, Inc., for the
lyrics on page 49 from "Chattanooga Choo-Choo" by Mack Gordon and Harry
Warren. Copyright © 1941 Twentieth Century Music Corporation. Rights
throughout the world controlled by Leo Feist, Inc.

FRIDAY NIGHT

1

Earl Kramer was wet and cold and his fingers felt as if they belonged to someone else.

He lay curled up in the rubber dinghy with his knees at his chest and his hands between his thighs. Rain collected in the hollows of his body and lay there, coldly absorbent, until his body suddenly rebelled and shuddered, shaking the water loose. He curled up again and at once the rain began to refill the hollows.

His head lay on the slick, rubberized canvas. From time to time a long swell eased under the dinghy, heaved it high and slipped away with an empty hiss. Earl Kramer felt these swells throb remotely past his head and ear, but he saw nothing. Rain drained out of the night and made a soft black screen all around.

He wondered where the hell he was. It could be anywhere. They must have been hundreds of miles off course when the Liberator ditched. Flak had smashed the instrument panel while they were still over Frankfurt, and then the engines began to quit on the way home. In and out of cloud, dodging fighters. Dusk before they ran out of fuel. The navigator said he thought it was the North Sea. Whatever it was, he was at the bottom of it now, poor bastard. When the Liberator hit the water and came to pieces, Earl Kramer was the lucky one. By the time he'd swum to the dinghy and crawled in, the bomber had gone and the rest of the crew with it.

The damn dinghy was filling up again. He felt water lap over his lower knee. He ought to bail, but then his hands would get cold, so he kept them between his thighs. Not yet. Let it get a bit higher. The flap of his ear was tucked under his head and his pulse beat into the cold canvas. Rain collected on his nose until a drop fell on his lip. He counted the pulsebeats between falling drops. Seven. Nine. Seven again. A stray current slowly turned the dinghy. His body shuddered and dislodged the icy little pools, but it was a much weaker shudder than before.

Now that was new. That was different. Earl Kramer thought back to all those survival-technique lectures. Sir, how long does it take a man to die of exposure? A fit young man? *That's an interesting question, Lieutenant. Can you supply further data, such as where this exposure is taking place . . . ?*

God damn this lousy dinghy. It was really filling up bad. Why can't they put drain-holes in the bottom? Typical Air Force foul-up. . . . Oh Christ: you don't want to be sick again, do you?

Earl Kramer forgot the water sloshing around his body and studied the unhappy prisoner inside him, a miserable bastard who once in a while tried to retch up something that wasn't there any more. Lie still, buddy. You don't really want to throw up. All that bending over and choking, just for nothing. Last time, you nearly fell in the sea, remember? Take it easy, buddy.

The dinghy stopped.

Immediately, the sea got annoyed and began tugging and heaving, working to jostle it free. The swell was stronger now that it had an argument. It rocked and wheeled the dinghy, thumped it, dumped waves in it, rolled Kramer about until he had to grab the rope handles.

Damn dinghy. Don't make 'em like they used to. Hellish uncomfortable. Lump sticking up in the floor. Right in the ass. Lousy sea's full of lumps. Don't make sea like they used to. Oh Christ, look out, another wave. . . .

As the swell reared up, Kramer rolled onto his stomach. The shift of weight made the dinghy slide across the tip of the submerged anti-tank obstacle and rammed its inflated ring onto the spike. Air galloped out, and he felt the tense canvas yield under his fingers. Unhurriedly, the boat collapsed and lowered him into the water. It was shockingly cold.

For a few seconds he clung to the wreckage, but the sea lunged and searched for his mouth, and the cold was numbing his body. He let go and swam. His flying boots felt like sewer-pipe, so he stopped using his legs and just thrashed with his arms. That was exhausting. His boots dragged his legs down until he was upright in the water, flapping his arms and straining with his chin, gasping. Waves washed over his head. Everything was a terr:ic effort. He had to rest. He couldn't go on. He deserved a rest. It was time to rest. . . .

His knee banged on a hot and violent rock, and the pain made him struggle. His boot kicked the rock, and as the next swell arrived he lunged for it and got a foot on top. The swell sucked him off, but he swam back and planted both feet. He was only chest-deep.

As he rested, he saw other rocks outlined against the weak phosphorescence. They were slimy with weed, a ropelike mass that slipped under his boots. But the beach shelved fast: he climbed clear of the sea in ten dragging steps. He lay face-down on the pebbles and listened to the rattling shuffle of the surf and thanked God he was here, wherever that was.

At the top of the beach he found a cliff. He patted the rockface and blinked up into the wet night. This could be Norway, Denmark, Holland, France, or Belgium. It could be Germany. It could even be England. It could also be mined.

If he waited here until daylight he might freeze to death. Or get captured. If he began wandering along the beach he might blow himself to bits.

At least death would be warm. He had to get warm. Under his soaking shirt his body was shuddering and cowering, trying to get inside itself. His feet were numb. He dragged off his flying boots and massaged his toes. They moved stiffly, like old piano keys. When he emptied his boots the survival knife fell out of its sheath, sewn to the leg of the right boot. He put the knife back and remembered his pistol. There ought to be a pistol in a holster on his belt. He found the holster twisted around behind him. The pistol was very wet. He tried to point it at something, but he couldn't see anything and his arm shook with cold.

All the same, finding the weapons made him feel better. Now that he had a knife and a gun he was in better shape for walking through mine-fields. He set off. Then he came back and put on his boots and set off again.

He wanted to keep close to the cliff but he kept walking into boulders which forced him to edge down onto the beach, where the mines would be. After ten minutes of cautious shuffling he was knee-deep in seawater again. Either the beach had vanished or the cliff had fallen into the sea or some damn thing.

He stood with his forelock dripping into his eyes and tried to see a shape or a skyline, anything; but the night and the rain cancelled everything. He turned and trudged back, no longer shuffling. The sand sucked at his boots and seaweed kept hooking itself around his ankles. He got sick of stopping to unhook the weed. Next time it happened he kicked out, tripped, and fell headlong.

For a while he lay, thinking *Jesus Christ, if there is a goddam mine anywhere on this beach I'm going to find it if I have to crash around all night.* Running water was splashing over his fingers, running down the beach. A stream.

He got up and followed it to a gap in the cliff. The stream-bed was steep and twisting: he had to clamber on his hands and knees. Water bustled over his fingers and pebbles scrambled away from his boots. His legs were bruised and greasy with mud, and still the hillside climbed invisibly and forever into the soaking blackness. When at last he groped and heaved himself over the top, he lay on his back, panting. Rain fell into his mouth; crimson and purple discs kept expanding inside his eyeballs. The taste of sickness revisited his throat. Earl Kramer was cold and exhausted and lost, and nobody cared.

2

The navigation lights appeared diffused and haloed by the drifting rain, hanging in the night like flares. They seemed to approach slowly and then gather speed. The runway lights came on, and the aircraft sideslipped a few feet into their dim glow. It was a Junkers 52, sturdy, capable, pig-snouted. Its three wheels touched down and raced ahead of three soft plumes of spray.

The plane taxied over to the control tower and stopped. First out was a boxer dog, frenzied with freedom. It bounced ecstatic circles around the guard of honour and chased after the officer who walked across to the aircraft steps. Next out was General Rimmer.

The officer saluted. "Good evening, General. I'm Major Wolff. I was adjutant to General Gebhardt."

"What a shame," Rimmer said. "Such a loss. And him only seventy-three. Well, you're my adjutant now."

He strode past the guard of honour, looking at their eyes and not their uniforms, and halted in front of the last one. The soldier was eighteen at most, bespectacled and lanky. Even when he stood at attention his knees were slightly bent. Rimmer pulled the bayonet from the man's belt and thumbed the edge. "Gardening going well, is it?" he asked. "Got your potatoes in early, I see."

The soldier's lips parted but he had no answer.

"Get that weapon razor-sharp, lad," Rimmer ordered. "If you can't shave with it you can't kill with it." He dropped it into the soldier's greatcoat pocket, and snapped his fingers. "Come, Dum-Dum." Rimmer, Wolff, and the dog got into a car.

"Congratulations on your appointment, sir," Wolff said as they drove away.

Rimmer found a hair misbehaving inside his right nostril and jerked it out.

"General Gebhardt was so awfully fit, sir," Wolff said. "The news of his heart attack came as a great shock."

"Gebhardt didn't have a heart attack, he had heart failure. He stopped a large rocket in the small of the back. A Mosquito strafed his car." Rimmer sneezed, and startled Dum-Dum. "But you're right: officially it's heart failure. What's your big problem here?"

Major Wolff glanced across. Rimmer's eyebrows were turned down in a small but permanent frown; the corners of his mouth were turned up, but in determination, not humour; he hunched his shoulders and thrust his head as if seeking challenge. "I'm very sorry to hear about General Gebhardt," Wolff said. "And I don't think we have any really big problem here, sir."

"Oh no. There never is any big problem. They told me the same story when I went to Greece, Italy, Poland, Russia, Yugoslavia. No problem here, General. Just partisans and resistance and saboteurs and spies everywhere. But no problem. Oh no."

"Things are different here, General."

"Different, are they? I've heard that before, too. Things are always different. Well, I'm not. I stick to the tried and true formula."

"What's that, General?"

Rimmer reached out a foot and rubbed Dum-Dum's stomach. "Retaliate first," he said.

Earl Kramer had lost the stream but he had found a wall.

It carried a five-strand barbed-wire fence planted on top of it. The whole thing stood about nine feet high. He couldn't climb over it and he hadn't the strength to break through it. He plucked at the second strand and stared. It looked like a lane on the other side.

He turned right and started walking. The ground was flat, so he stepped out confidently, keeping an arm's-length from the wall, until he tripped and landed on his face. Tears of pain and frustration came. He got up slowly and spat out bits of grass. He found the wire strut and gave it a kick. Its twang faded to a buzz which died as his fingers followed the strut to a steel post on the wall.

It marked a join in the wire. Eye-bolts held the ends on either side. He took out his knife, probed for the end of the lowest strand and levered it open. The wire was wet and tough and awkward but he persisted, standing in the rain like a blind man and swearing softly when the points spiked his fingers. At last he tugged the end clear and flung it away. It rattled softly on the roadway.

The second wire fought more stubbornly. Its end was needle-sharp and guarded by a cluster of barbs. It had a springy resistance to change. His hands were raked and scored before the first, crucial inch gave way, but the pain strengthened his obstinacy. When he got both hands on the wire it unwound more easily. A light flashed somewhere to his right.

Earl Kramer stood motionless, blinking at the blackness. A car? Too small. Maybe a distant car, then. With one headlamp? Okay, a motorcycle. Or a nearby flashlight. Or a very nearby cigarette lighter.

He held his breath and listened to the sigh and spatter of the rain. Slowly his stomach muscles relaxed. He turned back to the wire and carefully fed the corkscrewed end through the eye. He tried to throw the strand away, but it recoiled and slapped him on the arm, so he pulled it towards him and tucked it down against the wall. Now the gap was big enough for his head and shoulders. He smelled fresh tarmac. The light flashed again.

Kramer ducked. The light was a flashlight and it was coming up the lane. He crouched against the wall and thought about retreating down the hillside. Too risky, too noisy; better to stay here and let the flashlight go past. Sit tight and wait. For God's sake don't sneeze.

Heavy, unhurried footsteps approached. Occasionally they sent a stone skittering, or scraped a heelplate. Kramer squatted with his arms around his legs and his mouth pressed against a knee, and listened. The man passed the gap in the fence, and tramped on. Then he walked into the loose strand of wire.

Kramer heard a muttered exclamation, followed by scuffing and kicking and more muttering. The flashlight clicked on. Rain flickered across its aura and the beam swung to the fence above the wall. Kramer twisted his head to watch, and his toes curled as the beam found the half-empty post.

That discovery brought a grunt of surprise. Kramer edged away from the hole and found that he was dragging the other wire with him: it was hooked in his trousers. He tried to rip it loose, and made it worse.

The man came over to the post. He flashed his beam into the night, sketchily, as if he didn't expect to find anything, and found nothing. He placed the flashlight on top of the wall so that it lit up the post. He found the loose wire and brought it into the pool of light. He was a German soldier.

Earl Kramer stared up, stiff with cold and fright. That ugly coal-scuttle helmet, that grey greatcoat with the crazy eagle on the top, that damn great rifle: this bastard was a typical Nazi. Heavy face, big jowls, squinty eyes. Probably shot and looted his way all over Europe. He had a bayonet somewhere, and probably a couple of hand grenades too. A lousy sadistic fascist bastard. Kramer felt for his knife.

The German wrapped the wire around the eye-bolt and went along the wall, looking for the other wire. Kramer twisted desperately and felt the barbs rip loose from his trousers. He rolled away just as the German began pulling. The wire scraped over the wall and then stopped, caught somewhere. Kramer reached out and fumbled for the snag, while the German shook the wire. It wouldn't come. The German tugged and jerked, grunting with effort, while Kramer scrabbled at the stonework. Still it was jammed.

The German took a rest. Kramer prayed that the son of a bitch would give up and go. The German decided on one more try. He spread his elbows on the wall and leaned over to find out what the problem was. Earl Kramer saw the thrusting, armoured head and sprang at it. He grabbed its greatcoat collar and stabbed and stabbed in the back of the neck; stabbed and stabbed until Kramer was gasping for breath and the German was quite dead and too heavy for him to hold. The body folded at the knees and slid down its own side, leaving its helmet lodged against the wire.

Automatically, Kramer took the helmet. He stood with the steaming knife in one hand and the warm helmet in the other, panting, and blinking at the glow from the flashlight. It signalled the death, at the age of thirty-seven, of 32378196 Private Wilhelm Keller, B Company, 4th Battalion, 12th Regiment, 319 Division, German Army, while carrying out his six hundred and forty-eighth guard patrol. Private Keller, who left a wife and three children, was sadly missed by the guard commander, but not for another forty-five minutes.

3

General Rimmer came into the middle of the coffee lounge of the Hotel Bristol and looked around. In one corner three lieutenants and a captain stood stiffly beside a bridge table. "Very pretty, Dum-Dum," Rimmer said.

"Your suite is on the second floor, sir," Major Wolff said. "It faces the sea."

"Charming, I'm sure. When you've seen one sea you've seen them all. What's wrong with my operational headquarters?"

"There's not much more than a bunk and a washbasin over there, general."

"Whereas this place is like an overpriced Turkish brothel. Who lives here anyway?"

"Distinguished visitors. And Count Limner and his wife."

Rimmer walked over to the card table. "You mean the show-jumping Limners? How fascinating." He began turning over the hands of cards. "Send for them."

"Count Limner is Head of Civil Administration, General. He doesn't come under your authority." Wolff watched Rimmer stroll around the table. "In any case, he and his wife are out."

Rimmer nodded absently. He gave each hand a final glance, and pointed to the captain. "You win," he said. "Good night." The officers picked up their hats and went out. "We shall wait for the celebrated Limners," Rimmer said.

They arrived twenty minutes later, laughing. Count Limner was tall and lean, with thick grey hair and sleepy brown eyes looking out cautiously over a much-broken nose. With his tweed jacket, dark grey flannel trousers and cane, he had an easy elegance which made Rimmer look like an infantryman—and this despite the fact that Limner's left shoe carried a built-up sole two inches thick.

His wife wore a green silk dress under a white cardigan, with a raincoat over her shoulders. Her hand was tucked inside her husband's arm, and her head rested on his shoulder so that thick brown hair hid one eye. The other eye blinked lazily and lustrously. Count Limner and his wife were a little drunk.

Major Wolff performed the introductions. Nobody offered to shake hands. Rimmer made a small bow to the countess.

"Is it true that Gebhardt's dead?" she asked.

"A heart attack. While visiting France, you know. Quite sudden."

"Out of the blue," Major Wolff said.

"Thank you, Major, you may go," Rimmer told him.

"How very sad," she said.

"It was sudden, he didn't suffer. This is a great personal pleasure, Count. I was an admirer in your show-jumping days. Tell me: why was it you withdrew from the German team in the Berlin Olympics?"

Wolff paused at the doorway.

"Let's say I felt a bit lopsided," Limner said. He tapped his left shoe with his cane. "And those Olympics were sufficiently lopsided already."

"I understood that your riding accident took place in 1937. *After* the Olympics."

"Let's say I had a premonition."

"That would be very curious."

"Yes, let's say it was very curious."

Maria Limner swung her hair back and revealed a long smile that curled up on the right and dipped down on the left. "Michael has second sight, General," she said. "For instance, he knows what's going to happen to you. Don't you, darling?"

Limner screwed his face into a grimace of effort. He looked Rimmer up and down. "No," he said.

"He does, really," she said. "He's just too sleepy to try."

"A tiring evening?" Rimmer asked.

"Been playing bridge," Limner said. "With the de Wildes. Too good for us. We lost."

"The de Wildes?" Rimmer said. "Who are they?"

"He's what they call the Bailiff. He really runs the show around here."

Rimmer squared his shoulders. "That is no longer the case," he said firmly. "I run the show around here, Count. Let me make the situation crystal-clear." He handed Limner a piece of paper. "This is my appointment as Fortress Commandant, signed as you can see by the Fuehrer. I am flattered that he chose me. When invasion comes, we shall be the vanguard. I have given my personal oath that the enemy will be flung into the sea or we shall fight and die to the last man. Here we defend not just the coast of Europe but the whole future of the

Third Reich, and that is an honour and a responsibility I am not prepared to hand over to your Mr. de Wilde, who will do exactly what I tell him or blood will flow."

"Goodness gracious," Maria Limner said. "You do feel strongly, General."

"I speak as I see, Countess."

"Well, but things are rather different here," Limner said. "Let's say you and I and de Wilde will work things out."

"Let's say he'll do as he's told."

"Let's say nobody will wish to do anything foolish."

"Let's say good night," Maria Limner said. "Before the lights go out." Rimmer cocked his head. "The power supply is rationed," she explained.

"Ah," he said. "I thought for a moment you might mean sabotage."

"Dear me, no," she said. "We haven't had a case of sabotage since General Gebhardt's horse misbehaved itself during a parade for Hitler's birthday."

Rimmer reclaimed his written appointment from Count Limner's hand. "I believe I know how the beast felt," he said. "There are times when we all take more than we can stomach. Good night to you both."

The shaking was so bad that Earl Kramer had to tense his body to make it do things. If he stood still he began to feel dizzy from the fever of excitement racing around his brain; but when he moved, everything was very slow. It took him a long time to reopen the wire and get through the hole, and all the time, his memory was liable to release one of those frantic glimpses of a right fist, stabbing and stabbing: at first frantic with fear, and then frantic with triumph.

Kramer sat on the road in the rain until he heard his teeth chattering. He made himself get on his feet and walk over to the light. He found the loose wires and took them back and laced them up. The exercise calmed him and helped to control the trembling. He made a good job of the wire, tugging it tight and winding the ends to the last inch. It looked neat and secure. Earl Kramer, the local wire expert.

He shone the flashlight on the dead German. The body lay on its side, knees bent, one arm under the bald head. Kramer was surprised: Nazi soldiers shouldn't be bald. He got hold of the wrists and pulled. The body rolled onto its back, and the fingers flickered wetly against his forearms. He let go. Where the hell was he taking it?

On the other side of the road a field stretched into the night. Kramer walked into it, looking for anything: a barn, a haystack, a woodpile. Nothing. He turned back and fell into a trench, half-full of water. "Come off it, God!" he shouted hoarsely. He climbed out and sat on the edge and looked at the hole. "Okay, God, I get the idea," he said.

He got the body under the armpits and hauled it across the grass. The German rolled into the trench with a mighty splash. One of his boots had come off. Kramer found it and threw it in. The boot needed mending. For the first time Kramer shone the flashlight on the dead man's face. It was a night-shift face, tired and lined and ready for rest. Kramer dropped the rifle down the side of the trench, carefully, so as not to hit the face. Earth lay alongside in a smooth, weathered hump. He kicked it in. By the time the trench was full the rain was already at work, smoothing and blending. Kramer felt better now. Maybe it hadn't really happened after all.

He turned his back on the grave and walked inland. He knew what he had to do. He had to find the Underground Railway and go to Spain.

Large, soft, white discs kept appearing in the night. They vanished when the rain in his eyes made him blink. Then they appeared again. The funny thing was they didn't light up anything.

Kramer stumbled on a hunk of grass or something and his knees went wobbly, so he stopped. He seemed all empty inside. No warmth anywhere. Hollow belly, shaky shoulders, cold all over. Shaky all over. Better start walking again. Here come those damn lights.

He tried to swat them with the flashlight. It swung stiffly and slowly, and he nearly fell over. The lights in his head streaked and blurred and changed colour: shimmering blues, dappled mauves. Mustn't fall over. Got to keep walking. Mustn't use the flash. Good reason for that, goddam good reason. What? Can't remember. Had it just now. Gone again.

Oh yes. Got to find the Underground Railway and go to Spain. Long long long long way. Mustn't waste the light. Save the light to find the Underground and get on their little old Railway to Spain. That's what all the survival lectures said. Okay then. Keep walking. How many more fields? Christ, what a night. Jesus Christ, what a day and a night. Goddam shakes are getting worse. Just don't fall down. Please don't fall down.

A dog howled.

Kramer stopped and got his thumb working and switched on the flashlight. He saw a hedge, a gate. A sack. Faded printing. *Agricole,* it said. And *Pureté Garantie.* He turned it over. Address in Cherbourg. Well well. So this was France. Well well well. Lot of rain in France. Very wet country. Wet and cold.

He opened the gate and saw a house. The dog howled again. It sounded angry. Maybe it was a German dog. Maybe it belonged to the dead sentry. Maybe the house was full of Gestapo. He went up to the front door and knocked. The dog howled more loudly.

An upstairs window opened and a woman called: "Who's there?" Kramer shone the light on her. She was elderly, with curly white hair, worn long. *"Pardonnez-moi, madame,"* he said.

"Don't point that thing at me!" she cried. Kramer swung it away. He thought, *What's the French for "I'm sorry"?*

A man replaced the woman. "What the bloody hell d'you want?" he demanded.

"Voulez-vous . . ." Kramer began. That wasn't right. *"S'il vous plaît . . ."* No, that didn't lead anywhere either. "Um," he said.

"Here, let's have a look at you, Charlie," the man said. "Shine that lamp on your face." Kramer dazzled himself. "My God, Mary," the man said. "It's a drunk bloody German."

"Non, non, monsieur," Kramer said. *"Je ne suis pas* drunk. *Je ne suis pas* German." As he peered upwards the big German helmet slipped from his head and crashed onto the flagstones. He picked it up. "Did you drop this?" he asked.

Bolts slid. The door opened. The farmer held up a candle. He was wearing a raincoat over his pyjamas. "Who the hell are you anyway?" he asked.

"Moi," Kramer said, "Kramer, Lieutenant Earl Kramer."

"D'you speak English, or don't you?"

"Oui, oui. But *je parle . . .* um *. . . votre* language, too."

The farmer leaned out and took stock. He saw a white face in which the eyes were slowly closing and the mouth slowly opening. The shoulders were dragged down and the body swayed as if seeking something to lean against. The arms hung slackly and the feet in the flying boots were pigeon-toed from weariness. The farmer thought, *He could be a Jerry deserter, or a spy, or French Resistance, though how the hell he got here . . . Perhaps he's a Commando, but . . .*

"Louis!" his wife called down the stairs, "Send him away before he gets us all shot."

"Come on, come on," the farmer growled at him. "What d'you want?"

Kramer thought hard. "Railway," he said. "Underground Railway. To Spain."

"You daft bugger," the farmer said. Then his candle went flying as Kramer fainted across the doorstep.

They were climbing. They had to be climbing, because of the backward tilt. Also he could hear a steady buzzing. Nice regular climb, no turbulence, no vibration, must be through the clouds and into delicious warm sunshine, flickering across his eyelids. Beautifully warm. Wonderfully quiet flight, apart from that crackling. Just a quiet crackle. Sometimes a hiss or pop, but mainly crackle. Probably radio static. Funny smell, though. Sharp. Tangy. Can't be static. Must be the sunshine. The crackly sunshine. . . .

The whiff and crackle of burning grew stronger. Earl Kramer opened his eyes and saw fire: *The plane was on fire!* He tried to get up but hands held him down, he struggled and shouted in protest. Then a grandfather clock chimed.

Kramer turned his head and saw the clock standing next to a mantelpiece. It chimed again, with a sound like faded chintz. He looked farther and saw white walls, black curtains, an old deep-buttoned leather couch.

"You're alive, then." The farmer's voice did not celebrate the fact. "Drink this."

Kramer tried to reach out but he was wrapped in blankets. He got an arm free, and took the heavy tumbler. The arm was bare. Under the blankets he was naked. He drank some of the pale brown liquid and felt it lead a torchlight procession down his throat.

"Wow!" he whispered. The big old cane chair creaked as he stretched again.

Behind him, the farmer's wife said, "I tell you he'll get us all shot."

"In that case, shot is what we'll all get," the farmer replied.

"He comes crashing around here in the middle of the night. No consideration for others."

"D'you want him put back out there in that weather?"

"I never wanted him brought in here in the first place."

"He wasn't *brought in*, for God's sake! He collapsed."

"He'll get us all shot, you see."

Kramer felt the tingling of warmth reach all the cold, forgotten

ends of his body. He rippled his toes, slowly, in the heat of the fire.
He felt good. He wanted to thank somebody. He said, "I don't want
to put you folks to any trouble."

"No trouble," she said. "You'll get us all shot, that's all."

"Mary, hold your tongue," the farmer said. "What happened to
you?" he asked Kramer.

"My plane ditched in the sea. I got washed up in the dinghy."
Kramer sipped the liquor. "I guess I was pretty damn lucky to end
up here, eh? I mean, you speaking such good English and all."

"I ought to. I've spoken it all my life." He said this with such
finality that Kramer was silenced. He stared at his clothes, steaming
on the iron fender, and tried to make sense of it all. "Look," he said,
"straighten me out. This is France, right?"

"Not on your bloody life."

"He doesn't even know where he is." The farmer's wife sniffed.

"This is Jersey, chum," the farmer said. "Part of the Channel Isles.
We're all British here, except for about forty thousand German soldiers, and how you got through them without being shot I shall never
know."

"We're British, we are," his wife said. "Loyal subjects of King
George the Sixth." She pointed to a colour photograph on the wall.

"Jersey," Kramer said. "Gee . . . Where's England?"

"Ninety miles north of here," the farmer said. "That's the English
Channel you were floating in."

Kramer finished his drink and tried to remember the map of northern Europe. "How far to France?" he asked.

"Twenty miles. You can see it, on a good day. If you want to."

"My gosh. So I'm not really in Europe . . . but I'm not in England,
either. I'm in Jersey, a place I never even heard of before. Crazy."

"Glad you think so."

"I mean . . . it's crazy that you're all English but you're so far from
England."

"Well, you Yanks have got Hawaii, haven't you?"

Kramer stared into the fire and tried to accept the contradictions
of being in Occupied England, on the edge of France. "Well I'll be
damned," he said.

"You're not the only one," the farmer's wife said. She began turning over Kramer's clothes. "Are you feeling any better?"

"He's not going anywhere yet," her husband said sharply. "Look
at him, he's done in. D'you want to give him pneumonia?"

"He seems strong enough to me." She moved his trousers. "Anyway, he ought to be in hospital. There's blood all over the place. He's cut himself somewhere."

"I didn't see any cuts," the farmer said. His wife held up the trousers: the legs were caked and streaked with blood. "Crikey!" he said. "You hurt yourself, son? Cut your legs?"

Kramer felt himself under the blankets. "No. Just a few scratches from the barbed wire." He showed them his hands.

"You can't tell me that's not fresh blood," she said. "I've killed enough pigs in my time. Get him down to the hospital."

The farmer took the trousers and stood frowning at the stain. "You sure there isn't anybody else out there?"

Kramer shook his head. "I never even saw what happened to the rest of the crew." He put his hands inside and pulled the blankets snugly around his neck. "I guess I went one way and they went the other."

There was a short silence.

"Still and all," the farmer said, "you don't find a great gob of blood like this without someone's hurt. It *is* blood, isn't it? Not something you spilt in the aeroplane?"

Kramer leaned forward. "Oh," he said emptily. "That." They waited, puzzled and worried by his toneless voice. "See . . . I reckon I must have forgotten about that, because—" He studied the stain unhappily. It spread all over the inside of the legs, just where his knees and thighs had knocked and rubbed against the German's blood-soaked head and neck. He kept staring, not wishing to raise his face, to meet their eyes.

The farmer began: "How—"

"I killed a German sentry," Kramer said fast.

The farmer's wife screamed, shortly and faintly.

"God save us all," the farmer breathed.

"I had to. It was him or me," Kramer said flatly. "I didn't want to. He made me."

"A German murdered," the farmer said. "Oh my sweet suffering Christ." He sat down and reached for the bottle.

"A murderer," his wife said, "sitting in my own chair."

"I'm not a murderer, goddammit! There's a war on, he was an enemy soldier. Holy Moses, don't you think he'd have killed me, if he could?"

The farmer threw Kramer's trousers in the fire. It received them with a long and angry hiss. "If the Germans found you wearing those, you'd be a murderer all right and no mistake. God Almighty ... What in hell's name are we going to do now?"

Kramer lurched to his feet. "Give me some clothes. Let me out of here." He stood up too quickly: the blood pounded away from his brain, and the farmer's words reached him feebly, across a great gulf.

"You're going to need a lot more than clothes to help you survive, boy. For a start, it's curfew now. Anyone they see wandering around at night gets a bullet. Come daylight you might manage on your own, except you've got no money, no papers, no ration cards, and even the Jerries can tell you're no Jerseyman."

"I don't care. I'll escape."

"Where? This is an island, sonny. Nine miles long, five miles wide. The only way off is by boat. *German* boat."

Kramer sat down. He felt very, very tired. "I don't want to cause any trouble," he mumbled. "Maybe I'd better just go surrender."

The farmer scoffed. "In civilian clothes? They'd shoot you for a spy. They'd shoot us too."

"I told you so," his wife said.

Kramer put his head in his hands. "Oh Christ," he said. He was near to tears.

"It's too late to tell you now," the farmer said, "but you couldn't have got yourself into a worse spot if you'd personally bit Adolf Hitler on the arse."

"And for heaven's sake cover yourself up," his wife added. Kramer fumbled with the blankets. "Get us all shot, you will," she said.

SATURDAY

4

General Rimmer was up by six o'clock, and by six-fifteen he was having breakfast on the balcony of his room. The rain had gone with the night, the sea was calm, and the sky was a soft, serene cornflower-blue. Over Normandy the sun came up like a benediction. Rimmer turned his chair to face it and he felt its early warmth on his bare arms. Around and below him, the buildings and the streets were washed spotless for his inspection. Rimmer drank his coffee and allowed himself to feel a certain pride of ownership. It looked like a good day ahead.

Major Wolff came through the french windows and saluted. "Good morning, sir," he said.

"Hullo, Wolff. Splendid day, isn't it? Bright and early, like yourself. I trust you slept well?"

"No, sir."

"Oh?" Rimmer cocked an eye. "Were there things that went bump in the night?"

"No, sir. I never sleep nowadays. In fact I haven't slept at all for the last eighteen months."

"Indeed?"

"It doesn't matter, sir."

Rimmer looked more closely at his adjutant. Wolff was small, trim and middle-aged, with honest grey eyes in a simple and sensible face. "You look very well on it, anyway," Rimmer commented.

"Once in a while I doze, sir."

"Ah."

"Just last January I had a doze, sir," Wolff said. "And before that, in September 1943."

"I see."

"The second Tuesday, I think. Late afternoon."

"Well, if you ever feel like it again, don't let me stop you. God knows, you're entitled, if anyone is. . . ." Rimmer stretched, and felt the good, clean air fill his lungs. "I saw your records, in Berlin. Would you like some coffee, or will it keep you awake?"

Wolff smiled a gentle, forgiving smile. "I'd rather have some vodka, if you don't mind, sir," he said.

"Vodka? This early?" Rimmer searched the breakfast table. "I don't seem to have any vodka."

"I do." Wolff took a slim flask from inside his tunic. "I seem to have this stuff. Made from non-vintage potatoes. It's all right provided you don't get it on your skin."

He offered the flask to Rimmer, who sniffed the contents and made his eyebrows twitch. "No wonder you don't sleep," he said.

Wolff took a long swallow and put the flask away. "At the Front, the men used to call it electric soup," he said. He smiled at nothing and declared again, lip-smackingly: "Elec-tric . . . soup. . . ."

Rimmer paused for a moment, waiting while the memories faded, and then cleared his throat. "Tell me the real story of this island, Wolff."

"Electric . . . soup . . ." Wolff repeated softly. He saw Rimmer watching him, and he put the flask away and squared his shoulders. "Oh, it's very quiet, sir," he said confidently. "Nothing ever happens here."

"That's what they said at Pearl Harbor," Rimmer remarked. He rested one foot on the balcony rail. "D'you know where I was twenty-four hours ago, Wolff? In Yugoslavia, chasing partisans around mountains, and believe me there are large numbers of both, each uglier than the other. Then suddenly the phone rang and presto! I was in Berlin. 'Go and command the Channel Islands,' the Fuehrer told me. I hadn't the faintest idea where in the world the Channel Islands were. Adriatic? Baltic? The Fuehrer led me over to a map and showed me a few specks of land, all of them within artillery range of the French coast. 'Rimmer,' the Fuehrer said to me, 'those pips are the most powerfully armoured and heavily fortified outposts of the Third Reich.' Then he pointed to the sea-channel between England and France. 'This is the throat down which the enemy must pour his invasion,' he said, 'and those are the pips on which he will choke.' "

"I'm sure the Fuehrer knows best, sir," Wolff said, "but really, it's been very quiet."

"Well, that's not going to last, obviously," Rimmer declared. "The Fuehrer wouldn't have moved me a thousand miles overnight unless he knew my experience would be needed here. The Islanders must be expecting an invasion, so they must have an underground organization set up to help it. Right?"

"The only underground work I've seen performed here is planting potatoes, sir," Wolff said.

Rimmer grunted. "But they're all British, aren't they? This is the only British soil occupied by Germany. You can't tell me they enjoy that. You can't tell me they won't ram their potatoes up the exhaust-pipes of every German fighting vehicle the moment they get the signal from London."

Wolff blinked. "I'm not sure, sir," he said. "Food is short, and a good potato is hard to find."

Rimmer stood up. "One thing I've learned: they can't fight without orders. Who leads them?"

"You've already heard about the Bailiff, Daniel de Wilde, sir," Wolff said. "That's the lot, really."

"I don't believe it. He must have rivals, deputies, enemies, political opponents. Come on, come on, I want the whole picture."

Wolff thought for a moment. "Sir, the Bailiff is a known trou-blemaker," he began. Rimmer brightened. "He makes trouble for black-marketeers, for food-hoarders, for curfew-violators, and for Is-landers who paint V-signs on walls." Rimmer's brightness was fading. Wolff went on: "But he also makes trouble for Germans who cheat, steal, insult or harass the Islanders, or who break the law in any way."

"A busy man," Rimmer observed bleakly.

"Yes, sir. I suppose he's offended nearly everybody at some time or other, and yet if you took him away I do believe the island would go to the devil in a week. Maybe less."

"What about our fortifications and defences and so on? What's his attitude there? More trouble?"

"If necessary, yes. He stands by the Islanders' legal rights at all times, sir. As Occupying Power, we're entitled to defend the island and he accepts that. But when we wanted to blow up a house in order to improve some battery commander's field-of-fire, de Wilde fought like a tiger, and in the end we left the house alone."

"I want to see that house later today," Rimmer ordered. "It sounds dangerous."

"It belongs to an electrician," Wolff said.

"I don't care if it belongs to Merlin the Magician."

"If we blow up his home, sir, he might not want to go on wiring our bunkers," Wolff said.

"Oh," Rimmer said.

"As de Wilde pointed out, we have no absolute right to destroy civilian property. Once we start, sir, where do we stop? Every house could be considered a potential obstacle and—"

"Enough." Rimmer crumbled a piece of toast and bombarded some sparrows. "He sounds like a bloody nuisance. I'm not having this man interfering with my military decisions."

"I don't think he'd ever try to do that, sir. After all, he knows the Islanders can't survive on their own. Literally, their life depends on us. All the essentials have to be imported—medicine, fuel, clothing, most of the food."

"Ah! So we've got them by the balls, then."

"Not altogether, sir. It seems that we can't run this island without their help."

"*What?* Rubbish!" General Rimmer dragged his bushy black eyebrows together in a scornful stare. "You've gone soft, Wolff! Are you trying to tell me . . . Listen, the German Army conquered eight countries in two years—d'you mean to say the Third Reich isn't competent to manage a piddling, stunted drop-in-the-ocean like Jersey? Of course we can. It's a job for two companies of engineers and a one-armed captain."

"Yes, sir."

"Not even that. One company of engineers and a half-baked lieutenant."

"Yes, sir. I can't imagine what went wrong."

"What d'you mean?" Rimmer sat down. The sun was in his eyes. He stood up.

"Well, the army tried to take over the civilian management of the island once, but they couldn't make it work. The power station broke down, the gasworks kept catching fire, and the water supply tasted very strange. There was a lot of diarrhoea, I remember. The telephones worked fairly well, except when the power station broke down."

"That's too bad to be true," Rimmer said grimly. "I take it there was a court of inquiry."

Wolff nodded. "The general conclusion seemed to be that things are different here on Jersey, sir. You've got to have the right touch, that's all. It's easy once you know how."

"Once who knows how?" Rimmer demanded.

Suddenly Wolff sat on the balcony floor, dragged off his left boot and vigorously scratched his foot, using both hands. His face was screwed up in a grimace which combined tension and relief, and he sucked in a long, soft breath. "Sorry about that," he said. "Funny, but the toes that aren't there always itch the worst."

Rimmer sniffed. "That sounds like one of those damned meaningless Slav proverbs. I've had enough of those, thanks. . . . Come on, Wolff: who knows how?"

"The Bailiff, I suppose, sir." Wolff eased his foot into his boot. "Once the engineers pulled out, de Wilde's men got everything back to normal within a week."

General Rimmer thought about that as he went inside and put his tunic on. He buckled his belt and slid the pistol holster around to the hip. Inside his right boot-leg he thrust a stick-handled grenade: his personal trademark. "And so I suppose this bastard de Wilde thinks he's got us by the balls," he said. "Is that it?"

"Sir, if you want my opinion, I don't think the Bailiff is at war with anyone," Wolff said. "He's in a strange position. Has been ever since we arrived, four years ago. I mean, do you realize that he is not only Bailiff of Jersey but also acting Lieutenant-Governor, appointed by King George the Sixth of England?"

"Wolff, don't waste my time. I don't give an ersatz damn for King George."

"You do, sir! My goodness, sir, you give a most tremendous damn. After all, we still administer the Channel Islands in the King's name, and—"

"We do *what*?" Rimmer looked at his watch. "All right, explain. And for God's sake get a move on."

"It all goes back to 1940, sir," Wolff began. Rimmer snapped his fingers. "England was obviously going to be conquered soon," Wolff hurried on, "and then the British Crown would become part of the Reich, so we wanted to show them they had nothing to fear from a German Occupation. It would just be a sort of administrative reshuffle, everything was going to be in the best interests of the Islanders."

"You mean to say we're supposed to be fighting Winston Churchill in the name of George the Sixth?" Rimmer snorted. "Try again."

"Yes, sir." Wolff's missing toes began to itch again, and he ground his right heel on top of his left boot with a vigour which made Rimmer wince. "I'm only trying to explain the Bailiff's situation, sir. On the one hand, he's the King's Lieutenant-Governor here and so it's his duty to look after the Islanders. He can't do that without our help, so he's bound to co-operate, but, on the other hand, if he co-operates too much he's in danger of collaborating. And that's treason. So he's on a knife-edge. He's been walking that knife-edge for four years, sir. It's a fascinating performance, sir."

"I didn't come here to be fascinated, Wolff." Rimmer went downstairs and his adjutant followed, limping slightly. "I came here to beat off an invasion. Your Mr. de Wilde can juggle with his scruples until his arms ache, but the minute he gets in my way—"

"It's not quite like that, sir," Wolff said.

"I know, you told me: things are different here. Good, fine, splendid, you told me, I heard you, now forget it." Rimmer strode through the lobby.

"General, with respect—" Wolff skipped around a potted plant to catch up with Rimmer. "It won't do any good to forget it." Rimmer stopped, and his jaws clenched with impatience; but Wolff was curiously fireproof. "Sir, the way things are, you've both got each other by the balls. It's a very delicate relationship. Any sudden movement could be extremely painful, sir."

Rimmer stared down at him. "Have you finished?" Wolff nodded. "Good," Rimmer said. "Now let's get on with the war."

Two military policemen held open the double-doors of the hotel. Outside, the sentries presented arms. The general's driver stiffened to attention. "Airfield!" Rimmer snapped. Dum-Dum, waiting in the back seat, quivered with joy.

The general and his adjutant sat side by side in a Fieseler Storch. It was Rimmer's favourite form of transport: a sporty little high-wing monoplane with big windows to show him the ground he commanded. The pilot glanced over his shoulder and Rimmer nodded. The Storch rolled forward, hoisted its tail, and bustled down the runway. At fifty yards it angled up, sharply and boldly, as if the undercarriage had made one final downwards thrust, and quickly gained height in the mild morning air.

Rimmer looked down on a cluster of flak batteries and smiled his approval: this was better than studying maps or photographs. He turned to Wolff, but Wolff had his eyes closed. Rimmer shook him and the eyes hinged open, as wide and solemn as a doll's. "I wasn't asleep," Wolff said. "I don't like to see the flak, that's all. There's nothing you can do about it, you know, so it's best not to look."

"Flak? What flak?" Rimmer asked. "There is no flak."

Wolff took a good look out of both windows, and then put his mouth to Rimmer's ear. "Absolutely brilliant pilot, sir," he whispered hoarsely. "Simply superb." Rimmer shoved him away and wiped the moist breath from his ear. "Wolff, for God's sake relax," he said. "Everything's all right. Just point out the defences, that's all you have to do."

Wolff was silent for a moment. "It's not a bit like Russia, sir," he said. "The Russians down there don't wear fur hats. Maybe you can't see them from up here, but they don't. Take it from me, sir." As Rimmer opened his mouth he added: "And that's a divisional artillery strongpoint with six heavy-calibre guns under reinforced concrete. Very powerful, sir." Rimmer grunted.

The pilot climbed to five thousand feet and circled to give the general an overall view of the island. Rimmer studied it eagerly. Jersey was roughly kidney-shaped, tilted from north to south and curling protectively around a splendid sandy bay on the south side. At the eastern end of this bay was the island's only town and capital, St. Helier. Most of the northern coast rose steeply from the sea; even on a calm day like this, Rimmer could see white water worrying the rocks at the base of massive cliffs. No sane commander would send assault troops in there. The east coast was less impressive, but just as awkward: Rimmer could clearly make out line after line of ragged reefs lying in wait under the shallow sea. He turned and studied the big bay on the south side. It was completely dominated by headlands at each end; for good measure there was an island fortress out in the middle. Excellent.

That left the west coast. Rimmer looked down on its three miles of sands, wide open to the Atlantic. The rollers were lined up like a parade; they advanced endlessly, irresistibly, almost lazily, and discharged themselves creamily upon the beach. It was not hard to imagine landing-craft doing the same. Never mind; it was encouraging to know that the enemy had such little choice. Those sands might look inviting, but one could do various things to sour the invitation. Rimmer took a last look at his island as a whole. From this height there was little evidence of war. The coastal defences were well camouflaged, and a patchwork-quilt of fields, woods, hillocks, valleys, lakes, quarries, farms, and villages made a glorious confusion of rustic colour, enough to hide an army. Jersey looked so lush and fresh, and the seabed around it shelved so gently, that the edge of the ocean seemed to be stained emerald and purple by the island's richness.

Rimmer looked up, towards England, and saw the hazy shapes of other, smaller islands. He pointed. "Guernsey, Herm, Alderney, Sark," Wolff said. "All occupied and defended. You command the lot, but each one administers itself independently."

"Jersey is the biggest?"

Wolff nodded. "Then Guernsey, and the rest are just map-references. They don't have much to say to each other, usually."

"Why not?"

"Don't know, sir. After a thousand years perhaps they all know what they think, or maybe they've given up thinking."

The plane banked, and Rimmer looked again. The Normandy peninsula lay all along the eastern horizon, only a dozen miles away at its nearest point. Once there, you could drive for a thousand miles and still not reach the end of the German Empire. And in all that Empire, no other stronghold had so crucial a role to play; no fortress had been so powerfully armoured. Jersey was a military gem. Jersey was his. Rimmer nodded appreciatively. "It's a far cry from Yugoslavia, eh?" he said.

Wolff studied the island. "Different shape, too, sir," he pointed out.

Rimmer gave him a short, hard stare. "Wolff, are you feeling all right?" he asked.

"No, sir. Everything keeps going around."

"That's because everything *is* going around."

"Ah. Well, if you've got it too, sir, I don't mind so much."

Rimmer gave up. He tapped the pilot on the shoulder and pointed downwards. "I want a closer look," he ordered.

They dived to clifftop height and began a slow circuit of the island. Wolff at once lost all his vagueness and became a lucid and valuable aide. He described the skilful positioning of gun emplacements to give interlocking fields of fire so that an attacker would always be outflanked. He named each command bunker, each observation tower, and each bomb-proof infantry strongpoint as they passed it, giving its strength and battle plan. He pointed out the anti-tank walls at the top of beaches, the invisible mine-fields, the military railways by which supplies and ammunition were moved.

"Stop," Rimmer ordered. The pilot curled the plane around in a wide, slow circle. "Why are those barracks so exposed?" He pointed out a wired compound set in the middle of a stretch of treeless waste. "They're a sitting target like that. Not even camouflaged."

"It's really nothing to do with us, sir," Wolff said. "That's one of the Organisation Todt labour camps; there must be a dozen scattered about the place. The Todt people always stick them out in the wilds because it's easier to keep the workers under control, I suppose."

Rimmer examined the wooden huts: windowless, ramshackle, broken-roofed. Only the high wire fence around them was intact. "Squalid," he said. "All right, carry on."

Wolff showed Rimmer the array of ingenious traps and obstacles which awaited an invader. Along the clifftops there were "roll-bombs"—three-hundred-pound shells with long wires hooked to their detonators; release the shell and as it hits the beach the wire tightens and up she goes. In the fields there were "spiders"—webs of wires rigged so as to explode a heavy shell the instant a parachutist got entangled. The beaches were staked with girders carrying explosives which would erupt at the nudge of a tank. And so on.

Rimmer listened carefully and hid his admiration. So far the island had benefited from nearly four years of uninterrupted fortification. It was now his duty to bring it rapidly to a state of military perfection; and with luck it would soon be his honour to prove that perfection in arms against the enemy. . . .

When the Storch landed, Dum-Dum came bounding across the grass, followed by a dispatch-rider who carried a bulky envelope. "Returns of unit strengths," Rimmer grunted. "No good having strongpoints if you haven't the strength to man them, is it?"

"No, sir," Wolff said.

Rimmer tore open the envelope while Dum-Dum leaped and tried to grab it. He held the dog at bay and scanned the sheets of paper. One entry stopped him. "Hullo!" he said. "Or do I mean good-bye?"

Wolff tried to think of a useful remark and failed. "All present and correct, sir?" he asked.

"All except one," Rimmer said. "So maybe something did go bump in the night after all." He gave Wolff the paper. "Go and find out. Now."

5

Daniel de Wilde's single-breasted suits had all been converted into double-breasted suits, and still they were too big. That was how much weight he had lost during the war.

He had been a big man in 1940, when the Germans occupied Jersey. The Bailiff was virtually Prime Minister of the island then, and de Wilde had enjoyed his position: worked hard, entertained a lot, ate and drank his fill. Now he was tall and thin, with a long jawbone, slightly hollowed cheeks, and watchful grey eyes. He still had plenty of money; many of the Germans could not understand why he never used the black market; some Islanders didn't believe he didn't use it. He certainly needed extra food. The Bailiff's job was very demanding. De Wilde chewed on an empty pipe (tobacco was scarce) and survived on his rations.

Every morning at nine the Bailiff and the German Civil Administrator, Count Limner, met to sort out the day's problems. They met alternately in each other's office. Today they were in Limner's.

"First, we have a new Military Commander," Limner said. "General Rimmer replaces General Gebhardt."

"Nice chap?" de Wilde asked.

Limner took out his pipe and looked into the empty bowl.

He's a bastard, then, de Wilde thought.

"Next, your people must keep away from those Russians," Limner said. "It's for their own good, really."

"I suppose that means the Organisation Todt has lost some more."

Limner flicked through an untidy heap of reports until he found what he wanted. "Only three," he said, "two Russians and a Spaniard, but I don't need to tell you what they're like."

"Desperate."

"Utterly desperate. I do believe they'd kill for a crust of bread. They'll be caught soon enough, but—"

They sat on opposite sides of Limner's desk, each propping his head on his hand and looking into space, while he thought about the problems of slave-labour.

"I'll put another notice in the paper," de Wilde said. "But you know, when a man turns up on your doorstep, and he's bleeding, and shaking with cold, and starving, literally starving—"

"I know. I know. But the more the Islanders help them, the worse the problem will become."

"Why can't the Todt people at least feed them a bit better?"

There was silence while Limner scribbled his initials and put the paper aside. "I have nothing else," he said.

De Wilde stood and stretched. "The Island Finance Committee—" he began.

"Ahah," said Limner. "Ohoh." He began filling his pipe.

"They're complaining about the Occupation costs again."

"Good for them! I always feel happier when the Finance Committee starts complaining, it means things are normal. I thought we agreed on a percentage? So much to be paid by the island and the rest by Germany."

"We did indeed, but now they say your people are spending a lot more on defence works, and so our share has gone up, and they don't see why we should pay the extra. Damn it all, you can't say this is *normal.* You're turning the island into a concrete battleship." The Bailiff spoke mildly. He was looking out of the window, at a couple of tanks grinding along the esplanade, past the golden sweep of the mine-fields.

"The percentage is too high." Limner lit his pipe. "I'll try to get it reduced. Would that satisfy them?"

"Good God, no. Nothing will ever satisfy them, short of Germany paying for the lot, in gold bullion. I mean, these Occupation marks are a lot of nonsense."

"They're not worth much."

"They're worth damn-all. Once the war is over, we'll have to redeem them ourselves, which means exchanging them for British currency, so in fact you're not paying for anything."

"True. So why is your Finance Committee unhappy? If our Occupation marks are worthless, does it make any difference how we divide the bill? Ten per cent of nothing is just the same as ninety percent of nothing."

"It's a question of pride." De Wilde sniffed the air. "Also it's a matter of principle."

"Ah, Bailiff. You have principles the way Schumacher has gun emplacements: one for every situation."

"Sometimes I think principles are all we've got left." De Wilde sniffed again. "Count, what the hell are you smoking?"

"Aromatic, isn't it? So far I think I've identified dried tea-leaves and wild mint and perhaps nettle, but there's also something that tastes like licorice."

"Where d'you get it?"

"Boots the Chemist. They call it 'Aftermath.' Would you like to try some?"

"No thanks. I don't like the way your ears go green when you inhale." De Wilde looked at his notes. "Fred Green. When is he going to be let out of that shocking French prison?"

"I wish I knew. I have asked."

"What did they say?"

"Necessity of war."

"Necessity of poppycock! He's served his sentence, why can't they let him go?"

"Well, my guess is it's because he was suspected of spying. You know how nervous they've become."

"But you've just got to look at him to see that's nonsense. He's a gardener, for heaven's sake. What sort of spy d'you think Fred would make? All he knows about is dung and rhubarb."

"Excellent rhubarb," Limner said. "We bought some last year. First-class."

"There you are, then. All right, he listened to the BBC: it was wrong, it was illegal, he was guilty. But if Fred Green's a spy, then we're all spies. Anyway, he's served his sentence. Necessity of war's got nothing to do with it."

"Of course you are right, in principle," Limner said easily. "Mr. Green was not a spy. But there are those in the Gestapo who ache to find a spy. Captain Paulus, for instance, has quite made up his mind that there *should* be a spy. He considers it an essential part of the danger. And so Mr. Green must be a spy. Necessity of war."

"That's daft."

"Let's say it's the military mind at work."

"It's daft. If you go on keeping people in jail for no reason you'll make people angry, and then there *will* be trouble."

Limner smiled sadly. "Which will prove that Paulus was right all along. . . . But I will try again, I promise."

"Maybe this new chap Rimmer can intervene."

The telephone rang. Limner answered it, and listened. "By all means," he said, and hung up. "You can ask him yourself, if you like," he told de Wilde. "General Rimmer would like to see you at once."

Rimmer met de Wilde on the concrete roof of a gun emplacement overlooking a small and silent bay. They shook hands, while Dum-Dum sniffed de Wilde's legs. "I'm very pleased with your island, Bailiff," Rimmer said cordially. "Very pleased indeed."

"We like it," de Wilde said, "what's left of it."

"It's a gem. In all of Western Europe there is no place so magnificently fortified."

"No thanks to me." De Wilde looked for the cottage where they used to serve cream teas and found a machine-gun point instead. Without moving his head he could also see two pillboxes and a bunker. "All this is due to Colonel Schumacher and his slave-labour," he said.

"What? You're too modest, Bailiff. Major Wolff has been telling me about Jersey. It is—what was the expression you used in 1940? When you welcomed us?"

"I said I hoped it would be a model occupation," de Wilde said stiffly. "And let me make it clear that nobody welcomed you, especially after your planes killed nine people, all civilians, when this island had been completely demilitarized."

"Nobody told us that," Rimmer said sharply. "Your Government in London demilitarized the island and then kept that fact a secret, God knows why. You can't expect a soldier to walk into a trap, Bailiff, and the only way to find out if a place is defended is to attack it. Am I right?"

"I'm not going to argue. We surrendered because we had no means of resisting and because we were threatened—"

"Yes, yes, yes." Rimmer left the gun emplacement and led the way down a communication trench. "A model occupation. Exactly. If the other occupied countries had behaved as sensibly as you, Bailiff, Europe would be a happier and safer place, isn't that right, Dum-Dum?" The boxer wagged his stumpy tail and snorted with pleasure. "Major Wolff tells me there has not been a serious act of sabotage here in three and a half years! After serving in Poland, Russia, Greece, I find that record most impressive. I congratulate you, Bailiff. Ah!"

The trench turned a corner and led to a concrete tower fifty feet high, with observation slots sliced out every ten feet. Rimmer strode through the ground-level chamber, enjoying the echo of his boots, and

entered a large bunker built into the hillside. "Two metres of reinforced concrete," he said. "Even a direct hit cannot smash that. And
I have seen dozens just like this, all around the island! Literally
dozens."

"I think you should understand our position," de Wilde said. "We
don't *like* having you Germans here, but we're an island and there
is absolutely no way we can resist without hurting ourselves, too."

Rimmer was not listening. He had traced a length of tramline to
a room full of ammunition and found an empty truck. He released the
brake and watched it rumble gently down the track. Dum-Dum raced
it to the end.

"Schumacher tells me that your local craftsmen did all this."

"Only some of it."

"Excellent workmanship."

"I didn't encourage them. Your Organisation Todt pays them fifty
per cent more than anyone else is allowed to."

Rimmer shook his head in pleased amazement. "Can you imagine
the results if we tried this in Yugoslavia? Disaster! Those Slavs—half
are bandits and half are cretins."

"No doubt they resent being tyrannized every bit as much as we
do."

"Tyrannized?" Rimmer laughed. "That's a word they can't spell,
so I doubt very much if they can understand it." He opened a steel
door and found a flight of steps. "Shall we go up? After you, Bailiff."

They emerged in a stretch of young heather, intense with bees. "No,
I don't think your people have much in common with the Slavs,"
Rimmer said.

"Hunger."

Rimmer picked a buttercup and plucked the petals one by one. "I
was very good at arithmetic at school, Bailiff. That's why I have
earned so much promotion under the Fuehrer. Soldiering is fundamentally arithmetic. In France, for instance, I know that shooting ten
hostages for each act of sabotage will effectively discourage saboteurs.
In Norway the number is fifteen. In Poland, twenty. In the Ukraine
they can't count above twenty, so any large number will do." All the
petals were plucked. He twirled the naked stem between his fingers.

"By all reports," de Wilde said, "sabotage continues."

"I like this island. It proves what the Fuehrer has always believed:
that your people and mine have a great deal in common. We should
not be at war."

"General Rimmer, you're wasting your time."

"I hope not, Bailiff. One of my men is missing. A sentry on coast patrol."

"When?"

"Last night."

"I can't believe that an Islander had anything to do with it. There's a curfew, anyway."

"That proves nothing."

"I'm glad to hear that proof is important to you."

"Important, but not all-important. I can live without proof, but I'm not sure I can live without that sentry." Rimmer wanted de Wilde to ask why, but de Wilde had discovered con-trails high in the north-west, gradually growing southwards like tiny scratches that were slowly splitting open the white stuffing of the sky, and he was trying to hear the shadowy growl of the big, invisible bombers. Rimmer took his arm and said, "I think you should understand the facts of the situation, Bailiff." They strolled back to Rimmer's command vehicle, a camouflaged halftrack with a 7.9mm machine-gun mounted on a swivel next to the driver. "The situation is that the Third Reich is actual master of Europe."

"Not counting Italy."

"We are better off without Italy. Germany rules from France to Norway. Now, the Allies cannot defeat us unless they invade us. You know and I know that they are about to try. It's no secret, is it? And if their invasion fails they won't risk a second invasion, certainly not again in 1944, perhaps never. Well, the Fuehrer has made this island into an armoured spearhead on which the Allied assault will impale itself and die. He has made me responsible for that death. Failure here would jeopardize all Europe, while success here will guarantee the future of the Third Reich."

"Perhaps he fell down a hole," de Wilde said.

"Perhaps. If so, I hope it is a very small hole. If I lose any more of my men in the middle of the night, you, Bailiff, will lose even more of your Islanders in the middle of the following day."

6

Four hundred men looked for Wilhelm Keller. They formed a line with one end at the cliff road and the other a quarter of a mile inland,

and they set out to search every inch of ground, from the guardhouse where he began his last patrol, to the checkpoint which he never reached. They searched slowly and carefully, not because they gave a damn about Keller but because it was a beautiful morning, bright and cheerful as a chocolate-box, and they wanted to make the most of this holiday from drill and duty. Chaffinches and yellowhammers flew in front, complaining pleasantly, and a few swallows zoomed overhead, hunting the insects which fled the soldiers' boots. The sea was blue, the breeze was soft, the air was warm. "Don't rush it, lads," said an elderly corporal in the middle of the line. He sat on his heels and scrutinized a rabbit hole. "Let's do the job properly, now."

Twenty yards behind the line of men, Major Helldorf sat in his car with Major Wolff. Helldorf was lanky and restless, an ear-scratcher and eyebrow-tugger and trouser-hitcher. He had been a busy police-man doing nicely in Hamburg's thriving Homicide Department when the army claimed him and put him in charge of the military police on Jersey. That was two years ago: two years wasted on hunting down black-market potato-dealers and cyclists who pedalled on the wrong side of the road. Helldorf tried not to be resentful, but this damned island was a criminal desert; he saw his career slipping away, felt his brain slowing down.

"Waste of time," he told Wolff. "They won't find anything here."

"Tell that to General Rimmer," Wolff said. "He's taking a personal interest."

"Is he? Why? Because it happened ten minutes after he took over the island? Is he superstitious or something?"

The car crept forward another twenty feet and stopped. "I think he came here expecting trouble," Wolff said, "and now trouble has obliged."

"This isn't *trouble.*" Helldorf flapped a glove at the plodding sol-diers under the wheeling swallows. "I can smell trouble coming three weeks off and twenty miles away. This isn't trouble. They've forgotten what trouble tastes like here."

"They've forgotten what a lot of things taste like," Wolff said. "Nevertheless, we *are* short of one sentry."

"Murder, suicide, accident," Helldorf said. "Well, it wasn't acci-dent, was it? Not unless he lost his wits and just kept on going, in which case we're wasting our time here. Suicide? No body, but he could have climbed down the cliff and walked into the sea."

"Did you find a break in the wire?"

"No, but that proves nothing. Suicides can be very house-proud. If he did drown himself, we're wasting our time here." Helldorf turned a glove inside out and picked fluff from the ends of the fingers. "That leaves murder. Anyone desperate enough to break curfew and enter a Prohibited Coastal Zone wouldn't leave the body behind. So, again, we're wasting our time looking for it here."

"What's your guess, then?" Wolff asked. Off to the right, in the middle of a field, a police dog began barking and scratching at the earth.

"Oh . . . suicide. We normally get three a month, you know."

"I know."

A young soldier approached the car and saluted. "Yes?" Helldorf said.

"Keller's records, sir." The car moved forward and the soldier walked with it, while the two officers glanced through the papers. "Married, three kids," Wolff said. "Never been in any trouble. Catholic. He doesn't look much like a suicide, does he?"

"He could have lapsed. Maybe a bomb fell on his family."

"No, sir," the soldier said. Helldorf and Wolff looked up in surprise, and the soldier's face turned red. "Beg pardon, sir, I shared a billet with him, and there wasn't any bad news like that, sir. He was all right when he went on duty, sir."

A whistle shrilled and Helldorf looked past the man to where the line had stopped and a sergeant was waving his cap. "Come with me, lad," he said. "I may need you for a rapid identification."

The officers drank flask coffee and watched spades bite into the earth, while the rest of the search moved on. The grave was shallow; the body was soon uncovered. "That's not him," the soldier said, even before the face was visible. "Too skinny. Keller wasn't thin."

"Far too dead, in any case," said Helldorf. The corpse had begun to decompose. He threw the dregs of his coffee over it, and turned away. "Put it back, quickly," he said, "before the flies get here."

"So who was that?" Wolff asked on the way back to the car.

"Foreign labourer. Slav, by the look of him." Another whistle blew. Helldorf changed direction. "We had hundreds of them working up here," he said.

The second stop revealed a similar corpse: gaunt face, bloated limbs, dressed in rags, barefoot. Before the grave had been closed, three more whistles sounded. The police dogs were raucous with success. "For Christ's sake," Helldorf said. The line had come to a halt. Most of the men were sitting down, resting on their elbows, enjoying the sun. A sergeant came over. "We could do with some more spades, sir," he suggested.

"I knew it was a waste of time," Helldorf said.

"How many labourers died up here?" Wolff asked him.

"God knows." Another whistle sounded. "All right, all right!" Helldorf shouted. "Hold your peace!"

"Beg pardon, sir," the sergeant said. "I seem to remember one of the Todt supervisors telling me they buried forty-odd, all told."

"Thank you, Sergeant," Helldorf said bitterly.

"What killed them all?" Wolff asked.

"What the hell does it matter what killed them all? Nothing killed them, they just died. Pneumonia killed them. They weren't up to the work, that's all. Poor physical specimens, Slavs and Poles and Russians . . ." Helldorf pulled a map from his pocket. "They just died, that's all. Natural fucking causes. What the hell d'you think killed them?"

"I just wondered," Wolff said.

Helldorf was staring at the map. "How much of the ground have we covered so far, Sergeant?"

"Not much, sir." The sergeant could see that Helldorf was looking at the wrong section. "Only about a quarter, sir."

Wolff offered Helldorf a small cigar. He took it but did not light it. "Rather like looking for a body in a graveyard," Wolff said. "Must be a new experience for you."

"Keep six men and two dogs and go on searching," Helldorf told the sergeant. "Dismiss the rest."

They walked back to the car. Helldorf still had not lit his cigar. "Why be so angry?" Wolff asked. "It's not your fault."

"I can't stand people leaving goddamned bodies lying all over the place, that's all." Helldorf gave Wolff back the cigar. "It's the wrong way to do things. I don't care who they are."

"What a lovely morning," Wolff said. "It was just like this the day we went into Russia, you know. Blue skies, warm sun."

"Crime is indivisible," Helldorf said. "Makes no difference whether it's a duke or a dustman: every corpse has got to be accounted for. Otherwise you end up with this nonsense."

"You still think it was suicide?"

"Of course it was suicide."

"But why? He was a good soldier."
"So what? War is suicide. Maybe he got tired of waiting."

Earl Kramer awoke suddenly. He saw roofbeams, tiles, cobwebs, patches of sunlight. Not far away a man laughed, and boots marched across cobblestone. Kramer slowly remembered: he was in the barn. The farmer had given him clothes and a blanket and shown him a pile of straw in the loft of the barn. That was a hell of a long time ago.

He rolled out of the straw and scuffed over to a window. His shoes were too big. Below, in the courtyard, three German soldiers strolled towards the farmhouse. They wore steel helmets and carried rifles with bayonets attached. One man rapped on the door with the butt of a pistol.

Kramer saw the door open and the soldiers go in. He turned and scrambled down the ladder and ran to the barn door. The courtyard was empty except for a pile of dung on which a rooster slow-marched. Opposite Kramer an arched opening led to a road. Waiting wouldn't improve anything. He took off his shoes and reached the opening in ten stealthy strides. Nobody shot holes in him. The rooster started to crow, rustily, but gave up halfway.

Kramer put on his shoes and looked around. The farm was on the ridge of a steep hillside. Odd-shaped fields sloped down to a stream which flashed and flickered in the sunlight. Wildflowers grew everywhere. It was a lovely day for a manhunt.

To his left the road ran uphill and disappeared into a wood. To his right it ran downhill and a parked German Army truck blocked the view. It faced uphill and its cab was empty. Kramer scuttled between the truck and the wall. At the bottom of the hill a dozen German soldiers stood on a bridge over the stream. He scuttled back.

Decision. Down the road: crazy. Back inside: dumb. Up the road: they'd see him. Over the fields: no thanks, not after last night. Guttural voices sounded in the courtyard. A pig looked over a wall and curled its lip at him. Kramer decided.

He climbed into the cab and reached across the wheel and released the handbrake. Nothing happened. He thought, *Goddam it, they chocked the wheels.* Then he saw the gear lever thrust forward. He tramped on the clutch and banged the lever into neutral. At once the truck moved.

Kramer climbed out and dropped off. The truck rolled backwards, downhill. He ran for the pigsty and vaulted the wall. Both his shoes came off and he fell on a pig. It screamed with rage and terror, and bolted.

Kramer lay with his face in the muck and heard shouting, then running, then a chunky, splintering crash which made him grin; then more distant running and fainter shouting.

He looked over the wall. The truck was halfway down the hill and outpacing its pursuers. It veered right and hit a wall, veered steadily left and bounced off a concrete pillbox, straightened up and gained speed as it entered the last, steep plunge to the bridge. The soldiers stopped running. Kramer held his breath.

The truck wrecked itself on the left-hand parapet. The impact lifted its wheels waist-high and tossed the tail sideways, like surf flinging a small boat. For a moment the wreck turned heavily in the air. Then it fell onto the roadway, bounced, and slammed against the other parapet. Chunks of masonry tumbled into the stream. The truck exploded.

The blast reached Kramer like a warm, friendly shove in the face. He turned away and saw the farmer looking. His face was slack, his eyes were sick. "You did that," he said. Thunder re-echoed faintly from the valley.

"You're damn right I did," Kramer said. He climbed over the wall. "They'd have found me, that search party was gonna find me. It was a diversion, I had to do something."

"But they only wanted eggs," the farmer said. It sounded like a plea, and he looked at Kramer as if begging him to undo the damage. He pointed to a small basket, dropped beside the road. One egg had fallen out and broken. "That's all they wanted, man. Bloody eggs."

His wife ran past them and Kramer watched her go down the hill, arms windmilling and hair bouncing. Two German soldiers lay in the road, not moving. The third was crawling towards the wall. The truck blazed vigorously.

"They must have had something in the back," Kramer said. The words sounded empty and absurd, utterly out of proportion with the disaster they were meant to explain. He looked for the farmer, wanting to make it clear that he had not intended what had in fact happened; but the man was no longer there.

Kramer sat on the wall and picked bits of dirt from his hands. He felt curiously detached, as if he were high in the air, watching himself watch a performance. The farmer's wife reached the crawling German, knelt, stood, shouted something up the hill, but it was all part of the performance and Kramer did not respond. Down by the bridge a few soldiers cautiously approached the truck: more performers.

After a while a new sound took his attention, and the farmer drove a horse and cart out of the courtyard. He pointed to the back. Kramer climbed in. They rattled away, uphill, and the details of the scene— the bodies in the road, the flames above the bridge—receded and diminished and finally disappeared.

For a time Kramer just sat and watched the hedges go by. Then he suddenly remembered who he was and where, and what he had done, and he began to be afraid. Where was this man taking him? He wanted to ask and he nearly did, but checked himself just in time: if the farmer was planning to betray him he certainly wouldn't give a truthful answer; and if you couldn't be sure of the answer, why ask the question? Kramer found some ancient grains of wheat to chew, and worried.

The cart swerved and jolted onto the grass verge and stopped. He braced himself to fight or to run, but up in front the farmer had not moved. Kramer looked past the man's hunched shoulders and saw an open car coming fast, its headlights burning holes in the sunshine. The horn was blaring and the car was full of uniformed men. Kramer looked at the hedge and knew he couldn't get over it or through it or under it, so there was no escape. Fear lurched in his stomach; he wondered if they would beat him up, and whether he could stand that sort of pain; probably not; it was tough to be a hero when six big guys were busting you open, and Kramer didn't think he was that sort of hero anyway. He lay down on the floor of the cart and closed his eyes so they'd think he was unconscious. The car went howling past.

Kramer sat up and watched it go. It looked like military police. A few seconds later an ambulance followed the car, also going flat out with its klaxon screaming in pain: somebody else's pain. The farmer shook the reins and the cart jolted back onto the road. Kramer smiled with relief; he wanted to laugh aloud but he didn't know how the farmer would react to that, so he just took a deep breath and made himself comfortable.

They rolled through pleasant farmland, very green after the rain. Everywhere he looked, Kramer saw the German Army. At first he tried to keep out of sight; then he noticed that some of the soldiers waved, and the farmer waved back. Kramer sat up and joined in the waving. He waved briefly, almost curtly, just a waggle of the hand to

acknowledge their greeting. *Got to keep the bastards in their place.*
Their place was everywhere. Each crossroads had a bunker, each
road-junction had a strongpoint guarding it. They passed anti-aircraft
units, searchlights, troops drilling, troops washing, troops doing
weapons-training, troops digging trenches, troops living under canvas, troops manning artillery positions. It seemed that the entire
island was busy with soldiers. Kramer started to keep check of the
traffic and noticed one light tank, three or four half-tracks, seven
trucks, maybe a dozen motorcycles, before he lost count and gave up.

The cart swung off the road and jolted up a stony lane between an
avenue of lofty lime trees which made a cool, quiet tunnel. At the end
of the trees, there was a whitewashed cottage. The cart slowed but did
not quite stop. Without looking around, the farmer called, "Just say
Louis Betteridge brought you."

Kramer slid to the ground and hopped as his bare feet met a
pothole. The cart rumbled on.

"Say!" Kramer cried. "I want to thank you for what you've done!"

Betteridge did not respond. Kramer picked his way to the side of
the lane. "And please give my thanks to Mrs. Betteridge, too!" he
called. Betteridge swayed as the cart hit a deep rut. "I didn't want to
cause you folks any trouble," Kramer shouted. Betteridge nodded, or
perhaps he just shook the reins. It was hard to tell. The lane dipped,
and the cart moved steadily out of sight. Kramer was alone again, and
hungry.

7

Canon Renouf took his feet off the bicycle pedals and free-wheeled
down St. Peter's hill. He was lightheaded with hunger, and the rush
of warm air and the racing blur of fresh green hedges and trees tugged
at his reason.

His hunger was nothing new: civilian rations made no allowance for
size, and Renouf was a big man. But this morning, after listening to
the BBC news on his radio hidden in the church loft, he had stayed
to hear the last movement of Beethoven's Ninth Symphony. Its effect
on an empty stomach was intoxicating: the forthright, exuberant,
indisputable music still stormed in triumph through his head. The
bicycle bell tingled as he swooped down the slope. He filled his lungs
and boomed out the melody. Canon Renouf had a chest like a black-

smith's striker, and they heard him down in the village of St. Peter's. "Watch out," said Captain Paulus of the Gestapo, "here comes that mad bloody vicar again." Lieutenant Zimmerman turned his head to look.

Paulus and Zimmerman led the Gestapo counter-intelligence unit on the island. It was not a very rewarding job, but then neither of them had joined the Gestapo for reward. They were like two young priests, slogging away in a remote and humdrum parish, satisfied to know that they were serving a good cause. Paulus was slim and smooth and usually expressionless, like a professional ballroom dancer. Zimmerman was built like a bouncer, and looked at people as if gauging how well they might bounce. Both men were accustomed to unpopularity; they regarded it as a confirmation of their efficiency. Any unprovoked outbreak of popularity would have disturbed them.

Canon Renouf sang a few more vibrant phrases as the village green appeared around the bend and he coasted towards the old, familiar scene: Langley's Store, the George and Dragon, the granite war memorial, the flak battery under the chestnut trees, the machine-gun unit camped between the bunker and the church hall, now camouflaged and converted into a flame-thrower depot. Ted Langley stood in the doorway of his shop, while the two German officers looked in the window. "Morning, Canon," he called.

"Hullo, Ted," Renouf shouted. "The Russians are doing splendidly." He pedalled past the group. "Huge advances at Lublin."

"Well, I'd better get back to work," said Langley. He felt embarrassed for the Germans.

"I've warned him about that," Paulus muttered. They watched Renouf wave to a bunch of children. News of a thousand-bomber raid on Osnabrück reached them faintly. "Why must he make it so obvious?"

"My English isn't as good as yours," Lieutenant Zimmerman said.

"He said we're retreating at Lublin."

"Are we?"

"Of course we are. It was on the BBC at eight." Paulus saw a look of interest on the face of a soldier cleaning a nearby truck. He took Zimmerman's arm and steered him away. "We'll have to do something about this," he said. "I don't care if he is a parson, we can't have him going around like a damned town crier."

"What was that he said about Osnabrück?" Lieutenant Zimmerman asked.

"Get the car," Paulus ordered.

"I've got an aunt in Osnabrück, that's all," Zimmerman said.

"Think yourself lucky she's not in Lublin," Paulus said.

When they caught up with the minister he was cycling slowly past a couple of farmhands, who rested to hear him. "And the Japanese are taking a terrible pasting too," he told them. "The Americans captured Hollandia the other day. That's in Dutch New Guinea. And our chaps are pushing forward in Burma. Big raid on Osnabrück the other night. That's the third this month, you know."

"Canon Renouf!" called Captain Paulus. "You are coming with us."

"I say, that's most awfully kind of you," Renouf said. "Are you really going my way? Into town, that is."

"What about his bicycle?" Zimmerman asked.

Paulus got out of the car. "I've warned you before not to go around spreading alarm and despondency," he said.

"My goodness, I wouldn't dream of doing such a thing," Renouf said. He got into the car and left Paulus holding the bicycle. The farmhands had gone away. The car had no roof-rack. To an Islander a bicycle was invaluable, irreplaceable.

Paulus saw a civilian truck coming, and waved it down. "You will take this bicycle to Canon Renouf's home," he told the driver. "I make you responsible for it. Name?"

"Jack Greg."

"Papers?"

Greg gave him his papers. He got out and threw the bicycle in the back of his truck. "I suppose you've started taking bloody hostages now," he said.

"Hostages?" Paulus returned his papers. "Why should we take hostages?"

"Somebody knocked off one of your sentries last night, didn't they?"

"Did they? Who?"

"Well, it wasn't me, and it wasn't Canon Renouf, and it certainly couldn't have been the Commandos because they wouldn't dare, so I suppose it must have been the fairies."

"The fairies?"

"That's right. Elves and goblins and pixies." Greg tried to look surprised. "Don't you have them in Germany? I thought Germany was full of fairies."

Paulus took out a notebook and wrote in it. "You are aware of the regulation forbidding the spread of false and demoralizing information. The Fortress Commandant has authorized me to penalize offenders immediately. You are fined two days' pay."

Greg turned away. "Bastards," he whispered.

"Four days' pay," Paulus said. "Now shut your mouth, or I shall arrest you, too."

Earl Kramer was thirteen years old when he saw his first war newsreel. It showed German aircraft bombing somewhere in Spain, but the nationalities and the place had no interest for him. What mattered was the glamorous power of the bombers. They came as they pleased, arrogant in their mastery of the skies, destroyed their targets from an aloof distance with thunderous, majestic explosions, and flew home to a good meal. Fantastic!

From that moment, Earl Kramer's concept of war was established: there were the bombers, and the bombed. He was not an unusually violent boy; he was popular in the neighbourhood, cheerful, good-looking in a lanky wide-mouthed way, and he gave his parents little trouble; but what fascinated him was the big bomber. He kept a scrapbook of bombers in action: Japanese aircraft over China, German over Spain, Italian over Ethiopia. He was sixteen when the Second World War broke out and presented him with a flood of illustrations. Long before the United States joined the fighting his bedroom was a showplace of newspaper pictures and magazine spreads and balsa-wood models of the Junkers 88, the Bristol Blenheim, the Flying Fortress. If the war went on long enough, there was no doubt in his mind where he would be: up in the air, conquering gravity and distance and blasting the earth-bound enemy with a grand and God-like precision. To Earl Kramer it was all straightforward. The enemy had it coming to him, having started this war in the first place and then fought dirty all along the line, so the obvious thing to do was get over there and bomb the bejesus out of him until he surrendered.

Like a lot of people in Plattsville, Ohio, Earl felt pretty cheerful about the war, but then he felt pretty cheerful about most things. He was growing into a physically attractive young man, a slim-hipped six-footer with square shoulders. His hair had softened in colour from red to rust. His eyes were an untroubled blue, his skin was only lightly freckled, he danced well, and girls fell in and out of love with him at a flattering rate. He liked girls, girls were okay, girls were fun; but not as okay as bombers.

At school the teachers liked him personally. "Nice kid," one of them said. "Do anything for you. Except work." That wasn't quite true; Earl was smart enough to do the minimum of work. He was lazy but not stupid. He knew how to drift with the tide of learning, how to look receptive without actually pushing his brain. His academic performance was consistently mediocre. On his records a teacher wrote: "Never gets out of first gear." Underneath, a colleague added: "Maybe there isn't a second."

His father liked him—hell, everybody in Plattsville liked young Earl; you couldn't *not* like him—but he was dissatisfied too. Carl Kramer had built Kramer's Hardware & Garden Supplies into a healthy business and he hoped his son would help him run it. Yet plainly, when the boy graduated from high school (they gave him a deer rifle as a graduation present and he was delighted), he couldn't be trusted to handle any sale more complicated than a pound of nails. He was fine at meeting customers: he had a wonderfully welcoming grin; but when it came to figuring quantities or discounts, or adding up bills, or writing up orders, his father always had to check the work, and he usually had to correct it. "It's not that he's irresponsible," Mr. Kramer told his wife one day. "Is he stupid, then?" she asked. "He doesn't *act* stupid," Mr. Kramer said, "he just always gets things wrong." They thought about it for a moment. Mr. Kramer sighed. "Yeah, I guess he is irresponsible, at that," he said.

Then young Earl was startled out of his complacency. A neighbour's son, older than Earl, went cheerfully into uniform, assuming that he would be selected for aircrew, and found himself under training to become a records clerk. He was physically fit enough for aircrew duties; it was his mental equipment that let him down. The United States Army wanted only men with a good basic education to fly its complex and costly aircraft. What shook Earl Kramer was the knowledge that his neighbour's son had a better school record than he did.

The sudden prospect of not serving in bombers worried him severely, and the worry drove him to think hard, really hard, for the first time in his life.

After a week he went to his parents and told them he wanted to attend Ohio State University. They were surprised, pleased, sceptical, but certainly willing to help, if he could only meet the university's entrance requirements. They were impressed when he did just that, by studying in his room at night and on weekends to fill the gaps in his knowledge. He entered Ohio State in 1941 and applied himself especially to mathematics, physics and chemistry. He even mastered a little French and German. He enrolled in the ROTC. The work changed him, sharpened him, and his obvious determination marked him out from the run of students as someone who looked beyond the campus, and beyond the State of Ohio.

In January 1943 Churchill and Roosevelt met at Casablanca. The Allied aim, it was announced, was the unconditional surrender of the enemy. Already there was talk of opening a Second Front on the mainland of Europe. It was also the month when Earl Kramer passed his twentieth birthday, and he decided that now was the time to get over there.

He enlisted with a briskness which made his mother half-sad, half-proud. His induction into the U.S. Army Air Force raised him to a level of happiness and enthusiasm which he had never before experienced. He enjoyed every minute of his training, even when he failed the aptitude tests for pilot, navigator, and flight engineer; after all, what he really wanted to be was bombardier, the man who actually laid the eggs, hit the target, did the damage; and that was what he became.

Like all bombardiers he was commissioned second-lieutenant, and almost to his own surprise he found himself before long a valuable and well-liked member of a bomber crew. They all knew that he worked at his job and they respected him for it: what was the point in flying halfway across Germany and back if your bombardier couldn't hit the goddam target?

Earl Kramer enjoyed being in the U.S.A.A.F., and he even liked the discipline. Growing up in Plattsville, Ohio, had made him very law-abiding, very respectful of property; perhaps that was why he liked bombing so much. Until he got washed up on Jersey, Earl Kramer—for all his combat missions—had led a nonviolent life. In the air, he had aimed bombs at distant targets and hit several of them, but on the ground he had never so much as smashed a window.

Now, standing in the vacant sunshine outside this silent cottage in the middle of a foreign island, he felt ravenous hunger urge him to violence. The idea of housebreaking made him hesitant and nervous, but his growling, grumbling belly demanded urgent action. It was totally, achingly empty, and somehow he had a feeling that the cottage was empty too.

In the field beyond it a remote woodpigeon played its call-sign once; twice; began a third and gave up in the middle. Kramer walked up the front path. As he reached out to knock on the door, his ears sang, the world lurched, and the door seemed to recede. He made a clumsy grab and stubbed his fingers. The pain startled him. He knocked, and rubbed his hand. He knocked more loudly. The door was locked. Kramer stared for a moment, salivating freely. Then he found a stone and smashed a window.

By that act he finally left home in Plattsville, Ohio. Killing the sentry and wrecking the truck had been conditioned reflexes, imprinted on his behaviour by a hundred Hollywood movies, a thousand magazine articles. Smashing the window was pure Earl Kramer. He did it on his own.

It took him ten minutes to search the cottage and find no food. His stomach would not believe it and made him search again: the big, bare kitchen with smoke-streaks up the wall over the fireplace; the little parlour, smelling of dried lavender and bereavement; the dusty bedroom where an unmade bed sprawled like a tongue hanging out. No food. Some candlegrease; a restless, irascible bluebottle; blistered paint on the window frames. But no food. No food. His desperate stomach drove him on: someone lived here, there *must* be food. He opened the back door and saw an outhouse. He hurried towards it and felt his left ankle hooked and yanked backwards. His body hit the ground and someone's knee thudded into his back. "Thieving bastard!" growled a voice.

God help me, Kramer thought. He lay with his face in the dirt and gave up. This was too much.

The knee left his back. A hand gripped his shoulder and rolled him over. A man with bushy eyebrows stared angrily. He was in shirt-sleeves and he held a walking-stick like a club. "Well I'm buggered," he said. "Who the hell are you?"

"Kramer." He wiped earth from his mouth. "Earl Kramer. Don't hit me, okay?"

The man's forehead creased in disbelief. "You a Yank?"

"Sure." Kramer let himself go completely limp and made his voice husky. "U.S. Army Air Force. Bomber crew. I got shot down, and then I got washed up."

The man relaxed a fraction. "You bust my window," he accused. Kramer nodded, just once, feebly. "Sorry about that. Didn't want to, but . . . Just too hungry." He closed his eyes and whispered, "Too goddam hungry."

The man stood up and stared at him. "Look here," he said. "How do I know you're a bloody Yank?"

Kramer let his eyes flicker open and gradually produced a tired and gentle grin. "You want me to sing the national anthem?" he asked. He linked his hands behind his head and began, rustily, *Pardon me, boy . . . Is that the Chattanooga choo-choo? . . . Track twenty-nine . . . Oh won't you—"*

"All right, all right, shut up." He helped Kramer to his feet. "I thought you were another bloody slave-labourer. You're lucky I didn't smash your head in; there's plenty that would've. . . ." He brushed the dirt from Kramer's shoulders. "Well I'm buggered . . . A Yankee flyer wandering around my cottage in broad daylight. . . . Who would credit it? I'm Jack Greg." They shook hands. "What the dickens are you doing here? I thought for sure you were another of them bloody slave-labourers; you were lucky I didn't—Where's your uniform? What happened to you?"

"It's a long story," Kramer said. His stomach growled restlessly.

"You'd best come inside," Greg said.

He gave Kramer four cold boiled potatoes, a thick slice of ham, and hot tea in a mug made out of an old Tate & Lyle's Golden Syrup tin. The tea smelled odd, like old carrots, and it tasted lousy, really lousy. Kramer drank it. He ate everything, even the ham fat which normally he would have trimmed off. He didn't see where the food was hidden and he didn't ask.

Meanwhile, Greg left him in peace and got on with some household chores, which he did only sketchily. He was a discontented-looking man, in his late forties or early fifties; it was hard to tell which. He was balding and his narrow face was creased and lined like crumpled paper, but his movements were brisk. He kept his shoulders hunched, and often his fists were clenched. He wore working clothes and gumboots, smudged with grease and splashed with cement, and his forearms were as brown as a walnut, with fingernails that had trapped dirt like ten tiny hoes.

Kramer licked his knife and then his plate, but Greg did not take the hint.

"I guess you want to know how I got here," he said. "A guy called Betteridge brought me."

Greg was stacking bits of wood in the kitchen fireplace. He paused and stared at the blackened hearth. "Louis bloody Betteridge," he muttered.

"Right. He let me sleep in his barn last night."

"Rotten sod." Greg snapped a stick across his knee. "Lousy swindling bastard."

Kramer was taken aback. "Well . . . I expect you know him better than I do," he said.

"I know the bugger," Greg said savagely. "I've cause to know him. He owes me that bloody much, him and his fat-arsed wife. I wouldn't give them the time of day if I had two watches. Even though he is my kin. Cousin," he explained.

"Ah," Kramer said, as if that explained everything.

"He let you sleep in his barn, did he?" Greg laughed his contempt. "Generous. . . . Gave you his old shirt too, I see. What's the matter, couldn't he spare a pair of shoes, or did his missus want to sell them to you, tight old bag that she is?"

"I lost 'em in a pigsty," Kramer said. "Craziest damn thing you ever saw. I fell in this stinking pigsty, fell on this damn pig, and lost my damn shoes in the goddam mud!"

"You shouldn't've done that," Greg told him. "Boots and shoes are dreadful scarce."

"Well, I guess the pig ate them by now," Kramer said. "If I'd had any miserable brains I'd have eaten the crazy pig while it was in reach." He wondered if he should mention the runaway truck, and decided against it.

"And you just landed here last night?" Greg came over and sat at the table. "Didn't take Cousin bloody Louis long to get rid of you, did it?"

"Oh . . . I guess he got worried. Too many krauts hanging around his place this morning."

"I'm not surprised. I hear they lost a sentry last night, and not all that far from there, neither."

"Yeah? Is that right? Lost a sentry, eh?" Kramer tried to look surprised and impressed. "Holy cow. . . . that must be the Resistance, huh?"

"Resistance?" Greg scoffed. "God speed the plough . . . Not that there aren't some of us ready and willing to cut a few Jerry throats,

when the time's ripe. . . ." His voice sank to a cautious mutter, and
he glanced at the broken window. "No, he just disappeared, this one.
So they tell me. Not the first or the last, I dare say. I wish they'd all
just bloody disappear; they're a plague on this island, like rats. Dirty
grey rats, everywhere you look. Go where they like, do what they
want. . . ." Greg got up and wandered to the window. "They make
you sick," he said. Kramer looked and listened, for there was deep
anger in the man's voice. "Sick and bloody tired," Greg said. "They
take what they fancy, help themselves. What's the point of working?
They only rob you blind. Just this morning, one of them took a week's
wages off me. Stopped me in the middle of nowhere and . . . *Ach!*"
He spat out of the window. "I could've strangled the sod. One day
I will. But that won't bring my week's wages back, will it?"

Earl Kramer felt the need to be encouraging. It was an unfamiliar
need, and he cast around in his mind for the right kind of phrase.
"Don't worry," he said, "they'll get their comeuppance. You watch."

Greg wasn't listening. "Now they've even arrested the bloody parson," he complained.

"Why? What's he done?" Kramer had a vision of S.S. thugs pounding down an aisle and dragging a minister from his pulpit in mid-
sermon.

"Oh, nothing. Sweet sod-all. He just told the truth, that's all. But
that won't help him. Nor will the Bailiff. The Germans've got the
bloody Bailiff in their pocket, if you ask me. They'll put the bloody
parson on trial and the bloody Bailiff'll stand by and let 'em get on
with it. Makes you sick."

"What's the Bailiff?" Kramer found a piece of potato stuck to the
underside of his plate and carefully ate it.

"He's . . . sort of a glorified Prime Minister, or supposed to be."
Greg got a wooden spoon and began knocking bits of broken glass
from the window-frame. "He's just like the rest of them, he's given
in. They've all given in except me."

"And me," Kramer said, but again Greg wasn't listening.

"I tell you: when the Jerries landed here in 1940, there wasn't one
man with guts enough to stand beside me and fight," he said angrily.
"Nine hundred years we kept our freedom. We fought off the French,
the Vikings, the bloody pirates, the Spanish, and then we just let Jerry
walk in and take us. No resistance. That was de Wilde's very words,
I was there when he said it: no resistance, smile, be nice, give 'em
anything they ask for, lie down and let 'em stamp all over you.

Stinking Hun bastards." Greg looked out of his broken window and
glared at the wildflowers.

"The Bailiff said that?" Kramer asked. "He really told you to let
them—"

"Maybe not them exact words." Greg dismissed the American's
quibbling with a wave of his spoon. "No resistance, that's what we
were told. Surrender, quit, give up. D'you realize what they did? *They
gave old Hitler free run of this island.* Free run! We're part of Britain,
aren't we? Plenty of Channel Islanders went off to fight for king and
country against Napoleon, and the Crimea, and the Boers, and the
Kaiser, and plenty of 'em didn't come back! I should know: I helped
bury a few, on the Somme. And now look at us. In all the whole
British Empire, we're the only bit they let the Germans take. Doesn't
anybody over in England *care* what's happened to us?" Still jabbing
angrily at the fragments, he looked across at Kramer. There were
tears in his eyes.

"Sure they care," Kramer said quickly. "Everybody cares." He
tried to remember hearing or reading anything about the island.
Nothing came to mind. He thought harder, ransacking his memory.
"Jersey, where the cows come from, right?" he asked. "Hell, everybody knows how important this place is."

"Then when's the invasion coming?" Greg demanded. "When are
they going to set us free, for God's sake?"

"Any day now. Any *night*, more likely." Kramer jumped to his feet
as if to symbolize action. "Honest to God, that's all people can talk
about, back in England: the Second Front. It's got to come soon." He
grinned cheerfully and spread his arms wide. "Why the hell d'you
think we've been bombing the bejesus out of all them bridges and
railroads and stuff?"

Greg straightened up. His shoulders relaxed, and for the first time
he smiled. His teeth were stained and broken. "Good for you, lad,"
he said gently. "Blast the sods to buggery, every last one of 'em, it's
what they deserve. You did well."

Nobody had ever congratulated Kramer like that before. He experienced a moment of total happiness which left him convinced that
he was in the right place at the right time; that he was *meant* to be
washed up on Jersey, *meant* to end up in Jack Greg's kitchen. Memories occurred to him: the sun-drenched morning when he and five
hundred other brand-new second-lieutenants marched in a passing-
out parade under an impeccable Arizona sky; the first German fighter

he ever saw, a Messerschmitt 109 that rose and rose like a fish being wound in from a deep pool; the kick his heart gave when, ten thousand feet below, a small German town erupted into a colossal cumulus, balanced and symmetrical, snowy, silent, thrusting itself up as if in yearning or admiration: the fruit of a lucky strike on an ammunition train, maybe, or a chemical plant. "Hell, that's what we came over here for, wasn't it?" he asked cheerfully.

Greg was not listening. He had opened the window and was looking up the lane. Kramer heard brisk, masculine singing, underscored by the crunch of boots. He stood behind Greg and watched a company of German troops march past.

"They never stop bloody singing," Greg said. "Everywhere they go, they bloody sing. They need their bloody throats cut, the lot of them."

"Sure they do," Kramer said. "The sooner the better." On impulse, he added: "Matter of fact, I cut one of their throats myself, last night."

Greg's head swivelled. "You *what?*" he asked.

"Sure." He considered correcting himself: stabbing wasn't the same as cutting; but Greg's astonishment was too good to waste. "This kraut got in my way, so . . ." Kramer shrugged. "He had to go. So he went. Over and out."

"You mean, you killed one?" Greg looked stunned, bewildered; his mouth gaped; his face was suddenly empty of intelligence.

"Yeah. Sure. I had to." Now Kramer began to feel strong and decisive next to Greg. He also felt an inch or two taller. He smiled encouragingly, and realized that he really was an inch or two taller. "It was one against one, see, so I kind of took the initiative and cooled the guy."

"Jesus God, you killed one," Greg said weakly. He shut the window and drew the curtain.

"And that turned it into one against none," Kramer said. "Much better, huh?"

"He must have been the sentry they're after," Greg said. "You killed one of their sentries."

"I didn't stop to ask him what he was doing," Kramer said. He picked up a tableknife, flipped it in the air and caught it by the handle. "I just took him out of the game and moved on." He was impressed by his own calm professionalism.

"God Almighty." Greg washed his face with his hands, rubbing the shock away. "There's gonna be hell to pay when they find him. . . . Holy hell."

"Don't worry, Jack. I tucked him out of sight, he's safe," Kramer said. He balanced the tableknife by its point on his first finger.

"Maybe they'll blame the Commandos," Greg said, more to himself than to Kramer. "Maybe they'll think he got taken away to England."

"Sure. I mean, what the hell, it's only one sentry anyway. Your local S.S. Gauleiter is gonna have a bigger load than that on his mind before long. Right?"

"What d'you mean?" Greg asked. He was still taking in the death of the sentry.

"This island . . ." Kramer went to the doorway and looked out, his thumb testing the edge of the tableknife. "It's got to be the most beautiful target in the world. There's krauts everywhere! You can't toss a rock here without cracking some kraut on the skull! It's so easy, it's practically a crime."

Greg came over and peered uneasily at the dappled lane. "It's a crime what they've done," he said bitterly. "They took a lovely little island and turned it into the biggest Nazi battleship ever bloody built. Bastards. . . ."

"They're not so tough," Kramer said assuringly. "They can be creamed like anyone else. I just creamed three or four of them myself, before breakfast." Greg staggered, and bumped into the doorway. He sucked a deep breath into his lungs. He was very pale. "Hey, hey!" Kramer said, "take it easy! Gee . . . You been overdoing it, pal. Better sit down." He helped Greg to a chair.

"What d'you mean?" Greg asked. "What's happened?"

"Relax, okay? It was an accident. I just blew up this little old ammunition truck outside your cousin's farm, and a few krauts were standing too near the fire so they got themselves kinda flattened. They'll think it was an accident, somebody got careless. With all this military hardware lousing the place up, we might get a few more accidents like that, you think?" Kramer smiled, and patted Greg on the shoulder.

"I don't believe it," Greg said. He looked up, and his disbelief showed itself in a twisted, rueful smile. "You only just got here and already you kicked Jerry up the arse harder than any of us did in four years. I just don't believe it."

"Stick around," Kramer told him confidently. "Like the lady said: you ain't seen nothin' yet."

8

General Rimmer was eating his lunch at his desk when Wolff came in with Major Helldorf. Rimmer put the last piece of sandwich into his mouth and talked around it. "For a quiet little island, this is turning into a noisy little island," he said. "Things go bump in the night and then other things go bang in the daytime. It's all right for Wolff, he never sleeps anyway; but you, Helldorf, you must be very disturbed by this endless deafening racket, aren't you? As a conscientious policeman you must be thoroughly upset by it all. You must be conducting a most rigorous investigation with a view to obtaining a complete explanation and securing an early arrest, I hope. Aren't you? And when the hell am I going to see some results?"

"If you mean the ammunition truck, sir," Helldorf said evenly, "there's nothing to suggest that it wasn't an accident."

"Which means there's nothing to suggest that it *was* an accident," Rimmer said.

"We've just been over there and had a look at the evidence, sir," Wolff remarked, "and there's really not much left to suggest that it was even a truck."

"That's exactly what I don't like about it!" Rimmer barked. "It was a very thorough accident."

Helldorf tugged his lower lip and let it snap back. "Most of them are," he remarked. "We get a lot of accidents on Jersey, General. Narrow, twisting roads, heavy vehicles, German drivers: it's a lethal mixture. We get, on average, a wreck a week. This week's wreck happened to be carrying explosives, that's all."

"You know your trouble, Helldorf?" Rimmer picked up a magnifying glass and went over to Helldorf and studied his eyes. "Poor vision. You can't see your hand in front of your face." He lifted Helldorf's right hand and held it up in front of his face. "There you are. What's that?"

Helldorf frowned at the hand. "It looks like a bunch of bananas, sir," he said.

Rimmer released the hand. "And sabotage looks to you like pigeon-shit, because you've never seen sabotage before. Isn't that so?"

"No, sir. We've had evidence of sabotage on this island before now.

Several times." As Rimmer opened his mouth, Helldorf added, "But not by Islanders, sir. The sabotage starts hundreds of miles from here. A Frenchman drops a lump of black plastic explosive into a coal truck, say, and six weeks later one of our locomotives is chuffing along when it suddenly blows up: that sort of thing. A lot of our military vehicles are put together by foreign workers. Sometimes they hacksaw halfway through the brake cables. The Reich employs foreigners in its munitions factories too, which may explain a few premature explosions. And so on."

"That's where you're wrong," Rimmer said grimly. "No more and-so-on's on my island. Understand?"

Wolff raised his hand to attract their attention. "I remember once when the infantry were getting ready to attack near Demyansk," he said. "Our artillery fired off an enormous barrage and nothing exploded. Absolutely nothing. All duds."

He shook his head, smiling gently; and they looked at him, waiting for the unhappy consequences. "That can't have done you much good," Helldorf suggested.

"Actually it worked a treat," Wolff said. "The enemy assumed they were gas shells and he cleared off smartly. We just walked into his positions."

"War without tears," Rimmer observed. "A good trick. You should have tried it more often."

"Oh, we did, sir," Wolff said. "We tried it two hours later. Didn't work so well, though. The Russians sat tight and blew us to bits."

"Bad luck."

"Yes, sir. We all felt very disappointed. We thought we were on to something good, you see."

"Yes, I see." As he walked across to a wall-map of Jersey, Rimmer restrained an impulse to pat Wolff on the shoulder. "Look," he said, "here's the area where what's-his-name went missing, right? And here's where your fated ammo truck went off pop. Not a million miles apart, are they?"

"Well, it's a small island, sir," Helldorf said.

"Yes. But big enough to hide a lot of graves, apparently. How many have you found now?"

"About a dozen, sir. It's not finding them that takes the time; it's excavating them."

Rimmer sighed. "Amazing . . . Why does the Organisation Todt always do things the hard way? Why couldn't they just dig one big mass grave for everybody?"

"Perhaps they didn't all die at the same time, sir," Wolff suggested.

"What's that got to do with it?" Rimmer demanded.

"It's a matter of morale, I suppose," Helldorf said. "Workers might get depressed at the sight of a mass grave waiting for them every morning."

Rimmer sniffed his derision. "Morale! Depression! Everything's got to be psychologically tuned these days. Why can't people just do their job? That's what I've learned to do. Get on with it, get results, then good morale follows automatically. Bad morale is just an excuse for incompetence, Helldorf; remember that. You do your damn job and find what's-his-name. . . . What the hell is his name?"

"Keller, sir."

"Well, find him fast. Why are you standing around here? And if you can't find Keller, then find somebody who looks like him and stick a new label on his backside, but for God's sake *get some results.* Good-bye."

Helldorf saluted and went out. He did not hurry. "Open the beer," Rimmer ordered. He prowled restlessly around the room, stamping on a creaky floorboard, side-footing a chair out of the way, and ending up at his desk. He picked up a signal. " 'Northview four,' " he read aloud. "What's that mean?"

"It's the code-signal for invasion-probability, sir," Wolff said. He was pouring the beer carefully so as to protect the head. "Army Intelligence in Paris makes a new rating every day, on a scale of one-to-four."

"And four means? . . ."

"Improbable, sir."

"Bunch of pinheads." Rimmer took the beer and walked to the window. "They live in a permanent fog. Look here: clear skies and calm seas. Do they think Eisenhower is going to wait until it freezes, so that he can drive across? Intelligence? They couldn't tell Mata Hari from Hermann Goering."

"I could," Wolff said mildly. "Goering has bigger tits."

Rimmer snorted briefly. "Tell me, Wolff: where would you strike, if you were Eisenhower? You'd hit the town, St. Helier, wouldn't you? Grab the docks and guarantee your reinforcements a good place to land. Right?"

"No fear," Wolff said.

Rimmer drank some beer and studied him over the rim. "Use your brains, man," he said. "That's exactly the technique which the enemy has been trying to perfect in his landings at St. Nazaire and Dieppe."

"Tried and failed, sir. His men came an awful cropper. Two awful croppers, I suppose. . . . What is a cropper, anyway?"

"None of that alters the fact that he must have a harbour." Rimmer went over to the wall-map again. "If I were Eisenhower I'd drop every paratrooper I could find, with orders to grab this harbour and hold it for twenty-four hours, even if I lost every man in the process. Because by that time . . . I'm not boring you, am I, Wolff?"

" 'Cropper: one who crops.' " Wolff shut the dictionary. "Don't you wish you could write like that, sir? It's a gift, I suppose. Either you're born with it or—"

"Stop yammering, for God's sake."

"Yes, sir." Wolff came across and stood beside Rimmer. Together they looked at the map. "You know, sir, we could have done with something like this in Russia," Wolff said admiringly. "It's all trees and forests out there, you know. No seaside to speak of. . . . Would you like to hear what I think, sir?"

"If it's worth hearing."

"I think Eisenhower will wait for a patch of clear weather when the tide is really high just before dawn, and then he'll use it to get his landingcraft right up the beach. Once he's secured a good beachhead, he'll fan out and try to capture a harbour; after all, that's how he landed in Tunisia and Sicily and Italy, and it worked every time there. Moreover, a beach assault gives him added scope for air support, naval cover, tactical decoys, and flank attacks, whilst minimizing the danger to the civilian population."

Rimmer was surprised and impressed. "You seem to have considered everything except the price of apples, Wolff. Well done! I like officers who can think for themselves."

Wolff shrugged modestly. "I happened to read it in an American magazine called *Time,* sir. A copy got washed up on the beach last week. Probably fell out of an aeroplane, don't you think?"

Rimmer drained his beer. "I'll tell you what I think. I think you've swallowed their propaganda whole, which makes me more convinced than ever that they'll try to seize this harbour first." He handed Wolff the glass and went to his desk.

"It won't do them any good, sir," Wolff said, following. "The docks are wired for demolition from end to end, so they won't capture anything but a pile of rubble, which means they'll have to turn around and make a beach landing after all."

"Good." Rimmer sat in his chair and swung his feet onto his desk. "From what I've seen, all our beaches are perfect killing-grounds. We'll slaughter them, they won't get their boots out of the sand. Now shut up and fetch me this tame engineering genius."

Wolff ushered in Colonel Schumacher. He was a serious man of about thirty-five, an inch or two taller than Rimmer, handsomely dressed in a soft grey suit. His hair was black, cut short and brushed away from a domed forehead. Between his brows there was a blunt arrowhead of frown marks, the only lines on a face which was otherwise bland and untroubled to the point of being almost completely forgettable. It was saved by the eyes. Schumacher had wide-open eyes, enthusiastic and confident. One look at Schumacher's eyes and you were sure that he knew where he was going. He looked only for support.

He gave the party salute with his right arm at full stretch. His left arm should have remained pressed to his side, but he let it rise slightly, with the wrist cocked and the fingers delicately splayed. "Heil Hitler!" he said with feeling.

"Yes indeed," Rimmer said. "Heil Hitler." They shook hands. "Well, well. I've heard such a lot about your achievements, Schumacher, that I almost expected to meet a superman. I certainly didn't expect a civilian."

"Surely one can serve the Reich in a grey suit, sir," Schumacher said cheerfully.

"One can serve the Reich in a loincloth, Colonel," Rimmer said. "In fact we have a few battalions of Indians stationed in France right now who would be happy to do just that, if we paid them extra for it. But German colonels normally wear uniform."

"Mine is a sort of nominal commission, General. The Fuehrer insisted. He said my work here justified at least a colonelcy."

"Quite right."

"The Fuehrer is always right. But when I tried to wear my uniform, sir, it gave me a most painful rash."

Rimmer grunted. "How strange. And how long have you been on Jersey, Schumacher?"

"Over two years, sir. Since Fuehrer Directive Forty. The one that established the fortification of the Atlantic Wall, you remember."

"Yes, I was looking at FD Forty just now," Rimmer said. "A real landmark."

Major Wolff cleared his throat. "That was FD Fifty-one, sir."

"Are you sure? The one I saw was all about fortifications and so on."

"Yes, sir. That was Directive Fifty-one, issued November 1943. It confirmed Directive Forty of March 1942."

Rimmer made a note. "What did Directive Forty say, anyway?"

Wolff examined the point on his pencil. "Much the same as Directive Fifty-one, sir."

"Don't play the fool with me, Wolff."

"No, sir. It pointed out the danger of attack on the coastline of Europe and ordered that it be repulsed, and if it couldn't be repulsed it must be counter-attacked, and so on." Wolff met Rimmer's frown with a calm gaze.

"What d'you mean, 'and so on'?"

"Well, Directive Fifty-one added a few details. Like Field Marshal Rommel's appointment as C-in-C Channel Coastline."

"I'm glad you remembered Field Marshal Rommel." Rimmer's tone was biting. Wolff stopped playing with his pencil and looked as serious as he could. "Forgetting Field Marshal Rommel would have been dangerously casual. Has he been here yet?" Rimmer asked Schumacher.

"No, General. But we're ready for inspection at any time."

"Good. Now tell me all you've done."

Schumacher opened a portfolio and took out a stack of charts. "At present, sir, we're halfway through the Fuehrer's eight-year plan to fortify the Channel Islands. This chart shows the total amount of construction to date. The figures on the left represent tens of thousands of tons. It will give you some idea of the importance which the Fuehrer attaches to this work when I tell you that total excavations carried out in the Channel Islands are only slightly less than total excavations carried out so far in the whole of the rest of the Atlantic Wall." Schumacher paused and smiled at Rimmer, whose expression was concealed behind his cupped hands. "To make this possible required the building of twenty-five miles of railway line, which I myself designed," Schumacher went on. "Three more miles of line are under construction. Also, the dock terminals had to be enlarged. I did that too. This chart represents the total labour force brought to the islands ... approximately thirty-four thousand persons. .... The force requires constant replenishment, indicated by the dotted line here. . . ."

Schumacher piled statistic on statistic: coal, steel, cement, fuel, explosives, manpower. Rimmer's eyebrows rose to their limit and stayed there. Clearly Hitler had picked the right man to convert Jersey to an impregnable fortress.

"Excellent," he said at last. "You've done a magnificent job here, Schumacher. Admirable. When will you be finished?"

Schumacher's look of contentment faded as if someone had pulled a dimmer-switch. "I wish I could tell you that, sir," he said sadly. "It's a matter of materials. Last summer I was getting twenty thousand tons a month; now I'm averaging less than three thousand. It's very alarming, sir."

"What's the hold-up? Shipping? Red tape?"

"They *say* there's a scarcity on the mainland."

"Hmm." Rimmer's face gave a twitch of impatience. "What d'you need most?"

"Cement," Schumacher said at once. "I desperately need six thousand tons of cement, sir. It's months overdue."

"Right." Rimmer made a note. "Now I want you to do something for me. Wear your uniform, Colonel."

"But General . . ." Schumacher's body seemed to twist and withdraw inside his clothes. "The rash causes such pain. . . . I can't even work, or—"

"What's that suit made of?" Rimmer strode over and fingered it. "Flannel, isn't it?" Schumacher nodded, wretched with anticipation. "That's your answer, then, isn't it? Get your uniform lined with flannel! Suppose Rommel turns up here. How in heaven can I present a colonel in a spotted tie? It's quite unthinkable. We're running a war here, not a men's haberdashery. All right?" Schumacher nodded miserably. "Good man!" Rimmer squeezed his arm and Schumacher tried not to flinch. "It's a fine uniform, Schumacher. There are thousands who would give an arm and a leg for the chance to wear it."

"Well, half of it," Wolff said.

Rimmer ignored him. "What's that hullabaloo?" he demanded.

In the street outside, a car horn was blaring. It overwhelmed some timid cheering and a spatter of handclaps. Wolff went to the window. "Nothing special, sir," he reported. "Just Canon Renouf getting arrested again."

Rimmer joined him. The window overlooked German Field Gendarmerie Headquarters, where the Gestapo had its offices. Passers-by

were gathering around to watch the clergyman being escorted from
a car to the entrance.

"Again?" Rimmer said. "Is he so dangerous?"

"Indiscreet, I should say." Wolff smiled as Renouf paused to chat
with a sentry. When Captain Paulus impatiently put his hand on
Renouf's shoulder, Renouf cordially put his arm around Paulus. They
went in together, Paulus rigid with dislike. Wolff chuckled.

"Indiscretion is dangerous, wouldn't you agree, Schumacher?"
Rimmer said. The telephone rang, and Schumacher saluted and sidled
out while the general was taking the call. Already he was walking
uncomfortably.

"Don't apologize, damn you," Rimmer said. "I'll tell you soon
enough when you've wasted my time." He threw the receiver at the
cradle, and missed. "Get my command vehicle," he told Wolff. "That
was Helldorf. They've found a rubber dinghy on the rocks, and guess
where? Not a hundred yards from where that sentry went missing.
Now who was right?"

9

After the bright sunlight the cellar was cool and dim. A few half-filled
sacks lay in a corner. A man was sitting on one and sorting potatoes
from another. At the sound of footsteps he straightened, his thumb
still worrying mud from a potato; until he recognized Jack Greg, and
relaxed.

"Hullo then, Ted," Greg said. "This chap's . . . um . . . Earl
Creamer."

"Kramer," said the American. He squeezed his bare toes against
the cold granite floor and sniffed the ancient, faded smell of fruit and
vegetables.

"He's a Yankee pilot," Greg explained. "Got shot down last night.
This is Ted Langley."

"Hi," Kramer said. It sounded inadequate. "How do you do?" he
added.

Langley stood up: a short, stocky man, middle-aged, heavy-chested,
with powerful, hairy arms. His head merged into his shoulders without the luxury of a neck, and his face was as battered as an old boot;
so it came as a surprise that his voice was light and husky; almost
gentle. "Stone the crows," he said. They shook hands and he looked

closely at Kramer. "Bloody young, aren't you?" Langley asked. "Are all Yank pilots as young as you?" Kramer grinned and shrugged, slightly embarrassed, unwilling to reveal that he wasn't actually a pilot because that would diminish him just when he felt the need for approval. So he grinned and said nothing, and looked younger than ever.

"He needs papers, Ted," Greg said.

"That's a funny name, Creamer," Langley said. "Never heard that one before."

"It's just a regular old American name," Kramer said. "And it's *Kramer.*"

"Well, we're pleased to see you, of course." Langley took out a bundle of identity cards. "Staying long?"

"I don't seem to have a hell of a lot of choice. There's no way I can get to England, is there?"

"Depends how well you can swim. It's ninety miles, uphill all the way."

"You might get to France," Greg said. "Still a few ships going that way."

Langley screwed his face into a scowl. "Got any names and addresses in the French Resistance?"

"No."

"No. You wouldn't last long then, wandering around Brittany with nowhere to stay, no French papers, no French money, that red hair and talking broad Yankee. The Jerries aren't complete bloody idiots." As he spoke he was filling in an identity card. "What name d'you want?" he asked. The two men looked at Kramer.

"I kind of like the one I've got," he said.

Greg scoffed. "Not likely," he said. "You need a good Jersey name."

"Leroux," Langley suggested. "Eric Leroux."

"Leroux means redhaired," Greg explained.

"What the hell," Kramer said. "You guys know best." He watched Langley write in the name. "I guess this cloak-and-dagger stuff is all in a day's work to you," he said, making conversation. Langley waved the card to dry the ink, and handed it to him. As Kramer took it, Langley stamped hard on his right foot. Kramer screamed. Hot flames of pain seared his foot, shrank for an instant to a cold flicker, and surged back with a great gush of suffering which enfeebled his whole leg and turned his guts slack and useless. He sat down, more heavily than he intended, and tried to hide his raging foot in his hands. "Jesus fucking Christ," he whispered. "You lousy goddam chicken-shit bastard sonofabitch asshole." Suffering as he was, he was impressed by his own swearing.

"All right," Langley said. "Good enough."

"That's what you think," Kramer snarled. "Cunt."

Jack Greg tried to help him to his feet but Kramer refused to get up. "You're all right now, son," Greg said, "but suppose the first words out of your mouth had been '*Mein Gott*'? I don't know what we'd have had to do, I'm sure."

"I'll tell you what you can do. You can go fuck yourselves."

"That's all very well for you," Langley said. "A lot of Islanders have ended up in prison for helping people who turned out to be German agents."

"You didn't have to bust my goddam foot." Kramer used his sleeve to wipe the blood away. He picked bits of dirt out of the broken skin. "Christ, I wish I'd stayed out there in the goddam Channel. At least I could throw up in peace."

Langley scuffed his feet. "I forgot I was wearing these clogs," he said. "Sorry."

"Get me out of here," Kramer told Greg. "Keep this maniac off me."

"I had my doubts too, you know," Greg said. "No uniform, and smelling of pigs, and all. How could I be sure you were a Yank pilot?"

"That guy Betteridge knows." Kramer hobbled to the stairs. "Go ask him. Holy Moses, I'll never walk again."

"Louis Betteridge and me haven't been on talking terms for sixteen years," Greg said. "That's why he dumped you on my doorstep."

"Great," Kramer said. "Terrific. I come three, four thousand miles to fight for freedom and you bums aren't even speaking to each other. That's just dandy." He limped up the stairs.

"There's an old pair of shoes you can have," Langley called after him. Kramer said nothing. They watched him climb out of sight.

"Nice lad," Langley said. "He's got guts. Reminds me of my own boy. Last I heard of him he was in the Duke of Cornwall's Light Infantry. Corporal."

"He doesn't half eat," Greg said. "You should see him put away the spuds. What's Spam, d'you know?"

Langley shook his head. "Can you take care of him?"

"I'll manage somehow. Anyway, it's only for a few days. He says the invasion'll be here soon."

"Does he, by God?" Langley's eyes brightened. "Does he really say that? I can't believe—" His voice trailed away and he stood staring at the sunlight flooding down the stairwell.

"He eats enough for two," Greg said. "He eats like a bloody horse."

Langley took a loose brick out of the wall and fished out a bundle of ration cards. He gave Greg two and replaced the rest. "He really said that about the invasion, did he? My stars. . . . I think the Controlling Council ought to see him, then. A few days, he reckons?" Greg nodded. "I know they've got to come soon," Langley said. "Otherwise there's no point in going on, but still . . . Sometimes I don't know whether I really believe in it any more. Funny, that, isn't it?"

Greg and Langley stood with their hands in their pockets and looked at the dusty granite floor. Four years, each year with less to live on except hope of invasion, until hope itself was something you didn't dare look at too hard. "I'll get him those shoes," Langley said.

The rubber dinghy lay in the middle of the road like a great dead yellow poppy, a bit lopsided and more than a bit torn and stained by the attack of the sea. As the general's halftrack bustled around the bend and squealed to a halt, half a dozen troops came to attention. Rimmer vaulted out. Dum-Dum wriggled free from Wolff's grasp and followed him. Together they stared at the dinghy. Major Helldorf stood nearby and scratched his ear.

Watching the scene, Wolff felt the theatricality of it all. It was as if General Rimmer were a tribal chief and the dinghy some strange yellow totem. The scene looked arranged and designed: a splash of wrinkled saffron on the grey tarmac, flanked by tufted grass which shimmered under the invisible brushstrokes of the afternoon breeze. In a long, slow instant of discovery, Major Wolff realized that he did not take the war seriously any longer. For some time he had been treating it as a long-running bad joke; now he couldn't even give it that much importance. He had let his attention drift. He had lost his place in this war. He should now be standing one pace to the right and the rear of the fortress commandant, not sitting in the back of this halftrack with the throb of the engine gently vibrating up his left arm and through his fist into his jawbone. The war was significant, critical, tragic: but not for Major Wolff. It had gone on too long. He had run out of seriousness. From now on he was a bystander.

Major Helldorf stepped forward and saluted. "You asked to be kept informed, General," he said, "but really this is just a standard American rubber dinghy."

"Show me where it was found."

Helldorf went to the fence and pointed down at the beach. "That big black rock, sir," he said. "About three metres out from the water's edge."

"Why wasn't it reported earlier? I ordered a thorough search of this area."

"A thorough search was made, sir, but you'll remember it was high tide this morning."

"So what? Are your men afraid to get their feet wet?"

"The dinghy was under eight metres of water this morning, sir. It wasn't until low tide that we even saw it, and then it was jammed behind that rock."

"These things are awfully well made, sir, aren't they?" said Wolff, joining them. "Look, it's even got a little mast. Jolly clever, the Americans."

"Take Dum-Dum for a walk, Wolff," Rimmer said. He hooked his fingers between the barbs of the wire and studied the beach. "Finding this thing here, Helldorf. . . . It's too much of a coincidence, right?"

"Not necessarily, sir."

"Rubbish, man. We lose a sentry and find a dinghy, all in the space of twenty-four hours? It stinks to heaven."

Helldorf almost sighed. "Let me put it this way, sir. Suppose I organize a search on the opposite side of the island and we find another American rubber dinghy on the rocks. Would you expect to lose another sentry over there?"

Rimmer did not like the question, did not like Helldorf's relaxed and unmilitary style. He was not even sure that he understood the question. But he detected a professional competence behind the man's mildly dyspeptic expression, and that made him cautious. Rimmer had got where he was by knowing when to give his talented subordinates their heads. If things went wrong, theirs were the heads that got served up on a plate. "Are you saying the man was not killed here?" he asked.

"I'm not saying he was killed anywhere, sir. We haven't found his body. He might have deserted, he might be shacked up with some floozy in St. Helier for all we know. It's happened before."

Rimmer jerked his head at the dinghy. "And that just fell out of the sky?"

Major Wolff cleared his throat. "It does say 'Air Force' on it, sir," he said. He was sitting on the dinghy, beside the boxer dog.

"I told you to walk Dum-Dum, Wolff."

"Dum-Dum refuses to be walked, sir."

"Then make him."

"He's stronger than I am, sir."

"You two." Rimmer pointed at the nearest soldiers. "Help this officer move that dog."

Wolff stood up. The soldiers took hold of Dum-Dum's collar and lifted. The dinghy rose with the dog: Dum-Dum's massive jaws were fastened on the fabric. "Idiots," Rimmer said. One of the soldiers shook the dog by the collar until it began to make choking noises, and its hind legs scrabbled desperately at the dinghy floor. "Imbeciles," Rimmer said. The men looked at him for orders. "Oh, put the beast down," he said angrily. They lowered Dum-Dum to the road. The dog sprawled warily inside the dinghy, its eyes rolling and its teeth still clenched in the fabric. "Pair of cretins," Rimmer said. He turned back to Helldorf. "Well?"

"General, the temptation in this situation is to find a pattern just because one wants a pattern. We searched the area and found a dinghy. That in itself means nothing. Frankly, I should have been surprised if we had *not* found a dinghy."

"Then you must be easily surprised, Major."

"Perhaps not a dinghy, sir, but a liferaft, or a bundle of lifejackets, or *something*. The Channel is full of that sort of stuff. Inevitably some of it washes up around here."

"So you don't think it has any link with my missing sentry."

"It might, it might not. And there again perhaps the link isn't the obvious one. For instance, sir, it's not impossible that Keller himself had the dinghy hidden somewhere. Perhaps he took it down to the water last night, launched it, got wrecked on those invasion obstacles and was drowned."

"And why the hell should he do that?"

Helldorf sucked his teeth. "Last year, sir, a batman shot his officer and threw himself down a well. Why the hell he did *that* we never knew, but he did. Maybe Keller thought he could drift to England."

"Ninety miles? Ridiculous."

"This is a small island, sir, very crowded. There's not much to do.

People behave strangely when they're bored. Have you ever lived on an island, sir?"

"No, Major, and I've never had the time to be bored, either. What else have you found?"

"Nothing relevant. Just a lot of bloodstains." Rimmer's eyebrows twitched. "Too many and too old," Helldorf added. "The Organisation Todt used forced labour to dig bunkers and so on. No boots, of course, just rags on their feet, so they bled everywhere. It confuses the dogs."

"Are you confused, Dum-Dum?" Wolff asked. The dog wagged its stumpy tail, barked once, and cocked its leg against the dinghy. "Dum-Dum seems confused, sir," he reported.

"We're leaving," Rimmer ordered. He tapped Helldorf on the chest. "You don't think this is a case of sabotage because you don't *want* to think so. Believe me, I've had experience of sabotage and you don't get rid of it by looking the other way. I want you to find that sentry, Helldorf, and I don't care if you have to kick every man, woman, and child to death to do it."

Helldorf and the soldiers watched the halftrack speed away. "That should certainly do the trick, shouldn't it?" Helldorf said brightly to the nearest soldier.

"Don't know, sir," the man said.

"Very wise," said Helldorf. "Very wise."

Rimmer said nothing on the way back to his headquarters. He dismissed Wolff and sent for Captain Paulus. Paulus accepted the offer of a chair without giving thanks. He was not overawed by Rimmer: no general could outrank the Gestapo.

"I saw you bringing in that pastor," Rimmer said. "I'm glad to see you getting to grips with the troublemakers. You have my full backing, you know."

Paulus nodded politely.

"I'm not at all happy with the way Helldorf is handling this missing-sentry business," Rimmer went on. "I'm sure there are Islanders who know more than they've said. Helldorf's too meticulous, too painstaking. He thinks too much. Weighs all the options. I don't want options, I want results." He drummed his fingers on the desk. Paulus moistened his lips and waited patiently. "D'you think you could . . . scare up some action?" Rimmer asked.

Paulus nodded once.

"Good," Rimmer said. Nevertheless he felt, obscurely, that somehow the junior officer had contrived to take charge of the situation. "Good!" he repeated briskly.

Paulus tilted his head a little. After a moment Rimmer realized that Paulus wasn't simply waiting for final orders; he was actually looking at the Fortress Commandant, surveying him, taking stock of him. *Insolent bastard!* was Rimmer's sudden reaction, abruptly suppressed: there was nothing to be gained from a fight with the Gestapo. That was Rule One.

"Then all that remains to be said is . . . good luck," Rimmer said. He added a firm, positive gesture.

Paulus waited. He waited just long enough for his delay to begin to be offensive, and then he stood up. "General," he murmured. He went out.

That's the last time I ask you for anything, you smooth sod, Rimmer thought; but he was honest enough to add: *unless I really need it.*

10

Ted Langley had a van and a small petrol ration, granted so that he could collect provisions. He used part of his ration to drive Jack Greg and Earl Kramer into St. Helier. They could have walked—it wasn't more than three miles—but Langley wanted to make amends for Kramer's foot; and he decided that he deserved a little luxury. It wasn't every day that he took an American bomber pilot to meet the Controlling Council, even if the chap did look remarkably young. Besides, he might find some provisions to take back to his shop, if he was lucky. Very lucky. Unbelievably lucky.

Greg and Kramer rode in the back. It smelt of turnips and exhaust fumes.

"What the hell's the matter with that guy?" Kramer asked. He was still angry about his stamped-on foot. "He acts like he doesn't believe in the U.S. Air Force. What in hell does he think's been making all those loud bangs over in France? Champagne corks?"

"Ted didn't mean any harm," Greg said. "It's just—See, everybody here's been waiting, and waiting. You know what it's like, you wait for something so long, when it comes you don't seem to feel anything—"

"I felt something. I felt plenty."

"I believe you. Ted's got big feet."

"Terrific. I had small feet till I came here. Now I got one small, one big. Thank you, Ted. Nice guy."

"What it was, he couldn't believe you could be so young. Not and fly one of them big bombers. That's what he couldn't believe."

"Fourteen goddam missions," Kramer said. He knew he should really tell Greg that he was a bombardier, not a pilot, but not now; not after Langley had bashed his foot. "Yesterday was the fourteenth. Next time I'll bring along my eyeglasses and my hernia belt. Who did he expect, for Chrissake? Tyrone Power? Errol Flynn?"

"I don't know," Greg said. "Who are they?"

Kramer stared. "Movie stars," he said.

"Ah." Greg noticed a small, bruised potato lying on the floor and put it in his pocket. "All we get here is the Jerry films. Propaganda. I never bother. What's it like in England now?"

"Lousy," Kramer said. "Always pissing down with rain." He knew that Greg really wanted to know how the British were standing up to war, but right now he didn't feel like talking about other people's heroism and self-sacrifice and cheerfulness. "Our group had six missions scrubbed in the last ten days," he said.

"Yes?" Greg didn't understand, but he nodded anyway. "We're nearly there now," he said, as if that made up for the bad weather.

They were rattling through St. Helier. Kramer caught glimpses of narrow, twisting streets and solid, stone-built houses. Occasionally gulls flickered in and out of view, looking conspicuously white and well turned-out; by contrast the people were drably dressed, even shabby, and the buildings needed a coat of paint. There were surprising flashes of colour, but they came from the sea or from spilling tubs of geraniums. The place had an atmosphere that was half fishing-port, half market-town. Kramer observed how easily the civilians and the soldiers mingled. Take away the swastika flags and banners and he could be back in Cambridgeshire, in Market Deeping. He noticed a pub with a hanging sign, the Goat and Compasses. Then he saw a total contradiction: a policeman—a typical English bobby with his domed helmet and his thumbs hooked in his tunic pockets—talking to a German officer. The van turned a bend and the figures disappeared, but Kramer held their image in his memory: irreconcilables reconciled. He wondered what they had been talking about, and who was giving the orders. It was like a dream, it couldn't be real. But the van jolted over cobblestones until Kramer had to grab for support, and last night's barbed-wire scratches stung his hands; so it had to be real.

They stopped in a small Georgian square, lined with tall and purposeful buildings. Langley led them up a flight of wide steps and through a doorway that had been built for crinolines. "This is where the Bailiff has his offices," he said. "The Controlling Council meets here. He's Chairman, see." They climbed a spiral staircase, passing rooms where typewriters clacked. Kramer glanced past a half-open door and saw a grey-haired woman with a pencil in her mouth; she was frowning at something in a buff file. It was like being inside the City Hall in Plattsville, Ohio. Same colours, same smell. As if they kept the air in the filing cabinets and you had to fill in a form to get it changed.

Langley used the banister to help heave himself up the last few stairs, and he leaned, panting, against an ornate doorway. "That climb's going to kill me one day," he muttered. "Why can't old Dan work downstairs?"

"Self-protection," said a man's voice. "The climb keeps the riff-raff away. Well, usually."

"But since you're here . . ." said another voice.

"Sweet blind O'Reilly," Langley said. He took Greg and Kramer inside. Sitting by the window were two late-middle-aged men, one sandy-haired and sprawling, the other grey and elegant. The room was small but comfortable, an antechamber to a much bigger room. "What are you two doing here?" Langley asked.

"Waiting for Dan to get off the phone," the sandy-haired man said. "He's called a Council meeting. Dunno why."

"Never mind, I've got something we can talk about," Langley told them. He pointed at Earl Kramer. "Yank bomber pilot. He says the invasion's coming soon, probably tomorrow or the day after."

"Hey, wait a minute," Kramer said uneasily, but Langley was bustling him forward to be introduced. "This smooth bugger is Richard Labuschagne. He's a bank manager. Meet Lieutenant Kramer. He bombs Berlin."

They shook hands. Labuschagne was the grey and elegant one, dressed in the orthodox uniform of black jacket and pinstriped trousers. At closer range Kramer saw that black leather patches reinforced it discreetly at cuffs and elbows and lapels. The banker had thick and silvery hair, which he kept brushed to perfection. But his face was sunken and lined beyond repair. "Welcome to Jersey," he said.

"Nice to be here," Kramer replied.

"Ah, now that's a matter of opinion," Labuschagne said with a sad smile.

"And the shaggy bugger is Henry Beatty," Langley said. "Don't get ill, because he's the doctor."

Kramer shook hands again. Beatty was at least two inches taller, and he wore tweeds of old-fashioned cut which generously wrapped his angular, bony frame. The only characteristic he had in common with Labuschagne was the mark of overwork on his face: his cheeks were worn as hollow as a whetstone, and he had bags under his eyes like toy purses. "How d'you do?" he said.

Kramer flexed his foot. "You sure you really want to know?" he asked, with a quick grin that made Langley chuckle.

"Not unless it's constipation," Beatty said. "I can give you medicine for that. In fact, it's the only medicine I *can* give you."

"No constipation," Kramer said. "More like the opposite lately."

"Ah . . . Well, if you ever feel you'd rather be constipated, don't hesitate to ask."

"I'll surely bear that in mind, sir," Kramer said.

"Then I can cure you of it, d'you see," Beatty pointed out.

"Dick and Henry and me are the Controlling Council," Langley said. "Us and the Bailiff run the island, pretty well."

"Yeah?" Kramer said. "From what I saw, I'd say the krauts were pretty well in full command here."

"No, no. They run their part and we run ours."

"Sounds cosy."

"You see," Beatty said, "the islands have been self-governing for hundreds of years. Under the Crown, of course. We saw no reason to give up that tradition just because the Germans gate-crashed the party. We can govern ourselves better than they can. Maybe it's not comfortable, but it's tolerable."

Kramer sucked his teeth. "Maybe that explains something else. Maybe it explains why you folk don't seem too excited about getting yourselves liberated."

"Oh, I thought that was a joke," Labuschagne said.

"Well, 'tain't no joke over in England, no sir," Kramer told him. "We been treating it pretty damn seriously over there, believe me."

"Yes, of course you have," said Labuschagne. "Remarkably stupid thing for me to say. I do apologize."

"He's a banker, you understand," Beatty explained. "They never take anything seriously. You should see him trying to count on his fingers without moving his lips. Hilarious."

"It's not nearly as funny as my weekly trip to the German brothel," Labuschagne said. "Half the Islanders fall about every time they see me knock on the door."

"Only half?" Langley grunted. "What's wrong with the rest?"

"Ah, the other half are all my customers. They think it's disgusting; they can't understand how I can lower myself."

"Hey, you mean Jerry runs a regular sporting house here?" Kramer was just catching up.

"He does. The ladies are French, and they send all their earnings home. The bank used to be full of Les Girls and it was bad for trade, you see. So now I take the bank to them."

"He's lucky," Beatty declared. "All he does is count their change. Me, I have to examine them. Sometimes I even have to grope around inside their overworked plumbing. You can imagine what that thought does to my more fastidious patients."

"It's disgusting," Labuschagne sniffed. "I can't understand how you can lower yourself."

"I don't lower myself," Beatty explained. "The girls stand on a chair."

Labuschagne looked at his watch. "First he says it's urgent, then he keeps us waiting," he said.

"Hell, those French girls aren't being very patriotic," Earl Kramer protested. "They shouldn't behave like that, for God's sake."

"Oh, most of them do it for their families," Labuschagne said. "I'm sure the money's very useful. Besides . . . just about everybody on this island is in business with the Germans, one way or another."

"Yeah, but not like that," Kramer insisted. "I mean, that's encouraging 'em."

"I don't give a damn what the girls do," Langley said, "but the Jerry doctors ought to inspect them. It's their brothel, it's their bloody soldiers who stand to catch the pox. It's not fair on Henry."

"All's fair in sex and war." Beatty yawned. "If we let VD get loose inside their whorehouse it would soon spread everywhere. There's enough banging going on in this island to awaken the dead."

"It's disgusting," Labuschagne said. "I can't understand how they can lower themselves."

"Block and tackle?" Langley suggested.

"Ha ha bloody ha," Greg snarled. The sound was startling, for
Greg had been subdued and silent since they came in. Now he
straightened up and thrust his wiry shoulders back. The beginning of
a sneer tugged his mouth askew. "All a great big joke, isn't it? Bloody
witty lot of buggers, you lot. You'd sooner laugh than fight, you
would." He stabbed a dramatic finger towards Earl Kramer. "He
could teach you something about fighting. He could show you how
to sort the bastards out. Christ Almighty, the bloody liberation's
going to be here before we've lifted a bloody finger to help it!"

There was a short silence. Earl Kramer shuffled his feet and
frowned modestly. Ted Langley went over to Greg and patted his
shoulder. "See, Jack actually found our American friend," he told the
others. "Naturally, he feels more sort of . . . I dunno . . . involved."

"That's understandable," Labuschagne said. "All the same I'm at
a loss to know what exactly he expects us to do."

"Stop licking their arses," Greg rasped. He looked to Kramer for
support. "Start booting them up the arse instead, right?"

Earl Kramer found them all looking at him. "That's exactly right,"
he said. It sounded good, so he said it again. "That's *exactly* right.
Listen: there's more goddam targets on this island waiting to be
flattened than I've had hot dogs. What are we all gonna do? Sit around
and wait until the Allies hit the beach and watch 'em get a bloody
nose?"

"Let's get this right," Beatty said slowly. "Are you proposing
sabotage?"

"You bet your blue bootees I'm proposing sabotage," Kramer declared. "I'm proposing sabotage in spades with ice cream and chopped
nuts."

"And when d'you reckon on starting?" Langley asked.

"Yesterday," Kramer told him firmly. Greg nodded enthusiastically, but the other three men simply looked at Kramer blankly,
almost woodenly; and that irritated him. "How the hell do you guys
expect to get yourselves liberated unless you get off your fat duffs and
start swinging?" he demanded.

"Wait a minute, laddie," Labuschagne said, and knew at once that
he had used the wrong word, even before Kramer's head jerked
backwards. *Damn, I've gone and offended the fellow,* he thought. Too
late now. Besides, why should this American be so touchy? He was
obviously thirty years younger than anybody else in the room, so what
made "laddie" such a mortal insult? Labuschagne took a deep breath

and ploughed on. "I don't suppose you've been here very long. We have. Long enough to know that sabotage would be not only very easy but also very stupid."

"Yeah? Why?" Kramer's face was heavy with resentment.

"Because innocent Islanders would suffer along with the enemy, that's why. This is a very crowded community."

"So is London. So is Berlin. So was Stalingrad, remember? Nobody in those places decided to quit and lie low and tell funny stories till the war was over. Right, Daddy?"

"It's not like that here," Beatty said. "Jersey's different. We—"

"You want to get liberated, don't you?" Kramer challenged.

"Of course we do. The point is—"

"Yeah, I know the point. The point is you're ready to fight to the last drop of some other sucker's blood."

Labuschagne was shaking his head. "Let me try to explain." He gave what he thought was a sympathetic smile, but it reached Kramer as an ageing, patronizing smirk. "Things are not as straightforward as they may seem."

"Don't bother," Kramer retorted. "I understand fine. I understand just dandy."

Beatty began: "I'm sorry—"

"Yeah, I bet," Kramer cut him short. "I can just see how goddam sorry you all are. Goddam heartbroken."

Beatty raised his hands in a gesture of mild despair. The door to the next room was thrown open and Daniel de Wilde hurried in. "Dear, dear, dear, I'm so sorry, I do apologize," he said. He was massaging his right ear.

"Yeah, sure, everyone's sorry," Kramer muttered, but the Bailiff was too preoccupied to notice him. "We've got a really sticky problem, I'm afraid," he announced. "Please come in. . . . Ah, Ted, glad you could get here. . . . After you, after you. There isn't a second to waste." He ushered the Council Members into his room and was closing the door when Earl Kramer grabbed his arm.

"Sir, are you the boss around here?" he asked.

"Who's this?" de Wilde said.

"He's an American airman," Langley told him. "Jack Greg found him."

"Yes? Good. Are you all right? Not hurt?" Kramer shook his head. "Fine. Take a seat, I'll see you later." The door closed on Kramer with a crisp finality.

"Gutless lot of toffee-noses," Greg complained. "See how they treat you? You'll get no change out of them."

Kramer walked to the middle of the room and stood with his fists on his hips and his legs braced. "This whole set-up is screwy," he said. "Who's running the Resistance around here? Anyone?"

"Gutless bloody bunch," Greg scoffed. "The Jerries've got them in their pockets. They've given up."

Kramer looked at him and laughed. "That's what they think," he said. "Laddie."

"Well, it's short and not very sweet," de Wilde told the Controlling Council. "Canon Renouf's been arrested again and this time they're sending him to Paris, and you know what that means: Cherche Midi."

"God in heaven," Beatty said. "How long for?"

"Three months, so I'm told."

"That means six," Langley said. "Look at Fred Green."

"What's Renouf done this time?" Labuschagne asked.

"Same as last time," the Bailiff said. "Only louder."

Beatty squeezed his eyes shut and pinched the rumpled skin between his brows. "Well," he said, "he'll be dead in ten days, then."

Nobody spoke, and nobody showed surprise. Beatty pencilled a slow whirlwind across his blotter until it ended in a dense, black point. "They might as well shoot him here and now as send him to Cherche Midi," he said. "Remember what happened last time they put him inside: he nearly suffocated. Came out wheezing and gasping and looking like the underside of a toadstool. And that was only five days in the local lock-up. Cherche Midi's not a prison, it's a dungeon. I give him ten days at the outside."

"That's something I'll never understand," Langley said, "him being such a strapping great bloke."

Beatty made a face. "Asthma is no respecter of sizes, Ted. The bigger they come, the harder they choke."

"If only he would keep his big mouth shut," de Wilde said.

"Medically impractical," Beatty commented.

"Frankly, I think talking is what keeps him alive," Labuschagne said. He tilted his chair onto its back legs. "I think Renouf lives on fresh air and faith. He considers he's doing God's work—you know, spreading the good news, and so on—and as long as he keeps busy in the open air, his asthma stays away. . . . Still, that's not solving the problem. What exactly happened, Dan?"

"First, Count Limner telephoned me, said he'd heard a rumour. Then I telephoned everyone I could think of—our police, their Army Police, Field Gendarmerie, Secret Military Police, Justice Administration, Luftwaffe Police, even the Organisation Todt. Finally I got hold of Zimmerman in Counter-Intelligence and he said Paulus was interrogating Renouf at Gestapo headquarters. That was twenty minutes ago. Zimmerman says Paulus intends to have him tried and sentenced and off the island by tomorrow night."

"He can't," Langley claimed. "There isn't a boat."

"There is now. Zimmerman says the *Schleswig-Holstein*'s coming here tonight and going back to France tomorrow."

"What? They can't do that!" Labuschagne's chair came down with a bang. "We're not ready, the money isn't ready! That boat isn't due for another week. How the devil am I going to raise five thousand pounds by tomorrow? Can you get those tomatoes organized by tomorrow, Ted?" Langley shrugged. "Henry, what about your tame Jerry messenger?" Beatty threw his hands in the air. "For heaven's sake," Labuschagne complained, "why can't the Germans stick to their timetable?"

De Wilde rubbed his face. "Sounds as if you three are planning another of your Big Deals," he said.

"I thought we told you about it," Labuschagne said. "In fact I'm sure we did."

"Quite possibly. On average, two thousand people tell me about four thousand things every day. If I didn't forget most of them I'd collapse under the weight. So tell me again."

"Well, it's like all the other deals, only bigger."

"I see. You brought those off quite successfully. Can't you do the same with this?"

"It's more complicated. I think we ought to talk about it."

"Look, Dick," de Wilde said. "Canon Renouf's life is in danger. *That's* what we have to talk about. How you finance your deal is a technical detail. It's up to you to resolve it." He heard a note of impatience creeping into his voice, and made himself slow down. "Right?"

"Ah, but this is a matter of life and death too," Beatty argued. He spread his lanky arms on the table and tapped a heavy forefinger. "Take medical supplies. We're hard-up now; in a month we'll be desperate, even for things like aspirin and antiseptic. But that won't stop people going down with pneumonia or appendicitis, and if we lack the basic means to treat 'em they'll jolly well die, make no mistake about that."

"Yes, I know the problem, Henry," the Bailiff said. He glanced at his watch: five to three. "What's the solution?"

"Well, it's not regular channels; you might as well send a message in a bottle. But there's a German soldier stationed here whose father works for a medical wholesalers in Bonn. He's due to go on leave. He says if we can find the money, he'll bring back all the drugs he can carry."

"Good for him. Give him all the cash he needs."

"It's not as easy as that," Labuschagne said. "Occupation marks are no use in Germany. This lad needs genuine Deutschmarks."

"Well, you know where to go," the Bailiff told him. "See what's-his-name in the German Paymaster's Office, that crook who runs the black-market racket with his pal in Britanny."

"Schwarz," Labuschagne said. "I saw him yesterday. He wants a hundred cases of tomatoes as his fee, and he wants them sent to Britanny."

"Schwarz will get himself hung before this war's over. . . . Still, that's his funeral." De Wilde looked at Langley. "Ted, you can find a hundred cases of tomatoes, can't you?"

"No problem at this time of year." Langley folded his arms and let his chin sink until his jowls crowded. "No, the big snag's getting the stuff on the boat. The skipper's all right; a couple of chickens'll keep him happy. But there's that Jerry security officer in Harbour Admin, the one who has to sign the cargo manifest. Klopper."

"Klopper?" For no reason at all, de Wilde suddenly had an image of a glistening, tubby pork pie. He waved it away, literally waved; saw the others look, and pretended he was flapping at a fly. "What does Captain Klopper want?"

"He says he wants a pig."

"That's sheer greed."

Langley shrugged. "He says there aren't nearly as many boats crossing these days, so he's got to put up his rates. A pig or nothing, he says."

"And that's where the whole deal breaks down," Beatty said. "No pig, no tomatoes; no tomatoes, no Deutschmarks; no Deutschmarks, no drugs."

"Blast the man," de Wilde said. "He must know that his own people keep tabs on every damn pig on the island."

"Oh, he knows," Langley growled. "I told him they're all tattooed with numbers and every number's registered. That's our problem, he says. He wants a pig."

The Controlling Council brooded over the necessity and the impossibility of laying its hands on a spare pig. "Any suggestions?" de Wilde asked. No suggestions. "Well, we're not going to find a pig in here," he said. "Dick, you go ahead and get your Deutschmarks. Ted, organize your tomatoes, and Henry, make sure our German friend has the right shopping-list."

"We'll look right daft if we do all that and Klopper doesn't get his pig," Langley grumbled.

"We'll look even dafter if he gets it and we're not prepared," de Wilde pointed out. "Anyway, let's try and give our luck a bit of a nudge. You never know . . .. Now, what about Canon Renouf?"

"I suppose there's no point in our contesting the charge?" Labuschagne asked.

"Come off it, Dick; we've all heard him do it a dozen times," Beatty said impatiently. "Frankly, I'm not surprised the Jerries want him put away. I mean, if you were a Jerry officer trying to get your troops all keyed-up to meet an invasion, how would you feel about someone trumpeting enemy victories? It's just not on."

"Paulus is only a captain," Labuschagne pointed out. "Can't we appeal for clemency to a higher rank? What about this new Fortress Commandant, for example? He might want to make a good impression, you never know."

"Not a chance." The Bailiff sounded tired, and the others noticed it, so he put more vigour into his voice. "It seems that General Rimmer is something of a fire-eater. It seems that his answer to any problem is to shoot fifty hostages before breakfast."

"He can't touch me," Langley said. "I haven't had breakfast for eighteen months."

"And it seems that one of his sentries disappeared last night."

"Yes, I heard a rumour," Beatty said. "They say he deserted. He's supposed to be living with a tart, down by the Weighbridge."

"Rimmer doesn't think so. Rimmer thinks it's the start of a terror campaign by a resistance group, to soften up his troops before the invasion."

Their heads swivelled. For a moment the room was struck with silence.

"Surely he can't be serious," Labuschagne said.

"He'll be deadly serious if they ever find a body," said de Wilde. "In the meantime, he's got Renouf."

On the roof overhead a seagull screamed in bad temper, once, and shut up. A loose floorboard creaked as the Bailiff got up and walked across the room. "Any suggestions?" he said. Nobody spoke. He went to the window and looked down at the square, where a platoon was being drilled. They presented arms with a stuttering of boots. Not a patch on the ones who came here in 1940, he thought. On the other hand there were more of them now. A lot more. They infested the island.

"Two dilemmas, then," he said. "The pig, and the parson. Tell you what: if I tackle one, could you three take on the other?"

They looked surprised and wary. "Depends," Langley said. "Which one were you thinking of taking?"

The Bailiff silently counted to five, just to make them think. "Renouf," he said.

"Ah," Langley breathed. "Well, seeing as you've got by far the worst part of the bargain, I don't see as how we can refuse, can we?" Beatty and Labuschagne nodded. They were relieved to have the responsibility for Renouf lifted from their shoulders.

"Well, that's good," de Wilde said.

Something in his tone made Labuschagne glance. "Have you had an idea, Dan?" he asked.

The Bailiff waggled his hands. "It just might work," he said. "You never know. It's worth trying." Already he was heading for the door. "And if it does, Canon Renouf won't be in jail tomorrow. He'll be in jail tonight."

Jack Greg and Earl Kramer waited in the ante-room while the Controlling Council met. Greg wanted to go home; he certainly did not want to confront the Bailiff, who either knew or suspected a good deal about Greg's shadier activities on the fringe of various black markets, and whose glance made Greg nervous and stuttering. But Kramer was determined to meet the island's top man. "I want to put this guy in the picture," he told Greg. "When he knows the score, maybe we can get our heads together and you know . . . tie a coupla cans to Adolf's tail, or something."

And so they waited. They sat in silence. After a long while, Greg remarked that on second thought perhaps there was nothing to be gained from getting into a fight with the Council Members; after all, they were supposed to know better than anyone what was really going on, and anyway, if you upset them, they could easily get their own back. . . .

The midafternoon sun gently baked the air while Kramer sprawled back-to-front on a chair and let his chin rest on his hands. The tension of the last twenty-four hours was slowly draining out of him, and a pleasant fatigue was replacing it.

"Wonder what they're talking about in there," he murmured. Greg made no suggestion. "Sounded to me like something pretty hot," Kramer mused. "What did he say? Not a minute to lose? Right?"

Greg shrugged. He saw a pencil stub on the floor and put it in his pocket.

"You know, those guys in Allied Intelligence, they've got a pretty smart set-up with the Resistance all over Europe," Kramer said. "I mean, they don't fool around, those guys. They're real pros. You can bet they've got a masterplan all hooked up and ready to swing into action the minute the goddam balloon goes up! Or sooner, probably."

Greg watched and listened warily. He had felt good, earlier, when he told the Council Members what he thought of them, but now he regretted it. They weren't going to change their ways because of anything Jack Greg said, and his short temper might have got him into trouble. He was no good at apologizing, so the only sensible thing left was to shut up.

"Tell you something," Kramer said. "Those guys in there. Bet you they know one hell of a lot more than they said. More than they *could* say. . . . Bet you they're sitting right now on a whole mess of secret stuff, plans and signals and schedules and stuff." He yawned. "Gee, I could use about ten years in the sack," he said wistfully.

A few minutes later the door suddenly opened and de Wilde came upon Kramer with his arms hanging slackly and his eyelids drooping. "My dear chap, I do apologize!" he exclaimed. He took Kramer's limp hand and shook it briskly. "You've caught me rather on the hop, but I'm sure we shall have ample opportunity to—" Kramer never discovered what, for the Bailiff hurried out and was gone.

"Gee," Kramer said. "That guy is one ball of fire."

"I'm afraid that all of a sudden there's rather a lot to do," Labuschagne said. "And on top of everything the Germans have become rather touchy. They seem to have lost a sentry, which is remarkably careless of them, wouldn't you say?"

"Sure," Kramer said. He glanced at Greg, who looked away. "Sure is careless," he said.

"Anyway, that's not your problem." Labuschagne shook Kramer's hand. "Please forgive me for that stupid slip of the tongue just now." He put on a charmingly hangdog expression which he usually reserved for ingratiating very important customers of the bank. "I'm afraid senility is eroding my brain. The very last thing I would wish to do is give offence, even in the smallest way, to an Allied airman, and especially to an American."

"Hey, that's okay. Don't worry about it. Please." Kramer found himself smiling back.

"We're a rather peculiar lot here," Beatty said. He too shook Kramer's hand, and also squeezed his shoulder. "We have our own ways of doing things. It may look a bit odd, but it usually works out for the best eventually."

"Listen, I just wanted you to know I was around," Kramer protested. "I'm just so damn lucky to be here. I mean, if I can, you know, do anything. . . ."

"Get some rest, that's the first thing you can do," Beatty said. He held Kramer's head firmly in both hands and gently thumbed his eyelids back. Kramer stopped thinking and let Beatty take charge. "Nothing that a good warm bed won't cure," the doctor said. He steered Kramer out of the room and they all tramped downstairs. "This is some island you got here," Kramer told them.

"Beyond dispute," Labuschagne said.

11

General Rimmer was in his hotel suite having a massage when Major Wolff brought Count Limner and Daniel de Wilde into the room.

The general lay face-down on a towel-covered bed and grunted under the powerful hands of a sergeant P.T. instructor. He squinted up at Limner and de Wilde, moved his head to look at Wolff, and closed his eyes. "The last time I had a massage was thirteen months ago, Wolff," he said. "Since then I haven't been in one place long enough to arrange such luxuries. During the past thirteen months I have mounted and commanded twenty-eight separate operations in seven different countries. What you are watching now is not so much a magnificent massage as a decoration for long service and very, very, very good conduct. I sincerely hope for your sake that you have equally good reason for interrupting it. Otherwise I shall be obliged to ask the good Sergeant here to rip your arms off and beat you to death with them."

"Funny you should say that, sir," Wolff said. "We had a cook killed by somebody's arm in a wood near Byelgorod. It fell out of a tree and hit him on the head. Frozen stiff, of course."

"How sad." Rimmer groaned as his spine took a pummeling. "I hope he got a medal anyway."

"No, sir. It turned out not to be a Russian arm, you see. It was a busy little wood, that one," Wolff recalled. "Not an unusually big arm, sir. But a fairly tall tree. And a very cold climate."

"So they tell me."

"And now Count Limner has something he wishes to tell you, sir," Wolff said amiably. He gave a small but comprehensive bow.

"Does it involve a severed limb?" Rimmer inquired.

"It involves a general strike," Limner said. His voice was flat and unfunny.

Rimmer propped himself on his forearms. The masseur stood back and wiped his hands. "Thank you, Sergeant," Rimmer said. When the man had gone out he stood up and wrapped a towel around his waist.

"Now this is plainly impossible," he said, "because strikes are illegal, and only this morning the Bailiff himself assured me that his Islanders are tremendous respecters of the law."

"Call it a withdrawal of labour, then. Frankly, I don't think it matters what we call it. Do you?"

"No. No, it doesn't matter a damn," Rimmer opened a desk drawer and took out his personal stick-grenade. "But since we seem to be on the verge of a debate, I'd better call the meeting to order." He hammered the desk with the grenade until splinters of veneer jumped in the air. "Have I your attention, gentlemen? In ten minutes from now this problem, if it is a problem, will be solved, because in ten minutes from now I have another appointment." Crash! went the grenade. "Ready? Go!"

"It's all to do with Canon Renouf," de Wilde said.

Rimmer looked at Wolff. "That churchman, sir," Wolff said. "The one who got arrested this morning."

"Ah," Rimmer murmured. He gave the desk a token clout of remembrance.

"I understand that he's to be sent to Paris," de Wilde said. "To Cherche Midi. The man has chronic asthma, and even a short sentence there is bound to kill him. He's also hero-worshipped by many Islanders, so if you kill him you'll certainly make a martyr of him. I don't suppose that bothers you much, but I assure you it will bother a great many Islanders. To put it bluntly: if the Germans kill Renouf, the Islanders won't work for the Germans."

"And if I reverse every decision of my officers, before long my officers won't work for me, either," Rimmer said. "Unless, of course, you have some startling new evidence which proves Renouf innocent?"

"No, General, he's guilty. The law is clear enough."

"Then I'm surprised at you, Bailiff. Is this the famous British sportsmanship in action? Is this how you practise your ideals of fair play?" Rimmer made his eyes bulge with perplexity. "As soon as you find the rules of the game working against you, you demand to change them!"

"It's not a question of fair play," de Wilde said evenly. "And it's certainly nothing to do with sportsmanship."

Rimmer pretended not to have heard. He was shaking his head like a vicar who has found a washer in the collection plate. "After all I have been told about your being such good losers, too," he said. "Dear, dear . . ."

"Unless something is done very quickly, General, we shall all be losers. My people will lose Canon Renouf, and your people will lose their skilled workforce. It's as simple as that."

Rimmer laughed, and began to get dressed. "Oh no, nothing is as simple as that. Look: once your Islanders cease to work they'll cease to qualify for special rations. Correct? They'll also cease to have the extra money to buy extra food on the black market. Then they'll discover that they can't think of this man Renouf *and* their empty bellies at the same time. Hunger is very bad for the memory, Bailiff."

"Maybe," de Wilde said. He watched Rimmer pull on his breeches and fasten his belt with a muscular heave. "In your opinion, General, how long will it take for the Islanders to forget Renouf and go back to work?"

Rimmer thought it over while he buttoned his shirt. "At the most," he suggested, "what shall we say? Two weeks?"

"In two weeks, the Allies may be here," de Wilde said.

Rimmer said nothing. He shrugged on his tunic; added his wristwatch, keys, fresh handkerchief, wallet, notebook. Wolff brought him his boots and he stamped his feet into them. Count Limner watched these commonplace actions and noticed the tiny acts of emphasis: the little flourish as the handkerchief was tucked away; the slight, unnecessary flex of the knees after the boots were on. General Rimmer was giving a bit of a performance to conceal the fact that he was thinking.

The stick-grenade slid inside the leg of the right boot and the uniform was complete. Rimmer checked his watch against the clock on the mantelpiece. "Well, I don't suppose you're taking up my time just for the sake of hypothesis and speculation, Bailiff," he declared, "so please get on with whatever it is you wish to get on with."

De Wilde was surprised to feel his pulse leap and his breathing quicken. "I suggest that Canon Renouf's case be transferred from your military court to my civil court," he said. "In that way he can be convicted without becoming martyred." He had meant to say more, much more, but he suddenly decided to wait and see how that lot went down.

Rimmer walked slowly over to his desk and stood fingering its splintered surface. "Get me another desk, Wolff," he said. "This one looks as if it's been in a war."

"Yes, General." Wolff examined the desk and tut-tutted to himself.

"Bailiff, I wasn't aware that Renouf had broken a civil law," Rimmer said.

"He hasn't yet. But the Royal Court can always pass a retroactive law. If you agree now, I can have it done this afternoon and Renouf can be charged under the new law five minutes after I sign it. There need be no doubt that he'll be found guilty."

"Oh, I don't doubt it, Bailiff. It's just that I have a simple, arithmetical mind. I lose a sentry: you lose a churchman. The symmetry of it pleases me."

"There is, of course, another factor," Count Limner said.

"What's that?" Rimmer asked.

"The obvious one. The unavoidable one." When Rimmer still looked blank, Limner went on; "After all, it was Captain Paulus's arrest. The whole thing is, strictly speaking, Gestapo business."

"So what?"

"Well . . ." Limner spread his arms. "It's a matter of recognizing boundaries, isn't it?"

Rimmer uttered a loud and scornful hoot. "No, by God, it is not! I don't know how Gebhardt operated here, but I can tell you now that in my book the Fortress Commandant commands the Fortress, and that means *everything.*"

"Yes, of course," Limner murmured. "I suppose I had rather assumed that poor Gebhardt's policy would continue. That is certainly Captain Paulus's impression."

Rimmer chuckled. "Paulus is at an impressionable age, Count. He really believes that all he has to do is say 'Gestapo' and the whole world will wet its trousers. He has a lot to learn."

"Half the world doesn't even wear trousers," Major Wolff observed.

"Wolff, I want to see Paulus at eighteen hundred hours," Rimmer said. "Meanwhile get this fool Renouf transferred to the Bailiff's custody. I want him tried, convicted, and sentenced before sundown, Bailiff, and I make you personally responsible for publicizing those events to every Islander. In return, I expect an uninterrupted flow of work on all defence projects. Understand?"

"Yes," de Wilde said.

"By the way . . ." Rimmer paused in the doorway. "I've been reading about you Islanders. Racially speaking, you're really Celtic stock, aren't you? Not Anglo-Saxon. I'm surprised that you put up with the British for so long." When de Wilde said nothing, he added: "When exactly did England annex Jersey, Bailiff?"

"Never," de Wilde said. "They didn't capture us; we captured them. In the year 1066. William the Conqueror came from these parts, you see. England has always belonged to the Channel Islands and it always will. You're standing on the oldest piece of Britain, General. This is where it all began. We *invented* the country."

"Ah," Rimmer said. He went out. Wolff followed and shut the door behind him.

De Wilde heaved a deep breath. "Thank you for your well-timed contribution," he said to Limner. "I think it just turned the trick."

"Not at all. Glad to be of help, Bailiff." Limner pressed a button and cocked his head to hear the bell ring distantly. "Would you like some tea here? We might as well drink the Fortress Commandant's rations."

"I must get on with my dubious bit of lifesaving."

"Yes, of course . . . He's an odd mixture, isn't he? Bright as a button and not a great deal more intelligent. A typical soldier, I suppose. How they love to dress up and play with their noisy toys!"

"True," de Wilde said. He was nervous, twitchy, eager to act before anything could go wrong.

"I was surprised to hear that the Islanders feel so strongly about Canon Renouf," Limner remarked. "I didn't realize he was so popular."

"He's not," de Wilde said. "But Rimmer doesn't know that."

"I see. So there was in fact no threat of a strike."

"Rimmer doesn't know that, either."

"No, but Paulus might tell him." Limner rang the bell again. "You're living rather dangerously, aren't you?"

"Not as dangerously as Renouf."

Limner nodded thoughtfully. "One last thing: you seem to think that the invasion will come soon," he said. "Yet you have just assured Rimmer that work on the defences will not be interrupted. I find that paradoxical."

"Not so much a paradox," de Wilde said, "more of an optical illusion." He went out quickly, while Limner was still trying to work it out.

12

Felix Schumacher had few political beliefs and no religious faith. He did not need them, because he had concrete. He was in love with concrete.

He joined the Nazi Party in 1932—when he was an architectural student at the Institute of Technology in Karlsruhe—because he wanted a strapping girl called Lotte who was very keen on the Party. For her sake he worked hard, designing banners and stage-sets for Party rallies. He never got Lotte, but he made some contacts which paid off after he graduated. Party officials put work his way, and when war came Schumacher had a tidy little business going.

The first Commando raids on the coastline of northern Europe angered and disturbed Hitler. He issued Directive 40 and ordered a competition for the best-designed infantry bunker. Schumacher was invited to compete. Most of the other architects guessed that Hitler would need many thousands of such bunkers, so they kept their designs simple and economical. But Schumacher had recently met Albert Speer, Hitler's architect, and he knew about the Fuehrer's plans for a rebuilt Berlin: a colossal Reichstag in the form of one vast domed hall over seven hundred feet high, big enough to hold a hundred and fifty thousand people; grand boulevards four hundred feet wide; a triumphal arch more than twice the size of Napoleon's Arc de Triomphe; and so on. The other architects proposed bunkers with walls three feet thick. Schumacher's bunker had walls six feet thick. The others showed models. Schumacher built a full-scale prototype. Hitler inspected it and was impressed by its massive proportions. Schumacher won the competition. His prize was the Channel Islands, and the freedom to pour as much concrete as he liked, where he liked. In two years of happy, ceaseless work, Schumacher used up two hundred thousand tons of steel and cement; and still his love-affair with concrete was not exhausted. Even when the Allied bombing offensive seriously disrupted the supply of vital defence materials, the Channel Islands still got top priority; and other German commanders in Europe learned that it was useless to suggest any change, no matter how desperate their needs. The Channel Islands were Hitler's personal project. By the early summer of 1944 he was more concerned than ever that they should be impregnable, and Schumacher was still happily exploring the potentialities of this wonderful medium, concrete.

At four o'clock on the first full day of Rimmer's command, Schumacher was escorting the general on a tour of the rocky north-west corner of Jersey. They walked along gentle paths between softly droning slopes of heather, while Dum-Dum hunted rabbit-smells and snapped at insolent bees. Rimmer looked approvingly at the coastline: clean-cut cliffs two and three hundred feet high, cutting into the Atlantic like the bows of dreadnoughts. Schumacher talked of concrete.

"As you can see, General, the wonderful thing about concrete is the way it goes *exactly* where you tell it to. I experience no conflict between the material and the structure, because the material *is* the structure, all of it. Look, sir: isn't that superb?"

The bunker grew out of the hillside like a twentieth-century Sphinx: massive, blunt-headed and hulking, with one deep, square slit overlooking the empty sea. The afternoon sun cast one side in warm grey and left the next in grim shadow.

"It looks like a hippopotamus coming up for air," Rimmer said.

Schumacher's head retracted an inch or so. He shut one eye and looked at the bunker again. "Ah," he said. "Yes. I see what you mean, sir. The monolithic effect. Very true."

"What is the maximum direct hit it will withstand?"

"According to my estimates—"

"Your estimates? You mean you don't *know*?"

"Sir, short of actually testing a bunker to destruction—"

"Then test one, Schumacher! It'll give my gunners some practice. Now then: why did you build this bunker here?"

"To command the headland, General. I have built bunkers on every headland, with one observation tower for every three bunkers. Below the bunkers I've built machine-gun posts with reinforced concrete canopies; these are interesting, but I'm more proud of my work farther inland, where our gun emplacements have a certain sculptural purity of line. . . ."

As they walked, Schumacher explained his whole elaborate coastal-defence system, a gigantic complex of interlinked sources of fire-power, calculated to repel any form of invasion, from any angle. It took a long time, but Rimmer patiently heard him out.

"You've been working hard, Colonel."

Schumacher shrugged modestly. "Others have done more, sir. Besides, the Fuehrer is the real architect here. I simply follow his inspiration." Schumacher affectionately stroked the flank of a regimental command bunker. "You see how lean, how spartan, how utterly devoid of ornamentation and—"

"Yes, yes, yes. Now what if the invaders make their attacks *between* your splendid bunkers?"

"Between? Well, the crossfire will take care of them, sir."

"So you say, so you say. They would be even better taken care of if we put more bunkers in the gaps. Right?"

The landscape blurred as Schumacher felt tears pressing at his eyes. He had not experienced such excitement since Hitler shook his hand, two years ago. He had to clear his throat in order to get his voice under control. "That would be marvellous, sir. Can we get the materials? And the skilled labour?"

"Leave that to me. I don't believe in shortages. Is that

a race-course I see?" Rimmer pointed inland.

"Yes, sir. The transport battalion stables its horses there. I think that's Countess Limner out riding now."

"So it is." Rimmer watched through binoculars as Maria Limner cantered the shaggy mare in and out of gaps in the rails. She was wearing an open-necked shirt and breeches, and she was smiling and talking to the horse. "So it is indeed." Rimmer reluctantly lowered the binoculars. "Who else could ride such a poor mount so well?" He smiled at Schumacher. "Well, you have much to do, Colonel. How good to see you in uniform, by the way."

"Thank you, sir." Schumacher saluted. When Rimmer had gone, he went inside the bunker and opened his tunic. His chest was speckled with little pink lumps, like midge-bites. "Oh God," he whispered.

Maria Limner hooked her feet under the belly of the mare and leaned back until her head touched the horse's back. She looked up at the sky, a far-off, friendly blue with just a faint skim of milkiness here and there, like a perfect bowl which needed only rinsing to get it spotless. She was pleasurably uncomfortable. The saddle pressed against her spine, and made her arch her torso, while her arms hung down easily and her fingers scratched the beast's powerful hind legs. The mare ignored this and enjoyed the rich grass. She flapped her ears at the sound of thudding hoofbeats, but went on grazing. Maria Limner twisted her head to look. It was General Rimmer, riding an unsaddled grey, with Dum-Dum lolloping behind. She remained stretched out, half lazy, half tense, and watched him canter alongside. He was riding sitting sideways, with one foot held across the other knee. "Good afternoon, Countess," he called.

She propped herself on her elbows. "Good gracious, General. Are you advancing or retreating?"

He smiled. "That's something I never really know until the smoke clears," he said cheerfully. "However, I feel as if I'm advancing." His smile, as he sat sideways on that fat and foolish animal with one hand gripping its mane and his cap tilted back, was surprisingly youthful. "Do you often ride up here?"

"Yes, often. It helps to keep the horses in condition. And me, of course."

Rimmer glanced at her fluent legs gripping the mare, her trim waist, her understated breasts, her sunburned neck. "And Count Limner? Doesn't he ride with you?"

"Michael never rides any more."

Rimmer slid off the grey and walked over to her. "Will you give me a riding lesson, Countess?"

She sat up, and Rimmer raised his face to look at her. The sunlight bronzed his eyebrows and showed up a fine, weathered scar angling across his right cheek. "I didn't know you cared about the sport," she said.

"I may never have such an opportunity again, Countess. Seize the day, seize the hour! That's something this war has taught me."

Maria Limner looked at his horse. "She seems harmless, but one can never tell. You may end up getting thrown."

"All experience. One never knows how far to go until one has gone too far, Countess."

"Call me Countess just once more and you'll very soon find that out. My name is Maria."

"Good, good, that's a nice name." Rimmer picked a large dandelion and fed it to her horse. "I like Maria. My wife's middle name was Maria. She was killed in the bombing. My middle name is Karl but she never used it so it is intact and available in mint condition, so to speak." He walked around her horse and stroked its neck. "I ought to have a saddle," he said. "Yours is a saddle-and-a-half, Maria."

"It's a Western saddle. American, I expect. I found it here, in a junk shop." She stood in the stirrups to show him. "It's made to stop you falling out. That's why it sticks up so much behind and in front."

"This must be the pommel. Am I right?" He touched the polished knob which rose from the front of the saddle.

"That is the pommel."

"Big, isn't it?" He squeezed it thoughtfully. "And strong, too." He tilted his head and looked at the pommel. "D'you prefer—"

Maria Limner slapped her heels against the mare's flanks and Rimmer's hand banged her thigh as she sprang forward.

"Do you want a lesson or not?" she shouted over her shoulder.

Rimmer remounted, this time astride the grey, and galloped after her. By the time they had completed a lap of the old race-course he had almost caught up. She glanced back and swerved the mare towards a stretch of rough country. The track led into ancient surface mine-workings that had become overgrown with bramble and bushes.

General Rimmer successfully followed Maria Limner in and out of the first three gullies. The fourth ended in a steeper bank. The mare pounded up and over the top, with Maria Limner firmly held in her bucket-shaped saddle. Rimmer's grey saw how it was done and attempted the same thing, but she had a broad, well-polished back. Rimmer lost his grip half-way up and slid over the horse's tail. He fell on his backside and rolled ten feet to the bottom. "Stupid bloody bastard horse!" he shouted.

Maria Limner came back and looked down at him. "You should have had a pommel to hang on to," she said.

Rimmer lay on his back and squinted into the sunlight. "That shirt is translucent, I'm happy to say," he told her. "And I have a perfectly good pommel to hang on to." Dum-Dum came up and sniffed his feet.

She got off the mare, unstrapped her saddle and tugged a blanket out. "Look out, Karl," she said as she ran down the slope.

"But we hardly know each other," Rimmer said.

"We knew each other the moment we met," Maria Limner told him. She undid his tunic; he undid her shirt. "You are tab 'A' and I am slot 'B' and if you need any further instructions look on the box."

"Excellent idea," he said.

13

Dr. Henry Beatty looked down from his office window, saw Private Lang walking across the lawns in front of Jersey General Hospital, and was reminded of an athlete strolling across an arena—a runner or a hurdler, not a hammer-thrower or a shot-putter. The rumpled grey uniform couldn't hide Lang's easy, openchested manner any more than his boots could take all the bounce out of his stride. He met a nurse who was pushing a wheelchair, turned and walked backwards while he spoke to her and made her smile, caught his heel on something, stumbled, and contrived to make even his recovery look fluent and attractive. Henry Beatty had been an army doctor in France thirty years before, so he had seen plenty of ripped and ruptured bodies in field-grey. The sight of Private Lang revived a twinge of the rage he felt at the thought that such a superb piece of engineering as a man's body could be so savagely, so casually hacked about by reeking lumps of jagged, spinning metal. He turned back to his desk. A flicker of rheumatism grabbed his shoulder, and he felt a twinge of envy too.

Lang knocked and came in. Some people are born with the imprint of middle age on their faces; Private Lang was the opposite. Beatty found it impossible to picture this wide-mouthed and clear-eyed face looking anything but eternally, youthfully confident. It was a delusion, Beatty knew that; as Lang aged, so work and worry would leave their marks. But all that was unimaginable right now.

"The Orderly Room says you need me to help with an urgent operation, Doctor," Lang said. "So here I am."

"Good, delighted to see you. Don't bother to scrub up, it's not that kind of operation." Beatty pulled out a chair for him. "The *Schleswig-Holstein* is coming here tonight and going straight back to France tomorrow, so I'm told. If you're still game to help us, we'd like you to sling your leave application in now, fast, and bring back as much medical junk as you can carry."

"Yes, I will do that," Lang said. He gave a half-smile and looked away. "It's sudden, isn't it? I haven't been home for eighteen months, and now . . . I suppose they altered the sailing schedule? Yes, obviously. Well . . . I'd better go straight back tc the Orderly Room, then." He did not get up.

"I've made out a shopping-list." Beatty handed him a bundle of typewritten pages. "Some of it's just dreaming, I know, but if you never ask you never get, do you?"

Lang glanced through the pages, and pointed to some items which had been crossed out. "Toothpaste, invalid food, cough medicine," he read aloud. "It looks as if someone is a bit delirious."

"Yes, well, we've got our share of clowns and cretins too. Some people ran away with the idea that you were going to lead back a relief column, not hump a kitbag. . . . Anyway, we've got perfectly adequate substitutes for all those things."

Lang looked at the list again. "Ersatz toothpowder I know about: it's ground-down cuttlefish shell, right? We use it ourselves. Tastes like the bottom of the Dead Sea."

Beatty licked his teeth and swallowed. He did not particularly want to remember the taste of ground-down cuttlefish shell. "Invalid food is no great problem either," he said. "It's basically phosphate of iron, so you just chuck a few wrought-iron nails into a bottle of phosphoric acid. Cough medicine: we make that from carrageen moss. The stuff grows wild on the seashore. And so on."

"And so on." Lang tucked the papers away inside his tunic. "And so on and so on and so on. Everything repeats itself. I think that should be the motto of this place: 'and so on.'"

"Hullo," Beatty said mildly. "Do I detect a note of youthful, blis-

tering cynicism?" He found an empty pipe and put it in his mouth foɪ·
added company. "And I thought you were the only other sane person
on this island."

"There's no such thing as sanity, is there?"

Beatty shrugged. "There's no such thing as a horizon, either, except
in the eyes of the beholder, but we'd all be in serious trouble without
it."

Lang leaned forward with his arms resting on his thighs and he
looked at Beatty with a slightly speculative smile.

"You look changed, Private Lang," the doctor said. "You look as
if something has happened to you. Has it?"

Lang sighed. "I don't know. I think perhaps I lost my virginity."

"You *think?* God's truth, that's carrying absentmindedness too far.
Besides . . ." Beatty flipped open a folder and ran his finger down a
graph. "The rate of illegitimate births on this island has now reached
eleven per cent, which is more than double the pre-Occupation rate.
Far be it from me to suggest . . . Nevertheless, you have been here
a long time."

"Nearly three years."

"And you are not the ugliest soldier on the island."

"That's true."

"All things considered, then, I find it hard to believe that long ago
you were not seized by the throat and brutally raped by one of our
lusty young spinsters."

Lang said nothing, but now Beatty detected the tug of tension
keeping his smile in place, and he saw how Lang's fingers squeezed
his biceps. "My dear chap," Beatty said, "you are obviously bursting
to bounce your rubber ball, and what you need is a wall to bounce
it against. Believe you me, you are looking now at an old and experienced wall. Slightly cracked, some might say, but still too thick
to be harmed. Stop sitting there like a bump on an introspective log,
and fling your wretched ball!" Beatty wildly flung out his arm and
nearly fell off his chair. It was a self-effacing device which he had
perfected over the years, and it made Lang chuckle. The German got
up and wandered to the window.

"I'm very confused, Doctor. I don't know why I'm here or where
I'm going. I'm not altogether sure who the hell I am." He beat his
knuckles together. "I saw a man die this morning, but that doesn't
explain it. People die like that all over the place, all the time, and the
fact that I don't see them die makes absolutely no difference, does it?"

"No," Beatty said. "Who died?"

"You didn't hear the crash? One of our trucks went over a bridge and blew up. My unit was on duty. We got there in time to see the worst case die, which was just as well for him because everything was broken. Except his neck, I suppose. . . . He died while I was working on him. One moment he was blowing little red bubbles and the next he was gone for ever. Stopped like a clock. I gave him cardiac massage but it was absurd, he was so gone. Thumping his chest was like beating a steak. First time I ever saw somebody just *die* like that."

"You've seen operations fail," Beatty observed.

"Ah, but they were different! They simply didn't live, despite everything. This man got blasted to death. There's a difference, isn't there? He was *killed.*"

"Pneumonia kills. So does TB, diphtheria, typhoid."

"Not like that," Lang said. "Not like that." He looked out at the hot sunshine making the lawn a pool of vivid green.

"You sound as if you need this leave," Beatty said.

"I don't really want to go." Lang spoke unemotionally, as if he were giving evidence.

"You don't?" Beatty leaned back to enjoy a better view of Lang's face. "Why not?"

Lang turned and sat on the window sill. "I don't love my mother and father," he said, "and I know they don't love me."

"Not unusual. There's no law says anyone must."

Lang wasn't listening. "Maybe they hate me. I think my mother must hate me now, because my brother has been missing in action in Russia since February, so he's either dead or captured, which is the same as dead."

"That's not your fault."

"She thinks it is. Who else can she blame? She can't blame the Fuehrer, or the Army, or God. But here I am, safe and warm in the Channel Islands, where the snow never falls and the bombs never fall and nobody ever gets shot. Of course it's my fault." Lang heaved himself off the sill and made a militaristic display of squaring his shoulders and jutting his chin. "I'd better soldier on down to the Orderly Room . . . . By the way, how is your son?"

"No more news, so I assume he's well."

"Good . . . . A strange thought occurred to me this morning, after that man died. I was thinking about the future, and how everyone seems to think the Allies must invade soon. Then I thought that your son might be one of the invaders, and that I might be given a rifle and ordered to shoot, and . . ." Lang shrugged gloomily.

"You're a non-combatant."

"Am I? If some S.S. officer comes along and puts his pistol to my head I don't suppose I'll stop to ask him why I should be made to fight. I'll just blaze away at the enemy."

"Let's hope you hit the S.S. officer, then."

Lang laughed, and moved towards the door. "Don't forget the money, Doctor," he said.

"We're getting it for you now. Five thousand pounds in real Deutschmarks."

"Just think," Lang said. "If the Allies invade while I'm away, you may lose it all."

"I hope we do," Beatty said. Lang went out, and Beatty suddenly felt five years older.

14

Major Josef Schwarz ran the Paymaster's Office from a suite of rooms in the building which housed the island's telephone exchange. He made a great number of telephone calls, mostly to the Continent, and so he found it very useful to have the close co-operation of the Signals personnel. In return he made sure that the Signals canteen got regular deliveries of such luxuries as razor blades, gramophone records, and beer.

It took Schwarz only one and a half days a week to do his job as paymaster. For the other five and a half days he and a Luftwaffe colonel on the mainland bought, sold, and exchanged large quantities of anything that was scarce, which meant everything.

Schwarz did it because he enormously enjoyed making deals; he had a talent for long-range bargaining and bartering, and exercising that talent gave him pleasure. The Luftwaffe colonel, whose name was Bodenschatz, did it because he was bored. There were no Luftwaffe squadrons left to be administered in that part of France, and idleness made him irritable.

He and Schwarz had never met. They first came in contact when Bodenschatz telephoned Jersey to find out if anyone at the airfield wanted five hundred surplus gallons of aircraft-engine coolant mixture, and he got connected to Schwarz's office by mistake. Schwarz asked Bodenschatz to hold the line for a minute, telephoned Cherbourg, and talked to a French chemical company which had just supplied Jersey with fire-extinguishers. They offered him a quantity of copper tubing in exchange for the coolant. Schwarz kept the line open while Bodenschatz telephoned a nearby distillery and did a deal: Six cases of calvados for the copper tubing. Schwarz agreed. Seven minutes of telephoning had earned each officer three cases of liquor. Schwarz later sold two of his cases and made a week's pay, but what pleased him even more was the discovery that two imaginative men and a telephone could so rapidly resolve problems of supply and demand over such large distances. Even in wartime, individual initiative and mutual trust could be made to pay off. Schwarz and Bodenschatz set to work and developed the best black-market network in northern France.

Schwarz looked more like a greengrocer than a paymaster (or a black-marketeer). He was burly, a little shaggy, with receding black hair which curled untidily behind the ears; and he had an air of hopeful expectancy about him, as if the season's first avocado pears were due at any moment. When Richard Labuschagne came into his office, Schwarz was in shirt-sleeves and tieless, and he was talking on the telephone.

". . . all right, don't worry about it, leave it with me and I'll call you back. . . . Now: is this other stuff any use to you? . . . I see. . . . Well, what can you give us, then? . . . Boot polish. Colour? . . . Uh-huh. . . . Well, I'll look around. . . . Yes. . . . Fine. . . . Good-bye." He hung up. "Any idea what you make with 'calciferol'?" he asked.

"I'm afraid I haven't," Labuschagne said.

Schwarz grunted. "There's a two-hundred-litre drum of the stuff gathering dust in Avranches. . . ." He made a note and tucked it inside his blotter. "You've heard about the *Schleswig-Holstein*, obviously."

"Indeed I have. That is the sole reason for my visit. We now need the currency very urgently, Major."

"Yes, I thought you might. Five thousand pounds in Deutschmarks, right? Well, I'm sorry but I can't get it for you."

Schwarz made an unhappy face and opened and shut a couple of desk drawers. Labuschagne kept his expression politely blank, but he felt a chill of despair which made him realize how completely he had been depending on Schwarz. He carefully hitched up his trousers and crossed his legs. "Some unforeseen circumstance has intervened?" he inquired.

"What? No, no. The only thing that's intervened is one week." Schwarz was prowling around the room, searching shelves. "The money was due to arrive on the *Schleswig-Holstein* seven days from now. At this very moment, half of it's in Paris."

"I don't wish to appear to be interfering with your arrangements," Labuschagne said, "but whereabouts is the other half?"

"Bodenschatz has it." Schwarz found a Swiss pharmaceutical catalogue and thumbed through it. "Any use to you?"

"Oh yes, undoubtedly. Half is better than nothing, always."

Schwarz gave him an old-fashioned look over a pair of imaginary spectacles. "Not always, Mr. Labuschagne. Bodenschatz could introduce you to a man in St. Malo with twelve hundred left-footed seaboots. Interested?"

"How on earth did that happen?"

"The makers shipped the left and the right boots separately to discourage theft. Unfortunately they forgot to explain the idea to the thieves." Schwarz stuffed the catalogue back on the shelf. "Calciferol. . . . Sounds sort of medical, but . . ." His lips silently shaped the word again.

"Would this be an opportune moment to complete arrangements for transferring Bodenschatz's portion of the currency, Major?"

"It'll be on the boat. Hey! D'you want a diamond?" Schwarz turned to him with the gleam of invention in his eyes.

Labuschagne began to feel like a Methodist missionary in an Arab bazaar. "With all due respect—" he began, but Schwarz had already seized the phone.

"Get me Jean-Jacques Jensen in Caen," he ordered. The number was connected remarkably quickly. Schwarz talked briskly in a mixture of French and German, and then covered the mouthpiece. "He wants a Jersey cow," he said. "Can you give him a Jersey cow? You've got enough of them, God knows."

"Quite impossible, I'm afraid," Labuschagne said. "Difficulties of transport aside, there is the official registration of all cattle—"

"You're getting a wonderful bargain. Jensen's diamond is worth at least three thousand English pounds. How much is a cow worth?"

"The export of cattle is completely illegal," Labuschagne replied firmly.

"And diamonds are a universal currency." Schwarz tossed the receiver in the air and caught it with the other hand. "Don't worry about transport, just get the beast on the boat. Is it a deal?" His enthusiasm was irresistible; Labuschagne weakly shrugged his way into crime. "It's a deal," Schwarz said into the telephone. He hung up. "Now about those mushrooms," he began.

"Tomatoes," Labuschagne corrected. "You said tomatoes."

"Yes, yes, but that was for next week. Tomorrow I need mushrooms. Fifty boxes."

"Oh. . . . Well, I'll see what I can do. . . ." Labuschagne began to wish he had made notes. "So does this mean that you do not in fact require any tomatoes?"

Schwarz looked up from a tattered dictionary. "How many have you got?"

Labuschagne tried to remember. "However many it was you asked for," he said. "But we need a pig," he added quickly.

"Pig? What—a bacon pig, or a breeding sow?"

Labuschagne blinked and tried to visualize Klopper, the Security Officer in Harbour Admin. Klopper was fat. "Bacon pig," he said.

"Get me Betteridge," Schwarz said into the phone. He studied the dictionary while the call was being placed. "Ah, Mrs. Betteridge? Major Schwarz. Out working, is he? Quite right too. How would you like two bath towels and a box of real soap in exchange for one small, smelly pig?" He listened, nodding, and turned a page. "Lemon-scented? Why not? Tomorrow. Good-bye."

"I hope you aren't expecting us to furnish towels and soap," Labuschagne said quickly.

"Oh no, no. Your tomatoes will secure those goods from . . . Well, never mind; it's rather complicated; you don't really want to be bothered. Now then: you're buying these Deutschmarks with Occupation marks?"

"That was the understanding."

"At double the exchange rate?"

"That was not the understanding."

"Ah. . . ." Schwarz put aside the dictionary and began searching an encyclopedia. "It's one of those technical things, Mr. Labuschagne. Frankly, I don't begin to know how it works; Colonel Bodenschatz is the currency genius. I just do what he says."

"My problem," Labuschagne said, "lies in having to reconcile the purchase of two thousand five hundred pounds'-worth of Deutsch-

marks with the expenditure of five thousand pounds'-worth of Occupation marks. Inevitably, questions will be asked. The auditors—"
"Calciferol!" Schwarz cried. His forefinger thumped the page.
" 'Crystalline vitamin D, used in fortifying margarine.' " He slammed
the encyclopedia shut and grabbed the phone. "Get me Palassier in
Brest, quickly!" He turned to Labuschagne with an apologetic smile.
"Palassier makes margarine, you see," he explained. "I never touch
it myself, but . . ." His call was connected and he began talking.
Labuschagne gave up. He had the pig and a diamond, but now he
needed mushrooms and a Jersey cow. He went out, signalling good-
bye. Schwarz was laughing delightedly at something Palassier in Brest
had just said, but he gave Labuschagne a friendly wave too.

Langley stopped his van at the top of a rise. Ahead the road fell
away down a curling valley in which a small but shining waterfall
added a sprinkle of sparkle to a meadow that was fat with buttercups.
Halfway down the road a cottage rested against the hillside as if it had
been moulded from the natural stone. Rambler roses poured down its
walls, and soft grey wood-smoke climbed into the sky: a human
smudge to show off its heavenly perfection. The view looked like a
best-selling picture-postcard, and in peacetime it was. Earl Kramer—
now sitting in the cab while Greg travelled in the back—scored it ten
out of ten. "Holy cow!" he said respectfully.
"What's that?" Langley asked.
"Some panorama!" Kramer said. "I guess this one gets the gold
star, huh?"
Out of politeness, Langley gave the valley a broody stare. "I'd put
the whole damn lot under potatoes if I had my way," he said. "See
that telephone pole?"
Kramer studied it for abnormalities. "Yup," he said.
"I stood beneath that bugger every night for a week in January,
1941. Me and nine other Jerseymen. January, mind you. Pissed down.
Froze our bollocks off, we did. And all because some stupid sod went
and cut that telephone line."
Kramer examined the telephone line. "What was his big idea?" he
asked.
"Big idea?" Langley scoffed. "He didn't have a big idea, just a big
head. It was supposed to be sabotage, but all he did was inconvenience
a dozen farmers and get the Jerries mad. They made ten of us keep
watch all night for a week. Pissed down, it did."

"Unsmart," Kramer observed. "No gold star."

"Every time I see that pole I want to smash it down his throat," Langley said.

"Sounds like you know who the guy is," Kramer said. Jack Greg appeared at the side of the cab and stepped onto the runningboard. "What's up?" he asked.

"Who cut down that line up there, Jack?" Langley's voice was flat and his face was blank.

"What line? Oh . . . that line." Greg put his head on one side and cracked his knuckles. "Dunno. Must've been the fairies."

"Fairies?" Kramer said.

"That's right." Greg flapped his arms like wings and gave a grotesque smile. "You got fairies where you come from?"

"Oh, sure." Kramer looked from Langley, still pokerfaced, to Greg, foolishly beaming. There was a short, uncomfortable silence. "Leastways, I guess so," he added.

Langley grunted. "And I suppose that was fairy-piss we all got soaked in. I ought to be bloody lucky I didn't turn into a princess. Or a sodding great toad. Right?"

Greg began to chuckle, found that he was alone and gave up. Langley leaned across and opened the door. "I've got work to do," he said curtly, "so you two get off here."

They stood in the road and watched the van drive away. "Funny bugger, Ted," Greg said. "You never know where you are with him, do you?"

Kramer was looking at the telephone wires. "I bet a guy could make spaghetti out of that lot in five seconds, if he had a real mind to."

This time Greg laughed confidently. "You should've heard the Jerries howl!" he said. "They like dishing it out but they can't take it. No sir! They can't take it." He led Kramer over a wall and across a field.

Langley visited six farms in the next hour and collected a few boxes of tomatoes from each. The seventh farm was Betteridge's. He squeezed the van past a crew of German engineers rebuilding the parapet of the bridge, and saw the blackened carcass of the truck lying on its side in the stream. A military policeman sitting astride his motorcycle recognized Langley and beckoned him on. Langley stopped and put his head out. "What happened here?" he asked.

The policeman waved his white gauntlets at the wreck. "French rubbish," he said. "They don't know how to make trucks. You wouldn't get that with Mercedes-Benz."

"Anyone hurt?" Langley asked. The man shrugged. Langley handed him a couple of tomatoes and drove on.

Mrs. Betteridge was in the barn, scrubbing out a milk churn. She saw Langley watching from the doorway, dropped the churn with clang that raised sparks from the flagstones, and flung down a whip-lash of water from her scrubbing-brush. "We haven't got any," she said. "The Germans took it all."

"I haven't asked for anything yet," Langley observed mildly.

"No, but you're going to." She wiped her hands on a sack and threw it at a hen which was looking at her.

"Anything wrong?" Langley asked.

"You should know," she said. "You've got your nosy spies every-where, haven't you?"

Langley looked at her tight lips and narrowed eyes, and he felt like a prison visitor. Mary Betteridge lived in a cell of her own making. She knew she was falsely accused and wrongly convicted and unjustly sentenced and now she would never come out, even if someone brought her a royal pardon, because only she knew how wronged she was, and she was making the world pay for it. Or, at least, a little bit of the world.Her bit. *God help you, Mary,* he thought, *since you'll never lift a finger to help Him.* "It can't be easy for you here," he said. "Just the two of you. It's a lot of work."

"You standing talking doesn't make it any less."

Langley felt her anger begin to infect him, and he made himself absorb it and remain calm. Tolerance didn't come easily to him; he had to keep reminding himself that short rations made for short tempers, and that nobody could afford to waste energy on squabbling. "I've come to ask for help," he said.

"Try the Salvation Army."

"They don't grow tomatoes."

"Nor do we." She thrust a hose into the churn and spun a tap-handle. Water drummed frantically.

"No, I know you don't." Langley knew they did. "But I thought you might keep a few plants just for yourselves. Private stuff. And I can give you a good deal, you know. Double market-price plus a bonus."

"So you should." She rolled out another churn. "You're taking the food out of our mouths, aren't you? The price ought to be good."

"Well," Langley said, "how many boxes can you spare?"

She thought while she scrubbed. "You can have two dozen," she said, "but I want the boxes back."

"Twenty-four boxes?" He had hoped for six. "That's . . . fine. I must say—" Langley didn't quite know what he must say. He took a short walk on his short legs while he thought about it. "I didn't realize you and Louis were so fond of tomatoes," he said. "You sure you can spare that many?"

Mary Betteridge rested her weathered, freckled forearms on the rim of the churn. "Listen, Ted Langley," she said harshly. "We spare what we can, right? Now you spare what you can. If Jack Greg says anything to anyone about an American . . . Well, he's lying, that's all. You know what a liar he is." Her words echoed around the granite barn like birds seeking a way out. "A liar and a crook, that man. Always has been."

"What American?" Langley asked, but she shook her head and began scrubbing again, more furiously than ever. The other churn overflowed, and she let it. "God knows, it's hard enough just to survive," she said. "We do everything we have to. Isn't that enough? Why can't people leave us alone?"

"Well, I'm grateful for the tomatoes, Mrs. Betteridge," Langley said. "Is tomorrow morning all right?"

"There never was any American. It's not fair."

"We need them urgently, you see. It's to exchange for some medicines."

"People shouldn't be ill," she snapped. "D'you think Louis and me can afford to be ill?"

"I don't suppose you know where I can lay my hands on a spare pig?" Langley asked.

"There never was one," she said. Fury was shaking her voice. "That man is a damned, bloody liar and he's going to burn in hell for it one day."

"I'll see you tomorrow, then," Langley said. It was supposed to be a promise but she looked at him as if it were a threat. He gave up. If she wanted to spend her life rattling the bars of her cell, there was nothing he could do about it.

15

In the park at the end of the street, between the Queen Victoria Jubilee drinking fountain and the statue of John Carteret, Earl Granville (1690–1763), a German military band was playing selections from *Tannhäuser*. Canon Renouf stood at the window of the Bailiff's office and conducted the band. As with everything he did, he held nothing back. His large body swayed and bounced to the rhythm, he hunched his head in concentration, and his left arm was hooked upwards, the fingers throbbing with emotion, while the right hand stabbed and chopped imperiously. Floorboards groaned as he swung from one instrument to another. Occasionally he uttered hoarse, enthusiastic noises which were neither in time nor on tune. It was a powerful performance. Behind him Daniel de Wilde was struggling with a tricky piece of legal writing that should have been typed, checked, and ready half an hour ago.

Canon Renouf rose on his toes and brought in the trombones with a two-fisted flourish that made de Wilde spin around. "For God's sake, Canon!" he cried. "Can't you sit in the corner and write your sermon?"

"I've written it," Renouf said.

"Then write another. Write several. Only *stop hopping.*"

"Hopping? I wasn't hopping." Renouf raised one leg and hopped to the middle of the room. "That's hopping. What on earth makes you think I've been hopping?"

De Wilde waved a fistful of papers at him. "Listen; I'm desperately late with this, and you keep dancing around to that blasted music."

Canon Renouf gave a short, tolerant laugh. "If you think that's dance-music, Bailiff—"

"Never mind. Forget it. Just give me ten minutes' peace and quiet."

"Perhaps I can help." Renouf rested a hand on de Wilde's shoulder and leaned over the desk.

"I don't need any help. Only some silence."

"My dear chap, there's no need to be stiffnecked." Renouf straightened the papers, so as to be able to read them. "I am, after all, a graduate of the University of Cambridge and I did, after all, edit the college magazine. . . . Now, what's your little problem?"

"You are." The Bailiff got up and moved his chair to the other side of the desk. "You realize the Gestapo wants you deported to Cherche Midi? You realize that?"

Renouf flicked the suggestion away like the piece of fluff it was. "A crass misunderstanding. Don't you ever listen, Bailiff? I told you, Paulus got the whole thing wrong. I explained it to him most carefully in court; *Rome has not yet fallen.* I never said it had. Evidently somebody mis-heard me. As I told Paulus, the fall of Rome is imminent, the Allies are at the gates, defences are crumbling. That is the fact of the matter. Why should I claim differently? When Rome falls, then I shall say so. Not before. I told Paulus that, and he accepted my word. I also told him that the whole affair had been absurdly inflated and grotesquely distorted, which it has."

"I bet he didn't accept *that.*"

Renouf went back to his music. "He certainly made no mention of prison."

"Of course not. The President of the court said it."

"Not to me."

"In German," de Wilde said wearily. "He said it in German."

"Bad manners," Renouf pronounced. "I try to discourage that sort of thing whenever I can. People must learn."

There was a tap at the door. Major Helldorf came in and took off his cap. "General Rimmer wishes me to approve the wording of your emergency regulation, Bailiff," he announced.

"He hasn't finished writing it yet," Renouf said. "Wagner puts him off. Could you ask them to play some Gilbert and Sullivan, perhaps?"

"Shut up, Canon, and for God's sake *sit down.*" De Wilde gave Helldorf his handwritten draft. "Maybe you can help me get the damn thing right, Major. It's pure ballyhoo, you understand."

"Ballyhoo?" Helldorf scratched his ear. "Is that the same as tally-ho?"

"It depends." De Wilde felt his head start to throb. "Yes and no. Let's not—"

"What is the purpose of this regulation, Bailiff?"

De Wilde took a deep breath. "To make it an offence for an Islander to thumb his nose at a German."

"Ah." Helldorf took a pencil and began to write. For three minutes there was silence, while de Wilde skimmed through reports and letters and memos, and Renouf waved at friends in the square below.

"Try this," Helldorf said. His strong, italic script ran to three paragraphs.

"Good," said de Wilde. "Good. . . . Yes, that's fine. You don't mind
if I make it retroactive? Splendid. Many thanks."

"You really cannot use that word." Renouf's arm came over and
his forefinger tapped the page.

" 'Abhorrent'?" de Wilde said. "Why not?"

"It's so utterly pretentious." The minister smiled pityingly. " 'Abhorrent'. . . . Who ever spoke that sort of word? It's as bad as 'evince,'
or 'odium.' Or 'disingenuous.' I mean, nobody actually talks like
that."

"I do," the Bailiff said. "I talk like that all the time."

"Then perhaps you'd better include all those other words too,"
Renouf said stiffly.

"All right, I jolly well will," the Bailiff told him. He turned to
Helldorf. "I wish to add: 'or in any other way disingenuously evinces
odium'," he said. "D'you mind?"

"Not at all."

"If that's your attitude, Bailiff," Renouf informed him, "I have
nothing further to say."

"I'll believe that when I don't hear it," de Wilde said. "Now let's
get on." He signed the Order as Deputy Lieutenant-Governor and
Bailiff; Helldorf counter-signed it on behalf of the Fortress Commandant. De Wilde then went to a cupboard, put on his ceremonial robes
as Chief (and sole) Justice of the Supreme Court of Jersey, and for-
mally endorsed the Order. He took off his robes, and together they
escorted Renouf along the corridor to the office of the Attorney-
General, who officially charged Renouf with offenses against the Order that de Wilde showed him, taking care not to smudge the signa-
tures. They returned to the Bailiff's office. De Wilde put on his robes,
read the charge, and asked the accused if he had anything to say.

"I find this whole affair thoroughly abhorrent," Renouf declared.

"Fourteen days' imprisonment," de Wilde said. "You know where
it is. Don't be late."

16

"See the bullet?" said Jack Greg. He scraped with his penknife in the
rutted bark of an oak tree. Kramer heard the blade click on metal,
and he saw the dull glint buried in the wood.

"I see it," he said. "Looks like it came out of a .30 carbine."

"And there's another down here." Greg went probing and scratching.

They were standing in the middle of a field about a mile from the cottage. "What was he, some kind of spy?" Kramer asked.

"Spy? Don't be daft, he was only nineteen. Scaulnier, Pierre Scaulnier. He looked a bit like you, that's what reminded me. Never stopped smiling. . . . Here it is, must have gone between his legs, see the angle? Firing-squad didn't have their hearts in it, did they? Half of them went off and puked in that hedge afterwards. . . . I'm not surprised. Six in the morning is a bad time."

"Is there a good time?"

Greg missed the question; he was pressing his head against the trunk and squinting into the cracks in the bark. "Look, you can still see the blood," he said.

"So what got the Jerries pissed-off at this guy?" Kramer asked.

"He was trying to get to England, him and about a dozen other French lads. They didn't know a damned thing about boats or sailing, poor little buggers. Thought they'd reached England, so they came running up the beach, all laughing and cheering and singing, straight into a Jerry patrol."

"Couldn't they see? There's swastikas and stuff everywhere."

"It was night." Greg measured out handspans on the tree. "There's more bullets in here somewhere, I know it. . . . Scaulnier was the oldest so they shot him."

"Bastards," Kramer said.

"Or at least some of them shot him," Greg added. He was down on his knees, searching.

Kramer walked around to the other side of the oak. He stood with his back against it and his arms outstretched. It was a big tree, staunch, sturdy, holding up a fistful of hefty branches and a million whispering leaves. *Nineteen years old*, he thought. *Six o'clock in the morning*. "Did he die straight off?" he asked.

"The officer had to finish him," Greg said. "Put his pistol in his ear and pulled the trigger. At least, that was the story."

"I wish I'd been here," Kramer said savagely. "I wish I'd had a B-24 with a bay full of five-hundred-pounders. I'd've turned that whole motherfucking firing-squad into spaghetti sauce. I just wish." He got down from the tree.

"Could you do that?" Greg asked. "I mean, without hitting the bloke tied to the tree?"

"Man," Kramer said, "we can put a bomb down a pickle-barrel without touching the sides."

They walked on. "I wanted to show you that tree," Greg said. "To hear some people, you'd think the Germans were as nice as pie, all please and thank you and wiping their feet three times before they come in."

"Some people got rocks in their heads," Kramer said.

They went over a stile and along a cart-track. In the next field a mobile anti-aircraft unit was setting up its guns. A sentry leaned on a gate and nodded to them as they went by.

"Bloody good mushroom field, that," Greg complained. "Ruined now, I expect."

Kramer was silent. The sight of that sentry, in the middle of such a beautiful afternoon, made him suddenly realize how enormously lucky he was. First he didn't go down with *High Society*, then he didn't get blown up on the beach, then he didn't get shot near the hole in the wire, and finally he did get helped by a lot of new friends. And now here he was, strolling through the kind of countryside he generally saw in the colour photographs in *National Geographic* magazine. The hedges were rich with white lupin and purple foxglove, dog-rose and cow parsley. Butterflies flickered across his path, some patterned like Japanese shawls, some coloured a fragile yellow, some delicately spotted. Birdsong made soft and distant ravels in the quietness, and the air itself smelled cleaner and fresher than anything Kramer could remember. He was lucky; God Almighty, how lucky he was!

Just to be alive, fit and well and alive, in this lush and lovely place, made Earl Kramer grateful, and he wanted to give thanks for his good fortune. He glanced at Jack Greg, and saw the man's lips moving in some mute, misanthropic complaint. No point in thanking Greg. Greg wouldn't know what to do with it. "Just had an idea," Kramer said. "Think I'll go see old man Betteridge."

Greg was startled. "Louis? What for?"

"Say thank-you."

"After he chucked you out?"

"Well, he had to take me in before he could chuck me out, and I guess I owe him something for that."

Greg plodded onwards in silence. "Not me," he muttered. "I don't owe that bastard a damned thing."

"Okay! So stay away!" Kramer yelled. "Don't come. Who's asking you?"

Greg did not speak again until the track reached a narrow lane. "That way," he said, pointing right. "Take your first turning on the left and follow your nose."

"See you later."

Greg watched him set off. "He won't thank you for coming back," he called out. Kramer waved without looking around. "See if you can get some eggs," Greg shouted. "Get all you can."

17

The Controlling Council met again at five o'clock. The Bailiff explained what he had done to save Canon Renouf from Cherche Midi, and he distributed copies of the Emergency Order. "I had to take your agreement for granted," he said. "It's all signed, sealed, and delivered now, anyway."

There was a thoughtful pause while they read the document. De Wilde rested his head against the padded chairback and dreamed of not being Bailiff any more; of walking home and never coming back into this great, impressive, slightly dusty office to wrestle day after day with somebody else's problems. Everybody else's problems. Nearly four years since the Occupation began. He had been forty-nine when that first Luftwaffe pilot cautiously circled Jersey and landed at the airport with a loaded pistol in his hand, expecting all sorts of trouble, only to find that he had captured the island single-handed. Now de Wilde was fifty-three but he looked sixty-five and at this stage of the day he felt more like seventy-nine.

The other Council Members looked at each other. "Well, Dan," Labuschagne said, "I didn't know you had it in you. What can I say but . . . congratulations. This is, beyond dispute, the most sordid and vicious piece of legislation ever to emerge from the Royal Court. It's . . . it's indefensible."

"The way I see it," Langley said, holding the paper firmly in both fists as if it might try to escape, "we can accuse any bugger of anything we don't like, even if he did it before we made the law."

Beatty had rolled his copy into a spill and stuck it in his ear. "Not so much an Emergency Order," he said, "more a poke in the eye."

"All in favour?" de Wilde asked. They nodded. "Right." He collected the copies. "Renouf is off the hook and with any luck this will be the first, last and only time we'll need to use this Order. Now: what success have you—"

"Wait a minute," Langley said. He took back his copy of the Order. "What's in this for Jerry?"

"For God's sake, Ted. . . ." The Bailiff looked at his watch. "It's been a long day, we're all tired, there's still far too much to do, you can stop worrying about Renouf, and, besides, the agreement was that I took care of all that side of things. Anyway, it's over and done with."

"M'lord," Labuschagne announced, "I have here seventeen reasons why my client is innocent, and if you don't like those I have in my hip pocket a further twenty-three."

"Which are even better," Beatty added, "or, as the case may be, worse. Come on, Dan, cough up. You'll feel better for it."

De Wilde stood and stretched. "Renouf's prison sentence is to be publicized as a warning," he said shortly. "That's being done." He slid his empty pipe between his teeth like a bookmark.

"And that's all?" Langley asked.

"All that's new. The work on the defence projects will go on as before."

"Defence projects?" Labuschagne leaned back and frowned as if he were trying to get the words in focus. "Defence projects are nothing to do with us. They're the sole responsibility of the German Army and the Organisation Todt. Aren't they? So—"

"Yes, yes, yes, of course they are." De Wilde cut in brusquely, like a veteran schoolmaster anticipating a common error. "The whole thing was nothing but a debating trick, for heaven's sake. Rimmer believed that if Renouf got martyred, then the Islanders would boycott his defence work, that's all. So when he handed Renouf back, naturally he wanted an assurance that the work would go on."

"I'm sure he did," Beatty said. "The question is, did you give it him?"

The Bailiff thought back to the scene in Rimmer's room. "Not in so many words," he said. "Perhaps the implication was there."

"Stop slicing the bacon so thin," Langley growled. "Just tell us: what does bloody old Rimmer expect?"

De Wilde blew wheezily through his empty pipe. "I really don't feel that I can be called upon to read the Fortress Commandant's mind," he said.

"Listen, chum: if you can't, who can?" Langley demanded. His blunt fingers were worrying and shredding the edges of the

Emergency Order. "You were there, Dan, we weren't."

"All right! I was there." De Wilde's head came up; he was on the attack. "To save Renouf I held a gun to Rimmer's head, or so it seemed to him. It was a gamble but it worked. Good. When it was over, I had to unload the gun. What else could I do?"

"Nothing," Beatty said. He winced as he exercised his rheumatic shoulder. "But it means that Rimmer thinks you've guaranteed there won't be any labour problems on his defence works, doesn't it?"

"Well, there never have been any problems. He hasn't won anything extra."

"Exactly," Labuschagne agreed. "So why are my tired old scruples sending out hot little twitches of anxiety?"

"I'll tell you why," Langley said. "Suppose bloody old Rimmer does get trouble tomorrow. He'll expect us to put a stop to it, fast."

"Ah!" Labuschagne delicately touched his fingertips together. "Yes. Beware your IOU's will find you out."

De Wilde began: "We've no reason—"

"Don't be so sure, Dan," Beatty interrupted. "D'you know why the *Schleswig-Holstein*'s coming here a week early? Rimmer's getting a load of cement rushed across, that's why. And what's his hurry? He's worried about the invasion, obviously."

"How d'you know that?" de Wilde challenged.

"Well, the word's going around. Three different people told me."

"Rumours."

"So what?" Beatty said. "If enough Islanders believe those rumours, they may decide it's time to stop pouring concrete for Schumacher."

"And they may be right," Labuschagne added. "After all, even the least imaginative dunderhead amongst them can see that erecting obstacles is a curious way to welcome one's liberators."

Langley felt a sudden shiver of excitement. "Remember what that American said? 'Any day now,' he said. . . . It could be all over in . . . in a month! Or less! We could be free in a week!"

"No we couldn't," de Wilde said. He was still standing. He looked at the Council Members as if they were a long way off, shook his head, and said again: "No, we couldn't. Not in a week, not in a month. I'm afraid it's impossible."

Labuschagne was the first to recover. "Bailiff, are you telling us that you have received some kind of secret communication?"

"Secret?" De Wilde almost laughed. "No, nothing secret; quite the reverse. My information is about as public as it could be. Just go out and look around you, Dick. Look at the bunkers, look at the gun-sites, look at the tank-traps, look at the strongpoints! Jersey's a concrete hedgehog. In order to capture Jersey you'd have to destroy it first."

"Nobody ever said the invasion won't be messy," Langley argued, "but just you ask any Jerseyman if it'll be worth it."

"The Allies don't give a damn what Jersey thinks," de Wilde replied. Langley jerked as if he had been struck. "I'm sorry, Ted, but that's the obvious truth. All Eisenhower and Churchill and the rest want is to win the war. They're not going to waste an army on Jersey. Why should they? Even if they capture this place, it's no good to them."

"I don't believe that," Beatty said immediately.

"You mean you don't want to believe it. I didn't want to believe it, either, but now I can't open my eyes without seeing the proof."

"And when did you first succumb to this delusion?" Labuschagne asked.

"When? I don't know. Three minutes ago, perhaps. That was when it became blindingly obvious to me. But I suppose I've known for a long time. Liberation, the kind we've all been dreaming about —well, that's just what it was, a dream." De Wilde took his seat again and shuffled his papers together. "Now, shall we move on? We've spent enough time on that."

"No, we shan't bloody move on," Langley said angrily. "I mean . . . If we're not going to get liberated, what's the point of it all? What's going to happen to us?"

"God knows," the Bailiff said. "And I expect He's going to need all the help we can give Him, so let's talk about this *Schleswig-Holstein* business."

All the enthusiasm had gone out of the meeting. Their discussion dragged on for five minutes, with undertones of hostility from Langley, of disbelief from Labuschagne, of perplexity from Beatty. They were all tired and hungry, and irritated by Major Schwarz's complicated requirements. Nobody could suggest how to get a cow, and the news that Mary Betteridge was supplying the illegal pig made the whole deal seem shabbier than ever.

"All right, how about mushrooms?" de Wilde asked. "Can we get those?" Langley made a pessimistic face, and the Bailiff felt fatigue overhauling him. His telephone rang. It was the governor of St. Helier prison.

"I want to go home," he told de Wilde. "When's your criminous clerk going to get here?"

"Canon Renouf?" The Bailiff looked at his watch. "He should have arrived hours ago."

"Well, he hasn't turned up. That's against the law, you know. People can go to prison for not going to prison."

De Wilde abruptly brought the meeting to an end; the others left silently. He telephoned St. Peter's vicarage and got no answer. He called St. Helier Police Station, the editor of the *Evening Post*, and the island hospital. Nobody knew where Renouf was. His head began to feel leaden; thoughts moved slowly, like elderly fish in a bowl whose water hadn't been changed in a long time. Eventually one thought swam all the way to the side of the bowl and peered out. He telephoned the German Field Gendarmerie H.Q. The duty NCO answered.

"This is the Bailiff," de Wilde said. "I am trying to locate Canon Renouf and—"

"A moment," the man said. After a while an officer picked up the phone: lieutenant somebody who either couldn't speak English or didn't care to. He talked rapidly, mentioned Canon Renouf four times in thirty seconds and hung up.

De Wilde heaved himself from his desk and put on his hat. At the doorway he felt briefly faint. It happened to a lot of people nowadays. He tramped downstairs and across the square and rang the bell.

Canon Renouf was in a cell. He was sitting on the bunk with his knees up, reading a translation of Hitler's *Mein Kampf.* "This is all they could offer. Poor stuff, I'm afraid."

"You were supposed to go to the Gloucester Street Jail," de Wilde said. "What the blazes are you doing here?"

"Very carelessly I left my shopping basket behind, and when I looked in to collect it they locked me up." Renouf flourished the book. "Listen here: he says, 'The task of diplomacy is to secure that a nation does not heroically go to its destruction but is practically preserved. Every way that leads to this end is expedient, and a failure to follow it must be called criminal neglect of duty.' " Renouf looked up. "Significant, eh?"

"You can leave now, Canon," de Wilde said. "I've seen the officer. It was all a misunderstanding."

Renouf gave the book to one of the guards. "I showed them that passage, but I'm afraid they're not terribly bright. I doubt if they realize that Hitler is doomed."

"Let's get out of here," de Wilde said.

They walked through the streets to the town prison. Hundreds of German soldiers, plus a sprinkling of sailors and airmen, wandered about. They were off duty, there was nothing to do, nowhere to go, very little to buy with their Occupation marks. They looked bored. "If I were General Eisenhower," Renouf said, "I wouldn't bother attacking this lot. Wouldn't bother with the coast at all: I'd drop fifty thousand paratroopers on Paris, that's what I'd do."

"Could you do it quietly?" de Wilde asked.

Renouf lowered his voice to a gentle boom. "Liberate Paris, my dear Bailiff, and the rest of France will erupt like a volcano. You've heard the latest from the Russian front? It's full-scale retreat out there. Rumania—"

"Tell me about your organ left," the Bailiff said.

"Organ loft? What about it?"

"I hear it's got dry rot."

"Nonsense. I'd be the first—"

"Then it must be the bell-tower. Have you been up there lately?"

"Not lately, it's—"

"You should," the Bailiff said firmly. "You really should. Go up and check the timbers." As Renouf opened his mouth de Wilde said, "And I hear the view is quite breathtaking. Tell me about the view, Canon. I'm really most interested."

"For heaven's sake, Bailiff," Renouf barked. "We're in the middle of a world war and you want to talk about scenic views? I've no idea what the wretched view is like."

"Then make something up," de Wilde told him.

Renouf narrowed his eyes and looked sceptically at the Bailiff. "You've been working too hard again," he said.

"Splendid," de Wilde said. "Shall we talk about that?"

When they reached the Gloucester Street Jail Renouf hammered on the door. "Don't worry, I shall be all right now," he boomed.

"I'm sure you will," de Wilde said.

Renouf was admitted. The Bailiff sat on a pile of decaying sandbags. A gang of boys, pinchfaced and scabby-kneed, scuffed past. They jeered at him in their yelping, scratchy voices, blew raspberries, shouted "Crawler!" and, when he stood up, ran.

Three minutes later, Canon Renouf came out. He was holding a pink duplicated form. "They can't take me," he said. "They're full up. They told me to come back in three months."

"I know," de Wilde said. "Now, will you do me a favour? Will you please, for God's sake and for your sake, go home and stop annoying the Germans?"

"You really mustn't concern yourself about me," Renouf said. "Today was just a misunderstanding. You said so yourself."

De Wilde stared at the minister's honest, open face. "Promise me you won't go shouting out any more war news," he asked. "They won't stand for it. I know they won't."

"Come, come. There's no harm in the truth." Renouf patted him on the arm. "They never objected when I told people about German victories, did they? Well, then . . ."

The Bailiff watched him stride off. Halfway to the corner Renouf paused, turned, and shielded his mouth with his hands. "The Japanese are having rather a sticky time, too," he boomed cautiously. His smile gleamed in the sunset.

De Wilde wanted no more. He walked away, in the opposite direction.

18

"Wait," said the sergeant.

He used the little finger of his right hand to tilt the dressing-table mirror upwards, and looked at his reflection. There was no doubt about it; he was still losing weight. His cheeks were so hollow that it looked as if he were sucking them in, and the skin above his collar was loose and slack. It couldn't all be blamed on the food. His stomach ulcer must have started up again. His battalion was made up entirely of men with stomach disorders, so he knew all about ulcers.

He sighed, and straightened his helmet. It was a fine mirror, slightly speckled at the edge of the glass, but that only drew attention to its age and the beauty of its ornate gold frame. He smoothed his tunic. Perhaps there would be more milk soon. He stepped back and nodded. The soldier swung his rifle-butt and shattered the mirror.

Mary Betteridge stood in the bedroom doorway and watched. When the squad of six soldiers had begun their vandalizing search she had wept, but their violence had outlasted her tears. Now there was very little left for them to smash.

She stood aside as they tramped out and went downstairs, glass and debris crunching underfoot. In the farmyard the sergeant stepped carefully over a rich white stream of milk which was pouring softly out of the barn and feeling its way between the cobble-stones. He saluted Captain Paulus, shook his head once, and marched his men away.

Paulus and Zimmerman were standing with Louis Betteridge in the middle of the farmyard. Betteridge looked sick; his eyes were bleary with suppressed tears and his arms hung like scarecrow sleeves. The milk had found and filled a small hollow, where it was gently revolving. Paulus clasped his gloves behind him and watched a little paper boat sail around. It stuck on the edge, and he nudged it free with the toe of his boot. A lick of milk tipped the glossy black leather. All three men looked at the white smudge. *Go on, make me clean it off*, Betteridge thought wretchedly.

"Well, we mustn't keep Mr. Betteridge from his work any longer," Paulus said.

"You haven't left me any damn work," Betteridge mumbled. "It's all smashed."

"Not at all! Your telephone still works. You can make good use of that, can't you?"

Betteridge said nothing, but watched the milk overflow its hollow and carry the paper boat away.

"Please use the telephone," Paulus suggested. "It would be pleasant to be able to negotiate some kind of compensation, for instance. You'll be surprised how generous we can be."

The Gestapo officers drove away. Betteridge went inside. His wife was already at work, slamming the heavy yard-broom across the littered floor, and she did not pause. He said, "They were looking for that bloody sentry."

"Inside the grandfather clock?" She kicked its torn dial and twisted hands towards him. "Inside the cushions? Inside the teapot? Inside the gramophone?"

"Oh . . . God knows."

"It wasn't God!" She tred on a cracked gramophone-record and shattered it. "It was Jack Greg put them up to this! He's begrudged you the farm these last twenty years. This farm and this house and all that went with it. Talk about hatred and covetousness. . . . We've always got on well with the Germans, haven't we? Why should they suddenly do this to us? Jack Greg put 'em up to it. Cousin Jack!" She hammered the broom against the hearth with a thwack that made Betteridge jump. "Well . . . two can play at that game."

Betteridge opened his mouth, but he saw that she was weeping silently. He let her get on with it, and went out to see what could be salvaged from the barn.

In the yard he found Earl Kramer squatting on his heels beside the farm cat, which was feasting on the pool of milk. "What in the name of mercy are you doing here?" Betteridge cried.

"How are you, Mr. Betteridge? Good to see you." Kramer stood up. "Just came by to say my thanks to you and Mrs. Betteridge. Looks like you had a little accident here."

"Oh Christ," Betteridge said. He sat on the edge of a stone horse-trough.

"Hey, talking of accidents," Kramer said, "I guess I really fouled things up this morning. That wasn't too smart, was it? I want you to know, I feel really bad about all that. I really do. See, thing is, I'd just blown in here, so I was going kind of by the book, the way everyone does on the other side, you know? When in doubt, kill a kraut. . . . I see now, things are sort of different here. . . ."

"Just go away," Betteridge said. "Leave us alone."

"Okay, okay." Kramer raised his arms to demonstrate his harmlessness. "Only I felt really bad about what happened this morning. . . . I mean, I've been talking to so many people, like Jack Greg and . . . Well, not so much him, because he's sort of stir-crazy himself, you might say—"

"Jack Greg?" Betteridge's face twisted. "Jack Greg sent you here?"

"Hell, no! Fact is, he was sort of against it, dunno why. I mean, I don't aim to cause you folks any trouble, I'm just gonna keep my head down and enjoy your gorgeous sunshine . . ." A rattling, tinkling crash stopped him. Mary Betteridge was sweeping debris out of the kitchen door. Dust rose like an exhalation. "You folks spring-cleaning?" Kramer asked.

"Leave us alone," Betteridge pleaded. "Just go away."

Kramer noticed that the kitchen window was broken. "Hey, man!" he said. "You two been squabbling?" He went over to the window and peered inside. *"Cheese and crust!"* he breathed. He turned his head, cautiously, and saw more havoc. "Jeepers!" he exclaimed. "What in hell's name went on here?"

Betteridge's face was hidden in his hands. The cat, plump with milk, rubbed against his leg until he kicked it away. Kramer stared anxiously. The rattle of broken china sounded again, and he went inside.

Two minutes later he came out. Betteridge had not moved. "This is terrible," Kramer said. "I mean, this is really awful. They got no right to behave like this to folks like you, war or no war."

"Go away," Betteridge said.

"There must be something I can do, for God's sake." Kramer pounded his fist against his palm. "I wanted to help clean up, but she said—"

"Just leave us alone."

"Yeah. . . . Don't worry, they're not gonna be let get away with this. Sonsabitches." Kramer paused. "It was the krauts, wasn't it?" he asked.

"They wouldn't listen," the farmer said. "They wouldn't speak and they wouldn't listen."

"There's only one thing those lousy bastards understand," Kramer announced.

"Next time they come around here I'll kill them," Betteridge whispered. He hugged himself as if he were cold. "I'll kill them. Kill them all. Then maybe they'll listen."

Kramer patted him on the back and squeezed his shoulder. "Don't worry about them bastards, Mr. Betteridge," he said. "They're gonna get their comeuppance right soon. I personally guarantee that."

Betteridge pushed his hand away. "You're all the same," he said. "Just go away and leave us alone."

Kramer slowly walked backwards across the farmyard. He had come to make things right with the Betteridges and he hated to leave them in such distress. "Listen, you rest up now, Mr. Betteridge," he called. "Take it easy, you hear? Leave them lousy bastards to me. They'll get what's coming to them, don't you worry." He glanced at the trail of milk, now scummy with dust and fragments of straw; gave Betteridge a final, encouraging wave; and strode up the lane, his oversize shoes clacking.

General Rimmer lay in a hot bath and watched Major Wolff reading aloud from the daily War Situation Report. Wolff held the length of teleprinter roll at arm's length, like a scroll, and recited the familiar military jargon in a flat, unvarying voice. Wolff was not at all interested in what he was saying, but that was all right because Rimmer was not listening. He was thinking of the astonishing passion of Maria, Countess Limner in that sun-soaked, grasshopper-happy gully with the drowsy horses looking down at them.

Rimmer sighed with happiness. Wolff stopped reading. He glanced at the general's wistful expression, and went back a few lines to see what had disturbed him. Something to do with munitions production. "I don't think you ought to take all that stuff too seriously, sir," he said. "I mean, it's all balls, really."

"D'you know anything about women, Wolff?" Rimmer asked.

"Women . . ." Wolff rolled up the teleprinter scroll and breathed a soft foghorn-note down it. "They don't fight fair, sir."

"Neither do we, Wolff, neither do we."

"True, sir. But we do it deliberately, whereas they can't tell the difference."

It was not the sort of answer that Rimmer wanted. He curled the bath-plug chain around his big toe and tried to think of a wise and witty retort. Wolff sounded the opening notes of *The Blue Danube* on his scroll until a tap on the door stopped him. Major Helldorf and Captain Paulus came in.

Helldorf looked tired, rumpled, and gloomy; by contrast, Paulus looked scrubbed and pressed, as if he had just come on duty. Rimmer shut one eye and studied each man in turn. "I hear no cheers," he said.

"Keller hasn't turned up, if that's what you mean, sir," Helldorf said. "We're still digging."

"And so are we," Paulus remarked, "but in different places and in different ways. We expect the telephone to start ringing soon, General."

"My damn telephone is ringing already," Helldorf complained. "Paulus has been leading a wreckers' crew around this island, and not surprisingly the natives are getting restless. They'd like some police protection. Frankly, I can't blame them. Can you, sir?"

"Don't ask me, Major," Rimmer said. "I'm not interested in problems. I'm interested in solutions." He soaped an arm.

Helldorf was perplexed, and he looked for help to Wolff; but Wolff was busy weighing himself on the bathroom scales. He had found his true weight; now he was standing on one leg to see if he weighed any less that way. Helldorf turned back to Rimmer. "What Paulus's squad has been doing is a crime, sir," he said. "How can I—"

"Listen, Helldorf: there is only one crime in this world, and that's losing. The Fuehrer sent me here to hold the fortress of Jersey, and neither he nor I care how many flowerbeds get trampled in the process. Understand?"

Helldorf shook his head obstinately. "I can't do my work without the help of the people. Sir, if we tell them to obey the law and then we go and rampage through their houses, they won't believe anything we say. Crime is crime; it's indivisible."

"Aren't you thinking of peace?" Wolff asked. He was standing on the other leg now. "Peace is indivisible. I read that somewhere."

"Shut up, Wolff," Rimmer said.

"Yes, sir. It's probably obsolete now, anyway. They keep coming up with new ideas."

Paulus said in a bored, indifferent voice, "I see you allowed Canon Renouf to go free, sir."

"Then you need glasses, Captain."

"Like shooting the Jews," Wolff said. "They thought that was a good idea once." He tried standing on tiptoe.

"Canon Renouf was seen walking home less than an hour ago, General." Paulus spoke with a flat, absolute certainty.

Rimmer heaved himself up and sent the bathwater surging. "Then what the bloody hell is going on?" he demanded. "That damned priest was to be nailed and jailed in short order."

"So he was, sir," Helldorf said. "But the civil prison is overcrowded. It has been for some time. Renouf must wait his turn to get in."

"Nobody told me that." Rimmer scowled at him. "If I'd known—" He realized that the Bailiff and Count Limner must have known all along. "By Christ, that sort of nonsense won't happen again," he growled.

"Oh well," Paulus said. "No great harm is done, General. It's not as if the Islanders pay any attention to Canon Renouf. Most of them regard him as a buffoon."

Rimmer slowly lowered himself into the bathwater again.

"When we went into Russia, everyone wanted to shoot all the Jews," Wolff said. "It didn't last, though. I suppose it turned out to be too damned noisy." He sat on the scales and looked around the steamy room at the three men; Rimmer brooding, Helldorf scratching, Paulus apparently staring placidly into space.

Rimmer muttered, "No more of that nonsense." He wiped his hand over his head, plastering his damp hair down his forehead in spiky strands. It gave him the look of a minor Roman emperor, determined, confident, belligerent.

"The funny thing was," Wolff said, "we kept on running out of bullets in the Kursk campaign. Funny, that, wasn't it?"

Rimmer's uniform lay where he had flung it over a cane stool. Paulus straightened the breeches. "I associated you with the tank, not the horse, General," he said. "Do you enjoy bareback riding?"

"Yes," Rimmer said. He watched bleakly as Paulus picked a tuft of horsehair from his breeches.

"I see you took a tumble, General," Paulus said.

"No."

Paulus plucked burrs and grass-seed from the breeches and rolled them between his fingertips. "Oh," he said.

"That's all," Rimmer ordered.

"Ah," Paulus said. "Of course." He threw the seeds into the toilet. He and Helldorf left.

19

Daniel de Wilde walked home. He lived at the top of a long hill, a mile and a half from St. Helier, and before he got there he was dog-tired and bone-weary and he wanted nothing more than a long hot bath, only he knew there wouldn't be any hot water, so he made do with his second-best desire, which was to collapse in an armchair and rest his stockinged feet on a large green cushion and do absolutely nothing.

As he trudged around the last bend, he saw a silent crowd of about fifty waiting on his front lawn.

He recognized most of them: farmers, shopkeepers, craftsmen, a couple of schoolteachers. They gave off hostility like steam off a midden. He walked through them and climbed onto an old tree-stump. "What's up with you lot?" he asked. That wasn't a very diplomatic approach but it had been a long day and he was running low on diplomacy. He just hoped he wouldn't start to feel dizzy and fall off the stump.

Somebody at the back shouted: "Whose bloody side are you bloody on?" There was a grumble of agreement.

De Wilde said, "I should have thought that was obvious—"

"It bloody is!" the voice bellowed. A dozen newspapers were waved.

"Oh," de Wilde said. "That."

"We know you've got to lick Jerry's arse," called an elderly gardener, "but you didn't have to sling poor old Renouf in the nick just to please your Nazi friends."

De Wilde felt anger send blood pounding to his head. "The Nazis are no friends of mine," he snapped, "and Canon Renouf is not in jail."

"Rubbish!" shouted one of the schoolteachers. "You were playing poker with that bastard Limner all last night!"

"Bridge," de Wilde said.

"Oh, I *beg* your pardon," the schoolteacher mocked.

"I won half a dozen bars of chocolate." That caused a stir; most of them had forgotten what real chocolate tasted like. He smiled at their reaction and got a round of catcalls. "Which Count Limner sent, on my behalf, to the children's ward of the hospital this morning." He saw a hospital orderly in the crowd and pointed to him. "Right?" The man shrugged. "I also persuaded Count Limner to apply again to Berlin for a supply of Red Cross parcels."

"Fat chance," sneered a man who was standing on a flowerbed.

The Bailiff glanced at him: a farmer and black-marketeer, with a dewlap and a paunch. "You should know, Mr. Spalding," he said gently. "Fat chance is a subject on which you seem to be an expert."

That got a laugh. De Wilde unbuttoned his jacket and tightened his belt another notch. Spalding shoved through the crowd, red with resentment. "I'll tell you something else I'm an expert on!" he shouted. "Bloody Germans smashing down my crops and knocking holes in my buildings! And if they don't find what they're looking for mighty damn quick, we can all kiss our rations good-bye! Maybe you can live on fresh air, but—"

"Who was responsible for this?" de Wilde demanded.

"How the hell should I know? Some bloody jackbooted Jerry officer. He didn't leave his card, he was too bloody busy doing about five hundred quids' worth of damage while you were busy passing special laws to stop Canon Renouf picking his nose without a permit from your dear bleeding friend, the Fortress Commandant!"

Spalding spat the last two words, harshly and breathlessly. A tear of rage ran down his purple cheeks, and his head trembled like a toy animal's.

Without warning, his nose bled. The scarlet stream splattered his mouth and chin, sleeve and wrist, but he ignored it and went on glaring at de Wilde.

By some curious crowd-alchemy, the nosebleed aroused other people and set them shouting. Search-parties of German troops had systematically smashed up homes, farms, businesses. They were supposedly looking for the vanished sentry, but the way they ripped down doors, clubbed holes in plaster, flattened sheds, and made havoc of storerooms and workshops, it was obvious that the hunt itself was a form of reprisal.

No Islander had been attacked, but several who protested had been manhandled. De Wilde saw cuts and bruises and black eyes and one man who had stopped a rifle-butt with his teeth. The soldiers had left with this threat: unless the man was found soon, worse would follow. Worse already had: one of the searchers had cracked a gas-pipe, and the house had caught fire.

"Shocking," de Wilde said. "Appalling."

"We don't need you telling us that," the elderly gardener said bleakly.

"I know, I know. It must have been a horrible experience, and you all deserve the utmost credit for coming through this ordeal without losing your self-control or your respect for law and order." *If I say it firmly enough,* he thought, *they might believe it.*

"I could've strangled the bastards," said the gardener.

"But you didn't and you were absolutely right. Now as soon as I get inside I shall telephone Count Limner and demand a total and immediate cessation of this scandalous, brutal, and thoroughly illegal harassment."

There was a chorus of *Hear! Hear!* "Total and immediate!" de Wilde repeated, even more vigorously. "But before I do that, there are two things I want you to know. Two very important things."

Spalding took his bloody handkerchief from his nose. "Gimme a gun and I'll shoot the sods—" he began thickly, but the crowd shushed him.

"Three things, actually," de Wilde said. "First, I want you to know that I'm proud of you. I'm proud because you all chose to come together, in order to air your legitimate grievances—and God knows you have plenty—and in this way to decide what course of action is in the best interests of the island as a whole."

He blew his nose. That not only sounded a note of sincerity, it also gave them a moment to absorb his words. "Even if my marigolds have suffered in the process," he said.

That earned a few sheepish grins. "The Germans have acted tyrannically. You have acted democratically. That is what this war is all about. It would be a tragedy if we were to claim that we stood for freedom, justice, and decency and then let ourselves be stampeded by the crimes of others into behaving like a lot of selfish individuals—retaliating impetuously and irresponsibly and foolishly. That can only lead to disaster. Our hope is to stick at all times to the rule of law."

"Sod the rule of law," Spalding muttered.

"Have you got anything better?" de Wilde demanded. Spalding mopped his nose. "So that's the second thing," de Wilde told them. "The only weapon we've got to fight the Germans with is our legal rights as an Occupied Country, laid down in the Hague Convention. As long as we behave ourselves, they must treat us properly. I know it's not easy, but we've made it work for nearly four years now, haven't we? And we're still here, aren't we? Maybe not as fat as we once were, but alive and—"

"You getting at me?" Spalding shouted. His nose began to bleed again. "Oh Christ," he muttered.

The Bailiff noticed that the crowd had edged closer. Now nobody was standing in a flowerbed. He filled his lungs and tried to look as foursquare and confident as he could.

"Finally, the third thing," he said. "You can guess why we see so many hundreds of Allied planes in the skies every day. You can guess why the Germans spend so much time peering out to sea. You can guess what's happening on the south coast of England at this very moment, day and night, around the clock, seven days a week."

"Randy bloody Yanks," said the gardener. "They were the same in 1918."

De Wilde let the laughter subside. "D-day," he said. "D for Deliverance. It can't be long now. The Germans know it, and that makes them jumpy. They've started to do stupid things. They're nervous—and so they're just itching for an excuse to run wild. Let 'em itch! We're not going to oblige them, not us. Now, more than ever—now, when liberation is almost in sight—we must have patience, coolness, self-control, and, above all, legality. With those weapons we can win this war. And soon. *Soon.*" De Wilde raised his arms and shook his clenched fists. *"Soon!"* The gesture felt theatrical, but it raised a cheer. He turned and walked to his house.

His sister, Margaret de Wilde, was waiting inside the french windows. "Well done, Dan," she said, and kissed him. "Is that true, about D-day?"

"God knows," he said. "What do you think?"

She took his hands and looked at his weary face. "I think you need a drink," she said.

"There's only that little bit of whisky. We said we'd save it for the liberation."

She squeezed his hands and felt his fingers return the pressure.

"You're right," he said. "God blast the bloody liberation. Let's drink it now, every last drop."

20

Jack Greg was sitting on his one-hole privy, picking his nose, watching an elderly spider study a young fly, and waiting for his bowels to get on with it, when fists pounded the door and a harsh voice shouted: *"Raus! Raus! Donner und Blitzen. . . . Achtung! Achtung!"*

"Wait a minute!" he cried. His trousers were caught beneath his heels; he wrenched hard and heard something rip. "Hang on, I'm coming!" His fly was misbuttoned and his shirt hung out. The door-catch jammed under his hasty fingers; he swore, and knocked it loose with a blow that made the spider brace itself. "All right, all right!" he called urgently, as he stumbled into the soft evening sunlight. "What's the matter? What d'you—"

Sitting on a stump and aiming a carrot at Greg's stomach was Earl Kramer. "Ker-splat!" Kramer said. "You're dead."

Greg looked around. There was only Kramer. "You bleeding . . . madman. . . ." he said weakly. Kramer grinned and stuck the carrot in his mouth like a cigar. "Glad to see me back?" he asked. Greg glared, but his fury had to compete with his suddenly demanding bowels. He hurried back into the privy and slammed the door.

When he emerged he found Kramer standing beside a sycamore, whistling at a blackbird in the top branches. The blackbird heard him out and whistled back.

"Nice guy," Kramer said. "Not exactly Benny Goodman, but he swings all the same."

"Listen, don't ever do anything like that again," Greg told him angrily. "We don't make jokes like that, not here. Jerry's nothing to laugh at. He's had the last laugh too bloody often."

"Okay, okay, I'm sorry, I didn't realize you guys were so jumpy."
They walked back to the cottage. "Fritz is no goddam superman, you
know. I just walked through three of his checkpoints. All I did was
wave my papers. They didn't even look at 'em."

"They never do," Greg said. "Get any eggs?"

"Eggs?" Kramer had to stop and think. "Oh, eggs. No. . . . Hey,
that's what I wanted to tell you. The krauts busted up your cousin's
farm. Looks like a tornado hit. I guess I got there just after they left.
Chaos! You should hear the old lady. Mad? She's fit to be tied! Old
man Betteridge is ready to smash a few squareheads too. . . . Man,
they really did a job on his place. Disaster area!"

"Why? What for?"

Kramer shrugged. "Search me."

Greg opened his mouth, closed it, and then changed his mind again.
"Maybe they were searching *for* you."

"They don't know I'm here, even."

"Don't they? A lot of folk know you're here, my lad. It's no secret."
They went inside. "And I'll show you something else that's no secret,
too. Look what our patriotic bloody Bailiff and his pals were so busy
doing this afternoon."

A copy of the *Jersey Evening Post* lay on the kitchen table. The
front page carried a bold-type announcement in a heavy black frame
which was already smudged with Greg's fingerprints.

RELATIONS WITH THE ARMY OF OCCUPATION

I am pleased to announce that General Rimmer, who has been appointed
Fortress Commandant, has assured me that he wishes the pleasant relations
which have hitherto existed between the population and the Army of Occupation to continue.

In furtherance of this state of affairs, the Royal Court today passed a Law
prohibiting any statement or expression, whether written or spoken, which
is calculated to give offence to any member of the Army of Occupation. This
Law came into force with effect from 0900 hours today.

At a session of the Royal Court this afternoon Canon John Renouf, of St.
Peter's Church, Jersey, was found guilty of an offence under this Law and
sentenced to fourteen days' imprisonment.

In this connection, I have asked the Fortress Commandant to acquaint me
of any happening to which he may take exception, in order that I may
intercede on behalf of anyone who, unwittingly or without appreciating the
consequences, may offend against the German Military Code. I am sure that

nobody who has the interests of the island at heart will wish to endanger the harmonious relationship which both sides have so carefully constructed, and upon which our well-being and safety depend.

D. de Wilde
Bailiff

Kramer let out a whoop which made Greg jump. "He's a Quisling!" he exclaimed. "This guy is nothing but a lousy Quisling! For Pete's sake, why doesn't someone shoot him? Back home, we'd—"

"Shut your great noise!" Greg said. He closed the door and glanced out of the window. "You're not in Chicago now, you know."

"Ohio," Kramer said.

"And watch your tongue! De Wilde's no Quisling; he's been doing his job since long before they came here. You shut up about shooting. Someone hears you talk about shooting and I'll have the police round here in two shakes."

Greg tramped upstairs, scowling with disapproval. Kramer heard his boots clumping across the bare boards of the bedroom. *Here we go, in the doghouse again,* Kramer thought.

He threw down the newspaper and stood in front of the dead fireplace. In the early twilight the cottage looked bare and dreary, and he felt his spirits sink. His stomach was empty again, but his depression deadened even his appetite. It was twenty-four hours since *High Society* had ditched with that almighty roller-coastering, bouncing, tail-skidding, wave-smashing impact that ripped one wing off at the roots and sent seawater flooding through the fuselage as if someone had opened a sluice. Now he was alone. The base at Market Deeping was ten thousand miles away. Plattsville, Ohio, was fifty million miles away. He felt a longing for his room at Market Deeping, his cramped, untidy room with a copy of *Stars and Stripes* jammed in the window to stop it rattling, and Carmen Miranda and Betty Grable on the wall, and The Jack Benny Show on AFN, and a half-read letter from his mother in his locker on top of two Mars bars, two rolls of Lifesavers, and a Babe Ruth. Holy smoke, what he wouldn't give for a bite of that Babe Ruth right now. . . . When the Marines land on Jersey they better bring plenty of Babe Ruths with them. . . .

"You really think they're going to invade, then," Greg said. He had come down with a hammer and was nailing a board over the broken window.

"Yeah. Sure."

Greg went on pounding nails.

"Why not?" Kramer asked. "We've got to invade. Can't win unless
we invade."

Greg clawed out a bent nail and straightened it. "Then again," he
said, "they might invade and still not win."

Kramer's stamped-on foot began to ache. He sat in an old cane
chair, which wheezed.

Greg said, "These Germans are no fools, you know. They got this
island boxed up snug."

"It didn't keep me out."

"Aye, and they know it. I hear they found your rubber dinghy."

Kramer had completely forgotten where he'd left his dinghy, and
he didn't feel like starting to remember now. "What burns my tail,"
he said, "is all this goddam collaboration. I mean, that's not going to
help our guys when they hit the beach, is it?"

"I don't know," Greg said.

"Course not. Jesus, they're gonna need all the help they can get.
They need a Resistance kicking the krauts in the balls, not some
half-assed collaboration slapping them on the back."

"Look here: I've got to leave you now," Greg said. "I'm working
the night shift this week."

Kramer watched him put on a patched and tattered coat and an
elderly, ragged muffler. "I don't get it," he said. "What about the
curfew?"

"That's all right. I've got a job with the Organisation Todt, driving
a lorry."

Kramer twisted his face in astonishment. "You're working for *the
Germans*?"

"All right, all right, don't get your knickers in a twist. It's not the
German Army. The Todts are all civilians, they're just building con-
tractors. We're building a hospital, that's all. It's not going to win the
war for anyone."

Kramer got up and walked around the room. He raised a hand and
then let it fall, limply. "Holy cow," he said, "what's gotten into you
people?"

"Listen, the money's good and if I didn't do it, someone else
would." Greg fidgeted with his muffler, squinting down so that he
wouldn't meet Kramer's wide-eyed gaze. Eventually he had to look
up.

"You must be out of your minds," Kramer said. "We fly through seventeen different kinds of flak so we can bomb Hitler where it hurts, and all the time you guys—"

"Shut up, shut up," Greg snapped. "If you must know, there's more to it than that. Look here."

He dragged the table away from the wall and prised loose a section of skirting-board. Using the tips of his fingers he hinged up a floorboard. "Dynamite," he said.

The sticks lay in bundles, on a bed of wood-shavings; about forty in all; dull yellow, with blurred green lettering and dark red caps at one end. They might have been an exotic vegetable, stored away for the winter. Kramer stared. His mouth hung open, stretching spittle, until Greg reached across with a horny finger and shut it.

"I pinched it," Greg said. "A stick at a time. That's good German dynamite, that is, and when-and-if your invasion ever gets here it'll blow up a good few Germans."

Kramer watched him fold the floorboard down and tap the skirting into place. "Well, that's different," he said.

"And another thing." Greg put half a loaf of bread and a small piece of black pudding on the table. "If I didn't get extra rations because of my job, you wouldn't have any supper tonight."

"Ah," Kramer said.

"Don't stamp your feet," Greg said as he went out.

21

Greg had been gone only about ten minutes when Earl Kramer felt loneliness descend and claim him. It happened suddenly, as he stood at a back window. Dusk was draining all the colour from the day, and for the first time in his life Kramer knew the shrunken, tired insignificance of being a nobody, nowhere. The world looked bleak and indifferent, and there was no way he could alter it—no lights to be switched on, no radio to play, no magazines to flip through, no friends. Especially that: no friends. Kramer rested his forehead against the cold glass and thought about never seeing or hearing the rest of the crew of *High Society* ever again. Yet the dead refused to die: they still swung down from the hatches in the belly of the B-24 and strolled stiffly to the jeeps which would take them to de-briefing: whistling, singing, kicking the massive tires as they went past, shout-

ing insults at other crews whirling past on the long drive around the
perimeter track, yawning with the contentment of survivors. They
refused to die, but Kramer saw them as cheerful ghosts, and loneliness
sank deeply into him like an enfeebling disease.

Okay, so they were dead and he was alive: so he was alive: so what?
Who cared? It was all just luck, empty luck. Nothing made any
difference. The world didn't give a damn one way or the other. He felt
cold and hungry, but loneliness numbed his will to move. Nobody
cared about him, so why should he care, either? He shivered a little.

Somebody rapped on the front door. Kramer rocked back on his
heels and stood with his arms half-raised, holding his breath. The cold
cottage absorbed the noise and went back to its grey silence. He
resisted a flutter of panic that made him want to run: his footsteps
would give him away; besides, where could he run?

The rapping sounded again, and a man cleared his throat. Kramer
lowered his arms and let his breath escape. There was sweat in his
armpits and he wanted desperately to swallow, but instinctively he
was beginning to relax. An enemy would not have knocked twice, and
the Gestapo probably wouldn't have knocked once. He heard the door
open, and someone ask: "Anybody at home?" The voice was very
English.

"Jack Greg's out," Kramer said huskily. He turned and saw a man
who was built like a heavyweight but dressed like a minister. "He
won't be back till morning."

"Ah. . . ." They stood and examined each other, until the visitor
snapped his fingers. "Of course! You must be our transatlantic friend.
One of the intrepid birdmen come unexpectedly to earth, I hear. Too
bad, too bad. . . . I'm Renouf, the local dog-collar and Bad Influence."
They shook hands. "Tell me," Renouf said, "how good is the Focke-
Wulf 190?"

Kramer blinked. "You mean the fighter?"

"Yes, yes, the fighter. Is it much of a threat to you?"

"Well, hell, I wouldn't say that." Kramer felt unsure of himself
under Renouf's closely attentive gaze. "I mean, nobody likes to see
'em around, but—"

"I was thinking of its performance. How does it compare, for
instance, with the P51 Mustang?"

"Oh, the Mustang's a hundred per cent better," Kramer said confidently. Renouf rewarded him with a smile, and he went on: "The 190
is a neat little plane and it packs a real punch if you let it get in close

—I mean, twin cannon, twin MG—but above, say, twenty-one thou it goes all kinda woozy. Flies sloppy, you know what I mean?" Kramer made slack, loose-wristed gestures in the air. "Like it's swimming in Jello. I mean, gimme a Mustang any day."

"Ah." Renouf nodded thoughtfully. "And I suppose you fly above —what was it?—twenty-one thou?"

"Oh, sure," Kramer said.

"Obviously it makes sense."

"Yeah. . . . Of course, sometimes the weather kinda forces us down." He wondered if he should mention the new high-altitude four-cannon FW-190, which could outfly almost anything up to thirty-five thousand feet or more. He decided to forget it.

"Most interesting," Renouf said, turning away at last and taking slow strides about the room. "Thank you so much. One tries to keep one's flock apprised of the latest war news, and one finds that a little technical embellishment now and then helps enormously. The little leaven that leavens the lump, you know," Renouf smiled.

"Yeah," Kramer said. "I guess so."

"You wouldn't by any chance have any anecdotes relating to the Burma Campaign?" Renouf asked.

Kramer thought hard about Burma. He got images of Errol Flynn in a slouch hat. Was Flynn an Englishman? He wasn't sure. "I guess not," he said.

"What a pity, some of my parishioners have great difficulty in following the Burma Campaign. I try to paint them little word-pictures of steaming jungle and leeches and pagan temples, but it doesn't seem to be very effective. You haven't seen my bicycle, by any chance?"

"Bicycle?" Kramer looked around the bare cottage.

"Yes. Greg very kindly promised to take care of it for me today."

"Gee . . ." Kramer shook his head. He looked in the kitchen, although he knew no bicycle was there, and saw the evening paper lying on the table. His mind moved cautiously, and heavy shapes fell slowly into place. "Hey," he said. "You must be—" He found the Bailiff's announcement. "You must be this Canon Renouf, right?"

"Hah! In vain my dogged humility," Renouf boomed, "when all my infamies precede me. Yes, I am he, the very same desperado. Nevertheless, you quail not, neither do you cower! Such courage in the face of depravity. Brave lad, brave lad."

"According to this thing here, you ought to be in jail."

"Never believe everything you read."

"The Bailiff says—"

"The Bailiff has been working too hard. He is suffering from severe mental instability and delusions."

"Delusions?"

"Delusions the size of small elephants. They thunder through his brain, my boy, in a perpetual stampede of unreason, leaving their large footprints in the popular press." Renouf smiled broadly and marched his fists across the table.

Earl Kramer puzzled over Renouf's statement and gave it up. "Lemme get this straight," he said. "Are you saying the Bailiff is crazy?"

"Crazy?" Renouf's head rocked from side to side while he considered his answer. "Too strong," he decided. "The Bailiff has merely lost his grip on reality. His mind rambles, his sense of priorities is wildly askew. I still value him as a friend, of course, but I should have to question his judgement, even if he told me that the sun rises in the West."

"East," Kramer said.

Renouf turned through a half-circle, aimed his index fingers in opposite directions, and thought. "East," he accepted. "Correct. Not that it greatly matters."

"Well, it matters to me," Kramer said. "If the Bailiff hasn't got all his marbles, that makes a difference to me. For a start, it maybe explains why the Resistance is so thin on the ground around here."

Renouf was not listening. He had dragged a leatherbound autograph book, scuffed white at the edges, from an inside pocket and spread it on the table. "If you would be so kind," he said. "I consider it an enormous honour to meet the man who is come, so to speak, as the vanguard of our liberation."

Kramer took the fountain-pen and turned the pages. The last signature was Charles Lindbergh's. Before that, Humphrey Bogart's. He looked up worriedly. "You sure about this?" he asked. Renouf waved him on, using both arms. Kramer made a few practice swoops and wrote *Earl T. Kramer,* underlining his whole name by hugely extending the tail of the initial E. It looked good. He felt pleased and proud. Canon Renouf's visit was the best thing that had happened to him all day. This burly, booming man had the warmth of a friendly crowd, a warmth which dissolved Kramer's loneliness like the sun on a chill mist. He wanted Renouf to stay, to talk. "Hey, take a seat, why doncha?" he suggested.

"May I? You're very kind. I have a little time before curfew. Tell me: what sort of aircraft do you fly?"

"Four-motor job. What you guys call a Liberator."

"Ah, the B-24. We see quite a lot of them. A remarkably strong machine, I believe."

"A real big tough sonofabitch." He saw Renouf's eyes widen. "Toughest damn airplane in the sky, the B-24. I remember once we came back from Dortmund, there was so much flak you could get out and play hockey on it. They hit us in the wing, tail, everywhere. Had a hole in the side you could drive a jeep through. But she still flew, she got us home." (He didn't tell Renouf about the ambulance backing up to that jeep-sized hole to remove the bloody remains of one of the waist-gunners, all broken up inside his flying-suit like a rabbit that had stopped a double charge of buckshot. What was his name? Barnett? Barrett. Kramer knew that he wasn't telling the whole story, the true story, by leaving out Barrett's death. On the other hand, what was more important: Barrett getting flakked to bits or the B-24 holding together? Anyhow the guy's name wasn't Barrett, it was Bassett and nobody had liked him. His feet had stunk. Bassett had a quicker turn-round of room-mates than Eskimo Nell. Nobody could stand his feet. Going to war was bad enough, but coming back to share a room with Bassett's feet was too much.)

Canon Renouf was intrigued, He wanted to know what it was like to fly in a Liberator. For instance, was it very noisy? Kramer told him about the four mighty Pratt and Whitney engines and how they made the bomber shudder and strain while they were being run up. He described what it was like to thunder down a runway with five tons of bombs tucked inside the belly and feel the aircraft heave itself off the face of the earth. He talked about the great aerial spectacle as squadron after squadron of heavies went climbing and slowly wheeling to form their group, and then the wonderful sight as the group made its rendezvous with other groups until the sky was thick with bombers and more bombers, Liberators and Fortresses by the hundred, plus a few squadrons of mediums, like Mitchells or Marauders—two-motor lightweights thrown in for a diversion attack. All told maybe a thousand bombers, trucking freight to Germany.

Renouf listened intently. "And what happens when you encounter the German fighters?" he asked.

Kramer tried to describe their different tactics, such as the head-on slam-bang hello-goodbye attacks, when the fighters streaked through an entire bomber formation in just a few seconds. He remembered attacks by Messerschmitt 109's—resembling Spitfires only not so beautiful, except when they blew up, like that one on the Cologne mission; and Focke-Wulf 190's, always had those crazy yellow noses. . . . Once, on the Mannheim run, a 190 screwed up his pass and let himself get caught in the crossfire. Must have been forty or fifty guns chewing bits off that guy, knocking him back and forth, like he was a football or something. Finally the 190 came all undone at the seams, didn't explode, just fell apart, did a kind of strip-tease up there in the middle of the formation, until there was only the cockpit and the engine left, trying to fly all on its own! Hell of a sight. Then *poof*, down it went.

"Amazing," Renouf said. Kramer nodded. *Thank Christ we never got sent to Mannheim again,* he thought. *The squadron lost five planes that day. Twenty per cent. Forty-five men.* And *they missed the fucking target.*

"And presumably your actual bombing run is the most spectacular part of the whole business," Renouf said brightly.

"Sure. Well, sometimes. You got to remember: we're four, five miles *up* when those cookies hit. We don't *hear* anything, we just see them score. It's like . . . I dunno, it's like—" Kramer squeezed his eyes shut and tried to find words. It was like huge white flowers opening, all fresh-looking and crammed with life. Like rich, round blossoms suddenly emerging from dull, dead land. That's what bombing was like. It was beautiful, creative, touching, magical. All the wrong words. He opened his eyes and shrugged.

Renouf smiled understandingly. "I mustn't monopolize your time like this," he said. "You've been most kind. My goodness, I shall have to hurry or I shall get shot."

Kramer went with him to the door. "One thing I've been thinking about lately, padre," he said. "It's funny, I never thought about it during a mission, but just lately it keeps coming to me . . . I mean, what I've been doing, let's face it, I've been *killing* people."

"Ah." Renouf studied his face and saw bewilderment rather than guilt. "Contrary to the Sixth Commandment? Is that what worries you?"

"Blood is blood," Kramer said, looking at his hands. "I mean, who the hell am I to—"

"Now wait a minute. First, 'Thou shalt not kill' is a mistranslation. The correct version is, 'Thou shalt not murder.' "

"Is that right?" Kramer whistled his amazement. "Hey, I bet hardly anybody knows that."

"Second, the question you must ask yourself is what, if anything, is the alternative?"

"Kind of hard to think of anything else we *could* do," Kramer said. "I mean, they started it. I guess what bothers me is some of them are, you know, just ordinary guys who can't get out of the way." He remembered the night-shift face of the bald, dead sentry.

"Mr. Kramer," Renouf boomed, "you need not concern yourself for the enemy. God has seen fit to enrol you in a great war which is also a just war, and anything you can do to bring an Allied victory nearer is a righteous and a splendid thing. Anything."

"Gee," Kramer said. "You really think so."

"Praise God," Renouf told him, "and blast Hitler, early and often. Good night to you."

Kramer watched the minister stride down the path and fade into the deepening dusk. He felt restored, refreshed, recharged. *Anything you can do to bring an Allied victory nearer is a righteous and a splendid thing. Anything.* He filled his lungs with cool, fresh air. Maybe his real war was just beginning.

22

General Rimmer gave a small dinner-party to mark his arrival. There were six guests: Count Limner and his wife, Colonel Schumacher and his wife, Major Wolff and a visiting Luftwaffe general. The meal was simple: smoked eel, cream-schnitzel with mushrooms and egg noodles, a mixed salad, and apple pancakes. There was a choice of hock or burgundy. At the end, real coffee was served: enough for only one small cup each; but the brandy was Cognac and unlimited.

The wives wore long gowns. Beth Schumacher's was matte brown with full sleeves and a high collar which brushed her jaw. Maria Limner's was glossy red, with no sleeves and a deeply cut neckline. During the main course, while the Luftwaffe general was explaining the ethnic differences between the Chinese and the Japanese, Major

Wolff decided that Beth Schumacher looked as if she had taken a mudbath whereas Maria Limner looked as if she had been for a swim. He surprised himself by feeling more curious about the mudbath than about the swim. Beth was a dull, willing girl with hips like a cement-mixer, but right now Wolff would sooner slide into a warm quagmire with her than plunge into refreshing brine with Maria. That was odd. That was unsoldierly. He was not only giving in, he was giving up.

"Churchill's greatest blunder was not military," Rimmer said. He drank wine and glanced provocatively at his guests.

"He'd have to go some to beat Dieppe," the Luftwaffe general said. "What a massacre! I wasn't there, but—"

"Churchill's greatest blunder was political," Rimmer declared. "A fit of self-indulgence, a moment of complete bloody-mindedness, and I thank God for it."

"What was it?" Beth Schumacher asked. Somebody had to ask.

"The demand for unconditional surrender. It has stiffened the re-solve of our people just when the bombing was beginning to get them down. Now they will fight like tigers. They will never give in! Church-ill himself said it: 'We shall never surrender.' Does he really think we are weaker than his patchwork alliance? Silly man, he should have kept his mouth shut."

"And what was Hitler's greatest blunder?" Maria Limner asked.

Her husband sighed and stared at the ceiling. Nobody else moved.

"Well, the man's only human," Maria said calmly. "He does make mistakes, doesn't he?"

"Officially: no," Rimmer said.

"Then why aren't we winning the war?"

Schumacher said, "The Fuehrer has sometimes been badly advised by his generals, and also let down by his commanders in the field. For instance, at Stalingrad, where we—"

"Have you ever been to Russia?" Major Wolff asked.

"No, but from my experience of the Slav workers here on the island I know they are subhuman. One German soldier is worth fifty of them."

"Fifty?" repeated Major Wolff sharply.

"Yes." Schumacher half-expected Wolff to challenge the figure, but Wolff merely squeezed his chin until it dimpled, and let his eyes grow thoughtful.

Rimmer leaned back. "Wolff has something subversive to contrib-ute, haven't you, Wolff? Speak up, then. I've appointed him my devil's advocate," he explained to the others. "He's immune from prosecution."

"I was only thinking," Wolff said. "According to the London *Daily Mail*, one American soldier is worth five Germans. I'm quite sure our gallant Oriental allies believe that one Japanese soldier is worth at least three Americans. By a process of simple arithmetic which is too hard for my poor tired brain—"

"It comes to seven hundred and fifty to one," Maria Limner said. "One Japanese is worth seven hundred and fifty Russians."

"But they're not at war," Beth Schumacher said. "Are they?"

"No, my dear." Count Limner patted her hand. "They've already had their war for this century, 1904. It was a complete flop, Japan won easily. It was such a flop that they cancelled the fixture."

Rimmer was staring at Wolff. "How do you get the London *Daily Mail*?" he asked.

"From the Count. He also lends me *The Times.*"

"A colleague in our Stockholm Embassy sends them," Limner explained. "They're usually a week old, but at least they keep one informed about where the bombs are dropping."

"Yesterday it was Stuttgart and St. Cyr, near Versailles," said Maria. "Railway yards, a tank factory, and a Luftwaffe supplies depot. Last night it was Dusseldorf again, although God knows what they found still standing to bomb there, and various other places in France. Rheims and Amiens and some place near Orleans, I think."

"Salbris," the Luftwaffe general confirmed. "The explosives works. Went up like a volcano, so they say."

"Reichsminister Goebbels says it's unpatriotic to spread rumours," Beth Schumacher said stiffly.

"Oh, Maria doesn't listen to rumours," Limner said. "She listens to the bells. Like Joan of Arc. You've heard of Joan of Arc?" he asked Beth.

"Not bells," Schumacher declared before his wife could open her mouth. "No bells have rung on this island since 1941."

"Then it must have been something else," Maria said. "It must have been the deep, reverberating clang of field marshals knocking their heads together, or generals kicking each other in the balls." Schumacher stabbed himself in the mouth with his fork, and spilled sliced tomato and cucumber on his lap. "It went 'ding-dong,' " Maria said. "It was quite unmistakable."

"Was it as clear as, for instance, the BBC?" Rimmer asked.

"Do they play bells on the BBC?"

"You haven't answered my question."

"Well, you didn't answer mine."

"About the Fuehrer? There is no answer to a question like that."
Rimmer spoke quietly and confidently. "Remember how this war
began, Countess. Remember that in the space of two years, under the
brilliant leadership of one man, the German Army conquered the
whole of Europe, except Spain and Switzerland, which are more use
to us as neutrals. In the space of two years one man made Germany
the master of Norway, Denmark, Holland, Belgium, France, Poland,
Yugoslavia, and Greece. Remember that already this one man had
brought Austria and Czechoslovakia into the German fold." Rimmer
made an enclosing gesture with his left arm. "Then came Hungary,
Rumania, Bulgaria. Italy was our ally, Sweden and Turkey our
friends. The entire north coast of Africa was ours." He put his hands
together in an arrowhead and thrust outwards. "Our armies were six
hundred miles inside Russia! Threatening Moscow! All this in the
space of two years! All this, from the genius of one man!" Rimmer's
hands fell with a thud which frightened the wineglasses. His eyes were
bright with remembered glory, and the enthusiasm had brought colour to his face, showing up the shiny, zigzag scar. He let his guests
sit in silence for a moment while he looked at each in turn, ending with
Limner. "What did you do in 1932, Count?"

"In thirty-two? Dunno. I expect I played a bit of polo."

"In 1932 I worked in a chemical fertilizer plant, believe it or not."

"Certainly, certainly," Limner murmured courteously.

"In 1933 I joined the Party. I was twenty-nine, no prospects, no
confidence, no ideals. The Fuehrer changed all that. By 1939 I was
a lieutenant in the Reserve. They made me a captain in Poland, an
acting-major in France, a colonel in Yugoslavia. Twelve years ago,
Count, I was bagging phosphate in Saarbrücken. Now I am Commandant of what is probably the most vital fortress in the defence of the
Third Reich. Can you understand what that means? Without the
Fuehrer, the Third Reich would be nothing. Without him *I* would be
nothing. Without him none of us would be here now."

Rimmer sipped his wine and let them think about that. Then he
added, "So you see, Countess, I never think or talk of the Fuehrer in
terms of blunders. I have too much respect and gratitude for that."

"Hear, hear," Schumacher said. "I myself—"

"But yet," Wolff began. Schumacher gave up and poured himself more burgundy. "Sir, am I still devil's advocate?" Wolff asked.

"No," said Rimmer.

"Good. I just wanted to point out the absolute futility of an Allied invasion now, bearing in mind that we found it impossible to invade them in 1940, when they were much, much weaker than we are now, and personally I think that any apparent blunder on the part of the Fuehrer then can be largely blamed on the stupidity of the British, who made war when they shouldn't have and didn't make peace when they should."

"Thank you, Wolff."

"After all, he gave them enough chance. Weeks and weeks and weeks. They were utterly helpless. It was foolish of them to go on fighting."

"You've made your point, Wolff."

"The great advantage for us in this situation," the Luftwaffe general said, "is that we know their invasion plan already. Fundamentally, it's our 1940 plan in reverse. They'll take the shortest route, just as we planned to do, across the Pas-de-Calais. Twenty-odd miles. Just a skip and a jump."

"But I don't understand—" Beth Schumacher began.

"It's all settled," Rimmer said. "The Fuehrer has given orders. The main invasion threat is to the Calais area. Von Rundstedt has concentrated his main defences there."

"I wonder if Eisenhower knows that, " Wolff mused. "He must, mustn't he? With all those thousand-bomber raids flying back and forth, somebody must have looked down and seen the massed ranks of squareheads all shaking their fists at England. So perhaps he won't invade there after all. . . ."

"It does seem a bit obvious," Limner said. "If it were me, I'd go and invade somewhere else. Anywhere else."

"Exactly." Rimmer's forefinger smacked the table. "That is exactly what Eisenhower expects us to think. Because Calais is such an obvious place, it is also—apparently—the *least likely* place, which in fact makes it the only *possible* place! Believe me, the Fuehrer is no fool."

"The best place to invade is always the last place the enemy expects to see you," the Luftwaffe general added helpfully.

"Yes." Wolff spun his knife on the tablecloth. "Of course, Eisenhower is no fool either. What if he carries it a stage further and decides that the last place is therefore the *worst* place? Because it's obviously the best place, you see," he explained to Beth Schumacher, who was plucking nervously at her napkin.

There was a moment's silence while they waited for General Rimmer to finish eating a small piece of bread. "The Fuehrer has anticipated that," he said. "By keeping strong defensive forces in the Calais area he has constantly encouraged the enemy to believe that we expect him to invade elsewhere. I think we can safely assume that the *one* thing the enemy will *never* do is behave in the way he thinks we want him to behave. Correct?" Rimmer smiled the smile of the detective who has arrested the con man.

"But Eisenhower may have worked all that out too," Wolff said. "He may just do what he thinks we know he knows we want because he also knows we don't really want it."

"You're being tedious, Wolff."

"Anything's possible," Count Limner said sleepily.

"Not in war," Rimmer corrected. "Very few things are possible in war. The Fuehrer made that absolutely clear at a conference I was privileged to attend only recently."

"Then I don't understand what Felix is doing here," said Beth Schumacher. She looked accusingly at her husband. Schumacher had his hand inside his shirt, scratching. He withdrew it, guiltily.

"He's putting up dozens of spanking great bunkers, dear girl," Limner said.

"But if the enemy is going to invade Calais—"

"There will also be a diversionary attack," Rimmer announced. "The British will make a supreme effort to recapture the only part of their country which is under German rule. That is inevitable. It is what we would do, if we were in their place."

"Ah," Beth said. She looked reassured.

"The British haven't shown much interest in these islands during the last four years," Maria remarked.

"Exactly," Rimmer said. "Exactly." On a nearby rooftop an air-raid siren began its throaty wail. One by one, other sirens picked up the call, mechanical hounds baying at the night. Rimmer brightened. "And now an interest seems to be developing."

"Probably just seagulls sitting on the radar scanner," said the Luftwaffe general. There was still some apple pancake left.

"Wolff, go and give the radar scanner a good shake," Rimmer

ordered. "And while you're up, signal an immediate full-scale invasion alert."

Wolff went out. Limner said, "Anyone for a little bridge?"

Maria was watching Rimmer. "You're quite enjoying all this, aren't
you?" she said. "You look ten years younger."

Rimmer shrugged amiably. "These who can, must," he said.
"That's what makes the world go round."

23

Earl Kramer ate the bread and the piece of black pudding which Greg
had given him, and then wandered about the cottage, bored, restless,
looking for something to do. There was nothing.

Even for wartime, even for a single man like Greg, the place was
extremely bare. Where did he keep all his food? Kramer suddenly got
annoyed at this silly little secret; didn't Greg trust him, or what? He
set to and searched every inch and found nothing, not even crumbs.
He paced up and down, cursing Greg's stupidity, until the ill-fitting
shoes made him stumble. "Don't stamp your feet," Greg had said.
Kramer looked at the floor. A man like Greg wouldn't have room for
more than one idea in his head, would he? Kramer got to work.

In the bedroom, under a chest-of-drawers, he found a floorboard
which hinged up and concealed a small wireless set and an acid-
accumulator battery. On the landing, under a blanket chest, a hinged
board hid Greg's larder: the other half of the loaf, a few pounds of
potatoes, a piece of ham, some oatmeal, a jar of carrot jam. It didn't
seem much. Then downstairs, he shifted an old bureau and lifted a
hinged board which revealed a bundle of detonators and a box of
fuses. That altered everything.

An hour later he was sitting in a corner of the bedroom with a
candle for light, eating Greg's ham and trying to make sense of a
German leaflet which had been wrapped around the detonators.

Outside it was dark: an imperial purple. At his elbow Glenn Miller
finished "Cherokee," said a few words, and started into "Tuxedo
Junction." Even filtered through Greg's lousy little radio, the music
had a swing and strut that made Kramer hunch his shoulders, twitch
his head, and flick his fingers. He had a poor sense of rhythm—it was
all he could do to march in step—and the band was soon lagging

behind his eager, erratic beat. Kramer was half-aware of this but he kept twitching and flicking. He reckoned Miller would catch up with him again before the end.

Achtung! it said at the top of the leaflet. That meant Keep Off or Get Out or something. The only other word he recognized was a *verboten* in the middle of the text. Fortunately there were lots of pictures. Kramer held a detonator in one hand, a fuse in the other, gripped a stick of dynamite between his knees, and tried to figure out how the pictures wanted him to assemble them.

The snarl of a nearby air-raid siren startled him and he nearly dropped the lot. The snarl began low and throaty and soared raucously to a piercing shriek which made his shoulders rise and his scalp creep. Behind this one, other sirens began their whooping climb, ripping through the stillness of the night. Kramer pressed himself against the corner walls. His eyes widened, creasing his brow, and he tasted the same metallic surge of saliva which he got when flak bursts suddenly rocked the B-24 and sent shrapnel rattling against her skin. Earl Kramer had flown above plenty of air raids but this was the first time he had ever been caught underneath one: and it frightened him.

For a long time he was too scared to move. His twitching legs braced him against the corner and he let the terrible, bullying bellow of the sirens blast away at his brain. It was a warning that aircraft were coming to bomb and kill, and his helplessness left him numb and witless. Then the scream slid off its harrowingly high pitch and dropped, fading, to a gloomy moan, and Kramer instinctively relaxed. Glenn Miller's trumpets punched holes in the dying sound, and he realized that what had scared him was not the air raid but the siren. He got to his feet and heard the throb of aircraft engines, and again his heartbeats leaped into double-time. Fear tightened his throat. The heavy throbbing seemed to swell and fill the sky; as if there were planes everywhere. The cottage looked small; small and frail. Kramer ran downstairs. There was nowhere safe to hide. He began to run back upstairs and stopped halfway in a panic of indecision. Where was best? Upstairs the bombs were closer; downstairs the collapsing house might crush you. . . .

He scuttled downstairs and ran outside. The throb of the bombers swelled to a grinding roar. He stood under the faceless, naked night and looked for shelter. Nothing. He was helpless to save himself. The bombs might be falling now, tumbling out of the gaping bays, dipping nose-first as the tailfins caught the rush of air, hurtling faster and faster in an invisible cluster, as blind and senseless as a swarm of meteorites rushing towards a turning planet. They would kill and maim. Nothing could stop that. Kramer stared miserably upwards and remembered the moment when *High Society* bounced with relief as its bombload departed. Everyone felt better at that moment. Yet it marked the beginning of the last few seconds on earth of God knew how many people.

He found himself breathing shallowly, as if by disguising the fact that he was alive he might stand a better chance of not dying. It was impossible to keep it up; he stopped wishing, stopped fearing, stopped wondering, and took a deep breath of surrender. Okay, so let them kill him. Who the hell cared any more?

No bombs fell. The roar of engines receded to a dull thunder and grew again from a different angle. Kramer's fear had almost evaporated, but he wasn't going back inside that cottage. Too cramped, too cold, too much like a trap.

He put his hands in his pockets and walked cautiously down the path to the lane. The planes seemed to be circling the island. At odd intervals came the crash or bark of anti-aircraft fire, followed by the remote *woof* of exploding flak. Three searchlight beams suddenly created themselves and began tapping at the sky like blind men's sticks.

Kramer strolled down the lane, keeping close to the hedge. Once, in a pub, after too many pints of beer, the tail-gunner of an RAF Lancaster had revealed to Kramer how much he hated searchlights. He had tried to describe what it was like to be caught in a cone of beams, painfully dazzled by their starkly focused brilliance, pinned naked against the night for the benefit of a dozen flak batteries and any passing night fighter. He'd hated searchlights so much that Kramer had had to help him go outside and be sick. Or maybe that was the beer.

Kramer looked resentfully at the fingers of light wandering over Jersey and wished there were something he could do about them. He had a brief fantasy of himself on a hilltop with a high-powered rifle, blinding searchlights as fast as the krauts could mend them. . . .

Forty yards short of the road junction he stopped. Up ahead, by the dimmed lights of a truck, a dozen German soldiers were erecting a tank barrier: six-foot lengths of girder which they slotted vertically into readymade sockets.

They scattered as an aircraft roared out of nowhere, invisible in the blackness but attracting a sudden storm of flak and tracer. It climbed away and faded, and the soldiers ran back to their work. Beyond them Kramer could see a lot of military traffic bustling about. He climbed onto a log to get a better view, and watched half a dozen troop-carriers speed by. Why? Where were they going? Come to that, who needs a tank barrier in an air raid?

The answer struck him like a shout of joy: it wasn't just an air raid, this was the invasion! He slipped and fell off the log and sat in the lumpy, rutted lane, exulting. This was it! No wonder the krauts were buzzing like flies in a thunderstorm. The show was on the road at last! What a break!

He raced back to the cottage and stuffed six sticks of dynamite, six fuses, and six detonators into separate pockets. The lane was still empty when he hurried out, but the soldiers were adding barbed wire to the tank-trap, so he went through a hole in the hedge and made a detour across a field.

He reached the road at a point where he could look down on it from a steep bank. Not far away, the road forked. A military policeman with a flashlight in each hand was controlling traffic. Kramer watched an armoured personnel carrier halt to let a mobile anti-aircraft gun drive through. *Never mind the goddam searchlights,* he thought. *Let's really discombobulate the bastards.*

Various trees grew out of the bank. He chose the biggest, failed to climb it, and tried a smaller one with lower branches. That was easier, especially when he took off his shoes. Fifteen feet up he found a good wide branch which stretched over the road, and he crawled along it. When he looked down he saw, thirty feet below him, a captured British Bren-gun carrier, dimly lit by the truck behind it. Smoky-sweet exhaust fumes drifted up and made him cough, but the racket of engines was so great that he could scarcely hear himself. Another plane made a low pass, and the troops in the back of the carrier looked up. *Still no bombs,* Kramer thought. *Maybe they're dropping para-troops or something.* The carrier bellowed and rolled forward, its tracks spitting sparks.

Kramer made himself comfortable. He took out one stick of dyna-mite, one detonator, and one fuse.

The detonator would probably be no problem. He was pretty sure he'd figured out where that went: on the end, like a bulb in a flashlight. He tucked the fuse behind his ear and shoved the detonator into the explosive, thinking *If that's wrong I'll soon know all about it* and then realizing that if it was wrong he wouldn't know anything about anything, but now here he was, still holding the dynamite and trembling with excitement, so it must be right. He gave it a good hard shake. The detonator didn't fall out.

The fuse was trickier. How long would it burn? How much spark or flame would it make? Best to take no chances first time. He clipped the fuse into the detonator and looked for a good target. Down below was a halftrack towing a field-gun, with what looked like ammunition cases stacked behind the cab. No passengers. Perfect.

Kramer held the dynamite between his thigh and the branch, bent the fuse into a loop, and sat poised, with his matches ready. As soon as the military policeman began signalling, Kramer struck the match and lit the fuse. The halftrack was just moving off when he leaned over and lobbed the explosive into the well of the vehicle. The fuse made a glowing arc, but nobody shouted or fired shots. Within seconds the clatter of the halftrack was fading into the night.

Dead easy.

He hugged himself and waited for the payoff. It came after twenty seconds: a flat bang, as if someone had popped a giant balloon, followed by a *ker-rump* that travelled up through the trunk of the tree and made his buttocks tremble. A surge of hot orange flared beyond the leaves, and after a second they danced in the outer edges of the blast.

Kramer was impressed. The power of the explosive, and his own ability to exploit it, was very encouraging. This was real warfare. It was even better than bombing.

The military policeman vanished, presumably to investigate, but soon came back. Distant flames were flaring and crackling, and Kramer could hear men shouting. He primed another stick of dynamite and began searching for a second target: something big and elaborate and heavy, something that would really *block* this road. . . .

He chose a recovery vehicle. It had a vast, powerful engine and it carried a winch and a crane. It stood beneath him, shuddering gently, a massive workhorse which would need two workhorses to right it if it ever fell over. He studied it carefully and picked his spot. As soon as the truck moved he lit his fuse and lobbed the explosive neatly between its high sides. The dynamite curved through the air, bounced off something, and fell from the open tailgate.

Kramer thrust out his head to try to follow the rolling stick and

nearly fell off the branch. He grabbed, and raked his fingers across the
bark before they found something to grip. With an effort, he heaved
himself upright. He had to escape but he was facing the wrong way.
He swung his feet onto the branch, half-stood, half-turned, slipped,
again nearly fell, screamed, and clung desperately, face-down, living
out a nightmare. Twisting and twitching, he wriggled until his narrow
body was stretched along the branch, and then he tried to make it even
narrower. Below him, trucks and tanks, ambulances and police wag-
ons filled the roadway with noise.

1694er pressed his head against the tree and held his breath. He felt
a lurching, hasty pulse beat out the passing seconds. He counted to
twenty before his overworked lungs rebelled and made him gasp. The
roaring traffic-noise briefly faded each time he filled his lungs and then
surged back as they emptied.

After a minute he gave up thinking, hoping, wishing, wondering,
even looking. He shut his eyes and just lay there.

After two minutes he found the strength and the courage to raise
his head. Thirty feet below him the traffic still rolled. Either the stick
had been a dud or somebody's wheels had squashed the fuse. Or
something. Holy hell. What a break. Enough, enough, enough.

Kramer crawled along the branch, scrambled down some of the
trunk and fell the last six feet. He got up at once and started running,
and ran all the way to the cottage. When he stumbled through the
door and slumped into a chair he remembered that he'd left his shoes
under the tree. The hell with them; he wasn't going back there in a
hurry.

The flak was tailing off. The raid seemed to be over. Looked like
the invasion wasn't going to happen yet, after all. After a while
Kramer went to the porch and wiped his dusty feet on the old potato
sack in front of the door. Something sweet-smelling was growing
nearby; maybe honeysuckle or something. He enjoyed the scent. What
a night! Maybe everything hadn't gone exactly according to plan, but
what a night! At least he'd hit the krauts one good blow where it hurts.
Which was more than a lot of people could say.

The wrecked halftrack blazed and crackled enthusiastically, and its
flames kept leaping and grabbing for the branches of an overhanging
tree. Sometimes the branches caught fire but they always went out
after a few seconds. Then the flames tried again. It was an energetic
fire.

A bucket-chain under the command of Lieutenant Zimmerman was fetching water from a pond. Zimmerman was so busy that he did not see General Rimmer walk out of the night.

Rimmer watched six bucketfuls get thrown into the blaze. It swallowed them as a cart-horse might swallow little apples.

"Lieutenant!" Rimmer shouted. Zimmerman came running. "Dismiss your men," Rimmer said. "The alert is over."

"But the fire—"

"Leave it. What were you planning to do when you put it out? Clear the remains away? Let it burn. Then you'll have less to clear."

"Sir, there's a man in the cab, the driver."

"Is there? Well, he was very ill-advised to stay there. Put him on a charge."

"He's dead, sir."

"I'm not surprised. So what is your interest in him, Lieutenant? Are you a necrophiliac? Or a relative?" Zimmerman was outpaced. "A slightly charred corpse has nothing to commend it," Rimmer said. "I saw hundreds in Warsaw. Believe me, once the process of cremation has begun there is no point in stopping short of a handful of ashes."

"But, sir, the enemy aircraft—"

"The enemy aircraft have gone home. Follow their example."

Rimmer turned. Wolff, Helldorf, and Paulus were waiting.

"This halftrack seems to be the only thing the enemy actually hit, General," Wolff said. He pointed to an overturned motorcycle farther down the road. "That chap just got caught in the blast, it seems."

"Indeed." Rimmer strolled over and kicked the motorcycle tires. "Caught in the blast, was he? What bad luck. I want to talk to this man. Where is he?"

"God knows."

"I know," Paulus said. He hurried off into the darkness.

"Paulus knows," Wolff remarked. "Good old Paulus. I expect he's got a file on the chap." The blaze leaped and danced and flung its brilliance haphazardly across their grey uniforms. "Two files," Wolff added, "in case the first one gets lost in the wash."

"Don't be silly," Helldorf said. "Paulus has a file on the laundry too. Nothing could possibly get lost."

"Paulus has a file on Nothing," Wolff told him. "I saw it when he wasn't looking. So if Nothing happens to go wrong, Paulus is covered too. It's all in his Nothing file. Paulus is very thorough, you see. That's why—"

"I could swear I can smell hot food," Rimmer said. They all sniffed the night air.

"Well, the driver is still in there," Wolff pointed out.

"Not him. It's . . ." Rimmer sniffed and shrugged and gave up. "You've had no reports of other incidents tonight?" he asked Helldorf.

"Just damage from falling shrapnel, sir. And a couple of minor road accidents, but that's to be expected."

"So was this little brew-up to be expected. You might say that it followed as the night the day. . . . Ahah! Enter the victim of war."

Captain Paulus walked up with a young soldier who was holding a big white dressing over his right eye. "The motorcyclist, General," Paulus announced. Wolff threw his hat in the air.

"I want you to think carefully, son," Rimmer said. "Do you remember this explosion?"

"Yes, sir," the soldier said. His voice was faint, he was trembling, and blood was soaking through his dressing and staining his fingers.

"What do you remember? Do you remember hearing something coming? D'you remember the sound of a bomb? Like a whistle, for instance?"

The soldier gazed at Rimmer's eager face. A bright trickle of blood escaped and hurried down his cheek. "No, sir," he said. "If I'd heard something coming I'd have got my head down."

"Of course you would. All right, that's all." The soldier walked away. "At last, the non-whistling bomb," Rimmer said. "What will they think of next?"

"It could have been a parachute-mine," Helldorf said.

"Oh, it could have been lots of things," Rimmer said. "It could have been a rogue owl which had swallowed a hand grenade. It could have been a thunderbolt. It could have been an RAF chamber-pot on a very long piece of string. It could even have been a freak shell from the Russian front, which is, after all, only fifteen hundred miles away."

"But not a direct hit," Wolff said. "I mean, there are limits."

"Sir, there is no evidence that any Islander was involved in this," Helldorf said.

"Oh yes there is," Rimmer declared. "You're looking at it." He tapped himself on the chest. "The Fuehrer knew there was trouble brewing here, that's why he sent me. You remember Norway, 1940? He knew the British were going to invade Norway, he even knew *when.* And so he made damn sure that we got in first. Right?"

"By twenty-four hours," Paulus said. "The British arrived one day late."

"That is the genius of the man, and that's why I'm here. And now that I am here, I'm not going to tolerate this. Someone's going to pay for it. Stop scowling," Rimmer told Helldorf.

"I was thinking, sir."

"Scowling thoughts, obviously."

"I just don't think we can ignore the possibility of some new weapon, General. After all, this did happen in the middle of an air attack, and . . ."

Helldorf gave up. Rimmer had walked away and was sniffing the air again. "For an artillery halftrack, this smells remarkably like a field-kitchen," he said. He found a piece of fencing and poked at the edge of the blaze.

Paulus carefully put on a pair of dark glasses. "One wonders if sending a squadron of aircraft some hundreds of miles to destroy a single item of military hardware is the method Eisenhower would choose to test a new weapon," he said.

"Paulus has a file on Eisenhower," Wolff announced.

"There's no evidence—" Helldorf began.

"Then find some!" Rimmer snapped. "There's an invasion coming, for God's sake. Show him the late night news, Wolff."

Helldorf took a handful of leaflets, and read the heading: *Citoyens de la France!* He glanced at the signature: Charles de Gaulle. "Where did these come from?" he asked.

"St. Helier," Rimmer said. He found what he was looking for and raked it out of the fire. "Did you ever hear of a leaflet raid where they bombed their readers?"

"No, sir."

"No. One mistake at a time is enough, even for the RAF. . . . My goodness, we seem to have stumbled across a hotbed of crime here. The driver of this vehicle was obviously transporting black-market potatoes. And under your very nose, Helldorf."

Rimmer tossed a charred lump to Helldorf, who juggled with it. He tossed another to Paulus, who sidestepped and let it hit Wolff in the chest. Wolff fell down and lay in the roadway, looking at the stars. "Those damned Russian guns!" he said.

SUNDAY

24

Kramer was asleep when Greg got home from the night shift. Greg woke him with a mug of carrot tea.

"I see you had a go at the ham," he said.

Kramer struggled awake. The tea looked rusty and smelled soupy. "Gee," he muttered. "Wossa time?"

"Drink your tea."

Kramer pretended to sip it and accidentally drank some. It tasted worse than yesterday's: tacky; like some rotten old herb medicine; awful. "I got so damn hungry," he said. "I think maybe the shock or the exposure or something caught up on me. I got so damn hungry I couldn't see straight. Nearly keeled right over."

"Well . . . I don't suppose . . ." Greg shrugged. He was dusty and he looked tired. Clearly the ham mattered.

Kramer said, "Don't worry, I'll get you the biggest ham what am." He got out of bed. "Hey, this looks like one hell of a great morning!"

"Eggs for breakfast."

"Terrific!"

"You'd think so if you knew what they cost. Eggs are like the Crown jewels nowadays."

"I certainly appreciate it, Mr. Greg. Don't think I don't appreciate it. I do appreciate it."

Kramer got dressed and carried his tea downstairs, meaning to slip outside and throw it away. Greg was putting the eggs on to boil. "Hear the planes come over last night?" he asked.

"Sure did. Caused a big panic among the krauts."

"Aye. They thought it was the invasion starting, but nothing much happened."

Kramer walked to the doorway. "This sun is delicious," he murmured. He adjusted his grip on the syrup-tin mug. Greg came ovet and joined him. "It'll be hot again," he said, squinting at the sky.

"You sure do grow some handsome flowers on this island." Kramer strolled over to a clump of tall plants, hung with bell-shaped pink blossom.

"Foxgloves," Greg said. "Don't you have them in America? We can grow anything here. Wet and warm, see. Grow anything, provided the bloody Germans don't steal it off us first. Foxglove, that is."

He took Kramer around to the side of the cottage, where wildflowers were growing thickly, and recited their names: white bryony, lady's bedstraw, weasel's snout, cowslips, common stork's-bill, Aaron's rod, hawkweed. . . .

"Gee," Kramer said. His finger, hooked in the handle of the heavy mug, was growing stiff. "It's like a real garden here." *Wouldn't the eggs be done by now?*

"Some I put there myself, mind. They're all wild but cared for, if you follow me. . . . You ready for more tea?"

"Not yet, thanks." Now Kramer had to drink some. It seemed to coat his teeth with fine fuzz. Out in the lane, a car door slammed. Greg's head twisted as if jerked by wires. "German police," he whispered. "Bugger! You've been shopped. Get out of sight, now, fast."

"How d'you know?" Kramer asked. Greg grabbed his shoulders, spun him so that the tea went flying in a brown arc, and gave a shove that sent him sprawling head-first into a mass of grasses and cow parsley and thistles. Greg ran to the back door.

He had crossed the cottage and was opening the front door while Captain Paulus and two military policemen were still coming up the path. "You were expecting us?" Paulus asked.

"Did you think I couldn't hear you? The way you slam that door it's going to come off, one of these days." He let them in.

Paulus examined the eggs. "Brown," he remarked. "Some people believe they contain more flavour. You have a radio, Mr. . . . ." He took out a piece of paper and held it at arm's length, as if he were far-sighted. "Greg. We met yesterday, right? Now we meet again, because you have a radio."

Greg felt sick with a mixture of shock and relief. "Who says?" he asked huskily.·

"Oh . . . voices," Paulus said vaguely. "Go and fetch it, please."

Greg walked across the room, took the saucepan of eggs off the stove and drained it into the sink.

"Your brain is going chinkety-chonkety," Paulus said, "and exhaust smoke is emerging from your ears. Unless you fetch your radio, my men will tear your little cottage apart. That will damage their fingernails and your prospects."

Greg went upstairs and fetched the radio.

"Off we go," Paulus said.

"Aren't you going to take the eggs as well?"

Paulus picked them up and dropped them in Greg's pocket.

"If I took them and your Bailiff heard about it," he said, "he would hit me over the head with the Hague Convention until my skull was as square as the rest of the world believes it to be."

They walked, in the morning sunshine, to the car. Captain Paulus came last, playing with the radio. He got the BBC: a programme of popular songs. "Vera Lynn?" he asked. Greg nodded. "Charming," Paulus said, "quite charming."

"I surprised myself," Maria Limner said.

"Well, life is full of surprises," Rimmer remarked. They were riding back to the stables, letting the horses walk through grass which twinkled with dew, while Dum-Dum scouted for rabbits. It was half-past seven in the morning.

"Did you read that in a book or is it your own idea?" she asked.

He looked at her, and arched one eyebrow like a miniature bow. "You see: you obviously don't love me, otherwise you wouldn't make such discouraging remarks."

"Of course I don't love you. This is just a temporary infatuation. I honestly don't understand it. It's something I never expected to happen; it just happened."

"As long as we don't have to be nice to each other. D'you agree?"

"That depends on what you mean," she said.

"Well . . . I mean all the old sweet-and-loving-tenderness stuff. That's not our style, is it? We couldn't keep that up for five minutes."

They rode in silence for a while.

"The curious thing is I don't even find you awfully physically attractive," she said. "Not facially, anyway. I suppose you've got a good body, but that's not so all-important. . . ."

"Isn't it? It is, you know. You wouldn't share your tender loins with me if I were fat and smelly, would you?"

"Probably not. I've no way of knowing. This is the first time I've been unfaithful to Michael."

"Ah . . . I've been thinking about that." Rimmer chewed his lip. "Simply as a technicality, there's actually no question of unfaithfulness, is there? I mean, if your husband's impotent, then—"

"Michael's not impotent."

"Oh. I understood—"

"I'm sure you did. So do a lot of people. That sort of rumour is very hard to deny. All the same, it's not true."

"I see. Well, good for him."

Maria laughed, but not much. "My Christ, you can be cold-blooded," she said. "What is this to you: another military exercise?"

"Oh no! Sex is no exercise. Sex is as real as war. It's as natural as winning."

"And what happens when you lose?"

Rimmer gave it some thought. "So far, I haven't lost," he said. "What motivated you? Since I didn't seduce you with my roguish charm . . ."

"Oh . . . God knows. No, that's dishonest. It's so hard to explain. . . . Look, we've been on this island since 1941, and it's the biggest little nothing-happening place in the whole wide world. You turned up, and I suddenly felt as if I'd been holding my breath for three years, and—"

"Poof—you blew my trousers off."

"Yes. Sheer impatience."

"Or boredom."

"All right, boredom. I was bored and you were loaded. What does it matter?"

"Nothing," Rimmer said. "And everything." The horses saw the stables and broke into a canter, which suited him fine. This discussion was on the verge of getting out of control.

Daniel de Wilde reread the handwritten draft of his official protest as he walked to his office. It made all the points, he decided, but not strongly enough; Limner had to be made to see that the German search-parties had been a dangerous blunder. He paused and pencilled in extra words: *savage and brutal . . . utterly unprovoked . . . senseless. . . .*

Limner's limousine pulled up beside him and the rear door swung open. "Please get in, Bailiff," Limner said.

"I prefer to walk to my office," de Wilde said.

"I know you do. But General Rimmer wants to see you—see both of us—and he's miles away."

The Bailiff got in. "In that case you'll have time to read my protest against yesterday's harassment of civilians. I expect an immediate apology and full compensation."

Limner riffled through the papers. "Of course I'll do what I can," he said, "but I suspect that the situation has already gone far beyond all this."

They were driven out of St. Helier, along the great, curving southern bay, and up a steep and heavily wooded little valley which opened onto the massive and lofty promontory of the south-western headland. The big car turned off the road and followed a track over heathland dense with heather and ling. They were several hundred feet above sea-level, and the fresh breeze sent dozens of butterflies dancing before it. "They look so helpless," Limner said, "but I bet they could outlast the human race." De Wilde grunted.

A gun emplacement came into sight a hundred yards ahead, on the clifftop: but the car turned right and pulled into a clearing. General Rimmer's command vehicle stood in the middle. Rimmer was eating breakfast off the lowered tailgate. Half a dozen officers, including Wolff and Schumacher, stood around, enjoying the sunshine.

"Good morning, Bailiff," Rimmer called. "May I offer you coffee?"

"No," de Wilde said, more loudly than he had intended. "Thank you." It was real coffee, and the aroma—rich and burnished—made his nostrils twitch. Rimmer was eating fried bacon, too. De Wilde's mouth watered until he had to swallow. He walked to the edge of the clearing and looked down the cliffs to where the sea rolled and played amongst the rocks like a tireless, overgrown puppy. A quarter of a mile away stood the next headland, curling back protectively upon itself, with concrete bunkers sprouting like warts at the end.

"Enchanting," Rimmer said. He gestured with a strip of bacon and then ate it.

"Semi-enchanting," de Wilde said.

"You find it so? Perhaps you are right. Since last night I have a one-eyed soldier. Half a view would be enough for him, d'you think?"

"I don't know. If the behaviour of your search parties is anything to go by, soon everything on this island will be in half."

Rimmer stretched and filled his lungs. "Either it's this relaxing air, or it's the influence of your famous British understatement; but lately

I've become amazingly restrained. D'you know, I haven't had anybody shot for a week? I feel like St. Francis of Assisi."

"He was the one who talked to the birds," de Wilde said.

"I know how he felt!" Rimmer exclaimed. "Because you, my dear
Bailiff, are up there with the birds." He flapped his arms. "In the
clouds, out of touch. Saboteurs are at work on this island and you
distress yourself over broken tea-cups."

"What saboteurs? Where?"

"They blew up one of my vehicles last night. Killed the driver
outright. Other men were maimed in trifling ways, such as being
blinded in one eye."

"I'm sorry to hear that. I regret suffering as much as you do."

"More, I hope," Rimmer said. "For me, the novelty has long since
worn off. As the man said after the strip-tease: 'When you've seen one,
you've seen them both.' " He smiled amiably.

"Let's get this clear," de Wilde said. "Are you talking about what
happened during that air raid?"

"Correct."

The Bailiff stared. "And you're trying to tell me saboteurs did it?"
Rimmer nodded. "That's absurd. There were British bombers all over
this island for half an hour or more."

"They dropped no bombs."

"Who says? It was pitch-black. Or is the German Army clairvoyant
nowadays?"

"Bombs do more than go off bang. They whistle as they fall, they
make craters, they leave bomb splinters. None of those things has
happened."

"You mean your people didn't notice them."

"No, I mean they didn't happen."

De Wilde shrugged. "That still proves nothing. For all we know the
RAF may have a new kind of bomb. You Germans are always brag-
ging about your secret weapons."

Rimmer breathed upon the lenses of his binoculars and polished
them. "It's conceivable. What is inconceivable is that the RAF would
come all this way to drop one bomb and kill one man. I can't believe
it. Can you, Bailiff?"

De Wilde remembered the leaflets he had picked up on his way into
St. Helier, and his face gave an involuntary twitch. Rimmer noticed
this. "No, you can't," the general said. "Neither can I."

"It still doesn't prove an Islander was involved," de Wilde insisted.

"Sabotage could come from your own men; that's been known. Suppose—"

"It would require clairvoyance," Rimmer said. "Nobody knew those vehicles would be used last night. Not even me."

"Well, suppose—"

"Bailiff, you begin to irritate me." Rimmer walked back to his halftrack. "Understand this: I command here. I do what I like. I can have you shot, now; one word to that man with the Schmeisser and he will take you over to that patch of thistles and fire a dozen nine-millimetre bullets into your body. I can have twenty Islanders shot, fifty, three hundred, whatever I decide! What I cannot do is allow German soldiers to be blown up. You understand me?"

"Yes," de Wilde said. His legs were beginning to ache.

"I explained everything to you because I assumed that you want to stamp out this sabotage as much as I." Rimmer was raising his voice. "Now all you do is tell me that the nose on my face is all the time really my ear, and therefore the stink which I smell is actually the Moonlight Sonata! Right? *Right?*"

The Bailiff forced himself to meet the man's angry gaze. He suddenly realized that Rimmer was more than annoyed, he was deeply angry. Rimmer had not brought him out here just to give him another warning. And all these members of Rimmer's staff, who were standing around and pretending not to listen, must be present for a reason. A military reason. He felt afraid. They had such huge power, such total freedom to destroy; and he was just a tired old man whose hair kept blowing into his eyes. "No matter what happens," he said, "you cannot, under the terms of the Hague Convention, punish civilians for military acts."

"Sabotage . . ." Rimmer snarled the word, and licked spittle from the corner of his mouth. "Sabotage is a disgusting disease. Either it dies or it spreads."

Fatigue added itself to fear and began to pick at the edges of de Wilde's self-control. "You Germans have always prided yourselves on being good soldiers," he said. He tried to keep his voice quiet and level, but a tremor shook some words. "You have accepted all the fortunes of war. Are you incapable of accepting the misfortunes of war, too?"

Rimmer turned abruptly to Wolff. "Begin," he ordered. Wolff made a signal to a sergeant, who spoke into a field-telephone. The officers stopped talking and turned to look along the coast.

"What are they going to do?" de Wilde asked Limner.

"I'll try to find out."

Limner spoke in German to one of the officers, who reached out and squeezed Schumacher by the arm. Schumacher flinched angrily. He came over, carefully adjusting his uniform sleeve. "This is a demonstration," he said. Already pride was beginning to overcome discomfort. "We are demonstrating the virtual indestructibility of one of my bunkers. The one in the middle." He pointed across the bay, towards the cluster of strongpoints which guarded the tip of the next headland.

De Wilde tried to force his eyes to focus. It was all too far away; his eyesight wasn't good over long distances any more, and the glitter off the sea didn't help. But he knew that part of the island well. "Wait a minute!" he said. "There are people living near there. You can see the cottages."

The coastal battery at the end of the track boomed and belched. The breeze briskly swept the smoke away. Seabirds screamed, binoculars were raised. A hundred yards to the right of the target, a huge, brown fountain hurled itself upwards and outwards, hung poised, and slowly collapsed.

"For God's sake!" de Wilde said. "That's nowhere near."

"Never mind," Schumacher murmured. "It will be interesting to get the effects of blast."

"But there are people living there!" de Wilde cried. "General Rimmer, there are—"

The battery boomed again. De Wilde snatched Schumacher's binoculars and shoved them to his eyes. The headland sprang into being, clean and green, rich and sharp. A cottage chimney smoked. Cattle stampeded. The second shell-burst erupted in the middle of their field. De Wilde saw a cow tossed high, its legs splayed like a broken chair.

"Limner, for God's sake make them stop," de Wilde pleaded. His voice sounded feeble after the crash of artillery. He felt remote and helpless, watching this grotesque act of savagery dressed up as a test of military hardware. He heard Limner say, "General, please at least evacuate—"

"No-one is in danger," Rimmer interrupted. "The target is isolated."

"You're not hitting the target!" de Wilde shouted. "You're hitting—" The battery fired and blew his words away. The shell struck at least three hundred yards from the target bunker and destroyed a hen-house. De Wilde saw through the binoculars people running away from the cottages, away from the explosions, inland. They seemed to move with appalling slowness, drifting across the enormous spaces.

He barged through the officers, grabbed Rimmer's arm and dragged down the binoculars. "You must stop this, now, at once!" he cried. "You're killing civilians, you're murdering—"

Again the battery thundered. Rimmer gave the Bailiff a stony look. "Let go," he said. De Wilde was rigid with anger. Rimmer half-turned and kicked him on the calf, hard. Pain sucked all the strength from the leg and it collapsed. The officers moved aside to leave room for de Wilde on the grass.

The fourth shell nearly hit the target bunker. Thereafter the shots were aimed alternately at the bunker and at the cottages. After ten minutes the bunker was battered but unbroken. Schumacher was delighted. Six cottages lay in ruins and two were on fire. Most of the cows were dead.

De Wilde was resting against the halftrack, rubbing his leg, when Rimmer walked past. "Can I give you a lift into town, Bailiff?" he asked politely.

"That was a brutal and treacherous thing to do," de Wilde said. He forced himself to stand. "A contemptible and barbaric act."

"I don't think so," Rimmer said. He was quite at ease. "My guns fired at my bunkers. Any damage to your civilian property must have been caused by sabotage, under cover of our barrage. There's a lot of it about, you know."

De Wilde wiped tears of pain from his face.

"It's part of what you might call the misfortunes of war," Rimmer said. "Think about it." He turned away but then remembered something. "By the way, my dog has disappeared. You know the one? Dum-Dum, the boxer. You'll keep an eye open for him, won't you?"

25

Earl Kramer hid in the woods for half an hour. Everything was wet with dew, and there were nettles which stung if he moved. He was hungry, too, but he couldn't be sure that the Germans hadn't left someone to wait inside the cottage.

A spider's web stretched between the broken branches of a fallen tree. Each strand glistened and sparkled like a jeweller's dream. Kramer lay on his side and admired it. He tossed a twig at the web. The spider scrambled out to investigate, but the twig was too heavy and it dragged down the web and broke it. "Gee, I'm sorry," he said. "I didn't mean to do that." Nevertheless it gave him an idea.

He got onto his knees and flung a big piece of wood, so that it fell in front of the cottage and made a loud thump.

He held his breath. Nothing happened. He threw a stone onto the roof. Still nothing. He threw another stone but it slipped in his fingers and broke an upstairs window. He crouched and ducked, but the cottage was silent.

Kramer stood up with his hands raised. They wouldn't shoot a man who was surrendering. A black cat came around the corner and stood looking at him. It yawned. Kramer lowered his hands and went inside. The cat turned back.

The cottage was empty. Upstairs, where Greg hid his radio, the floorboard was up and the hole was empty. Kramer slumped with relief: he'd half-expected to find Greg spread-eagled on the floor with a Nazi bayonet stuck through his throat. But obviously they just came for his radio, that was all; just his goddam beat-up crappy old radio. Everything was okay after all.

He folded the floorboard down and stamped it flat, thinking as he did so that Greg had probably left the hiding-place open as an explanation of what had happened. He wondered what they would do to Greg. Fine him, probably. Maybe knock him about a bit first, ask him a load of dumb questions. . . . Kramer stopped at the top of the stairs, one foot reaching, one hand touching the banister, while he worried about that. They'd surely question Greg; no doubt about it. And how good would Greg be at answering questions? Not too smart, that was for sure. Greg was a nice guy, but any six-year-old bedwetter could smash him at tic-tac-toe. Suppose they asked him what he knew about an American airman? He'd give himself away in ten words. Give them both away.

Kramer ran downstairs. For all he knew, Greg had talked already and the car was on its way back, only faster. This place was far too risky; he had to get right away from it. He sneaked out to the lane and saw nothing coming, but while he was looking his stomach groaned and hunger overwhelmed his anxiety. There was no point in escaping and starving. He ran back inside and ransacked Greg's secret larder. Underneath the fibrous, lopsided hunk of bread he found a small flat key. An ignition key. Greg's truck.

Kramer whooped with triumph, tossed the key in the air and caught it. Now he had wheels! All he had to do was find them. He cleaned out Greg's cache of explosives while he was at it, dumped everything inside a dirty pillow-case, and hurried out. Still no sight or sound of the enemy.

Fifty yards up the lane, he came across a falling-down barn, half-hidden by trees. Inside it was Greg's truck. There was a bicycle in the back, and a pair of patched, cut-down gumboots which fitted him where they touched but were better than bare feet.

He got behind the wheel and started the engine. It coughed, and fired sluggishly. He stamped the accelerator to the floor two or three times and jerked the choke in and out as if he were raking a boiler. The engine backfired savagely, and settled down to a raucous shout. The barn filled up with smoky black exhaust.

He trod on the clutch and stirred the long, black-knobbed gear lever until he found a hole somewhere down there in the clattering, vibrating guts of the truck. The windshield was cracked, starred and yellowed with age. He released the handbrake and discovered that his door was open, so he banged it good and hard and it was still open, but the engine was backfiring like the Lone Ranger, so he decided to leave.

Driving out of the barn wasn't easy, what with the unfamiliar pedal-pressures and having to hold the door shut. The lane seemed narrower, too. He cut the wheel hard across and fed her a burst of power. The truck turned out to be longer than he thought and its tail slammed the side of the barn. Kramer heard the smash and instinctively trod on the accelerator. The truck ripped out a main beam and spun clear as the barn slowly collapsed behind it.

Kramer caught a glimpse of falling timbers and billowing dust. The engine-racket drowned all but a bass rumble. He was going too fast because he was in the wrong gear, steering wildly to miss potholes, smacking into low branches which raked loudly against the cab.

The road junction came up in a hurry and the brakes felt woolly, so he made a quick decision and didn't stop, just swung right and hoped nothing was going that way. He was lucky.

He drove for fifty yards in the right-hand lane before he remembered that he wasn't in America and hurriedly switched to the left. The road ahead was clear. He began experimenting with the gears.

A klaxon blared, and Kramer looked up to see an army truck

coming at him, head-on. He floored the clutch and brake, grabbed for the hand-brake in the wrong place, panicked, ran into the hedge, and stalled. The oncoming truck swerved across the road and roared past in a blast of anger that made Kramer flinch. "Crazy bastard!" he shouted. Exhaust smoke swirled around the cab. Ahead, a motor-cycle-combination came around the bend, also on the wrong side of the road. Kramer watched it drift sideways and speed past him. "Looking for an accident?" he bawled. The driver swung back to the right-hand lane. "Now wait a minute," he said aloud. Which side of the goddam road did they drive on in this goddam island?

It had to be the right, after all. England drove on the left, but Germany drove on the right, right? Goddam krauts. He restarted the engine and ripped and trampled his way out of the hedge.

A quarter of a mile down the road he passed the burned-out wreck of a halftrack. It looked terrific, just like the pictures in *Life* magazine, with one of the front wheels broken right off and a jagged hole in the side. Two German officers were examining it. Kramer was so pleased that he forgot to be scared. "Strike one, you bums!" he shouted as he went by. His words were lost in the din.

The countryside was green and pleasant, like an English travelogue. He wondered where he was going and how much fuel the truck had —the gauge kept bouncing from Full to Empty like a metronome. Well, hell, he could always ride the bike. That reminded him of something. Somebody wanted a bike. Someone came looking for a bike. Poor bastard wanted his bike, couldn't find it, had to walk. That church-guy, the gentle giant. Renouf. Kramer slowed down and got his mind working really hard on remembering the report in the news-paper. . . . Yeah, St. Peter's Church, that was it. St. Peter's. There was a St. Peter's Episcopal back in Plattsville, Ohio, got struck by light-ning. The Baptists and the Catholics all reckoned it was a Warning, until Father Mulcahy found termites all through St. Theresa's crypt and the Reverend Clatworthy ran off with a janitor's daughter and the Baptists' bank account.

St. Peter's Church had to be nearby. Kramer drove around in wide circles and found it after ten minutes. Woodsmoke curled from the vicarage chimneys. He parked in a lane and pushed the bicycle to the front door. Renouf opened it before he could reach for the knocker, and once again Kramer felt a heartening sense of inevitable, onward-driving rightness, that this whole thing was meant to be.

"My dear boy!" Renouf cried. Both arms went out in gesture of surprise and welcome. "How very kind. How *very* kind. You have, at a stroke, trebled—nay, quadrupled—my mobility. Do come in. Are you alone?" He took the bicycle and wheeled it inside.

"Yeah, I'm alone," Kramer said. "Jack Greg just got arrested."

Renouf was testing the bicycle bell and squeezing the brake-grips. "What has he done?" he asked.

"Well, they took his radio."

"Radio. . . ." Renouf sighed theatrically. "How often have I told the Germans that you do not convince people by silencing them. Not that it makes any difference."

"No? They did arrest him," Kramer pointed out.

"That matters not. I myself was arrested only yesterday. Twice, in fact." Renouf came outside to look at the church clock. "I'm just on my way to listen to the BBC news," he said. "Would you care to join me?"

They strolled through the churchyard, Renouf pointing out mossy, tilted tombs which might be of interest to the American visitor: here lay a Charles de Carteret, related to the man who governed New Jersey in the sixteen-hundreds . . . there lay a Fanny Le Breton, sister of the famous actress Lillie Langtry. . . . The day was beginning to be hot. Kramer looked up as they passed under the hefty, red-brown branches of a yew tree, its bark gently sweating beads of resin, and saw patches of forget-me-not-blue sky looking a million miles away.

The church was old and dark and smelled faintly of roses. Streaks of stained-glass light soaked through the air like wine-stains. Renouf led the way to the loft and assembled his radio, which developed a low, soft buzz as it warmed up. They heard the tail-end of a talk on how to make the most of dried eggs. "We could do with several tons of those," Renouf rumbled. Then came the time signal and the news. *Last night RAF squadrons carried out attacks on a wide variety of targets in Germany, Belgium, and France. Widespread damage was done to the marshalling yards at Rouen, the aircraft factories at Augsburg, and . . .*

Augsburg.

Kramer closed his eyes and remembered Augsburg. The raid on Augsburg in March. When a bunch of Me 110's just stooged about, outside gun-range, and kept lobbing in rockets. Most of them missed but one hit was all it took. *Treat Me Nicely,* flying behind *High Society,* stopped a rocket and blew up so badly she took out the B-24 next to her too. Just simply knocked it out of the sky. One rocket, two

kills, and nothing anyone could do except weave and pray. The entire
attacking force lost 64 planes out of 738 that day. Afterwards everyone felt pretty pissed-off with deep-penetration raids. If that rate kept
up you didn't have to be Albert Einstein to figure out how your
personal war was going to be entirely all over in ten missions. Or less.

After Augsburg he had stopped worrying about whether or not
Mom and Dad were worrying about him. He decided that they'd
never given much for his chances of surviving anyway. You couldn't
blame them for that. In a twenty-five-mission tour, all it took was a
four-per-cent loss-rate and you had a whole new squadron by the time
anybody's tour was over, which in theory it never would be, on
account nobody would live that long, although some crews did. And
four per cent was chickenshit compared with Augsburg.

All the same, what Kramer remembered best from that mission was
looking down and seeing a really beautiful bomb-strike. For a few
seconds it just completely fascinated him, it was all so pretty and
perfect. A long stick of bombs kept marching across the target area,
one hit blossoming in front of the last, all in perfect march-time, like
someone down there was going along turning on fountain-heads, big
and clean against the flat grey city. Kramer was counting the strikes
out loud. They built to a perfect natural climax: six white hits heading
to a scarlet seventh, which sprang out like a magician's bouquet. Pow,
pow, pow, pow, pow, pow, crump! Unforgettable.

The news ended. Renouf switched the set off and put it away.
"Excellent!" he said. "Most encouraging. The German Air Force
seems to have quite given up. Tell me—"

The massive timbers of the loft trembled slightly, and the thunder
of a distant explosion beat ponderously against the church like a
single, huge drumbeat.

"My goodness," Renouf said. "That's their coastal artillery."

"Sounds like big business," Kramer observed. They listened in
silence, and this time they heard the eruption of the gun and the
louder impact of its shell. "Hey, that's got to be bad news for someone," he said.

"I shall go and see," Renouf decided. "You will be quite safe here
for a while."

"Horsefeathers! I'm coming, too."

Renouf looked doubtful. "It is not a very strong bicycle," he said.

"I've got Greg's truck."

"But how enterprising!" Renouf exclaimed.

"Just Yankee know-how," Kramer told him. "That's what's gonna win this war. Good old Yankee know-how."

26

Ted Langley had set out at 6 a.m. to collect the tomatoes and mushrooms for Paymaster Major Schwarz. He drove his tired and jolting van up and down the island, from the breezy heights of the Parish of St. Ouen, thrusting into the Atlantic, to the patchwork fields of Trinity and St. Martin, from where he could just see France blurring the eastern horizon. He picked up loads of three or four boxes at each farm and paid for them on the spot, peeling grubby Occupation marks from a wad that stretched his hip-pocket. Everywhere he went he asked if they knew where he could get a cow, any cow, age and condition immaterial; and everywhere he got the same dusty answer. It wasn't that they didn't trust him. The risk was too great. Every beast on the island was counted, and last time the Germans caught someone trying to beat the system they fined him five hundred pounds.

The heavy tang of overheated oil filled the van as it laboured up the hill to the Betteridges' farm. Langley had left them to the last, in the hope that he might get enough elsewhere and not have to face Mary Betteridge's morose and lacerating defeatism; but he was still two dozen boxes of tomatoes short when he pulled into the courtyard and saw Louis Betteridge sitting on the edge of the stone horse-trough.

Langley unhooked the bit of wire which held his door shut, and swung his stubby legs out. Betteridge didn't move, didn't look. Housemartins stunted in and out of the courtyard, flipping from wingtip to wingtip faster than thought, chirping with casual exuberance. Langley loosened his shirt from his broad, sweaty back and eased his thumbs under his leather belt to stop his trousers binding. Still Betteridge didn't move. Langley walked over, flexing his left leg to get rid of some pins-and-needles. A small fly was resting on Betteridge's face, just below the left ear. He had not shaved and there was a lot of dried blood on his hands.

"Well, Louis," Langley said. "It's hot again. I've come for the tomatoes."

Betteridge moved his head slightly and looked at Langley's feet. "I don't know what we're going to do," he said softly. "God knows what

we'll do now." He began picking scabby flakes of blackened blood
from his fingers.

"I heard they caused you a lot of needless harm," Langley remarked. "You must've had a nasty shock, eh?"

"It's the end," Betteridge whispered.

"No, no. The Bailiff is going to make them pay compensation.
Don't worry, everything will be put straight soon. Have you got the
tomatoes?"

"It's the end for Mary. She won't go on. They've done for Mary,
Ted. She's not very strong, you know. She looks strong, but that's just
her manner. Inside she's weak as water. They've finished her, Ted, she
won't go on. Why did they do it? We had no quarrel with them, they
always paid cash on the nail, not like some, and now . . . It's like her
own brother came up and hit her. She's finished, she—"

"Louis, Louis. Don't take it to heart." Langley put a hand under
his arm but the farmer refused to stand. "She's not been hurt, has she?
Well, then, she'll get over it. Where is she? Where are the tomatoes?"

For the first time, Betteridge looked directly at him. He had the
eyes of a refugee; hiding fear, hiding hope. "Behind the barn," he said.
"Where we keep the hens."

Langley made his way around the barn, treading between knee-high
docken and waist-high nettles. He found a smooth hollow tucked into
the side of the hill, big enough for a couple of henhouses. In front of
one henhouse sat Mary Betteridge with a small domestic axe in her
hand, the kind used for splitting firewood. Fresh, glistening blood
spattered her dress, which was of white lace, and coated her hands
with a red mess. There was a pile of slaughtered chickens beside her,
some of them still twitching and kicking. She had her legs spread so
that she could brace her feet against the earth, and her left hand was
struggling to get a good grip around the body of a terrified chicken.

"For the love of God, Mary!" called Langley. She worked her
fingers around the animal's ribs and thrust it down between her knees.
The axe swung, half-severed its neck and slammed through the white
lace and into the ground. Blood sprayed and squirted in tiny, frothy
fountains; the claws scrabbled, the wings flailed. Slowly and frown-
ingly she levered the axe out of the ground, took aim again and swung.
The axe-handle slipped in her bloody hand and she battered the
chicken's head. "Oh Christ," Langley groaned. He stood and watched
her wipe her hand on her breast and carefully hack off the mutilated
head. She tossed the carcass onto the pile and slipped the head down

inside her dress. The skirt between her knees was slashed until it scarcely held together. She half-turned and reached inside the henhouse.

"Mary!" Langley cried. "Mary, what the devil d'you think you're doing?" He moved closer but not too close; ready to dodge that axe.

She looked up and smiled, still rummaging around for another chicken. "Finishing off," she said. "They didn't manage to break everything so I'm doing their job for them. I never believe in leaving something half-finished. If we're to be ruined, why, it must be done properly. Smash everything, spoil everything, kill everything."

"You're not well, Mary. Why don't—"

"*Everything.* It's all got to go, all of it. Nothing's worth keeping, that's why they came and broke it all up." She dragged out a chicken and smiled again: dry-eyed, bright-eyed, full of confidence. "Not all. They missed some of it, so that's got to be my job. Can't leave it half-finished. Wouldn't do." She transferred the chicken from right hand to left. "The devil finds work for idle hands."

Langley tried to think of words which would move her, make her lay down her feathery axe and go indoors and sit quietly in a room; but she was beyond his reach. "I came for—" he began, and gave up. It was obscene to worry about tomatoes when this woman was in such appalling distress, and yet a part of his mind was at work on that purely technical problem. The pig, too; it was almost certainly lost. . . . "I'll try and send someone to help you," he said.

She shook her head. "I can manage. It's got to be my job."

Langley watched helplessly as she beheaded the squirming chicken and deposited the parts. He felt a great need to leave, and an equally great duty to stay. The decision was made for him by the sudden boom of an explosion, followed by a deeper, louder blast.

"What the hell is that?" he asked. Mary Betteridge smiled brightly and licked her fingers. Again the explosions roared. Langley turned and ran for his van.

Schumacher's driver slowed to a crawl and wound up his window to keep out the swirling smoke and the wind-blown embers. He edged the staff car onto the grass to get around a shell-crater and jolted across a tangle of splintered fencing. Daniel de Wilde looked down into the crater and saw that the raw earth was still gently steaming. *The heat of the explosion,* he thought absently, *or perhaps some delayed chemical reaction.* The car lurched back onto the roadway.

"Please let me out here," he said. Schumacher tapped the driver on
the shoulder with his cane. "Thank you for the lift," de Wilde said
automatically as he got out. Schumacher nodded eagerly; he wanted
to get on and inspect his bunkers.

The Bailiff looked around. He had never before stood in the centre
of such concentrated havoc. The burning cottages flung great rippling
banners of smoke against the twinkling sea and the soaring, seamless
sky; black velvet on blue silk. Each blaze created its angry crackling
and growling, like animals tearing at their food, loud in the quiet of
the morning. Several other cottages were in ruins, either sliced in half
as if a giant foot had kicked them, or collapsed into rubble as if giant
hands had shaken them. Blast from the shelling had flattened sheds
and scattered haystacks. The carcasses of cows and poultry lay about
in untidy, awkward attitudes. Craters savaged the smooth green turf
without pattern or purpose.

It was all so spectacular, so vigorous, so costly; de Wilde wanted
to believe that this was a lavish film-set, not an act of remote and
calculated savagery. But when he approached the nearest cottage a
black and shaggy farm-dog, half-mad with terror and hoarse with
barking, drove him away and de Wilde saw the body which the dog
was guarding. It looked like an old man, face down in a lettuce-patch,
and he looked dead.

The Bailiff tried to think of a way to distract the dog, and failed.
In fact, there seemed to be nothing at all he could do except curse the
Germans, and he knew that would do no good. Nevertheless, he stood
in the middle of that pitiless devastation and cursed them at the top
of his voice. "Fucking Hun bastards!" he roared.

"That's right, Dan, you tell 'em," shouted Ted Langley. He
stumped down the road, kicking bits of debris out of his way. "Only
not so bloody loud, or you might end up in jail. We just passed a law,
remember. What happened here?"

"Reprisals." The Bailiff did not look Langley in the face: he had not
uttered such language in a public place for at least thirty years, since
he gave up playing rugby. "Plain, straightforward reprisals, Ted. This
fellow Rimmer still has it in his blasted head that there's sabotage
going on."

"They haven't found their sentry yet?"

"Sentry? What sentry? Oh, *him.*" The jerk of his head and the
hunch of his shoulders revealed how reluctant de Wilde was to think
about the lost sentry. "No. . . . One of their vehicles got blown up last

night and killed the driver. And it wasn't a bomb, either; or so Rimmer says."

Langley looked around and grunted his disgust. "Hasn't he ever heard of accidents? Bugger me, I've seen Jerry drivers who couldn't pick their nose without stripping their gears! How does he know—"

"He doesn't need proof, Ted."

"Doesn't he? By Christ, he'll get plenty if he goes on like this. He'll get more sodding sabotage than he can count. . . . Who's hurt here? Anyone?"

De Wilde pointed out the body of the old man.

"Looks like old Tom Nicholle," Langley said, standing on his toes to get a better view, "only I thought he passed on years ago." Together they succeeded in luring the dog away, and while de Wilde distracted the animal by waving a broken spade, Langley hastily rolled the body over. "Yes, it's old Tom," he called. "Stone dead, too." They retreated and left the dog snarling and sniffing around the corpse.

Figures were appearing in the distance: Islanders who had fled their cottages, friends who had come to offer help. A taller figure strode forward, vigorously waving the others on. "Oh, hell," de Wilde muttered. "Him again."

Canon Renouf stopped twenty yards from them and raised his arms like a prophet. "This is not the end!" he declaimed. "This is not even the Beginning of the End! But this is the End of the Beginning!"

The Bailiff glanced nervously towards the bunkers where a couple of German officers were staring. "Ted," he said, "try and get some search-parties organized, while I keep him quiet." Langley hurried off.

"Winston Spencer Churchill," Renouf boomed. De Wilde approached him warily. "You got here fast, Canon," he observed.

"Had I the wings of an angle, my dear Bailiff, I would have been here much faster. . . . Well, not precisely *here,* but certainly close enough to see the ungodly take the beating they so richly deserve."

"What the devil are you talking about?" de Wilde asked wearily. "And keep your great voice down."

"I am talking about Deliverance, Bailiff." Renouf smiled at him patiently. "Relief. Salvation. *Liberation,* for heaven's sake! The new day dawns, the benighted Hun shuns its joyous light. He cowers and he licks his beastly wounds. See!" Again he waved at the shell-scarred bunkers and the curious officers.

"I don't know what you're talking about," de Wilde snapped, "And

I certainly don't find anything here to rejoice in. It's a disaster, a tragedy."

"Poof. We must take our lumps like men now that we are in the front line of war. You can't expect the navy to be perfect. Sacrifices like this—"

"Navy? Who said anything about the navy? What navy?"

"The Royal Navy," Renouf explained. "Surely you remember? My dear chap, it hasn't been *that* long."

De Wilde stared. "The Navy had nothing to do with this. The Germans fired these shells themselves, from over there. As a reprisal."

"Ah." Renouf shaded his eyes with his hand and looked where de Wilde was pointing. "From over there, you say? An odd sort of reprisal. They seem to have made rather a nasty mess of their own defences, haven't they?"

"They were just testing the damn things. It was all a charade, for God's sake."

"Is that what they told you?" Renouf chuckled amiably and patted the Bailiff on the shoulder. "You don't think perhaps they might be feeling a little bit touchy about having let the Royal Navy come in and soften them up?"

"Oh, for God's sake," de Wilde muttered.

"Not quite yet the End of the Beginning," Renouf announced reverberatingly, "but very obviously the Beginning of the End. Don't you agree?"

"I don't give a damn one way or the other, but I do wish you'd keep that thundering foghorn of a voice down."

"You worry too much, Bailiff. It comes of spending so much time with the enemy. They worry, and so they should. Is that Tom Nicholle I see lying over there? What a shame. I expect his heart gave out. Ninety-three, you know. Splendid fellow. He kept trying to tell me he was an atheist, but I could see his heart wasn't in it."

Ted Langley came back. "No need for search-parties," he said, "everyone's accounted for except old Tom."

"In that case I'll just stroll down and have a word with the Germans," Renouf said. "I expect they're feeling a bit low."

"You stay where you are," de Wilde growled. "I'm sick of winkling you out of jail. You're more trouble than a drunken sailor."

"The Bailiff is feeling a little tired," Renouf explained to Langley. "The strain of office, you see. I think he needs a chance to rest, and catch up on events."

"I've caught up with events, dammit," snarled de Wilde. "Now I'm trying to control a few of them. I'm trying to stop this kind of madness from happening."

"The Bailiff's been telling me that the Germans did all this," Renouf told Langley, and winked so ponderously that even Langley was embarrassed. "Frightfully bad planning. They must be losing their grip."

"It's perfectly obvious to me," Langley said.

"Of course it is, my dear chap! It's a signal from the Lords of the Admiralty: 'Plenty more where this lot came from.' "

De Wilde saw Colonel Schumacher approaching them. "Haven't you got a sermon to preach or something?" he asked angrily.

"Not for hours," Renouf said.

"Hey, Canon, you're just the chap I need," Langley put in swiftly. "Give us a hand with that cow, will you?"

"Cow?" Renouf tipped his head back and studied the upturned beast as if it were caught in the middle of performing some trick. "Not so much a cow as an ex-cow. Are you quite sure you want an ex-cow?"

"Yes, yes. I want it put on the roof of my van."

"Indeed?" Canon Renouf turned his attention to Langley's van, parked beyond the cottages. He looked from the van to the cow and back again, while Schumacher walked closer. "Why not inside the van?" he asked.

"Full of tomatoes. Come on, let's—"

"Wait. You wish to transport this beast?"

"Yes, yes, now. Come on."

"I have a superior vehicle. I have a *lorry.*" Renouf strode away as Schumacher arrived. The German was shiny with sweat and self-satisfaction.

"No appreciable damage," he announced. De Wilde tightened his lips and said nothing. "What was that clergyman saying about the Royal Navy?" Schumacher inquired. Langley wandered off to his cow.

"He was saying that its ships sail on the sea," de Wilde said curtly.

Schumacher waited, scratching his stomach. "That is all?" he asked. The Bailiff nodded. "It hardly seems relevant," Schumacher observed.

"He is an extremely stupid man," de Wilde said.

Schumacher thought some more. "Do you think it was relevant?" he asked.

"It was relevant to the Royal Navy," de Wilde said.

Schumacher glanced at his bunkers, then searched the empty sea. "We are not worried about the Royal Navy," he said.

"Neither are we," de Wilde agreed. Schumacher looked at him suspiciously and walked away.

Greg's truck came bouncing and crashing across the hillside, with Renouf on the runningboard. It swung around in a dramatic skid and backed up to the dead cow. The Bailiff watched Langley, Renouf, and three or four local men heave the carcass into the back. A small corner of his mind wondered why Jack Greg should take the trouble to drive Renouf all the way out here, but the question was crowded out by other, bigger problems: Rimmer, the *Schleswig-Holstein,* the infectious risk of violence. . . .

"Bailiff!" Schumacher was back, pointing accusingly at the lorry. "What are those men doing with that cow?"

"Taking it to be butchered," de Wilde snapped. "For meat. To be eaten. As part of the ration. Or haven't you finished shelling it yet?"

Schumacher suspected something, but he could not define it. "They are acting very quickly," he said.

De Wilde clasped his hands behind his head and gazed unblinkingly at Schumacher. "If you require the carcass to be unloaded and left to decay," he declared, "please inform me where, and for how long. In writing."

Schumacher worried over it for a moment and decided it was none of his business. "All cattle must be accounted for, dead or alive," he said, and walked away before the Bailiff could answer.

Langley came over. "There's nothing more you can do here, Dan. I'll give you a lift into town."

"All right." De Wilde took a last look at the burning cottages, "If this is war, it makes about as much sense as an earthquake. . . . What are you going to do with that cow?"

"Hide it in the mortuary."

De Wilde gave up. "You know best," he said.

Earl Kramer drove the lorry to St. Helier, following Langley's van. "So what the heck happened back there?" he asked. "I haven't seen flames like that since *Gone with the Wind.*"

"If you listen to the Bailiff," Renouf said, chuckling, "the Germans did it. Presumably in a fit of masochism."

"Well, sure they did it. Who else would do a dumb, lousy thing like that?"

"Why . . . uh . . ." Renouf reconsidered the matter while Kramer drove and glowered at passing swastikas. "I am, of course, no expert in matters military. You feel convinced . . . ?"

"Yeah, yeah. Target practice. They get a kick out of it."

"How appalling."

"I see your boss-eyed Bailiff was having a good long chat with some big-shot Nazi," Kramer said. "What was all that about?"

"I have no idea. But I'm sure he means well."

"Yeah. So did the captain of the *Titanic.*"

Langley dropped de Wilde near his office, and drove on to the mortuary. As the truck was being backed up to its rear doors, he noticed that Kramer was behind the wheel. "Hullo!" he said. "Where's Jack?"

"Persecuted for his love of truth," Renouf boomed. "Incarcerated by the frightful Hun. . . ." He rumbled on, but Langley wasn't listening; he was thinking of Mary Betteridge, and of her distrust and sick fury and final, uncontrolled disintegration, dragging her world down with her.

27

It was midmorning when Major Helldorf drove along the North Coastal Road with Captain Paulus and an Organisation Todt supervisor called Hippel.

"I hear you swooped again this morning, Max," Helldorf said.

"When information is received one acts upon it," Paulus said.

"Oh, indubitably," Helldorf said. "Unquestionably. Captain Paulus is a great swooper," he told Hippel. Paulus looked out of the window. He was impervious to mockery.

After a while, Hippel, to appear interested, asked, "As a matter of interest, how much do you pay for such information?"

"Fifty or a hundred marks. It depends on the value," Paulus said. "In this case it was free. An anonymous letter."

"Free. . . . I shall never understand this place. They betray their own neighbours, and not even for money. At least Judas took the silver."

"Family feuds," Paulus said. "There is a lot of inbreeding here."

"Also a lot of boredom and frustration," Helldorf added. "Keep people on a poor diet and enforce a curfew, and they brood. All the same, you were lucky to get that letter, Max. The people at the Post Office destroy most of them."

"It was delivered by hand," Paulus said.

"Astonishing," Hippel said. "I sometimes wonder whether the British are really of the same Aryan stock as us after all."

Helldorf hooted with laughter. "Aryan bullshit! Has the Fuehrer got blond hair and blue eyes? Is the blubbery Reich Marshal Goering our ideal physical specimen? Are we breeding Hitler Youth to look like weedy Goebbels?"

Hippel had a moon-face with a small, tight mouth. Now he pursed his lips until they almost disappeared.

"Nevertheless," Paulus said, "the German people would never betray each other in this way."

"Of course they wouldn't. They'd do it in block letters and triplicate, with a copy to the victim." Helldorf changed down for an S-bend. "But they'd do it all the same, believe you me."

"What makes you so sure, Major?"

"People are people are people, that's what."

"But they're not all alike. You won't dispute that the French are racially inferior to us? We conquered France in fifty-six days."

"So we did," Helldorf said. "And then we turned around and we didn't conquer Russia in six weeks. All those sub-human Slavs, it was going to be a walkover. Remember?"

"This is most interesting," Hippel remarked. "I had no idea you felt so strongly, Major."

"You see, Max?" Helldorf thumped Paulus on the knee. "Hippel is getting ready to betray me! *Now* do you believe?"

Hippel chuckled, disliked the sound, and turned it into a cough. "Policemen always suspect everybody," he said. "It's a professional disease."

"If I've got to have a disease, my friend, that's the one I want." Helldorf pulled onto the grass verge. "At least it keeps me alive, which is more than you can say for some."

They walked across a field to where a working party was shovelling soil into a hole. One man gave the job a final slap with his shovel, and the sergeant planted a small white flag. The breeze made it stream perkily, the vanguard of a squadron of similar flags marking forty or fifty freshly turned patches of earth. Two chained alsatians stood up and stared at the visitors. The sergeant came forward and saluted. The dogs sat down.

"Any luck, Sergeant?" Helldorf asked.

"So far we've bust three shovels, sir, and one bloke's gone and herniated himself. But we haven't found Keller."

Paulus waved at the flags. "I suppose these indicate dead-ends."

"Yes, sir. In a manner of speaking."

"What the Sergeant means, Max, is that they indicate graves of non-Aryan origin. You are looking at some corner of a foreign field which will be forever Smolensk."

Paulus looked blank.

"Forget it," Helldorf said. "Sergeant, this is Organisation Todt Supervisor Hippel. He carried out this melancholy project."

Hippel frowned. "That's not quite—"

"No, no, of course it isn't. I mean the workers did the actual carrying-out, not Supervisor Hippel; but Supervisor Hippel kept them company and generally—uh—supervised."

"Beg pardon, sir," the sergeant said to Hippel, "but can you remember how many it was you buried?"

"Records were not kept," Hippel said. "It was not my responsibility. There was no need."

"Sort of a rough idea, though?" the sergeant asked.

Hippel shrugged. "We were extremely busy, the defence work was behind schedule and there were serious problems. Of a technical nature."

"Oh, come on, Hippel, make a guess," Helldorf said. "Was it more than two but less than a thousand?"

"Yes," Hippel said.

"Aha! Now then: more than four but less than nine hundred?"

"This is ridiculous," Hippel said. He walked away and made a show of surveying the area. "As far as I can remember," he said, "the total did not exceed two hundred and seventy-five."

Four members of the working party slowly sat down.

"And roughly where?" Helldorf asked.

Hippel gestured with both arms. "Wherever," he said.

"Ah. Of course. Silly question."

"Two hundred and seventy-five, eh?" the sergeant said thoughtfully.

"I don't suppose . . ." Paulus began. "There's no way the dogs can be trained to discriminate between . . . ?"

"No, sir," the sergeant said. "To dogs a body is a body."

"It wasn't my fault," Hippel said. "Don't blame me for all this. We needed all the manpower we could lay our hands on, for God's sake. We were behind schedule from the very start. The very last thing we wanted was to have our labour force keeling over with TB and dysentery and pneumonia and typhoid fever and God knows what else." His face was flushed at the injustice of it all.

"Typhoid fever," the sergeant said.

"I thought I caught a whiff of something funny," Helldorf said.

"Hadn't we better get some gas masks, sir?" the sergeant asked. "And plenty of disinfectant?"

On the way back to the car, Helldorf said, "I take it most of these workers were part of that tattered column which got marched all the way here from Russia."

"Probably," Hippel said.

"I remember watching them come ashore. They took an hour to walk from the docks to the Royal Square. What is that, Max? Half a mile?"

"I couldn't say," Paulus said.

"It's curious, that's all," Helldorf said, "the way the Reich goes to enormous lengths to make the worst of its conquests. One can't help suspecting a vast inefficiency at work somewhere."

"There have been no complaints," Hippel said.

De Wilde lodged his formal complaints with Count Limner, did some hard telephoning, and got the Controlling Council together in his office. He briefly described Rimmer's breakfast-time artillery shoot, and asked for suggestions.

"Well, he's got to be stopped, that's obvious," said Richard Labuschagne. "We can't let this sort of nonsense go on."

"The worrying thing is that he sounds a bit mad," Dr. Beatty said.

Ted Langley sat and chewed his thumb.

"Listen," de Wilde said. "Don't tell me he's got to be stopped, don't tell me he's mad. Tell me what the devil we're going to do." His leg throbbed savagely.

"All right, Dan, all right," Beatty said. "Give us a few seconds to get all our ducks in a row. You know by now there aren't any quick answers to these things."

"I know that if we don't do something fast, Rimmer's likely to blow up three schools and the cottage hospital because he doesn't like the way the tide comes in."

"He's clearly violating the Hague Convention," Labuschagne said, "The Protecting Power—"

"No good," de Wilde snapped. "Too slow. Takes a week to get through. Besides, Rimmer's not going to listen to the Swiss or the Red Cross, is he? Come on, let's *think.*"

A squad of soldiers marched past, singing. The Bailiff limped over and shut the windows.

"We've never yet tried to threaten the Germans," Beatty said. "But if they're not going to respect our rights, maybe that's the only way to make them behave."

"For instance," de Wilde said.

"Withdraw all labour. General strike."

"Hopeless!" de Wilde exclaimed. "Worse than useless."

"It would show 'em we mean business."

"It would prove to Rimmer that everything he suspects is true," de Wilde declared. "The man's got sabotage on the brain. If we start messing him about now he'll know we're all troublemakers. Then look out."

Labuschagne sighed. "There's talk of trouble already, you know. Some of those people who got so-called searched yesterday are saying they're going to get their own back."

"Suicide," de Wilde said. There was a short and gloomy pause. "What's on your mind, Ted?" he asked.

Langley was still chewing his thumb, denting the stained and leathery pad. He raised his eyes, and his eyebrows.

"You're thinking that perhaps Rimmer's right, aren't you?" de Wilde said.

"Well, hell . . ." Langley stood up and exercised his heavy shoulders. "It's a big coincidence that all this started when that American turned up here. Kramer. I mean, look what's happened since."

"One German sentry missing," Beatty said. "Not even proved dead, just missing, that's all."

"Yes, but look where he went missing: around the corner from where that rubber dinghy came ashore. And then not twelve hours later an ammunition truck blows up near Betteridge's farm and makes a bloody awful mess of three men."

"Accident," Beatty said.

"Kramer spent the night at the Betteridges'," Langley said.

Labuschagne groaned.

"I had the impression that Greg was looking after the chap," de Wilde said.

"He was, after Betteridge had had enough of him. And you know where last night's trouble happened."

"Not an awful long way from Greg's place," de Wilde said.

"And now Jack Greg's gone and been arrested," Langley added. "Paulus picked him up this morning for having a wireless. That was Kramer driving Greg's lorry, by the way."

"What the devil is he doing that for?" de Wilde asked irritably. "Blast the fellow. He's all over this island like a jumping bean. Why can't he sit quietly and read a good book?"

"Oh, you know what the Americans are like," Beatty said. "It's their Frontier Spirit."

"I hope not. I sincerely hope not." The Bailiff scratched his jaw and felt the stubble. It was hard to get a good shave with a blade that was in its eighty-seventh day. "We've got no room for freelance warriors here. This is a peaceful community."

"We're not peaceful, we're paralysed," said Labuschagne.

De Wilde waved away the distinction. "Nobody asked him to come here and blow things up."

Beatty laughed shortly. "I wonder what he'd say to that. Until a couple of days ago we were only too happy to have him and his pals blowing things up all over the place."

"Other places," the Bailiff said firmly. "Jersey is a special case."

Beatty grunted. "I bet everybody would be a special case, if they could."

"Excellent idea," commented Labuschagne. "No more war. By the way, are we going to do anything about Greg?"

"No," de Wilde said. "He'll get fourteen days, maybe a month at the most. He's a single man, he's all right."

Langley was growing bored and impatient. "Look," he said, "I'm not saying definitely that Kramer's behind it all, I'm just saying it looks funny. Anyway, I don't know what we'd have done without him this morning. That cow was too heavy for my poor old van."

"You've acquired a cow?" Labuschagne asked. "How marvellous!"

"It's dead."

"Oh." Labuschagne's cheerfulness faded. "Will that do the trick, d'you think? I mean to say, Schwarz is no fool."

"It'll be alive by the time he sees it. I've arranged with my brother-in-law to swap it for a real cow. His beast is due to be slaughtered, you see."

"Yes, but . . ." Beatty leaned forward. "According to German records, we'll still be short of one cow. Won't we?"

"I know what to do," Labuschagne suggested. "Let's tell them it got blown to bits by one of their shells. Direct hit. Total loss." The others thought about the idea. "They can't disprove it," he pointed out.

"Might work," Langley said. "Anybody got a pig yet? We can't depend on Mary Betteridge after all."

The Bailiff banged the table with the flat of his hand. "Can we please leave cows and pigs to another time? It seems to me there are two things we must do at once. First, we must get hold of this chap Kramer and make sure he behaves himself, put him in cold storage somehow. Ted, that sounds like your job."

"Right."

"Second, we've got to do something about General Rimmer, cool him down, make him relax, persuade him there's nothing to worry about. If we can sidetrack him somehow, maybe things will get better. But we need to win some *time*." He looked hard at each man in turn, impressing them with his urgency, willing them to offer a solution.

At last Beatty shrugged. "Well, I hope you've got an idea, Dan," he said, "because I'm damn sure I haven't."

"I've got half an idea," de Wilde said. "It's a pretty desperate long shot, but it might work. It won't be easy, because for a start I need a body. A corpse."

His words startled them. This was the Establishment speaking, the Bailiff and acting Lieutenant-Governor of the island, representative of His Majesty King George VI, a man to whom melodrama was as alien as mumbo-jumbo. There was nothing melodramatic about his appearance now. He sat with his shoulders hunched and his hands interlocked, staring at the wandering grain of the tabletop.

"I'd better see what's in stock, then," Beatty said.

The Bailiff stood. "And I'd better come with you," he said.

Earl Kramer drove Canon Renouf back to the vicarage. He parked in the lane and they walked towards the house.

"Such wanton, murderous savagery on a lovely day like this," the minister complained, beating his fists together. "It makes one want to tear the sun down from the sky and smite the devils dead with it."

"That's the only sort of language these guys understand," Kramer said. "They'll tramp all over you if you let 'em."

"Those poor innocent folk," Renouf grieved. "Assaulted without warning! Life snuffed out! Utterly blameless, totally helpless. Blasted from afar, rendered homeless, reduced to a state of beggary at the idle whim of some godless Gauleiter. . . ." He threw up his hands in furious dismay. "When will this suffering end?"

"Damn soon," Kramer said. "Just as soon as the Leathernecks hit the beach."

"One can only hope that you're right." Renouf looked at the church clock. "And, until then, pray for sense and sanity to prevail. . . . But now I must attend to my flock. We shall meet again, I hope."

He hurried away, using both hands to shape his disordered hair into fresh and different disorder. Kramer sat on a tree-stump and watched him go. He admired Renouf's spirit and vigour. The man knew his own mind and he wasn't afraid to speak it. This island could use a lot more like him: men who stood up for what was right and damn the torpedoes. . . .

He was too restless to sit still. The day throbbed with energy: sunlight, birdsong, rustling greenery, and swaying flowers. He got up and turned towards the truck, knew at once that he had no place to go, and made for the vicarage instead. Two of its windows were broken, which reminded him of the shattered, smoking cottages again, and a heady anger fluttered inside him like a caged bird. *Bastards! Where the hell did they think they got off, bombarding innocent civilians?* Reprisals, Renouf had said. *Reprisals for what? For getting their ass kicked? Who started this ass-kicking war anyway?*

The front door was half-open. The hall table carried a few bills, a stack of broken-backed hymnals, and a telephone. Kramer plucked the heavy black instrument, using a firm and positive action. The mechanism purred busily. He rubbed the earpiece against his neck and thought of the people he could call: the Bailiff, the Betteridges. . . . Suddenly the purring had stopped and a woman's voice was asking what he wanted.

"Get me the top German," Kramer ordered, and felt a light-headed thrill of excitement.

"The what?" she asked.

"The guy in charge here, the boss. The whaddaya-callim: Fortress Commandant. Him."

"Hold the line, please." She sounded uncertain, but after a moment Kramer heard: "General Rimmer's office. Major Wolff speaking."

"Good for you. This is Lieutenant Earl Kramer, U.S. Army Air Force, and I've got a message for your General Rimmer."

There was a pause; then Wolff cleared his throat. "This is bad military form, you know," he said. "I don't think General Rimmer would approve."

"I'm damn sure he wouldn't," Kramer said briskly. "As it happens I'm not so crazy about his military form. You tell him to lay off the reprisals, is that clear? Any more attacks on civilians and I'll start blowing this island in half."

"In half?" Wolff said.

"In half. To bits."

"I thought two bits made a quarter," Wolff said.

"Save the gags, smart-ass. Just pass the word to your boss. No more reprisals, or else."

Wolff straightened his left leg and exercised his missing toes. "No, I can't do that," he decided. "This is all too much for me. I'm not nearly strong enough for it. Let us just forget all about it."

"Look, I'm serious," Kramer protested.

"My dear friend, you are more than serious. You are tragic," Wolff said. "That's what I can't stand. Please let us—"

"Thirty minutes from now," Kramer rasped. "You listen for the bang. Then you'll know I'm serious!" He crashed the telephone onto its cradle. "Shit-head krauts!" he muttered.

In the ante-room to the Fortress Commandant's office a clerk glanced curiously at Major Wolff. "What was all that about?" she asked.

Wolff shook his head unhappily. "I tried to telephone Stalin once," he said. "But I was drunk and he was out."

28

Langley came down the steps of the Bailiff's building with Beatty and Labuschagne. "Sod my old boots," he said. "It's not yet eleven o'clock and I feel as if I've done a full day's work."

"Where do you expect to locate this lad Kramer?" Labuschagne asked.

"Oh . . . Renouf's place, I suppose. That's where he was heading anyway. . . . Mind you, he's probably halfway up the Eiffel Tower by now. Bloody Americans."

Beatty said, "You sound a mite weary, Ted."

"We're short of tomatoes for Schwarz, we're short of mushrooms for his mate Bodenschatz, and we still need a pig for Klopper. Christ knows how we'll get everything ready in time." Langley stretched.

"Never fear, something will turn up," Beatty said. "It always does."

"It's cutting it bloody fine this time," Langley grumbled.

They parted. Langley walked over to his van and made sure that the back doors were locked. A black Mercedes slid alongside and stopped. "Mr. Langley?" Captain Paulus said. "We need you. Please get in."

Langley took a step backwards. He suddenly felt isolated and helpless in this empty, sunny square. The rear door swung open and checked at the end of its leather strap. The dark·discs of Paulus's sunglasses gleamed obscurely. Langley looked for his friends and was just in time to see them turn the corner. "If you please," Paulus said.

Langley got into the back. The leather seats were cool and comfortable and smelt of polish. Paulus opened a briefcase. "Are these your shoes?" he asked.

Langley recognized them immediately. "Dunno," he said.

"They have your initials inside: E.G.L. Put them on, please."

They fitted perfectly. "Cinderella rides again," said Lieutenant Zimmerman, watching from the front seat. He reached back and closed the rear door.

"What's this all in aid of?" Langley asked. He felt a tightness grip his chest and stomach.

"Those shoes were found in the area of last night's sabotage," Paulus said. "Nearby was this." He opened a cardboard box and showed Langley a mashed and battered stick of dynamite. "Defective," he said. "Like your little operation."

"I've never seen that before," Langley said. "Anyway, I gave these shoes away, years ago."

"To whom?"

Langley thought desperately, and the desperation showed. "I forget," he said.

Paulus nodded. "Headquarters," he ordered. The car moved off. Langley saw the familiar, reassuring, sun-warmed buildings slip by, faster and faster. He sucked his knuckles and closed his eyes. *God stone the crows*, he thought. *This is just one damn thing after another.*

Half a mile from St. Peter's vicarage, on a stretch of quiet road bordered by rustling chestnut trees, Earl Kramer found his target. It was surrounded by a stout palisade of logs topped with barbed wire, too high to be overlooked. Overhead power cables, as thick as his arm, looped down from a pylon and vanished inside. The whole place was spotted with signs that said ACHTUNG and DANGER and KEEP OUT. Kramer didn't know what was inside and he didn't need to know. One glance told him that anything worth such protection must be worth destroying.

He drove on, turned the truck, and parked it on the grass. Greg had bound the steering wheel with black insulating-tape; Kramer peeled off a yard and bound six sticks of dynamite together. He became so preoccupied with remembering his Boy-Scout knots that he did not notice the platoon of soldiers until they were actually marching past, just a few feet away, and then he started so violently that he banged his kneecap on the wheel. The jolt made the horn give a feeble bleep, and one of the marching men called out something which made the others laugh. Kramer gave a sickly grin and hid the dynamite under his knees until they had gone. When he picked out a detonator he found that his hands were clammy. He wiped them on his shirt and felt his heart thumping.

To make sure of success, he fused all the sticks and wound all the fuses together. He put the charge in his lap and drove the truck to the target. With the engine running, he lit the fuses, lobbed the parcel of dynamite over the fence, and drove away. It was all extremely easy.

"How many did we kill?" General Rimmer asked.

"That is not the point," Count Limner said. "You cannot measure human lives against each other like a grocer weighing slices of sausage. The whole idea is inhuman."

"So is death, so is war. We soldiers, my dear Count, are in the business of being inhuman. So how many did we kill?"

Rimmer was looking out of his office window, while Limner stood in the middle of the room, gripping the texts of the official protests sent by the Bailiff. Somewhere in the distance a German band was playing Wagnerian selections. Mingled with the cry of gulls, the music gave a spurious hint of pier-end jollity. It grated on Limner.

"You have killed one old man," he said. "The rest got to safety in time."

"Never mind. We showed willing."

"The victim was innocent of any offence. It was a completely random killing, totally without justification."

Rimmer took the stick-grenade from his boot and scratched the back of his neck with the handle. "Don't be too hasty, now," he advised. "Ask me again tomorrow, or better yet next week. Then we'll know if it worked."

"It was contrary to the Hague Convention, which forbids reprisals against the civilian population for military actions."

"Yes, I expect so." Rimmer spun the grenade in the air.

"It was also a flagrant breach of our promise in 1940 when we solemnly guaranteed—"

"Yes, yes, I'm sure. And de Wilde is going to protest to the Swiss and to the Red Cross and to the Society for the Preservation of Jersey Cows, is he? Good. That will keep him occupied. Tell him that if he promises to write a stiff letter to *The Times*, I'll write one to the *Koblenzer Zeitung*."

"Koblenz?" said Limner.

"Yes." Rimmer picked up a file from his desk. "Home town of this unhappy soldier who got fried in the line of duty last night. Shall we have a little weep for him, too?"

"There's no evidence that an Islander was responsible," Limner declared.

"You should get that set to music," Rimmer said.

"The fact remains," Limner persisted, "that this whole island is delicately balanced. The Islanders cannot survive without our supplies, and we must have them to run the place. Random attacks will destroy that balance in no time."

"Exactly!" Rimmer exclaimed. "And there were two such random attacks yesterday, both of which blew up German Army vehicles! And inside them were *my* men, under *my* command, defending *my* island! So if you must preach, Count, for God's sake go and preach to the feebleminded sabotaging blunderers out there who think they can chuck explosives around like drunken jugglers and get away with it!" Rimmer ripped the file in half.

Limner allowed ten seconds for the angry echoes to fade and die. "Nevertheless—" he began; when the door opened and Major Wolff came in.

"Captain Paulus wishes to see you, sir," he said.

"Ah!" Rimmer breezed forward. "Come in, come in, come in.

Please don't go, Count." He tapped a chair. "Sit down, this may interest you. What luck, Paulus?"

Paulus strolled to the exact centre of the room. He watched Wolff close the door and move to a position behind Rimmer. He looked at the Count and noticed his stiff and angry face; looked at Rimmer and saw his tense expectation. Quite deliberately, he let his gaze move from one man to the other and back again.

"Paulus has been checking out some evidence which he found at the scene of last night's atrocity," Rimmer said, like an impressario introducing a prodigy. "Well?"

"The man responsible has been arrested," Paulus said quietly, almost carelessly. "He is in my custody."

"An Islander?" Limner asked.

Paulus moistened his lips and slowly swallowed, savouring the best bit kept for last. "A member of the Bailiff's Controlling Council," he said. "Mr. Langley."

"I don't believe it," Limner said.

"He left his shoes there," Rimmer told him briskly. "How's that for feebleminded blundering?"

Limner was shaking his head. "It must be a mistake, that's all. I've known him for years. A more sane, level-headed—"

"No mistake," Paulus said. "The man who last repaired the shoes positively identifies them as Langley's."

"Then—"

"Then I think we should allow you time to go off and reassess your position," Rimmer said firmly. "Wolff, see Count Limner out."

When Wolff returned, the general and the captain were drinking dry vermouth and discussing arrangements for Langley's trial. "Can you get it laid on for this afternoon?" Rimmer asked.

Paulus nodded, using the minimum effort.

"Splendid. Excellent. Now then; what are we to do with him? I think a concentration camp, don't you? That will remind his friends—" Rimmer stopped. A short, heavy thump shook the air, as if ten thousand blocks of cement had been dumped all at once. "What was that?" he asked.

Wolff looked at his watch. "That must be Lieutenant Kramer," he said. "He telephoned half an hour ago."

"Kramer? What unit?"

"American Army Air Force, sir."

Rimmer looked sharply as if Wolff were a child who had innocently spoken a filthy word. *"American* Air Force?"

"So he said, sir. He said that if you carry out any more reprisals he will blow the island in half. This was a sort of a demonstration, I suppose."

Rimmer stared unblinkingly at his adjutant while he got his jangled thoughts in place. "What astounding insolence!" he said. "Not just sabotage, not just threats—*practical jokes!* God save me, I'll show this joker how to raise a laugh!" He aimed his forefinger at Paulus. "I want that prisoner, what-the-hell's-his-name—Langley—I want him tried and convicted in record time."

"Yes, General?" Paulus said.

"Yes. And then shot." Rimmer gave Wolff a shove in the direction of the telephone. "Find out what your idiot comedian has blown up. Hurry!"

Earl Kramer had covered about a quarter of a mile and the truck was up to its top speed of about thirty-five when the roar of the explosion overtook him. It crashed past as suddenly as a hedgehopping squadron. The yellowed windshield rattled in its loose fittings. Kramer relaxed, slowed down, took a deep breath. Scratch one enemy installation, whatever the hell it was. That should help to even the score a bit.

He made left and right turns at random, concerned only to get clear of the area. From the people he passed who were standing in doorways, staring back along the road, he guessed there must be smoke or flame showing. "Don't you concern yourselves, folks," he muttered, "Ain't nobody but the good Lord, trampling out the vintage where the grapes of wrath are stored." He swung around a bend. Up ahead, someone ran out of a driveway and started waving. A girl. Her arm was raised and her face lifted as he barreled past. She looked young and pretty and anxious, but mainly pretty. He tramped on the brakes.

Before he could back up she had reached him, running. She threw a blue canvas bag into the cab and climbed after it. "What happened, d'you know?" she asked.

Kramer saw a red cross on her bag. "I guess something blew up," he said.

"It sounded like Whitehouse Corners. D'you know the way?"

"No." He thought: *Jesus H. Christ, man, you don't want to go back there. Not back there.*

"Keep turning right," she said. That seemed to be that. He shut up and drove.

During every straight stretch he glanced sideways. She looked about seventeen. She was fairhaired, not movie-star-blonde but light brown streaked with straw, pleasantly untidy now because she had been running. Her hair was short enough to reveal a slim and sun-tanned neck. She wore a faded blue work-shirt with the sleeves rolled up, a patchwork skirt, and paint-splashed tennis shoes with holes in the toes. Her face was serious and simple; her skin was smooth: no make-up, no freckles. But what Kramer couldn't get enough of was her eyes. They were hazel, flecked with gold, and he had the strange impression that they gave back as much to the sunlight as they took. He had never seen eyes so intense.

There was no need for directions: a soaring column of black smoke gave Kramer all the guidance he needed.

"My God!" she said as they got near.

"You said it," Kramer remarked modestly.

They were stopped by a German military policeman. She took her bag, gave Kramer a quick smile, and jumped out. The policeman shouted something, then recognized her and waved her on. She ran down the road.

For a moment Kramer just sat and watched. He felt weak and strong at one and the same time. The policeman banged his fist on the hood. Kramer woke up, backed the truck until he could turn it, and carefully drove back the way he'd come. He slowed to a crawl when he recognized the stretch of road where the girl had appeared. Be-tween a pair of cracked pillars he saw a long and crumbling drive which curved away behind a tangle of bushes. Cautiously he drove up it and, at the top, found a large stone house with a long conservatory facing the sun. Tall beech hedges surrounded what had once been a formal garden.

Kramer parked in a turning circle and got out. The atmosphere was quiet and serene, and he stood and stretched. The front door opened and a tubby old man shuffled out in carpet slippers.

"I expect you're looking for Nancy, aren't you?" he said cheerfully.

"Yes sir," Kramer said. "I sure am."

"She'll be back presently. She's gone for my *Times.* You don't mind waiting?"

"Oh no," Kramer said. They stood and enjoyed the sunshine for a while.

"Warwickshire aren't doing very well, are they?" the old man said.
"Is that right?" Kramer said.
"They need a decent fast bowler, if you ask me. Somebody who can make the batsman twitch. I used to bowl a bit, you know. Slow left-arm. D'you play much cricket?"
"Not a lot, no," Kramer said.
"Ah well, you're still young. Practice, that's the secret. Did you hear that thunder?"
"Thunder?" Oh yes; thunder. "Yes. Sure did."
"Treacherous weather." The old man squinted at the cloudless sky. "Treacherous."

29

Daniel de Wilde followed Beatty out of the spring sunshine and into the mortuary. It was made of Jersey granite and it smelt like a cold December in the Stone Age.
"You're in luck," Beatty said. "We got a fairly young, fairly fresh male only yesterday." He flipped back the sheet from a slab and read the label tied to the big toe. "Washed up near Gorey Castle. My guess is he's either a merchant seaman who got torpedoed or a Frenchman who tried to sail to England and sprang a leak."
"Who found him, Henry?" de Wilde asked.
"German beach patrol."
"That's bad. There's a risk someone might see him again and recognize him."
"Oh, I don't know. There's not all that much left to recognize." Beatty tugged the sheet off the head; the face was so badly battered that almost all the features were destroyed; it looked like a papier-mâché mask that had been left out in the rain.
"Oh my Christ," de Wilde said. He found a chair and sat down. "Cover it up, for God's sake."
"Sorry." Beatty replaced the sheet. He came over and took the Bailiff's pulse, then fingered back his eyelid and squinted into the eye. "You look almost as shaky as that poor bugger, Dan," he said.
"I'm all right," de Wilde mumbled. He felt dreadful: heart pounding, skin dank, ears singing.
"Too much strain," Beatty said. He brought a bottle from a filing cabinet. "Too much work and worry. You've got to let go occasion-

ally. Otherwise the elastic snaps and your underpants fall down. Drink this slowly."

De Wilde took the glass and sipped. Beatty made himself a drink too. "Calvados," he said. "Bootleg calvados. Cures everything from broken legs to biliousness."

After a while de Wilde felt better. "What happened to his face?" he asked.

"Probably had an argument with some rocks. I don't think you need worry about anyone recognizing him. It's not the kind of thing most people look at more than once. I can always take off his ears or half an arm, if you want him disguised a bit more. Take off the whole head, if you like."

"No," the Bailiff said. "I just want him to look like an American."

Beatty went back to the body. "I'd better give him a haircut," he said, "and trim his nails." He found some scissors and began snipping. The Bailiff went out to Beatty's car and got the clothes. He took his time over it, and when he returned Beatty had almost finished. They dressed the corpse in an American flying jacket, shirt, and trousers. Beatty slipped an identity tag around its neck and looked at the name. "Francis X. Ryan?" he said. "I don't remember him."

"It was a long time ago. His plane crashed on the sands near the lighthouse. I think he died on the way to hospital."

"Ah yes."

They wrapped the body in a small, black tarpaulin, tied it with string, and carried it to the back entrance. Beatty drove his car around and they slid the load onto the back seat. De Wilde looked at his watch. "Twelve noon," he said. "They'll be waiting at the harbour." His left eyelid kept flickering, like a light with a bad connection.

On the way, Beatty turned a corner sharply and the body almost rolled off the back seat. De Wilde reached over and straightened it. The body produced a clear, unmistakable fart.

Beatty laughed. "No actor," he said, "but what a critic!" De Wilde tried to smile, but didn't succeed.

When Count Limner came home for lunch he found his wife sunbathing, naked, on the balcony.

"God, what a morning!" he said. "First the Fortress Commandant decides to reconquer the island, starting with an artillery bombardment which wipes out a herd of cows and the oldest inhabitant. Then, of course, the Islanders bombard us with protests. Meanwhile Paris is sending its usual blizzard of fatuous signals: 'State stocks of football boots,' would you believe. Marked 'Urgent,' too. And to cap it all, Paulus decides to make the world safe for fascism by arresting the master-saboteur who's been causing all these nasty bangs, and surprise, surprise, that provokes the nastiest bang of all. Also Dum-Dum's missing and my foot hurts. I must say you look rather spiffing." He went inside and took a camera from his desk. "What is there to drink?"

"Only the brandy. And some burgundy." She stretched, and he photographed her stretching. "There's some sherry, too, I expect."

"Not for long. I saw in the London *Times* the other day that the Allies have got Spain to promise not to send us any more wolfram." He kissed her on the nape of the neck, and she arched her back. He photographed her again.

"That's terrible," she said. "No more wolfram. No wonder Paris is getting worried about football boots. Soon the German Army will have to play soccer in its tennis shoes, and then we shall definitely lose the war."

"What are you burbling about? Wolfram is the stuff we get tungsten from, it's absolutely vital."

"Don't worry, dearest. I speak fluent tungsten. My nurse taught me. She grew up in wolfram."

"That must have been very uncomfortable."

"Well, she did scratch rather a lot."

Limner stood on a chair and took another picture. "Wolfram makes tungsten, makes steel very very hard. No wolfram, no tungsten, no, for instance, armour-piercing shells. No aircraft engines. No radio valves."

"No sherry?"

"Well, it certainly looks as if Madrid is now backing the other horse. Our consul in Tangier has had his marching orders. Your left breast is bigger than your right. Not that I'm criticizing," he said, climbing down. "Each is delightful, in its way. The fault lies with this viewfinder, which is a shade too small."

"My goodness, it's hot," Maria said. She stood up slowly, to avoid dizziness. "People shouldn't be allowed to fight on days like this. War ought to be reserved for grimy, grubby weather. It's bad enough to be killed, but to be killed in sunshine is rotten bad taste on somebody's part."

"Yes . . . That reminds me: General Rimmer is coming to lunch.

Now *please* be nice to him, Maria. He can't help being the way he is, and really he's not such a bad fellow, deep down."

Maria Limner walked into the coolness of the room. Her lithe body was tanned an even, all-over *café-au-lait.* She curled her toes around the edge of a creamy rug and plucked at it.

"I can't help being the way I am, either, Michael. And you can't help being the way you are."

"Perhaps not, but I have to be damned careful about the fights I pick with the Fortress Commandant."

"You never pick fights with anyone, Michael. That's why everyone likes you. That's why they all say you're so good at your job."

Count Limner put his head on one side. He felt slightly at a loss. "Um," he said.

"I suppose you did pick one fight, but that was a long time ago. When you had your accident."

He looked at his left foot; then at his wife. "I wasn't *picking a fight,* for heaven's sake," he said. "I picked the wrong horse for the wrong jump, that's all. Sheer stupidity, that's all."

"The horse was stupid, but you were angry, Michael. I didn't know you very well in those days, did I? Otherwise I might have tried to stop you."

"It wasn't such a huge jump," he mumbled.

She laughed. "Michael, it was massive, it was like a prison wall! You were the best horseman in Germany, you knew it couldn't be done, not on that horse. Who were you fighting that day? Me?"

"Not you."

Maria Limner stood in silence. She flinched when a bumblebee dashed into the room and flew a noisy circuit, but the sunshine lured it out again.

"This is the first time we've ever really talked about it," Limner said. "Why is that, d'you think?"

"You were the best horseman in Germany. You were a national hero. And you just . . . smashed it all to bits."

Limner shrugged. "1937 was a strange year," he said. "And I'm not sure I was cut out to be a national hero."

The doorbell rang. Maria went into her bedroom and shut the door.

Count Limner's lunch did not go well.

He took an early opportunity to stress the necessity of treating the Islanders with courtesy and consideration. Rimmer nodded and talked of the necessity to keep front-line troops at constant battle-readiness. An army, Rimmer went on, was like a boxer: unless it regularly got into a fight it lost the taste for aggression, the instinct of attack. To be in training was not enough; one had to spill blood occasionally. Otherwise, he said, one never knew whether or not the bayonet was really sharp. And so on. Maria was no help, either.

"I take your point about keeping the troops alert," Limner replied, "but I must protest when the price of their alertness is a whole herd of cows, as it was this morning."

"Double the beefsteak ration," Rimmer suggested.

"Oh, don't worry; what's left won't be wasted. But what then? We need milk and butter and cheese more than we need meat. We *depend* on these farmers, General, make no mistake about that. Your garrison couldn't survive without them."

"All farmers are liars," Rimmer said easily. "They've been swindling you out of your proper share of milk ever since this occupation began. You watch: overnight their other herds will miraculously increase their yield to make up for the loss."

"Is that why you blew the cows to pieces?" Maria asked. "To make the farmers honest?"

Rimmer smiled, and helped himself to more smoked mackerel and tomato salad.

"Nevertheless," Limner said, "there are certain things which only genuine trust and co-operation can achieve. For instance, we cannot force the children here to speak good German. We can order the schools to hold classes in German, yes, but we can't compel the children to learn with enthusiasm. We can order the Islanders to play football against army teams, yes, but we cannot make them play well. All the same, many children have become fluent in German, and many enjoyable football matches have been played."

"Why?" Rimmer asked.

"Because . . ." Limner won himself time to think by refilling their glasses. "Because it makes sense. People cannot share an island for four years in stiff, cold silence, can they? Besides, friendliness is more efficient. What's the point of being hostile to each other in these circumstances? I remember the time we banned all fishing. It was in reprisal for something or other."

"Two Islanders had sailed away to England," Maria said.

"That's right. And what good did our ban do? It just meant no fish for anybody. Utterly self-defeating."

"But that's no reason for having German-language lessons and football matches," Rimmer said. "Why bother?"

"It's part of a long-term policy," Maria explained. "The aim is to breed a sportsman who can say 'Fuck you!' in two languages."

Rimmer smiled.

"My wife has a bizarre sense of humour," Limner said, looking out of a window.

"What I find curious, and also rather touching," Rimmer said, "is the way you persist in looking at war as if it were peace. The great value of these islands to the Reich is that they prove that Britain can be conquered and occupied just like France and Norway and Greece."

"Yes, and Yugoslavia and Russia," Maria said enthusiastically, "and Tunisia and Russia, and Libya and Russia, and Sicily and Russia. And Russia and Russia and Russia."

"Maria, please," Limner said.

"And Russia," she added.

"Countess, may I ask you something?" Rimmer said. "Was the Reich wrong to invade Russia?"

"I don't recall that the Reich ever made that decision."

"Well, you know what I mean."

"You mean that Adolf Hitler gets the credit for victories and the Reich takes the blame for defeats."

Count Limner sighed, and laid down his knife and fork.

"Let me put it another way," Rimmer said. "Was the invasion of Russia a mistake?"

"When I was a little girl, a circus clown once sold me a raffle ticket for an elephant." Maria took her napkin and wiped a speck of mayonnaise from Rimmer's lapel. "Then, when he'd got my money, he asked me what I was going to do with it if I won it."

"Maria, you're telling fibs again," Limner said.

"Of course I am. It's the only thing soldiers understand. The truth frightens the breeches off them, which is not a sight I can recommend."

"You must forgive my wife's manner of speech," Limner told Rimmer. "She spent far too many years hanging around stables."

"Well, Countess, suppose you tell me the truth," Rimmer suggested, "and we leave history to judge what happens to my breeches."

"Oh, the truth is simple: Adolf Hitler delayed until midsummer of 1941 before he declared war on Russia. June 22: we were in Paris for the races; remember, Michael? The weather was delicious. . . . And

the first snow of the Russian winter fell at the end of the first week
of October, just as von Bock opened his offensive on Moscow. That
is the truth. Are your trousers comfortable, General?"

"Bad luck, that snow," Rimmer said. "Winter came phenomenally
early that year. Damned bad luck."

"Oh, horseshit," Maria said. Count Limner closed his eyes. "Did
Hitler think the snow was going to wait until he was ready for it to
fall? General Guderian himself told me he kept asking for winter
clothing, again and again and again, until they told him to shut up.
His troops never got so much as a woolly muffler. Twenty degrees of
frost, and the German Army is fighting in its summer uniform."

"Guderian was a very good man with tanks," Rimmer said, "but
he talked too much. The Fuehrer was right to dismiss him. One
doesn't win battles by complaining."

"That's all history, anyway," Count Limner said. "What con-
cerns us right now is the efficient administration of this island.
Now take those raids by your so-called search-parties yesterday.
They've done a tremendous amount of harm. Two of the Islanders
who suffered hold vital jobs at the telephone exchange and the
waterworks. Neither of them turned up for work today—not surprisingly—and as a result we've had failures in the telephone system and the water supply."

"Good," said Rimmer. "That will give our troops a little taste of
battle conditions."

"I thought I heard a little belch of battle conditions about an hour
ago," Maria remarked.

"Yes. Some idiot destroyed an electricity sub-station. Fortunately
it only supplied the civilian population, but all the same this is obviously more sabotage, so now I shall have to shoot someone. It's a
pity."

"There is a pregnant deaf-mute grandmother living on the island,"
Maria said. "She has a doctorate from the Sorbonne, she is a concert
pianist, and both her legs are crippled. Why don't you shoot her?"

Rimmer smiled. Limner was standing, his knuckles tapping the
table. "There must be no random executions," he said urgently. "Everything must be done in accordance with law."

"I certainly intend to stamp out random executions," Rimmer
declared. "Ever since I arrived here someone has been randomly
executing healthy young soldiers who might otherwise have been
spared to play enjoyable football with your smiling Islanders. Well,

I am as tolerant and broadminded as the next butcher, but obviously this must stop."

"Shooting the wrong man won't help."

"No, but if we keep shooting the wrong man the Islanders will eventually produce the right one."

"I forgot to tell you," Maria said. "This pregnant deaf-mute grandmother has a kitten with advanced tuberculosis."

"Be quiet, Maria!" Limner snapped.

"You could always shoot the kitten," she said. "You know what the British are like. That would upset them more than shooting the grannie."

"Maria, *be quiet.*" The telephone rang, and Limner answered it. The call was short. "If you will excuse me, I must go," he said. "That was the Bailiff. For some extraordinary reason the Military Court is hearing Langley's case *now.*"

"Yes, I ordered it," Rimmer told him. Limner permitted his eyebrows to reveal a flicker of disapproval. He kissed his wife and went out.

"I don't suppose you engineered that," she said. "To get him out of the way."

"By no means. Which is the bedroom?"

"Don't be presumptuous."

"Presumption has nothing to do with it. I have a conference in forty-five minutes, that's all."

Maria stretched, and put her feet on Count Limner's warm chair. "Admit you were wrong about Russia."

"Certainly not. In 1941 we had no alternative but to attack Russia. England was bound to look for an ally on the Continent, and there was only Russia. Besides, the army was standing around getting bored. You either use an army or you disband it. And we nearly won, remember."

"Rubbish. You didn't even get to Moscow, and you know how much of Russia there is beyond Moscow? *Three thousand miles.* That's all of the elephant from the ears back. What did you intend to do with the beast, even supposing you won the silly raffle?"

Rimmer eased his boots off. "I didn't realize you took such an interest in the Eastern Front, Countess, otherwise I'd have brought my adjutant along. Major Wolff was flown out of Stalingrad a week before it fell. Strapped to a stretcher and weeping continuously, I believe."

"Do you ever cry, Karl?"

"Only at the cinema."

"Yes, you're right; crying does no good. The last time I cried was when I got a letter from my cousin Freddy. Such awful writing I could scarcely read it, and then I found the reason: he'd lost most of the fingers of his right hand through frostbite. He wasn't anywhere as big as Stalingrad, just some ruined Russian village. 'No food, no fuel, no water, not even a name.' That's what he wrote. 'Just cold, cold, cold.'"

Rimmer looked at her and she looked at him, each waiting for the other to concede some emotion. "Yes, it was indeed extremely cold," he said at last.

"He used to be a pianist," she said. "I still have some of his records somewhere."

"Ah." Rimmer stood up. "So that was why you wanted me to shoot the pregnant grandmother." He took her hand and helped her up.

"Was it?" She put her arms around him and rested her head. "I suppose it was. Sometimes I think I'd like you to shoot the whole damn world. Everyone. The whole stupid idiotic pointless pack of them."

"Is that the attraction I have for you?"

"My dear Karl, you attract me in exactly the way the plate-glass window attracts the brick." She sighed. "That sounds like a lyric by some decadent Jewish-dominated American propagandist, such as Cole Porter. The bedroom is to your right."

"Oom pa pa, oom pa pa," Rimmer said. He waltzed her, backwards, through the doorway.

"So I asked the skipper to give me another fielder in the covers," Uncle Dudley said, "and he nearly had a fit, he said, 'Good heavens, Dudders' (that's what they used to call me), 'good heavens,' he said, 'you've already got six men fielding between point and mid-off,' but I told him I knew what I was doing, and the next ball I bowled was a beauty, it came off that damp spot and broke two feet if it broke an inch, and the batsman had to take a swing because it was the last over and they still needed ten runs, remember, and he popped it up in the air, straight to that extra fielder I'd asked for, sweet as kiss-your-hand. Have another scone. Sorry about the tea. I can't seem to find any tea. Nancy must have put it away somewhere."

"Don't mention it," Kramer said. They were sitting in the kitchen, a big, friendly room. "These scones sure hit the spot." He took another: his sixth. "So you won the game, huh?"

"No." Uncle Dudley scratched his ear. "No, he dropped it, silly beggar. Never forget those days, though: golden age of cricket. Mind you, the weather was different then. Sunny, reliable. Not like now. Did you hear that thunder?"

Kramer nodded, his mouth full.

"And last night, too. Boom! Just like the Somme." He chuckled. "That took me back. . . . Hullo, dear, we were just—"

"So I see." Nancy came in. "Have you eaten all the scones?" Her voice was hard and flat as a breadboard. Kramer swallowed guiltily.

"Course not!" Uncle Dudley said. "Plenty left."

She tipped the last two scones into a tin, and slammed down the lid. "Don't you ever *listen?*" she demanded.

Uncle Dudley beamed. "Isn't she pretty?" he said. Kramer, still swallowing, nodded: pretty wasn't the word, wasn't anywhere near the word; she was a knockout! "Did you get my *Times?*" Uncle Dudley asked.

"Yes. You stay here." She took Kramer's arm and he stood up as if on springs. The way her fingers pressed on his biceps made his eyes widen and his lungs inflate.

They walked across the hall and up the staircase. "Those scones had to last us to the end of the week," she said curtly. "What are we going to do now? Eat cake?"

"I'm awfully sorry," Kramer said.

"I suppose you weren't to know. But the damn rabbits keep eating my lettuce and this morning there wasn't a bloody bunny in the traps, either."

My God, thought Kramer. *Maybe she's not as young as she looks.* "That's too bad, ma'am," he said.

"It certainly is. Do you have to talk in that ridiculous accent?" They went into a bedroom.

"Look, I'm sorry about the scones but this is my natural voice," Kramer protested. "I'm from Plattsville, Ohio, I mean this is the way we speak, that's all. I'm an American. I didn't aim to end up here but my B-24 got shot down in the Channel so here I am. I'm sorry about the scones and all, and I'll make good just as soon as I can, I promise. I can't change my voice, though."

She seemed neither softened nor impressed by what he said. He felt disappointed. She merely stood and looked at him, thoughtfully, like a gardener examining an unexpected plant. Then she closed the door. "Does he know about all this?" she asked.

"Your uncle? No."

"Don't tell him. Have you told him anything? What have you told him?"

"Nothing. Not a goddam thing." Kramer shook his head definitely. "All we talked about was cricket, and what the hell do I know about cricket?" He paused, and glanced at her. "To tell the truth, sometimes your uncle acts kind of . . . you know . . . sort of . . . well, like he's three bricks shy of a load."

"Three what?"

Kramer shuffled uncomfortably. "Well, he comes across sort of screwball at times," he said. "It's just his manner, I guess." She frowned. "Oh Christ," he said. "Forget I ever said anything."

"There's nothing wrong with his manner," Nancy said. "He's off his head, that's all."

"Ah," Kramer said.

"He got blown up too often in the First World War. So now I look after Uncle Dudley. He can't leave here, he's not strong enough; he hasn't been farther than the bottom of the garden since the Germans came. In fact he doesn't know anything at all about the Germans being here."

"Yeah, I kind of gathered that."

"He doesn't know about the Germans, or the war, or anything, and he's not going to know, d'you understand? If he realized the island was occupied, he'd blow a fuse. The doctors originally sent him here for peace and quiet. He's very . . . patriotic."

"And you've kept the war from him, all these years? That's some going . . . uh . . . Nancy, isn't it?"

She shrugged impatiently. "Uncle Dudley never goes out, and the Germans leave us alone. This place used to be a TB sanatorium and all Germans are terrified of TB. They treat us like a leper colony."

"What about the war upstairs?"

"He's short-sighted. He can't see the markings on the planes."

"But he must hear all the flak and stuff."

"I tell him it's fireworks."

"Or maybe thunder?"

"There you are, you see: he believes it all. He doesn't remember

things. He's happy just gardening and reading his *Times.*" She opened
a deep linen chest and took out a folded newspaper. "Before the war,
Uncle Dudley used to keep every copy of the *Times*, and when the
Germans came we started giving him the old newspapers to read
again, one a day."

"That's a real smart idea," Kramer said. "That's brilliant."

"Oh, I don't know about brilliant." She unfolded the copy and
refolded it lengthwise. "Uncle Dudley forgets everything. Besides, all
he's really interested in is cricket, and cricket's always the same, isn't
it?"

"I wouldn't know," Kramer said. "We don't play a hell of a lot of
cricket in Ohio."

For the first time she really looked at him. Her eyes still had the
searching intensity which he found so unsettling, but now he also
noticed a slight, shielded wariness about them. Experience or inex-
perience? He couldn't decide.

"I'm sorry," she said. "I haven't given you much of a welcome,
have I?" She sat on the edge of the bed and rubbed her face. "I didn't
get much sleep last night, and then this awful explosion. . . ."

"I guess you're a nurse," Kramer said. She nodded. "I reckon
nurses do a terrific job," he said. "I mean, fighting's one thing but
nursing is a whole lot tougher. It's a different war."

"The pain is what I can't get used to. I don't mind the blood so
much, but people in pain, real pain . . . They make me feel so helpless
and stupid."

Kramer nodded. "Yeah, pain can be pretty lousy," he said softly.
He examined the barbed-wire scratches on his hand. There was a
question which he didn't want to ask, but he knew there was no
dodging it. "That explosion," he said. "Was anybody hurt? I mean,
badly hurt?"

"No." He felt enormously relieved. "Some people got knocked over
by the blast," she said. "Cuts and scratches. A bit shaken-up. That's
all."

They sat in silence while he looked at her and she looked at nothing.
Eventually she gave her head a shake and stood up. "Oh well," she
said briskly, "I can't sit here wasting your time all day."

Kramer was taken aback. "Listen, my time is your time," he said.
"Aren't you going somewhere?"

He made an empty gesture. "Where would I want to go?"

"I don't understand." She was looking at him curiously, and

he realized a couple of his flybuttons had popped.

"Pardon me," he said, turning his back while he fastened them. "I'm kind of on the lam, you might say. I was hoping I could stay here awhile." He turned around and saw that she was not smiling. "I'd appreciate it, Nancy. Just for a few days, till we get liberated."

"What's your name?"

"Earl Kramer. It's Danish, so my old man says. Not the 'Earl' bit. That's English. Like Duke Ellington."

"Duke who?" Nancy asked.

"You know, the bandleader? 'Mood Indigo'? 'Don't Get Around Much Any More'?" He doo-dah-ed a few bars. She looked blank, so he stopped. "What the hell," he said.

"I'll have to find somewhere for you to sleep." She gave him the *Times*. "You'd better give that to Uncle Dudley."

Kramer went down to the kitchen, jaunty with exhileration. "Here you are," he said. "Hot from the press."

"Thank you," Uncle Dudley said. "Have we met? I'm Nancy's Uncle Dudley."

"Earl Kramer." They shook hands.

"Well now." Uncle Dudley took a deep, contented breath. "Let's see how Warwickshire are getting on."

30

Five fathom beneath the keel of the fishing boat *Hyacinth* lay the crest of a granite ridge. It rose forty feet from the seabed and stretched for about two hundred yards, pointing roughly north and south. As the tide came flooding up the English Channel it hit this ridge and was forced upwards and sideways, turning the surface into a restless wandering of currents and sudden, unexpected eddies. When, in addition, an on-shore wind blew across the tidal flow it created a busy chop, which jerked and twitched like a hiccuping drunk.

The *Hyacinth* wandered over this patch of water at an angle which was calculated to make the worst of everything. She was a short, stolid craft, flat-bottomed and open-decked, and the German soldier sitting amidships never knew where the next jolt was coming from. Somehow the *Hyacinth* was contriving to pitch and roll and toss and yaw, all at once. He braced his feet against a thwart and swallowed hard. The sun blazed down approvingly.

"Bad water!" the soldier called to the two fishermen.

They smiled and nodded. "Good fish!" one shouted. *"Gross Fisch! Beaucoup de gross Fisch!"*

The soldier tried to look at the horizon and ignore the jerky lurch and slither. Half a mile to the south, the bright grey cliffs of Jersey stood firm and fair. He loosened his belt and unbuttoned his collar. *Why didn't they send sodding sailors on these sodding guard duties? Oh Christ. . . .*

One fisherman stepped down the boat, sure-footed and cheerful, and lifted a handful of fish guts out of a tin. "Okay, matey?" he asked.

The German grimaced. "I eat *Wurst* at twelve," he said. "Not good, I think."

"Ersatz, was it?"

The German nodded and hugged his stomach. The *Hyacinth* rolled and he nearly fell off his seat.

"Oh well," the fisherman said. "If the *Wurst* comes to the *Wurst*, you know what to do." He began baiting hooks with the fish guts.

The German watched. The guts were slimy and multicoloured. He turned to his left, leaned over the side, and waited to be sick. The other fisherman moved the tiller a fraction and a wave flicked spray in the German's face. He straightened up, blinking, and swearing weakly.

"Try the other side," the hook-baiting fisherman said. "Get the wind behind you." He helped the German to the starboard side and held his shoulders until he began retching.

The two fishermen came together and pulled some old nets away from the rolled, black tarpaulin. They hoisted the tarpaulin over the side, kept hold of one edge, and let it unroll quietly into the sea, releasing a yellow-lifejacketed body which revolved twice and then floated on its back, legs hanging down, arms drifting out, waves washing its obliterated face.

The fisherman went back to the tiller and the *Hyacinth* curved gently away. The breeze found the swollen lifejacket and tugged at it. The German soldier rested on his forearms on the side of the boat, and spat miserably into the English Channel. He would never eat *Wurst* again. Or fish. Or any damn thing.

Count Limner met the Bailiff outside Field Gendarmerie Headquarters.

"They won't let me in," de Wilde said. "They won't even take a message to Major Helldorf, and that's never happened before." Sweat dotted his forehead. One of his shoelaces was coming undone.

"Let me try." Limner walked over to the guards, who stamped to attention and saluted. He talked for a while and got short answers; smiled; came back. "Total security until the court completes its hearing, I'm afraid," he said. "What is he being charged with, do you know?"

"Sabotage. Murder. Destruction of military property, breach of curfew, theft of explosives, just about everything you can think of short of dumb insolence."

"Good heavens. Who told you that?"

"Paulus sent a message. I think he wants publicity." De Wilde took out his handkerchief and wiped his face. "What's all this rush and panic, anyway?"

"General Rimmer's orders. Not surprisingly he is concerned about the explosions."

"Langley had nothing to do with them. It's absurd to accuse an Islander, a shopkeeper.... It's insane! How does Rimmer know it isn't some poor bloody slave-labourer on the run?"

"Be calm, Bailiff. Please."

"Or one of your own men? You've got more than your share of maniacs on this island, haven't you? Look at that chap who went mad and started rolling artillery shells down Trinity Hill! Look at—"

"Please, Bailiff." Limner took his arm. "We must be calm. Now come and sit in my car. I have a flask of coffee, or something that claims to be coffee."

"No, no, I can't do that." De Wilde breathed deeply and slowly exercised his fingers. "Thanks all the same. Too many people believe I'm on your side as it is. I shall wait here."

Twenty minutes later, Paulus and Zimmerman came out, pulling on their gloves and chatting.

"What has happened, Captain?" Limner asked.

"Ah." Paulus squinted at the sunlight and put on his gold-framed sunglasses. "Good afternoon, Count. You mean Mr. Langley? Guilty, inevitably."

"Has he been sentenced?"

"Oh yes." Paulus's face was as blank as a blind man's. "The death penalty. Inevitably."

"Excuse me," de Wilde said. "Have I permission to see him? Now?"

Paulus stared. He used the tip of his little finger to nudge the sunglasses up to the top of his nose, and stared again. Patiently, Limner folded his arms and took the weight off his damaged leg. Paulus looked up the street, and then down the street. A seagull landed on a nearby rooftop and screamed harshly. Paulus looked at the seagull. De Wilde felt his heart thumping and the blood pulsing uncomfortably in his head. He knew that his anger must show in his face, and that was something which he had never allowed, but today he didn't care. Years of being endlessly reasonable and balanced and courteous with jumped-up corseted cockroaches like this arrogant mannerless young bastard, and where had it got them? De Wilde opened his mouth and Paulus shouted.

A sentry came running. Paulus murmured a few words. The sentry went over to de Wilde and searched him thoroughly, being needlessly painstaking with the armpits and the crotch. Several passers-by stopped to watch. The soldier found a small penknife in de Wilde's fob pocket, and gave it to Paulus, who gave it to Count Limner.

"Permission granted," Paulus said pleasantly. De Wilde had a violent image of himself wielding something massive, like a railroad tie, and slamming Paulus in the stomach with it. Curiously, the image made him feel weaker, not stronger.

On the way up, Limner gave him back his penknife.

Langley was in a windowless room with walls which had been washed as high as a man could reach and left dirty above. The air smelled of many different feet. Jack Greg was there too, looking bitterly resigned. Langley looked feverishly alert. His face was tinged with grey about the mouth, and his eyes had a staring, searching intensity. He shook hands with the vigour of despair.

"Don't worry, Ted," de Wilde said. "We'll soon straighten out this nonsense."

"They wouldn't even let me speak to Peggy," Langley said. "She's probably still at the shop, she doesn't know. It's absolutely daft."

"The whole thing's a colossal mistake, Ted. Don't worry about it, don't worry about Peggy; we'll look after her. Now listen: did you ask for permission to appeal?"

"How the hell could I? It was all done in German. I didn't even know they'd sentenced me until I was brought out here."

De Wilde turned to Limner. Limner said, "That, of course, is quite improper. You must appeal on the grounds of mistrial."

"Did you hear about the shoes?" Langley asked.

"Paulus told me," the Bailiff said.

"Well, that's the answer, isn't it? Find out who left those shoes there, and . . . and get your hands on him." Langley's eyes were bright with desperation.

"Yes, I know," de Wilde said. "Don't worry, we'll do that."

There was a tense pause. Limner said. "If I can help—"

"Oh Christ," Langley said. "I've got to go again."

"Die Herrentoilette!" Limner said. The guard opened the door. Langley hurried out.

Greg scowled at the Bailiff.

"Look, don't think I've forgotten about you," de Wilde said, "but your case isn't nearly so serious. Have they heard it yet?"

"I got two months."

"I see. Well, the jail's still full, so—"

"And you're full of talk, aren't you?" Greg said disgustedly. "Blah blah blah blah blah."

"What d'you mean?" De Wilde felt Greg's contempt sour the air.

"I mean if you're going to even *try* to do something you'd better bloody hurry," Greg said, "because they're talking about shooting that poor bugger at tea-time."

"God in heaven," de Wilde said. "Does he know?"

Greg jerked his head in the direction of the lavatories. "What d'you think?" he said.

While Uncle Dudley was finding the sports pages, Kramer sneaked a look at some envelopes tucked behind a teapot on the kitchen mantelpiece. Nancy's other name was Buchanan. Nancy Buchanan. Now he felt he knew her a lot better. Nancy Buchanan. He tried it under his breath. It suited her perfectly, it was a swell name, terrific. Miss Nancy Buchanan.

Uncle Dudley talked about all the county cricket scores in *The Times.* Warwickshire, Leicestershire, Worcestershire, Gloucestershire, Nottinghamshire, Derbyshire, Northamptonshire, and a lot more. He was deeply concerned about them all.

"Worcestershire had better buck their ideas up," he said.

"They sure had," Kramer agreed.

"If they're not awfully careful they'll miss the boat."

"You don't say?"

"I do say." Uncle Dudley took out a small magnifying glass and studied the batting details. He pursed his lips. "Mind you, it's not too late to pull something out of the bag, if they're quick about it."

"Well, that's something."

"Yes." Uncle Dudley nodded seriously. "I must say Gloucestershire seem to be sitting pretty."

"I guess they deserve it." *Where was Nancy?*

"They could still come a cropper, mind you."

"No two ways about it."

After fifteen minutes of this, Uncle Dudley reluctantly put the paper aside and announced that it was time to mow the lawn. Kramer followed him out and found Nancy half-asleep in a hammock strung between two apple trees at the end of the garden. Her right leg hung down so that her toes brushed the grass, and the patchwork skirt was pushed up her smooth, slim flanks. The whole scene was beautiful in a clean, fresh, healthy way; it reminded him of a Norman Rockwell cover for the *Saturday Evening Post,* except that Rockwell wouldn't have shown so much thigh. Unless the girl was in a bathing-suit. Kramer wondered what Nancy would look like in a bathing-suit. He wondered what she'd look like *without* a bathing-suit. The thought made his stomach dip, the way it did when *High Society* hit an air-pocket.

"Hi there," he said.

"Hullo."

Kramer sat on the grass with his back against a tree, and watched her toes ripple the grass. After a while he had to see her face again, so he stood up. "Sure is peaceful here," he said.

Her eyes were almost closed. She blinked a couple of times. He took that to mean agreement.

"It wouldn't hurt to spend a long time in a place like this," he said. No response.

"No sir, wouldn't hurt a bit." He felt awkward, standing there, but he couldn't lean against the hammock. He linked his hands behind him, braced his shoulders, and rocked on his heels. "Reminds me of my uncle's farm, back home," he said. She touched her lips with her tongue and they shone like ripe fruit. "That's in Kentucky. State of Kentucky." She nodded, or maybe she just moved her chin to make it more comfortable.

Uncle Dudley came by, pushing his lawnmower. "Damn greenfly on the roses again," he said, over the chatter of the blades; and turned to attack another strip of lawn.

Kramer watched her trim, slim body move gently as she breathed. Everything about Nancy Buchanan entranced him, from her slightly shaggy hair to her slightly dusty feet. Just looking at her was an endless pleasure; like drinking beer after beer without getting drunk.

"Makes you sort of wonder why one guy should be so lucky," he said. "Maybe I wasn't so lucky to get shot up over Germany in the first place, and then shot down in the ocean in the second place, but I sure was luckier than the rest." That opened her eyes.

"What d'you mean?" she asked.

"The rest of my crew went down with the airplane. I just got wet. They got dead."

Nancy linked her hands behind her head and stared at the last of the apple-blossom. "What a waste it all is," she said. "You know they keep saying you bomb women and children."

Kramer was astounded. "Who say?" he asked.

Uncle Dudley arrived at the end of another strip, and turned. "You should have seen my daffodils this year," he called. "What a show!" He trundled away.

"Who says what?" Kramer demanded.

"The Germans. They say you don't care who or what you bomb, you just . . . 'Terror raids,' that's what they call them."

"But that's garbage!" He gave her a puzzled half-grin. "I mean . . . Gee, Nancy, you don't think we fly five, six, seven hundred miles and then just drop those cookies on anything, do you?"

"I don't know. I don't know anything." The depth of her feeling surprised him. "I'm just a girl. All I can do is roll bandages."

"Hey, come on, you know that's not true. The trouble is you don't get any real newspapers here, you don't realize what's happening! There is one heck of a fight going on, which let's face it they started and we've got to win it *or else*. I mean, they're not going to fall down unless we really hit 'em." Kramer clenched his fists and punched the air. "That's how Joe Louis beat Max Schmeling, right? It's the same with us."

Uncle Dudley clacked towards them. "I must remember to prune that clematis," he called. "Before it smothers the house." He turned and went away.

Nancy said, "Like Lübeck, you mean?"

"Lou Beck? I don't think I—"

"Lübeck used to be a town in Germany." She got out of the hammock and smoothed her skirt. "Very old and very pretty. So I'm told. I never saw it. I've never been to Germany."

"Lübeck?" Kramer shook his head. "News to me."

"It got bombed two years ago. Two hundred planes came over one night and bombed it, and it burned all next day and the next night."

"There you are, see," Kramer said. "Accuracy. Must of hit a munitions factory or something."

"No, there weren't any factories. Just houses."

"Yeah, but if it burned all that time—"

"They couldn't put it out. Lübeck was very old and the houses were all made of wood, and the streets were too narrow, and there's only one way to get into the town because it's surrounded by water on three sides. So once the bombs set fire to it, that was the end."

"Gee," Kramer said thoughtfully. "Gee whiz. I don't remember anything about that. Two years ago . . . I was in the States two years ago."

"The bombs killed more than five hundred people. Just ordinary people, not soldiers or anything."

"Sounds like somebody goofed. Maybe a bum navigator or something. That happens, time to time."

"The Germans didn't think so. They thought it was a deliberate experiment, to try out ways of setting a whole town on fire."

Kramer shook his head. "The brass wouldn't do that. Not unless they knew there was something down there worth destroying."

"It was like Toytown," she said. "Lovely old wooden houses, like doll-houses, and funny little narrow crooked streets. Nobody ever expected it to be bombed."

"Well, *they* bombed London, didn't they? What do they expect?"

"Is that why you bombed Lübeck? Because they bombed London?"

"We didn't bomb Lübeck, for Pete's sake! It was a night mission, it had to be the RAF." Kramer felt the conversation running away from him. He forced a grin. "How come you know so much about this Lübeck, anyway?"

"My aunt at St. Brelade had a German doctor billeted on her. His family lived in Lübeck. Seven of them."

"Holy smoke," Kramer whispered.

Uncle Dudley reached the end of the lawn, moving more slowly and looking tired. "You don't realize what a slope there is," he called,

"until you have to push up it." Kramer nodded. The lawn was absolutely flat.

"I was only fifteen when it happened," Nancy said. "I didn't understand it then and I don't understand it now. Everybody else is so sure
of themselves, but God knows why. I'm not sure of myself." She
started back to the house.

Kramer caught up with her and allowed his bare forearm to brush
against hers. It was the first time he had actually touched her, and his
skin glowed. They walked in silence while he worked out his thoughts.
"Still and all," he said, "there's a lot of important things at stake here.
I mean, it's too bad some people get hurt, I mean I feel as badly about
that as you do, but still we've got to stand up for freedom, right? Let's
face it, you don't want to live under a lousy dictatorship all your life,
do you? I mean, just look around. This is your *home.* Maybe nothing's
perfect, but . . . I mean, like it says in the song, 'This is worth fighting
for.' "

"Oh please!" Nancy turned on him with a mixture of passion and
pleading. "I don't want anyone to *fight* for me. Why does everybody
have to *fight*? I just want to live and be happy: isn't that enough? Isn't
there any other way to do anything, except by *fighting*?"

Kramer was momentarily speechless. Nancy turned sharply and
hurried indoors. *Dames,* he thought. *Show me the man who can figure
a dame and I'll show you a certified genius.* He stared at the roses and
the greenfly, but what he was seeing was Nancy's amazing face. He
was so in love with that face.

31

Richard Labuschagne and Canon Renouf got off their bicycles at the
foot of a gentle slope on the North Coastal Road.

"Wait a minute," the banker said. His leg muscles were flickering,
and tiny sparks kept racing across his eyeballs. He was forty-nine and
he felt like ninety-four. "Turnips," he said weakly. "They fill you up,
but they don't give you much go."

"Do look lively," Renouf said. "I've got to take Sunday school at
three o'clock."

Labuschagne rested for a moment on the handlebars, and began
pushing. "Not far now," he whispered.

"I'm dashed if I can fathom what's going on in the Bailiff's mind these days," Renouf said. "He's never shown any particular interest in this sort of thing before."

"He thinks it might be a sort of broad hint to the Germans to behave a bit more decently," Labuschagne replied. "Show that we care about these poor devils. No man is an island, and so forth."

"But they're all dead."

"Yes. Still, it's a gesture. We've got to keep our end up."

Renouf grunted doubtfully. "I must say I sometimes wonder about de Wilde, whether he's buckling under the strain. Yesterday he kept rabbiting on about dry rot in the organ loft. Is he all right, d'you think?"

"Tired, perhaps. That reminds me: d'you know what's happened to this chap Kramer?" Renouf shrugged. "Well, if you see him, we want him," Labuschagne said. He rested his arms on the handlebars and leaned into the hill. "I don't suppose you know where we could lay our hands on a spare pig, do you?"

"Is this in addition to, or alternative to, Mr. Kramer?"

"We need 'em both."

Renouf grunted sceptically. "Too much strain, that's the Bailiff's trouble. He reminds me of that chap who used to be on the music-halls, the one who juggled with strange things. A cigar box, an orange, and a dagger. Completely incompatible, you see."

"Yes, I see."

"*And* he whistled 'Annie Laurie' while he did it."

"Sounds impossible."

"He used to end up by catching the orange on the point of the dagger. Just to prove it was really sharp, I suppose."

"That's one thing nobody here needs to be reminded of," Labuschagne said. He remounted his bicycle. "What a waste. I don't think I've tasted an orange in three years." His mouth watered so much that he swallowed.

They pedalled along the clifftop road, Labuschagne behind Renouf: the Germans had made it illegal to ride two-abreast; nobody quite knew why. After a while, the minister turned his head. "I may have been doing the man an injustice," he said. "It may have been an apple."

Two hundred yards farther on they reached a checkpoint. Labuschagne produced temporary passes to enter a Prohibited Zone. The

sentry let them through. Up ahead they could see a flickering field of
white flags, over a hundred of them, like toy yachts scattered across
a green lake.

"Those are they?" Renouf asked.

Labuschagne nodded. "Trust the Hun to make it look neat."

The working party was refilling a hole when they got there. "We
might as well let them finish," Labuschagne said. "Then you can
include that one too." He walked across to the barbed-wire fence and
looked out to sea. "Isn't that the *Hyacinth*?" he said. "She must be
heading for home, I suppose."

"I can't see that far without my glasses." Renouf shaded his eyes
and stared. It was all a blue-green blur.

Labuschagne searched the sea between the fishing-boat and the
shore. The breeze was blowing directly into his face, so presumably
the bogus body had to be down there somewhere. "How far *can* you
see without them?" he asked.

"About a hundred yards." Renouf checked his watch. "Come on,
they've nearly finished now."

"Hang on a minute. I thought I just saw something." Labuschagne
pointed at a patch of empty water and furiously scrutinized the sea
around it. *Dammit,* he thought, *how can anyone miss a bright yellow
lifejacket?* "Something out there."

"No good asking me, old chap."

"Well, put your glasses on."

"I didn't bring them."

"Oh Christ . . ."

Renouf raised his eyebrows and expected an apology. Labuschagne
made one last, despairing survey and saw the speck of yellow, away
to his left, as lost as a single buttercup in a meadow. "There it is!" he
shouted. "Look! Over there!"

Renouf politely followed Labuschagne's wavering finger. "I see
nothing," he said.

"Yes, yes. That yellow thing. There's something bright yellow floating on the water. See? *There.*"

Renouf blinked, and shrugged. "Frankly, no."

"Look. . . . It's straight out from that rock. Near those gulls.
Yellow, bright yellow."

"You may be right. I couldn't say." Renouf turned away.

"For God's sake!" Labuschagne grabbed his arm. "It's a damn

great yellow lump of something or other. It's coming this way, it might be dangerous. Surely you see it now?"

"You amaze me," Renouf said. "I don't know what's come over you. If you want this object reported, then go and report it yourself."

Labuschagne heaved a deep breath. The whole point of bringing Renouf was to allow *him* to spot the body. It might look suspicious if a member of the Controlling Council found it. "Do me a favour, Canon," he pleaded. "Just for once, suppress your scruples and say you saw something yellow down there."

"Never," the minister said. "Never in this world or the next."

Labuschagne turned away in despair. The bogus body was rapidly drifting inshore. In a few minutes it would be on the rocks, perhaps hidden by the overhang of the cliffs.

"Was ist los?" called the sergeant in charge of the working party, attracted by Labuschagne's gesturings.

"Nothing, nothing," the banker said. "My clerical friend thought he saw someone in the water, but his eyesight is not reliable."

"How dare you," Renouf snapped.

"My dear chap, you just admitted as much."

"Yes, but—"

"Bitte, bitte!" The sergeant led Renouf to the fence and indicated the sea. "Show me. Show."

"I haven't the slightest idea," Renouf said.

"Come, come," Labuschagne chided him. "Don't be childish. It might be some poor soul in distress."

"Here?" the sergeant suggested. "Here? Here?"

"Oh, for heaven's sake," Renouf muttered. He picked up a stone and hurled it at the English Channel. *"There!"*

"He said it was yellow," Labuschagne said. *"Gelb.* Bright *gelb."*

The sergeant saw it. *"Ja! Ja!"* he said excitedly. He shouted orders to the fatigue party. A man set off at a run for the checkpoint. "Good, good." The sergeant was pleased. "We go, we look," he said.

"That's most reassuring," Labuschagne said. "Now, then. Canon Renouf is here to consecrate the graves which your men have so diligently marked."

They went and stood in the middle of the field of flags. The soldiers removed their caps. "This is all quite absurd," Renouf said huffily. "We haven't the faintest idea how many of these wretches were Anglicans. For all we know they could have been Greek Or-

thodox or Muslim or Plymouth Brethren or anything."
"Don't worry," Labuschagne said. "Nobody's going to get up and
walk out."
Renouf eyed him bleakly, and got on with it.

Colonel Schumacher, walking with his knees carefully apart because the insides of his thighs were raw, led General Rimmer into the
dank and echoing tunnel. The first thirty yards were smoothly con-
creted, but after that it was all broken rock and dripping water. "You
see," Schumacher said.

Rimmer saw an Organisation Todt overseer and six slave-labourers.
The overseer wore a safety helmet, heavy overalls, a waterproof cape,
and rubber boots. The labourers wore rags and home-made clogs.
They were so filthy that it was difficult to guess their ages and impossible to guess their race or nationality. In fact they were three Russians,
a Spanish Republican refugee seized in France, a Polish soldier, and
a French Jew. None was older than thirty and the three Russians were
less than eighteen. Their skin was black with dirt and bruises and
scabby at knees and elbows and knuckles. They did not look up at the
officers. As the overseer saluted, those labourers nearest to him
cringed.

"Carry on," Rimmer said. The labourers had not paused. They
were shovelling rubble into a wheelbarrow. A shovelful was too heavy
for one man, so another man heaved on a piece of rope tied to the
handle. Together they lifted the shovel onto the barrow. A third man
used his hands to push the rubble off.

"Yesterday I had five craftsmen working here," Schumacher said.
"Two carpenters, two concrete-layers, and an electrician. Today they
just didn't turn up."

"So send for them. If you want troops—"

"I sent for them, sir. They weren't to be found."

Rimmer walked over to the tunnel wall and traced the woodgrain
imprint created in the cement by the shuttering. "What's all this for,
anyway?" he asked.

"Ammunition store, sir. It completes the central bunker complex
in the ninth zone of the primary defensive perimeter."

"Not yet, it doesn't. Can we manage without it?"

Schumacher shrugged and immediately regretted it: the rash on his
shoulders was very painful. "That's a difficult question, General. It's
hard to say."

"No, it's not. Either we can or we can't. Yes or no?"

"No, sir."

"That's what I thought. Why not?"

"Well, sir, we've increased the firepower in this zone fourfold, and now the existing ammunition chambers haven't sufficient capacity to service all the batteries simultaneously."

Rimmer wasn't listening. "The work's got to be done, then." He waved at the shuffling labourers. "What about these clowns? Can't they do anything except drool?"

The lights went out.

"Don't worry, sir," Schumacher said. "There's an emergency stand-by generator."

They stood in the darkness, listening to the coughs and sniffles of the labourers. No lights came on. After a while the two officers made their way back to the tunnel entrance, preceded by the Todt overseer, striking matches.

"That's never happened before," Schumacher said. "Of course it may be just a local fault." He went into the overseer's hut and picked up the telephone. The line was dead. He gave the receiver a good shake and rapped it several times on the desk.

"If you are planning to communicate by Morse code," Rimmer said, "perhaps we should open the windows."

Schumacher replaced the receiver. "There's another site which I'd like you to see, sir, about three hundred yards away," he said. "I'll send someone up here to put this right."

They walked to the next site. Soldiers froze and relaxed as they went past gun emplacements, infantry strongpoints, armoured machine-gun turrets, mortar pits.

"Ah!" Schumacher said. The next tunnel had come in sight and its mouth was bright with electric light. Near the entrance, two men were feeding a noisy concrete mixer. One shovelled gravel while the other added water from a hose.

"And what will this be?" Rimmer asked.

"Flamethrower depot, sir. As you appreciate, it must be well protected. Normally there would be a dozen craftsmen working here; today, just these two."

"What makes them different? Bad breath?"

"No, sir. They're Irish. We have quite a few Irishmen here. They don't like the English very much." As they approached the tunnel, a telephone began to ring in the site foreman's shed. Schumacher brightened. "That will be the overseer to say that the power has been restored," he said.

As he opened the shed door the telephone stopped ringing, all the lights went out, and the man with the hose gave a cry of surprise. No water was coming out. He went over to the tap and kicked it.

"Obviously an Irish university graduate," Rimmer said. "Come on, Schumacher, don't just stand there. Bash the telephone."

"This is most extraordinary, sir. I can't understand it."

"Can't you? I can. Is there another site you want me to see?"

There was. When they reached it the lights were going on and off at fifteen-second intervals, and all work was at a standstill. "Well, well," Rimmer said. "Well, well, well, well, well."

"Obviously a freak fault, sir; we'll soon track it down. But you see what I mean about the skilled labour. Frankly, we're in trouble." Schumacher scratched himself anxiously, and jerked his hand away as he felt his rash burn.

Rimmer turned his back on the site. Half a mile away and two hundred feet below, the sea creamed sweetly against a splendid crescent of sand. It was the best beach on the island, and if he were planning an assault this is where his best men would storm ashore. Already, Rimmer had mentally fought the battle for the island, and he knew that here the slaughter would be greatest. The enemy must assault this beach and their destruction was inevitable. Rimmer could visualize it all: hidden machine-guns stitching the attackers to the sand; mortar shells steepling out of nowhere; the survivors—desperate for cover—forced to run forward into the mine-fields; while the artillery barrage marched and countermarched across the arena. Rimmer braced his legs and squared his shoulders until the joints clicked. *The battle was coming and he was certain he could win*: that was the finest feeling any military commander could have. Certain, that is, provided Schumacher got these damn tunnels finished fast.

"Do you think the craftsmen are staying away because of yesterday's search-parties?" he asked.

"Yes, sir," Schumacher said.

"Well, how do we get them back? Double their pay? Double their rations? Or maybe we should just halve everybody else's rations?"

Schumacher chewed at his lower lip and looked gloomy. "I don't know if that will do the trick, sir. Frankly . . . Well . . . Sir, I'm an architect. I don't pretend to know anything about war, except what the Fuehrer has said, of course."

"For God's sake, get on with it, Schumacher," Rimmer said. "Eisenhower will be here at any minute."

"Sir, if you have this fellow Langley shot," Schumacher said, "there isn't a man on the island who will work for us ever again, and that's flat."

Rimmer sucked his teeth. "Surely the Irish will work for us."

"No, they won't, sir," Schumacher said, "because Mrs. Langley is Irish."

Rimmer screwed up his face until his eyes closed. "It was all much simpler in Yugoslavia," he said.

The sergeant planted another white flag and stamped the earth flat around it. "Just one more, lads," he said, "then you can fall out for a smoke and splash your boots or whatever you want."

"Aren't we having a brew-up?" one of the soldiers asked. "Where's the mobile canteen?"

"No petrol," the sergeant said. "They need it all to make sure our brave Luftwaffe comrades never get caught with their cigarette lighters empty."

"Luft bloody waffe," said another man. "Couldn't organize a fuck-up in a brothel." The other soldiers were all too tired to complain.

The sergeant unleashed the police dog. It saw a low-flying wasp and gave chase, bounding and snapping and missing until the wasp suddenly climbed away. "Got a brain as big as a rabbit's turd," the sergeant said, "only not so useful." The dog sniffed at a patch of bare earth and began scratching. "Off we go, then," the sergeant said.

At twelve inches, one of the spades struck something metallic. "Hullo," the sergeant said. "This one's got his armour on." As he spoke, another spade exposed an army boot. "Hullo, *hullo*," he said. Then a rusty bayonet poked out of the soil. "Go easy, lads!" he warned. "Go careful, don't damage him." He turned and ran towards the checkpoint. The dog strained at its leash and yelped. It had never seen the sergeant run before. It wanted to join in the fun.

It was midafternoon when General Rimmer got back to his headquarters. Major Helldorf was waiting for him.

"Organize some tea, would you, Wolff?" Rimmer said. "Major

Helldorf has the flushed appearance of one in need of a mild sedative."

"That's very kind of you, sir," Helldorf said. "I didn't realize you were such an Anglophile."

"Well, I'm a great believer in understanding one's enemy. Did you know that when the British introduced a tea-break at their armament factories, production actually went up, despite the loss of time?"

"No, sir."

"Well, it did. The British have an extraordinary faith in the healing powers of tea. Faced with any kind of disaster—fire, flood, mass unemployment, hoof-and-mouth disease, unwanted pregnancy, Dunkirk, you name it—the British call for tea. They drink it, they rub it on their joints to cure rheumatism, they read their fortunes in the bottoms of the cups, and sometimes they even dry the tea-leaves and smoke them. By then the disaster has receded and a fresh catastrophe is upon them, so they call for more tea. I tell you, it's quite extraordinary."

"Yes, sir I'm sure."

"You don't give a feeble fart for British tea-drinking, do you, Helldorf?"

"No, sir."

"No, I thought not. Well, if you're determined to be determined, let's hear it." Rimmer sat down.

"Sir, in my opinion it would be a grave mistake to have this man Langley executed in . . ." Helldorf checked his watch; it was three-twenty. ". . . in forty minutes."

"Oh, balls!" Rimmer exploded. He got up, stiff with anger, and booted the wastebasket high in the air. It hit the brass knob on the end of the curtain-pole and lodged there. Rimmer shook the curtains but the basket would not fall. "Useless bloody thing!" he shouted. He tried to jump for it, and failed. "Aaah!" he cried, grimacing with pain. He walked awkwardly back to his chair, rubbing his ribs. "Pulled a bloody muscle," he groaned.

Major Wolff came in with an orderly. "Tea, General," he announced.

"Just in time," Helldorf said.

"Fetch me a brandy," Rimmer snapped. "Fetch me two brandies. And bring an anti-aircraft gun to shoot down that stupid basket." He waved away the orderly's tray. "I don't want any damn tea," he said. "Pour it down Helldorf's breeches."

"Cream but no sugar," Helldorf said. He looked at his watch again. "I know, I know," Rimmer said impatiently. "God almighty . . . I've only been here two days and already this place has given me mental dry rot." He stood up again, wincing. "What am I doing, listening to Helldorf's waffle? Is it the sea air? Or am I going ga-ga? This is a firing-squad matter, for Christ's sake. On the one hand we have sabotage, on the other hand we have a saboteur. Simple! In Yugoslavia this would be routine, automatic, do-it-and-forget-it! Shoot the silly bugger and get on with something more important, like has the platoon been examined for pox this week? The battalion commanders looked after this sort of flim-flam; not me. I must be going soft in the head. Here we've got jokers planting bombs the way sacred Jersey cows drop cow-pats, and I'm not supposed to shoot *one man*? Bless my soul, in the Ukraine we'd be shooting whole villages! Dear old Helldorf has a fit of the vapours because I want to flatten one wretched civilian. Why not, for God's sake?"

"Because he's innocent," Helldorf said.

The orderly brought in the brandy.

"The court found him guilty." Rimmer drank one brandy and sniffed the other.

"On the evidence of a pair of shoes," Helldorf said.

"It was enough for Paulus to convince the court. That's enough for me."

"When I was in Russia I used to wear two pairs of shoes," Wolff said, "Sometimes three. But it didn't do much good."

"Paulus keeps his monocle screwed firmly up his ass," Helldorf said.

"He seems to have discovered more than you, at any rate," Rimmer said.

"Paulus," Wolff announced, "leans over backwards to get hold of the wrong end of the stick."

"I don't care," Rimmer said. "I don't care which end of the stick he holds so long as he fetches somebody an almighty thump with the other end. Then maybe the local jokers will quit."

"Shooting Langley won't achieve anything, sir," Helldorf said. "If this is sabotage the man behind it is a tearaway, a death-or-glory merchant; you can tell that from the risks involved. Langley is a middle-aged shopkeeper. His idea of a big risk is going to bed without cleaning his teeth."

"Then he shouldn't be running around at night in his stockinged feet," Rimmer said.

"I wonder," Wolff said. "Did Paulus produce those stockinged feet in evidence?"

"No, he didn't," Helldorf said.

"That's bad," Wolff remarked. "That's ignoring half the entire case. How could Paulus be so sloppy? Come to that, where was Paulus at the time of the crime? How does he know so much about it all? Have you noticed that his eyes are too close together and his palms are always sweaty?" The major's face was tense, his eyes glittered and his hands trembled. "What about—"

"*Wolff!*" Rimmer cut in. "For Christ's sake. Leave it alone. I don't mind a joke," Rimmer went on, "but just remember there are men lying dead on this island, soldiers, comrades of yours and mine. Dead, killed, blown to bits."

"Oh well," Wolff mumbled. He had tears in his eyes. "At least they won't get sent to the Russian Front." He sat hunched, with his fists pressed between his knees.

Rimmer sighed. He handed his second brandy to Helldorf to give to Wolff, who looked at it as if it were a strange flower. Helldorf put the glass on a nearby table. There was a pause. Helldorf looked at his watch. Thirty-two minutes. "Paulus really should have looked at his stockinged feet, sir," he said.

"Go on, astonish me."

"Langley lives two miles from where his shoes were found. It was night and he couldn't use the roads, so it must have been more like three miles over rough country. Yet his feet are unmarked."

"Perhaps he carried a spare pair of shoes."

"Why? And why leave his shoes there in the first place? To betray himself? Strange behaviour for an ace saboteur."

"I don't know. Who can make sense out of these clods anyway? Rub two of them together and you might get a halfwit, but you won't get a spark of intelligence." Rimmer lifted the lid from the teapot, sniffed, grimaced. "All right: what's your theory?"

"I believe someone tried to incriminate Langley as an act of spite. He's not alone, either. I spent all morning checking out these." Helldorf displayed a handful of letters. "Informers. They accuse six different Islanders of causing six different acts of sabotage, and they're all nonsense. Here's one from a tenant farmer, sir; he says his landlord's been seducing young German soldiers and we'll find our missing sentry stuffed down his well. The landlord is bedridden and he has no well. . . . This one's from a spinster who says her brother keeps a secret weapon in his bedroom; you can imagine what her problem is. . . ." Helldorf spread the letters on Rimmer's desk. "If you're going to shoot Langley you might as well shoot these, too."

Rimmer grunted. "Meanwhile, the sabotage goes on, and on, and bloody *on.*"

"I think it's a maniac, sir," Helldorf said. "That's the only explanation that makes any sense. Some roving, raving lunatic."

"Then *find* the bastard!" Rimmer snapped. His telephone rang and he listened to the caller. "All right. Yes, now." He hung up. "Limner's on his way over with the Bailiff. Get Paulus. And Zimmerman, too. You never know, someone might want to take a vote or play ring-a-roses or something."

Wolff looked up as Helldorf hurried out. "They could still send me to the Russian Front, you know," he said seriously. "Only trouble is, nobody knows where to find it any more."

"Oh, shut up," Rimmer said.

"Ask General Zeitzler," Wolff said. "He had it last, at Stalingrad."

"Go to bed, Wolff," Rimmer ordered.

32

Colonel Schumacher's stomach looked as if someone had been prodding it all over with a red pencil.

He stood in Dr. Beatty's surgery, holding his shirt around his chest and looking at Beatty with an expression of deep anxiety relieved by only faint hope. "I'm covered, Doctor," he said. "Everywhere except my hands and face. And it itches so. My God, how it itches!"

"It looks very nasty indeed," Beatty said. "I'm glad I haven't got it. Thank you for showing me. *Very* nasty."

Schumacher delicately tucked his shirt inside his trousers. "Do you know what it is, Doctor?"

Beatty was tidying his desk. He looked up in mild surprise. "Know what it is? Well, at a guess I'd say it was a bad rash, wouldn't you? Bad, itchy rash. All over. That's what it looks like."

"I was hoping . . ." Schumacher ducked his head bashfully, as if he were about to borrow money. "I was hoping that you could suggest a cure, Doctor."

"Me? Oh, you don't want to trust a worn-out old civilian quack like me, Colonel." Beatty came over and patted him on the shoulder. Schumacher flinched. "Sorry. . . . Go and see one of your own doctors. They're a lot better."

Schumacher walked to the window and squinted unhappily into the sunlight. "I should much prefer you to treat me, Doctor. We have good doctors, I know, but this . . . this trouble which I have is . . . I mean it is not . . ." He sighed. "It would embarrass me, that's all. Please understand."

Beatty put his feet on his desk and began flipping through a medical dictionary. "It's not the pox, you know," he said. "It's not leprosy, it's not measles, it's not adolescent acne, psoriasis, eczema, incipient anthrax, or a dose of mild carbuncles. As far as I can see, all you've got is a large number of angry spots. I wonder what the right collective noun would be? A rage of tumours? A horde of pustules? Anyway, that's what you've got. A bloody great rash." He slapped the book shut and smiled.

Schumacher came over to him and tried to look six inches shorter than he was. "If you would agree to treat me, Doctor," he said. His brow was crumpling and uncrumpling. "I should be extremely grateful. You see, it is all caused by an unfortunate allergy." He spoke the word *allergy* as if it were an administrative error.

"Well, of course it's an allergy." Beatty gestured broadly. "But it could be anything, couldn't it? Cats, cream cakes, feather beds, bootpolish, who knows what? You toddle off and get your doctors to—"

"I know the allergy," Schumacher broke in. "It's this uniform. I am allergic to my uniform, Doctor. That is what is so shameful, so embarrassing."

Beatty reached across and fingered the material. "Try some other fabric. Experiment, my dear chap! Linen, cotton, silk. Perhaps a new outfit in gingham—"

Schumacher was shaking his head. "It is not the cloth, Doctor, it is the *uniform*. I cannot wear the uniform because . . ." He turned away in distress.

"Because it disagrees with you," Beatty said flatly. "Well, I think I can sympathize with you there."

Schumacher sat on the most distant chair. "It's so puzzling. So painful. All I want to do is accomplish my work and this . . . this is like sabotage. I feel as if I am betraying myself, betraying everything decent and desirable."

"Maybe that's it," Beatty suggested. "Maybe, deep down, you have a very healthy sense of what is decent and desirable. Perhaps you are secretly worrying about your work."

"We are behind schedule, that's true. Secondary Defence Complex B—"

"I don't mean that. I mean things like the slave-workers. The beatings. The brutality, the starvation. The disease. The appalling death-rate."

Schumacher looked at the backs of his hands. They were still unspotted. "The Organisation Todt is responsible for all that side of things," he said in a low voice. "It has nothing to do with me."

"It has to do with your uniform," Beatty said.

For a while neither man spoke. Beatty sprawled with his feet on his desk and watched Schumacher sit upright, impassive, looking at the empty air.

"Well, you know what the cure is," Beatty said. "That's up to you. All I can do is give you some stuff to help reduce the itching." Schumacher's head turned. "Of course, treatment like this is very irregular," Beatty went on. "I don't suppose your people would approve of it, and I certainly can't enrol you as one of my normal patients, on the regular basis, can I?"

"Whatever fee you consider appropriate I shall be more than happy to pay," Schumacher said.

Beatty reached for his prescription pad. "I want a pig," he said.

Earl Kramer laced up the brown boots, checked his fly again to be absolutely sure, and came out from behind the screen. He was wearing a very old cricket blazer, a tattered Fair Isle pullover, heather-mixture trousers, and odd socks. He said, "I feel like Daddy Warbucks."

Nancy looked him over. "Daddy who?" she said.

"Warbucks. In *Little Orphan Annie*. You know, the rich old guy?" Nancy shrugged. "In the funnies," Kramer said.

"D'you mean like Donald Duck?"

"Well . . . sort of."

"That's all I can remember. It's a pity about your hair, isn't it?" Kramer looked in a mirror. "Kind of red, I guess."

"It makes you stand out, rather. Try this."

Kramer put on a boater. "Leapin' lizards, Sandy," he muttered.
"Not much better. Oh well, nobody's going to look twice at you.
People have to wear any old clothes they can get nowadays. Is there
anything else you need? You can borrow Uncle Dudley's shaving kit."

"Let's see. I could use about a pound of medium-rare T-bone steak
with a stack of blueberry pancakes on the side, and a pint of chocolate
ripple ice-cream to follow."

She smiled, and he smiled too and felt good. "Our meat ration is
two ounces per person, every other week," she said. "Not that it's all
meat, either."

He stopped smiling. "I forgot about that," he said. "What the heck
do you guys live on?" He felt bad about his food-joke.

"Oh . . . bread, vegetables. Let's not talk about it. Talking only
makes it worse. Food doesn't really matter anyway."

Kramer went downstairs and found Uncle Dudley in the conservatory, talking to a young man. The visitor had dark hair and a pleasant
face, and he was making gentle practice swings with an elderly cricket
bat. "Ah, there you are," Uncle Dudley said. "This is Michael."

"Martin, actually," The young man smiled. Kramer liked him at
once; he had cheerful eyes and an unusually broad mouth, which
seemed constantly to be widening in search of humour. He wore
sandals, grey flannel trousers (much patched at the pockets) and a
short-sleeved shirt of faded blue. He was an inch or so shorter than
the American, but broader in the shoulders. Kramer introduced himself and they shook hands. Martin's grip was firm but not aggressively
so.

"I was just showing Michael how Bonzo Bassett used to tickle 'em
away down the leg side," Uncle Dudley said. "Lovely stroke. Anything pitched outside the leg stump went lickety-split to the boundary,
four runs and no mistake! You remember old Bonzo?"

"What a man!" Martin said warmly. He spun the bat in his hands.

"D'you play this game?" Kramer asked.

Martin laughed. "You are looking at the world's worst cricketer,"
he said.

"What nonsense!" Uncle Dudley scoffed.

"It sure is. Nobody's worse'n me," Kramer said morosely: so
morosely that they were amused, and he brightened. "I can't hit
worth a damn. Remember the guy who shot an arrow in the air? I
tried that once and missed."

Martin chuckled. He had good teeth and his lips were clean-cut and firm. "You should practice with Uncle Dudley's patent flea-killer," he said.

"Yeah? What's that?"

"Two bits of wood," said Uncle Dudley immediately. "You place the flea on one and hit it with the other."

They all laughed. Kramer thought about it and saw how crazy it was and had to laugh again. For a moment, he almost forgot his hunger.

"Yes," Uncle Dudley said. "That's the way to do it. Place the silly flea on one bit of wood and give it a jolly good biff with the other! That'll soon sort the little blighter out! Eh?" He laughed so much that he had to sit down.

"I guess you live around here?" Kramer asked.

"Oh yes, I do," Martin said. There was something faintly sing-song about his speech that reminded Kramer of a second-generation Danish family back in Plattsville. Maybe Martin was a refugee. . . . The daughter, what was her name? Ingrid; now she made some of the best deep-dish apple pie in the entire state of Ohio. . . .

"I suppose you saw what happened to Warwickshire," Uncle Dudley said, picking up *The Times.*

Oh Christ, here we go again, Kramer thought. But Martin turned to the old man with every sign of keen interest. "I did indeed," he said, "and if you ask me, Warwickshire had better watch their step." He stretched out on a deckchair and gave Kramer a look of profound significance.

"They're not out of the wood yet, you know," Uncle Dudley said. "I mean to say, Leicestershire will have a thing or two to say about that. What?"

"If Leicestershire buck their ideas up," Martin said, "things could become very interesting. Very, very interesting." He linked his hands behind his head and glanced sideways at Kramer. "Wouldn't you say?"

"Oh, sure," Kramer said. Martin raised his eyebrows at him. "Well, let's face it," Kramer said, "in this game, anything might happen." Uncle Dudley nodded approvingly. Martin smiled, and Kramer felt encouraged. "What d'you think of Worcestershire's chances?" he asked.

"Worcestershire had better buck their ideas up," Martin said.

"Now Gloucestershire, on the other hand," Uncle Dudley said, "seem to be sitting pretty."

"If they don't relax, they can't lose," Martin said.

"Hey!" Kramer cried. "Let's hear it for Gloucestershire!" A Plattsville High School football chant popped into his brain. "Boys got the muscles, Teacher got the brains, Girls got the sexy legs, We won the game!"

Uncle Dudley lowered the newspaper and stared in amazement. "Good gracious," he said. Kramer shrugged modestly.

As soon as the sentry had turned the key, Major Helldorf flung open the cell door so that it crashed against the wall. Langley was sitting on the bed, hugging his stomach. He had been sick into the wash-basin and the air was foul. Helldorf dragged him to his feet and shook him.

"You have thirty seconds to tell me the name of the man to whom you gave your shoes," he said. "If not in fifteen minutes you will be dead."

Langley was dull with terror. His lips moved sluggishly against each other, shifting wet fragments of food which he had not had the strength to wipe away. His eyes were weary with fear, and the lids kept drooping.

"They are going to shoot you, Langley," Helldorf insisted. "Now tell me. Tell me the man's name."

Langley had thought so much in the past hour about being shot that part of him was dead already. What was still alive tried to speak, but the sounds sobbed out in a stammer. Helldorf let him go and went to the door. He came back with the sentry's rifle.

"Have you ever seen someone shot, Langley? It hurts, the bullet rips a horrible hole in the flesh and smashes the bone. When you are shot it will be ten times more painful and more agonizing because ten bullets will tear ten horrible holes in your flesh. Do you understand? Watch!" He loaded the rifle and fired it at a table. The crash made Langley jump. "That is what you will be like in fifteen minutes," Helldorf said. "Now tell me the man's name."

"I don't know," Langley whispered.

Helldorf seized Langley's hand and forced a finger, any finger, into the bullethole, hammering at the knuckles with his fist. Langley screamed with pain. Helldorf whacked him with the rifle-butt. "Tell me his name, tell me!" he shouted.

Langley sucked his bloody, splintered finger and sobbed something incoherent. Helldorf knocked the hand away and grabbed Langley by the face. "What?" he demanded. "What did you say?"

"Kramer, Kramer, Kramer!" Langley cried. "His name's Kramer. I don't want to die. *Please.* I didn't do anything."

"Kramer. Where is he? Where is Kramer?" When Langley shook his head Helldorf punched it. "Yes you do know! Where is Kramer?"

"Anywhere. Don't hit me. He could be anywhere."

"You fool!" Helldorf bellowed at him. "Can't you see I'm trying to save your life? Where did you last see Kramer?"

Langley shut his eyes. If he said Renouf that would be the end of Renouf. If he said nothing that would be the end of him. He had to say something. Anything. "Jack Greg," he said. Greg was in prison, he was safe. "Greg's place. Cottage. Please, I didn't do anything, I don't want to die. . . ."

Helldorf looked at his watch. Twelve minutes. He threw the rifle to the sentry and ran.

It was eight minutes to four when Helldorf rejoined the meeting in Rimmer's headquarters. Paulus and Zimmerman were seated, expressionless, arms folded, ankles crossed. Rimmer was behind his desk, head propped on one fist while he used a long, thin, ivory paperknife to roll a stub of a pencil back and forth across his blotter. Count Limner leaned against a wall, resting his leg. The Bailiff stood in the middle of the room. He was speaking to Rimmer.

". . . simply cannot, with all due respect, accept this. I am sure, General, that you have been made aware by your staff of the remarkable record of—I was going to say 'harmony' but perhaps 'compatibility' is a better word—which has been maintained between the occupiers and the occupied during the past four years. Thanks to a great deal of self-control and sound common-sense on both sides there has been scarcely a case of serious friction, let alone an incident of violence. The value, indeed the absolute necessity for this sane understanding has already been demonstrated and accepted—hundreds, thousands of times. Therefore it is inconceivable that any Islander could be responsible for this outbreak; inconceivable. The so-called evidence against Langley is so flimsy as to be meaningless, and the irresponsible manner in which he was tried—hastily, secretly, with no chance for a proper defence to be offered—makes a mockery of any pretence at justice." De Wilde looked at his watch. "General, there is very little time, but there is still time. If you make wise use of your powers, we on our part shall make every effort to help end this violence, which threatens us as well as you. However, I must tell you now, with all the urgency I can command, that if Langley is executed, there will be such a revulsion of feeling on this island that, inevitably, violence will rapidly beget more violence, and both you and I will be trapped in an endless cycle of brutal retaliation."

De Wilde stopped. There was silence in the room. Rimmer went on rolling the pencil-stub across his blotter. Helldorf looked at his watch: six minutes to four. He took out a notebook, scribbled a few words, tore out the page and folded it.

"I agree with the Bailiff," Count Limner said. He limped forward. "In any case, since Langley was tried, Captain Paulus has found new evidence."

Helldorf walked behind Rimmer and put his note on the blotter. "Well, Paulus?" Rimmer said.

Paulus uncrossed his arms and recrossed them the other way. "New evidence?" he said. "That depends what you mean by 'new,' and what you mean by 'evidence.' "

"You know what I mean. The corpse."

"Well, Paulus?" Rimmer said. He had seen Helldorf's note and was tapping it from side to side with the paperknife.

"A corpse has been found this afternoon, General."

"Where?" Helldorf asked.

Paulus pretended that he had not heard. "It is not in the best condition, sir. I doubt if its own mother would know it now."

"Where was it?" de Wilde demanded. Rimmer was trying to unfold the note with the tip of the paperknife, and failing.

"However, we have established, sir, that the body is not that of Private Keller," Paulus said. "The feet are the wrong size and the hair is the wrong colour."

"Also, sir, the build is different," Zimmerman added.

"The build and the scars, too," Paulus said. "Keller had a hernia operation, and this corpse is unscarred in the relevant area. All in all—"

"So where was it?" Rimmer asked.

"This particular corpse, General, was recovered from the sea at the base of the cliffs, below the North Coastal Road."

"Near where the American rubber dinghy was found?" Limner asked.

Paulus shrugged. "Not precisely. Some little distance away."
"Who is it?" Rimmer asked. His attitude had not changed.
"An American airman. He was wearing an inflated lifejacket. His name is . . ." Paulus searched three pockets and eventually found the identity disc. "Francis X. Ryan."

"This is obviously the man whose dinghy ended up on the rocks," de Wilde said impatiently, "so that means he's been dead for days and he *couldn't* have been on the rampage here, so Langley *couldn't* have sheltered him." It was four minutes to four. "Correct?"

"Quite correct," Rimmer said. "I am in complete agreement."

"Thank God for that," Limner said.

"But I don't see what difference it makes," Rimmer went on. Helldorf could no longer stand to watch the general toying with his note; he looked away. "The unpleasant facts are that there has been sabotage, that much German military equipment has been damaged, that German personnel have been killed. You now tell me that Francis X. Ryan was not responsible, and you expect me to stand up and cheer. When you tell me who *was* responsible, Bailiff, I promise you I shall be duly grateful."

De Wilde met Rimmer's gaze and tried not to blink. Rimmer was right, of course. Yet Ted Langley was going to be taken out and shot to death in only a couple of minutes, and that was absurd, insane, obscene, unbelievable. There must be some alternative, some way to end this silent nightmare, if only his tired and ageing brain could produce it.

Rimmer unfolded the slip of paper on his blotter and read it. It said: *Langley says he gave shoes to man called Kramer.* Helldorf was looking at him. Rimmer smiled sadly, rolled the paper into a ball and flicked it across the room. "There is no person of that name living on this island, Helldorf," he said. "It's a local joke. Wolff investigated it this morning. . . . Now then, Bailiff: am I to have the chance to be duly grateful?"

God help me, de Wilde prayed; and for a moment it seemed as if God had done just that, for an extraordinary, a wonderful, a miraculous solution created itself in his mind: a shining golden key to turn this hulking lock. "Obviously Keller did it," he said.

Everybody moved. Paulus and Zimmerman stiffened; Helldorf and Limner turned; Rimmer sat up. "You surely are not joking, Bailiff," he said. "Not at two minutes to four."

"Of course it's Keller," de Wilde said. "All this trouble began the moment he disappeared. Clearly, the man has deserted and run amok. Keller wouldn't be the first German soldier to go off his head and start blowing things up; ask Major Helldorf. Keller vanishes and trouble starts: that's no coincidence. And look at the advantages he's got!"

As de Wilde advanced on his desk, Rimmer leaned back. "He can beat the curfew, he knows where to get explosives, he knows how to use them. It's your own man, General. It's Keller. It stands out a mile."

The General and the Bailiff stared at each other in silence. Helldorf held his breath and listened to his heart pounding out the seconds.

The door opened and Wolff came in. "It's snowing again," he said.

"Wolff, go to bed," Rimmer ordered.

"Can't find it," Wolff said. "General Zeitzler had it last."

Without taking his eyes off the Bailiff, Rimmer picked up the telephone. Count Limner saw the Bailiff's shoulders rise and fall in a great breath of relief. *What a showman Rimmer is*, he thought. *Full of cruelty and compassion. A great performer.*

"Send in a doctor," Rimmer said. He replaced the telephone.

Limner felt as if he had floated away from his body, as if he were watching this scene from an upper corner of the room. His body was a shell, taking part but not joining in, because the whole affair was unacceptable. If it was unacceptable then there must be an alternative; for instance, *Send in a doctor* was a codeword for *Cancel the execution*. But Limner knew that it was not.

De Wilde looked around for his hat. "God help us all," he whispered.

"Well, you certainly tried," Rimmer said. He stood up and stretched. "I particularly enjoyed your Keller story; that was quite inspired. Mind you, I don't suppose poor Keller would have liked it much."

Paulus said, "We found Keller this afternoon. He had been murdered. Stabbed in the neck."

Somewhere nearby a mellow, leisurely clock struck four, and Rimmer checked his watch. A muted volley of shots punctured the mild afternoon. Helldorf relaxed. Now that it was all over he felt a twinge of admiration for Rimmer's timing: theatrical, but very effective. And very wearing. Now it would be nice to go and sit in the sun with a cool drink for ten minutes.

"Well now, Bailiff," Rimmer said briskly, "now that we know

each other a little better, let's get down to business."

"I have nothing more to say." De Wilde wanted to get out, to be in the fresh air.

"No? Look here: I don't want to go through all this again tomorrow, but I shall if I have to."

Paulus said, "Keller was not killed by Langley. We know that."

"We know several other things," Rimmer said. "You know that I have power and am prepared to use it. I know that there is organized resistance on the island, economic as well as military. Everywhere I went today, the lights failed. That is sabotage."

"No, it's not," de Wilde said, "it's a polite warning from people who refuse to be bullied."

"Call it what you like; I'm not going to tolerate it. Unless you tell me who is responsible I shall have somebody shot tomorrow at noon."

"In that case it had better be me," de Wilde said.

"Oh no. I need you, Bailiff, to draw up a list of all women and children for deportation to Germany. Besides, I already have a candidate. I intend to shoot Mr. Langley."

The doctor came in. "Major Wolff?" he said.

"Can't find him," Wolff said. "General Zeitzler had him last."

The doctor took Wolff away. The Bailiff looked from Rimmer to Limner and back again. He felt sick and elated at one and the same time. "You mean he's not dead, then," he said.

"Not yet."

"I don't understand."

"I'm sorry to hear that. I hoped my demonstration would help you to understand very clearly."

The Bailiff was still struggling to catch up. "You cancelled the execution before I got here. This has all been a sham, nobody got shot at all."

"But it concentrated your mind wonderfully, I hope. Bailiff, let me tell you your problem. We are at war, right? And the currency of war is death. I spend lives to buy success. This is what you can't understand; but you must, or we'll never make any progress. I like to think that I'm a humane and intelligent soldier, so I use the currency carefully. I try to get full value for every life I spend. Not to do so would be an act of contempt for the whole purpose of war, don't you agree? Life is a wonderful, beautiful gift to be enjoyed to the full. You

must admit that you appreciate that gift now more than you did five
minutes ago."

De Wilde nodded. The man was right again.

"Good. So now you understand. Unless I have the information I
need by tomorrow noon, I shall shoot Mr. Langley, and thereafter
every tenth name on your list of deportees, at intervals of one hour."

"I protest," de Wilde said. "This is contrary to the Hague Convention." The words sounded foolish even as he spoke them.

"You are absolutely right," Rimmer said. "Believe me, if I could
I would shoot the Hague Convention, too." The meeting was over.

Helldorf could not find Jack Greg at Field Gendarmerie Headquarters. Paulus was not there, and Zimmerman said he knew nothing.
Helldorf drove to the civil prison in Gloucester Street, then to Greg's
cottage, then back to Field Gendarmerie Headquarters. Someone told
him that Paulus had gone to the airfield on the other side of the island
to organize a redoubling of security. Helldorf telephoned him.
"Paulus, what in hell's name is going on?" he asked.

"The airfield is at full red alert until further notice. That's a direct
order from Seventh Army HQ. What do you want?"

"I want Greg."

"Really? Why?"

You snotty little bastard, Helldorf thought. He said, "This is a very
bad line, Captain. If you forget you ever asked that question, I'll try
to forget I ever heard it. Now where is he?"

Paulus clicked his tongue thoughtfully. "I suppose it can do no
harm. Greg is on board the *Schleswig-Holstein*, Major. She sails at ten.
He is to serve his sentence in Paris, in Cherche Midi."

"That's ridiculous. Who decided that? Cherche Midi is packed
full."

"Then presumably he will be sent elsewhere."

"To Germany? To a camp? For having a radio?"

Paulus clicked his tongue some more. "You're absolutely right,
Major. This line is very bad." It went dead.

The *Schleswig-Holstein* was still being unloaded: a line of slave-
labourers shuffled up one gangplank and down another, stumbling
and straining under sacks of cement. It was such a familiar sight that
Helldorf scarcely noticed it. He found Greg on the foredeck, handcuffed to the rails. A soldier was guarding him.

"You know that Langley has been reprieved," Helldorf said.

Greg turned away and looked down at the quayside. "Yes, I heard the shots," he said.

"That was just a bluff."

Greg spat down into the greasy water.

"Listen," Helldorf said. "It doesn't matter whether you think Langley is alive or dead. He told me that you know the man to whom he gave his shoes. Do you?"

"To whom," Greg repeated mockingly. "To whom."

"Pay attention, for God's sake. We must find that man. He is very dangerous, do you understand? I don't mean dangerous to us Germans, I mean to all your friends and countrymen here on the island. They will suffer severely unless we find this man, this lunatic. This has nothing to do with the war. It's simply a matter of crime, vicious crime. Protecting innocent people. Do you understand?"

Greg said nothing. He was staring at the nearest gangplank. It was steep and ribbed with wooden bars to give a better grip. The slave-labourers were barefoot, the sacks of cement were heavy, and there was no guardrail. Halfway down, one of the men had slipped and stopped to get a better footing, but his feet were cut and bleeding and the gangplank itself was slippery with blood. He was so thin that his clothing flapped like a flag around a pole. The Todt overseer shouted at him, and he set off again, each overloaded foot jarring against a crossbar. When he was three steps from the bottom he slipped again, lost his balance and tumbled head-first. His desperate fingers were so locked into the sack that he could not let go and the weight drove his head against the dusty granite dockside with a soft crunch. The overseer threw up his arms in disgust. He walked over and kicked the man until his body was out of the way.

Greg turned his head and looked at Helldorf. His eyes were wide and unblinking, and his face was stiff with buried hatred. "Don't you talk to me about crime," he said. Helldorf nodded. He knew when he was beaten. He walked away.

33

Uncle Dudley fell asleep after the analysis of the English county cricket championship. The two men moved to the other end of the conservatory, and they were playing cards when Nancy came in. "Martin!" she exclaimed. "I didn't expect—"

"Shush," he said. "We are playing Medical Poker, which I have just invented, and I am on the verge of a bloodstained victory." He dealt Kramer and himself about a dozen cards each. The pack was made up of playing cards, Happy Families, and cigarette cards depicting either warships or film stars.

Nancy stood behind him and put her hands on his shoulders. "You two have met, it seems."

"Sure," Kramer said, sorting his cards.

"Martin's a nurse," she remarked.

"Yeah?" Kramer gave her a quick smile. "I guess you two work together?"

"Sometimes."

"This is not so much a hand as a foot with unusually long toes," Martin said. "Nevertheless, I shall open the bidding with one broken leg."

"You're lucky," Kramer said. "This hand looks like it's got frostbite. Okay, I accept your broken leg and I raise you . . . uh . . . I dunno, a couple of black eyes, I guess."

"Your black eyes, and cirrhosis of the liver."

"Jeez! That's pretty heavy stuff."

"What on earth are you two doing?" Nancy asked.

"We are bidding to the point of total collapse," Martin said. "The first one who fatally weakens his system, loses. So far I have only one broken leg and cirrhosis, so I am in no danger." He reached up and patted her hand reassuringly.

Kramer announced, "Your cirrhosis, and I raise you bronchitis."

"Bronchitis? That's not much compared with cirrhosis. You must have rotten cards if they're only worth bronchitis."

"Hell, when my uncle had bronchitis he was real sick," Kramer protested. "Bronchitis can be a bitch."

Martin considered. "Did he cough up blood?"

Kramer thought about lying, but he liked his uncle too much. "Not as I heard," he said.

"It doesn't sound like bronchitis. More likely the after-effects of influenza, or maybe just a sore throat. Is that all you are going to bid?"

Kramer felt challenged. "Hell, no. Bronchitis and food-poisoning and three busted fingers."

"Very well. I raise you a severe concussion."

"And I raise you a dose of malaria."

"That's it!" Martin claimed. "You're dead. You've got a high fever and respiratory complications so you're bound to catch pneumonia, and the food-poisoning has weakened your resistance." He snapped his fingers.

"Shoot!" Kramer said. He enjoyed losing when he had Nancy looking down on him. "Okay, whatcha got?"

Martin spread his cards. "Seven aces, of which four are spades; two battleships; Clark Gable, Marlene Dietrich, and Miss Bun the Baker's Daughter."

Kramer chuckled. "You don't stand a chance, fella. I got the ace of diamonds three times; then some garbage; a couple of aircraft-carriers; Mr. Snip the Barber; Fred Astaire, Ginger Rogers and—get ready to eat your heart out, pal—I got *John Wayne.*"

Martin picked up the cigarette card. It showed a cowboy with a faint, pitying smile and smoking revolver. "Is he so good?"

"Good? He's terrific! You shoulda seen *Hell in the Desert.* He can shoot lousy krauts faster'n they can breed!" Kramer grinned to show that he didn't take John Wayne as seriously as all that. Nancy looked away.

"You win," Martin said. He scraped the cards together and began sorting them into heaps.

Kramer slowly lost his grin. The game had gone sour and he didn't know why. The conservatory was quiet and nobody was looking at anyone. Martin's face was empty, maybe even sad. Kramer cleared his throat, and Uncle Dudley woke up. "Hell," Kramer said, "who cares about John Wayne anyway? He can't act his way out of a wet paper bag."

Nancy went over to the windows and stood looking at the garden. The afternoon had become overcast and the western sky had a grey restlessness.

"My goodness!" Uncle Dudley said. He was looking at the foreign news page of *The Times.* "Nasty business in Danzig."

"Yeah?" Kramer said. Anything to break this silence. "What happened?"

"Chap called Grübner seems to have got himself shot and now there's the devil to pay. International incident. The 'Kalthof Incident,' so *The Times* says, and they should know."

"Kalthof?" Kramer said. "You said his name was Grübner."

Martin stood up suddenly. "It happened at Kalthof," he said. "Kalthof is a little village on the border between Danzig and East Prussia."

"Ah, you've seen this, have you?" Uncle Dudley said. "Shocking how-d'you-do. It seems that a crowd of German Nazis went after the customs house at Kalthof the other night and smashed it up completely. Naturally, the Poles didn't take a shine to that sort of behaviour, and I don't blame 'em. Dash it all, Danzig's a free city, isn't it? League of Nations, and all that? Can't allow a lot of undisciplined Huns to go around shooting people. I mean, whatever next?"

"Goddam cheek," Kramer agreed.

"I think you'll find, sir," Martin said gently, "that it was the Polish Commissioner's chauffeur who shot Grübner."

Uncle Dudley read farther into the report. "Good Lord, so it was," he said. "Following day, too."

"In self-defence, I believe. He was investigating the affair, wasn't he? And a crowd of Danzigers attacked him, I believe."

"More or less," Uncle Dudley mumbled.

"All the same," Kramer said, "who started it? The goddam krauts, right?"

"I don't wish to argue about it," Martin said, and Kramer was surprised to hear a trace of distress in his voice. "I just would like to point out that there are always two sides to everything."

"Of course there are, my boy," Uncle Dudley said. He turned the page. "Anyway, I don't suppose anything will come of it. People are always having international incidents; I can remember several when I was a lad. . . . Ah! Now this is more like it. Come and take a squint at this."

Kramer and Martin crossed the room and looked. " 'Germany signs Non-Agression Pact with Denmark,' " the old man read out. "Somebody's got a bit of gumption, eh? 'The two countries will in no circumstances resort to war against each other.' Now why can't they *all* do that?"

Kramer looked at the date of the newspaper: June 2nd, 1939. He felt utterly lost, as if he were acting a part and he had forgotten his lines. After a moment his stomach spoke for him: a long, resonant gurgle.

"That reminds me," Martin said. "I brought some food. Just jam and biscuits, I'm afraid."

"Splendid! Tea-time." Uncle Dudley tossed the paper aside.

"You're an angel," Nancy said. She hugged Martin, and he recovered some of his former cheerfulness. Kramer scarcely noticed. He was licking and cleaning his mouth in readiness for biscuits, large crunchy biscuits, smothered with thick, fruity jam. "Let's hear it for Martin!" he said.

After tea they played boule on the freshly mown lawn. Uncle Dudley surprised Kramer with his skill; he lobbed the wooden balls accurately and added an expert back-spin which effectively checked their run. Unfortunately he kept forgetting his score. Nancy and Martin played a relaxed and carefree game; Kramer's aim was off and he broke several marigolds.

Three games were enough for Uncle Dudley, and he toddled off to have a nap. The others sat on the grass and talked about what they would do after the war. Martin planned to become a ski-instructor. "If I can't be a bird, I want to ski," he explained. "Ski-ing is the next best thing to flying."

"The next best thing to flying," said Kramer, "is flying."

"You can ski all you want," Nancy said. "I'm going to find a place where the sea is so warm that I can swim as much as I like. Just . . . slip in and out of the water all day long."

"Florida," Kramer told her. "You'd love Florida. Never been there myself, but—"

"Then in the winter I'd live in London. And go to all the dances."

"Great if you like fog," Kramer said.

Martin smiled. "What will you do when the war ends, Earl?"

"Well, first of all I reckon I'll eat three or four hundred double giant hamburgers with all the trimmings. That's just to get my system back to normal. After that . . . I don't know. I might set up in the demolition business."

"Demolition? As a career?"

"Well, it's sweet and simple. You just plant fifty bucks' worth of gelignite in the right spot and ten minutes later *boom!* Another satisfied customer."

"You make it sound easy."

"Sure, it's a cinch. *And* a service to the community."

Kramer rested on his elbows and enjoyed the big quiet garden, guarded by dense, square-trimmed beech hedges. He kept Nancy in his field of vision so he could always see her without actually looking direct. This was a good place to be; a different world; as if it had always been this way and nobody could ever get in and change it. Damn fine people, too. Nancy was a brilliant nurse and Martin was an ace medic; you could tell by their hands. Kramer had a momentary fantasy in which his stretcher was gently laid down and the blood-stained blanket pulled away and firm, friendly fingers touched and tested his body and he opened his eyes and it was . . .

"I must go," Martin said. They all stood up. "Good-bye, Earl."

"You'll be back, yes?" Kramer said hopefully.

Martin smiled, shook hands, and gave Nancy a quick, Continental-style embrace. They watched him walk away until he was out of sight.

"Nice guy," Kramer said.

"Yes. He's going to France tonight, you know, on the ten o'clock boat." Nancy turned back to the house. "He's got two weeks off and he's going to try and bring back some drugs and medical supplies. We're awfully short of everything."

"What does he do? Just buy the stuff?"

"Yes. There's a Purchasing Commission for the whole island, and they've given him five thousand pounds to spend."

"Holy Moses! . . ." Kramer did some calculating: it was twenty thousand dollars. "You mean they just hand him the money and wave good-bye? That sounds like living dangerously."

"Is it? I suppose it is. All living is dangerous. Last time he went over, he brought us back one thousand pounds' worth. He certainly helped save a few lives."

They walked in silence for a while. Kramer was puzzled and intrigued by Nancy; sometimes she was mature and assured, other times she was the youngest fourteen-year-old on the block. She could be high-spirited or serious. Right now seemed to be a serious time.

"Would you do me a favour?" she asked.

"Name it," he said seriously.

"I have a headache, I want to lie down. Could you peel and cook some potatoes? You'll have to light the fire, I'm afraid."

Nancy went upstairs, looking tired, and Kramer headed for the kitchen. He found potatoes, water, salt, cooking-pot, but he couldn't find where they kept the knives. He thought of scrubbing the potatoes and cooking them in their skins, but they were pretty banged-up potatoes; they really ought to be peeled. He decided to go and ask Nancy, before she fell asleep. Just as he reached the hall she went out of the front door.

Something about her manner made him halt and keep silent. There was stealth in her cat-footed movements; she looked alert and intent. He stood in the shadows and watched through the tall windows as she ran across the lawn and disappeared into the bushes beyond the hammock. So what did she keep down there? What was the big secret? And why did everybody have to keep Earl Kramer in the goddam dark all the time? He went after her.

The bushes had been allowed to overgrow what had once been a formal, ornamental garden. Between and beneath them, old mossy paths strayed and met, divided and disappeared. Kramer tried to keep a rough heading down the middle, but the going was confusing and he came to an unexpected wall. He turned away, lost the path, and finally blundered back onto the lawn. By now four or five minutes had passed; she could have reached the road, or gone back to the house: anything. He wandered into the bushes and broke a blossom off a rhododendron. As he did, Nancy laughed. Kramer turned his head like a radar dish. She was not all that near, but she wasn't all that far, either. He stepped carefully towards the sound. After twenty yards he paused. The first breeze of the evening bustled overhead and made the bushes whisper. He was lost again. Then he heard a light mutter of voices, and he moved. He ducked under the branches of a sprawling laurel and stopped in front of the ruins of a summerhouse. Its roof sagged and its windows gaped, and he knew that Nancy was inside.

Kramer went over to the summerhouse and looked in. He was not ready for what he saw, and for an instant his brain went into shock. It was like an atrocity photograph.

Martin, naked on his back. On a blanket. Eyes shut, smiling. Nancy, naked, on top of him. Arms around his head, cuddling. Moving her body against his, pressing, sliding, rubbing. Her neat, round buttocks bouncing. A happy, crooning sound in the air.

Kramer took a pace back. He felt a little lightheaded and he could taste something metallic in his mouth, except that there was nothing in his mouth but saliva, too much saliva. He looked away from the atrocity and saw their clothes. Hers on the floor, his on a broken wicker chair. The sandals, the slacks, the shirt, and a grey uniform. On the right breast of the tunic was a spread-eagle emblem. Nancy was giving herself to a kraut. Martin was a kraut, a fucking kraut. Kramer backed away, walked away, ran away. It was horrible, filthy, sick, like a kick in the stomach. He ran all the way back to the kitchen and smashed the first thing he saw: a milk jug. With milk in.

34

The Controlling Council met ten minutes after de Wilde left General Rimmer's headquarters. The news that Langley was still alive encouraged them, but only briefly: they had been rescued from a grim today, only to face a gruesome tomorrow. Nobody expected Rimmer to indulge in the luxury of mercy again.

"The really absurd part about it is that he knows Ted's not responsible for all these explosions," de Wilde said. "Damn it all, that electricity station went up *after* he'd been arrested."

"I hear that Helldorf's latest theory suggests there is some kind of lunatic abroad," Labuschagne said.

"He's not far wrong," Beatty growled. "Billy the Kid. . . . And to think we had him right here, yesterday afternoon!"

"I suppose there is no doubt that Kramer was responsible?" Labuschagne said. "I've heard that the Germans sometimes attach a certain amount of explosives to important installations for the purposes of demolition. Possibly some fault occurred and—"

"No, no, no, he did it," the Bailiff said. "We can't go on telling Rimmer all these things are accidents. Not four in a row, that's impossible."

Beatty looked at his watch. "He's about due for his fifth," he said.

"*Please*," Labuschagne said.

"Anyway . . . Your Francis X. Ryan wasn't exactly a sweeping success, was he?" Beatty said to de Wilde. "A lot of work for nothing, that turned out to be."

"All I can say is it seemed like a good idea at the time," de Wilde replied. "Rimmer was so obsessed with that damned rubber dinghy."

"Well," Labuschagne observed, "he now accepts that it really was Ryan's dinghy, but unfortunately that is no longer the problem. In fact, by eliminating the dinghy and its owner from consideration it would seem that we have merely placed the Islanders under even greater suspicion."

Beatty sucked gloomily on an empty pipe. "Maybe we ought to get the *Hyacinth* out and float another empty dinghy ashore," he said.

"I'm afraid I'm not much good at this sort of thing," de Wilde sighed. "Cloak and dagger . . . I should stick to what I know."

"All right, cheer up, Ted Langley's not dead yet," Beatty told him. "Question is, what do we do now?"

"I'll tell you what we do," de Wilde said. "Three things. First, this monkeying about with the power supply and so on has got to stop. Second, Schumacher's workers have got to get back on the job. And third, we've got to catch this man Kramer. If we can do all that by tomorrow morning there's still a chance."

"We have one clue: Greg's lorry," Labuschagne said. "Kramer took the vehicle; in all probability he still has it. I propose we organize an intensive search."

"Agreed," Beatty grunted.

"The glass is dropping," de Wilde said. "Let's hope he's got the sense to stay in out of the rain." He stood up. "One or more of you ought to get down to the *Schleswig-Holstein,* you know."

Labuschagne clasped his brow. "I knew things were going too smoothly," he said.

By late afternoon all the cement was off the *Schleswig-Holstein* and the slave-labourers had been marched away to their verminous barracks and their pint of thin cabbage soup each.

Meanwhile Labuschagne had been busy. He arranged for Langley's brother-in-law's cow to be brought to the docks, and also for Langley's van to be driven there and unloaded.

Schwarz and Beatty met him on the quay. The major was cheerful, the two civilians were worried: they were still short of mushrooms and tomatoes. Schwarz was unconcerned. "Make it up next week," he said breezily. "I never expected to get it all anyway. Like a drink? The Captain has a case of sherry for me, I hope." He went loping up the gangplank.

The captain had a great deal more than sherry (which was excellent) for Schwarz. While Beatty and Labuschagne drank, the other two discussed a long list of items which, it seemed, Schwarz had ordered and which his partner, Colonel Bodenschatz, had or had not supplied. Eyeglasses, shaving brushes, creosote, lipstick. . . ."Electric fires?" Schwarz said. "I don't remember anything about electric fires. He's sent me two dozen. In June, for God's sake." He hunched his shoulders at the challenge.

"Maybe they're meant to be used for cooking on," the captain suggested.

"Excuse me," Labuschagne broke in.

"Help yourself, help yourself," Schwarz said.

"No, we should really be getting along. If we could complete the transactions . . ." He unbuttoned his waistcoat and shirt and pulled out a foolscap-size envelope. "Your Occupation marks," he said.

The captain went to his safe and produced several wads of Deutschmarks and a small leather bag. Labuschagne untied the drawstring and tipped the diamond onto his palm. It was tiny and irregular and it burned with the fury of a bit of broken glass. "Are you sure this is worth all that much money?" he asked.

"Full refund if not completely satisfied," Schwarz told him. "It may not look like much, but then neither do I. More sherry?"

As they were walking back to the dock gates, Labuschagne gave Beatty a discreet nudge. "So far, so good," he murmured. Beatty nodded. He was exhilarated, and he knew why: after so many recent setbacks and crises it was marvellously rewarding when something went right for a change. It gave him strength to cope with tomorrow. They went through the dock gates and met Captain Klopper. Klopper was in a towering, quivering rage.

Fatness was a profession for Klopper. His job in the Harbourmaster's Office gave him a unique power to extort bribes from anyone who wanted something shipped in or out. Throughout the years of strict rationing he had taken his payment in food, until he flaunted his fatness like a badge of office. It was proof of his power: he was still only a captain after four years on the island but he was going to make damn sure everyone knew that he was no ordinary captain.

Now, stamping up and down outside the dock gates, Klopper exuded rage like hot air trembling above a brazier. As soon as he saw Schwarz he swung towards him and began a furious, cheek-trembling harangue in spluttering German.

"Oh, oh," Labuschagne muttered. "I knew our luck couldn't last. I bet you this dreadful fellow didn't get his pig."

"Yes, he did," Beatty said. "I saw to that."

"Indeed? You never said."

"Well, I forgot. But I certainly remembered to get him a pig."

"In that case why is he throwing such a tantrum?"

Schwarz waved Captain Klopper to a twitching silence and turned to them, looking sad but brave. "The honour of the German Army is at stake," he explained. "Captain Klopper has been cruelly mocked by persons unknown who have sent him four pigs. This he says is a slur on his character. Maybe even three slurs, since all he wanted was one pig."

"He should be bloody glad to get 'em." Beatty snapped.

"Well, Captain Klopper is sensitive about this sort of thing," Schwarz said. "He suspects a plot to embarrass him with pigs."

"But where did all these pigs come from?" Labuschagne asked.

"I certainly supplied one," Schwarz said. "That was the arrangement, wasn't it?"

"Yes, but I understood that Mrs. Betteridge was . . . uh . . . indisposed," Beatty said. "So *I* got hold of a pig, instead."

"Well, that was thoughtful," Schwarz remarked, "but as far as I know she is still in business. So who sent Captain Klopper the other two pigs?"

A hearty shout made them all turn. It was Canon Renouf, bicycling towards them and waving. "So there you are, Labuschagne!" he called. "I've been looking for you everywhere. Did they arrive safely?"

"God stone the crows," Beatty said.

"You've no idea how much trouble you've put me to," Renouf boomed, as he dismounted on the run and forced the group to scatter. "I finally tracked down the Bailiff and he told me to send the beasts to some grossly overweight German officer, I forget his name."

"This is Captain Klopper, Canon," Labuschagne said.

Renouf parked his bicycle. "A thoroughly unhealthy young man," he observed.

"You delivered two pigs to him?" Labuschagne asked.

Renouf looked impatiently at Labuschagne. "You asked me to get you a pig, didn't you? Earlier this afternoon? Well then, that was what I did. I made certain inquiries and I got you a pig. Only, as they were rather small, I decided to get two." He dusted his hands. "I trust your little problem is now solved."

Major Schwarz patted him on the shoulder. "I can't tell you what a difference your help has made," he said. "And now I suggest that you all go away and leave me and I will make everyone happy, which is my mission in life."

Beatty hesitated, caught between admiration and disbelief. "Everyone?" he said. "Does that include the Fortress Commandant?"

Schwarz smiled like a baby. "My dear Doctor," he said, "who do you think got hold of all this lovely cement for him?" He took Klopper's arm and led him away.

Canon Renouf was about to call after them when Labuschagne

grabbed his arm. "Please," he urged. "Let them go."

"But Rome has fallen," Renouf said. "The news has just come through. Don't you think they'd like to know?"

"Another time," Labuschagne said.

35

A bluebottle scrabbled against the bedroom window, skidded away, hit its nose on the frame and ricocheted furiously across the glass, drumming up rage to overcome this blind, invisible obstacle.

It had been trying to get out for half an hour. The window was open at the top but the blubottle couldn't find the freedom which it saw and smelt and heard, and that made it furious. It rested and then attacked again.

Earl Kramer heaved himself off the bed and walked stiff-legged to the window. He rapped at the bluebottle with his knuckles and missed. It flew a frenzied zigzag. He got hold of the curtains and mashed the bluebottle against the glass. Immediately he wished he hadn't done it. As one flyer to another, he should have helped the poor bastard escape.

The evening was fading into a damp dusk. Kramer felt bad, about as bad as he could be. He couldn't stand thinking about Nancy; yet nothing else was worth his thought. He suffered brief tortures when her face unexpectedly slid into his imagination. He rejoiced in longer tortures when he punched and stomped and smashed that creeping, smirking kraut, while she watched and wept and begged him to forgive her.

Nobody cared. That was the worst of it. To be lonely and betrayed and with nobody to talk to, nothing but foreigners, pacifists, collaborators. . . . You risked your life, you fought Jerry fighters, flak, drowning, armed guards; and at the end of the day nobody cared, nobody gave a good goddam. Alone. Lonely. Cheated.

Kramer turned away and dropped on the bed again. Christ, she was so lovely. . . . He rolled off the bed and paced about the room. How could she do it? And what a God-awful waste! He remembered how he had touched her, just brushed her golden arm, how it had felt on his skin: electric. A tear ran down his cheek. He wanted to cry; it would be right to cry; he deserved to cry; stinking bitch! Lousy cheating filthy whore! His fists were clenched, the thumbs worrying the knuckle. They wanted to hit, to pound, to break. Presumably she was nearby, in her bed, sleeping it off, maybe. Smiling in her sleep. That torturing smile.

He went downstairs, his jolting footsteps thudding in the gloomy silence. Outside, the air made him shiver and hunch up. He took three sticks of dynamite from the toolbox in Greg's truck, ripped open a seam in the lining of his blazer and dropped the sticks inside the lining. A hunger for action was growing in him like a fever attacking a disease.

Ten minutes steady walking took him past several good targets, all too well guarded, all too close to home (Nancy's home), until he rounded a bend and saw a village green with a pub, a granite war memorial, a general store. He recognized the scene. This was where Jack Greg had taken him, the previous day, when the sun shone and he was not sick with love. So that had to be Ted Langley's shop, the place with the cellar.

Kramer checked the name, faded and blistered but still clearly readable, and knocked on the door. Nobody came. Blinds were drawn over the shop-window and no lights burned upstairs. A pair of German soldiers strolled past and made him nervous. He looked around the green and counted a dozen Germans just hanging about. At least one of them was certainly watching him. This was crazy: what the hell was he doing here anyway? Looking for someone to talk to. Would the krauts believe that? He knocked again, longer and louder. The racket split the evening quiet like gunshots.

Still nobody came. Kramer groaned to himself; now he would have to walk away, past all those eyes. A chain rattled: he was saved, there was somebody here after all! The door was unlocked and pulled open, and Kramer smiled gratefully at a woman, not young, in a long, dark coat. She was holding a shawl around her head and she held onto the door as if she needed its support.

"Is Mr. Langley in, ma'am?" Kramer asked.

"No," she whispered.

"Oh." Kramer shuffled his feet. "Is he somewhere around? I mean, could I find him nearby?"

To his horror she was weeping. "Hey, please, don't be like that . . ." he began, when a man's footsteps came pounding from the back of the shop. He was burly and balding, in breeches and shirt-sleeves.

"What the hell's going on here?" the man demanded. "Go back inside. Go back." He took her hand away from the door and gently pushed her towards the back. "Who are you? What d'you want?" he asked in a harsh whisper.

"I'm a friend of Ted Langley," Kramer said. "I just thought I'd—"

"Ted's not here. The Germans have got him. He's going to be executed tomorrow."

Kramer's smile shrivelled. "Oh no," he breathed.

"I'm his brother, I should know. Now leave us alone, for God's sake." The door slammed.

Kramer wandered away, across the green, between the groups of idling soldiers. Now he didn't care if they noticed him or not. Life was so bad that nothing could make it worse. If only someone could invent a bomb that would blow up this whole lousy island and kill everyone on it in one clean flash. That would be good. That would at least stop all this reprisal crap.

He found himself walking along a lane. The breeze was colder and sometimes he felt a drifting raindrop touch his face. There was a small bridge over a small stream, so he stopped and leaned on the parapet. The dynamite pressed against his hips. Would three sticks be enough to blow this lousy thing up? He decided he might as well try it and see. You had to keep showing the bastards that you weren't beaten yet, for Christ's sake. If you didn't fight back you might as well give up.

He swung over the top and ran down a grassy bank. It was dark under the low bridge but there was enough room for him to get in and plant the explosive. He ducked his head and edged alongside the stream, looking for gaps in the mossy masonry. Watery chucklings resounded in the enclosed space, and someone's wiry fingers seized him by the throat.

Kramer stumbled, more from surprise than from the violence of the attack. He felt the fingers slip as the man lost his balance, so he dropped to his knees and grabbed the wrists. They were bony and skinny, like a child's, and he easily jerked them apart. As he turned to face his attacker the man hacked him on the legs, repeatedly, in a frenzy of blows, until the pain made Kramer let go of his wrists and scramble away. At once the man rushed him, fists flailing, and Kramer had to defend himself. He punched with his right arm, using all his strength, and the man's mouth rammed against his clenched knuckles like a mallet striking a post. Kramer felt the teeth bend and the lips split, and then the man crumpled like a bag of old clothes.

Kramer stooped, panting and rubbing his fist, and waited for movement which never came. He rolled the man onto his back and saw a starved scarecrow, gaunt in the face, unshaven, so emaciated that Kramer could feel the bones between his fingers. The man was wearing rags that were more filth than rag. His pulse said he was alive but he looked ready for death. A runaway slave-labourer. This bridge must be his hideout. As Kramer's breathing returned to normal he saw what a horribly pathetic little fight it had been: a non-fight. He had delivered a massive knock-out blow to a feeble little piece of human wreckage. He felt ashamed and deeply sorry, and determined to help this man who had suffered more than he could ever imagine.

Kramer hurried to Nancy's house and raided the kitchen for food. When he got back to the bridge the man had gone. There was no trace of him except a little blood and a sour smell in the niche where he must have been hiding.

Kramer gave up, went home, put the food away, went to bed. This day had gone on long enough.

Half an hour before curfew the Controlling Council met at the Central Police Station, where the search for Greg's lorry was being organized.

"I've got everybody out looking," de Wilde said. "I don't see who else we can raise." He listed the unpaid officers who managed the island's twelve parishes: Constables and Rectors, Centeniers and Vingteniers, Constable's officers, Almoners. "They've recruited from all over: Chamber of Commerce, football clubs, schoolteachers, fire brigade. . . ." He shrugged.

"Golf Club?" Beatty asked.

"Yes," de Wilde said.

"Contract Bridge Circle? Amateur Dramatic Club?" The Bailiff nodded each time.

"For such a little island it takes a great deal of searching," Labuschagne said. "We need a week, really."

"The bloody thing can't be on the road anywhere," de Wilde said. "So that means he's hidden it." He sounded weary but his movements were restless.

"Marvellous," Labuschagne muttered. "What if it's in a barn? Or a garage? There's scores of them."

"We mustn't give up," de Wilde said. "We can't give up."

Beatty stretched and yawned. "When we find this cowboy I think I'll amputate his head. He obviously doesn't use it."

"That reminds me," said de Wilde. "Is your messenger-boy safely on board?"

"Done." Beatty thought of his farewell handshake with Martin Lang, the evening mist softening everything except the pang of parting. "You must speak as you find. They're not all bad, and that one's a remarkable lad."

"Let's hope so. All right, go home. We'll start again first thing in the morning."

36

It was the Schumachers' turn to give a dinner party in honour of General Rimmer. The other guests were the Limners; a visiting naval commander named Hoffman; and Major Wolff, who appeared in full-dress uniform, including sword, spurs, and medals.

When Rimmer arrived, Wolff was leaning on the mantelpiece, smoking a short, square cigar, and absent-mindedly raking one of his spurs up and down the Regency wallpaper.

"What on earth is he doing here?" Rimmer muttered.

"We invited him, sir," Schumacher said anxiously. "I mean, we took it for granted . . . Is something wrong? I could always—"

"His nerves gave way this afternoon, that's all. I thought he was in hospital by now."

"Oh dear. We had no idea, sir. I've been out all day, and nobody told Beth. . . . Oh dear. He's had a couple of drinks, too. . . ."

Wolff came over to Rimmer and clicked his heels. "Everything is all right now, sir."

"I'm glad to hear it. This isn't a full-dress occasion, you know, Wolff."

"It is for me, sir. It's my mother's birthday."

"Indeed! Well, please give her my best wishes when next you see her."

"I'm afraid she's dead, sir. Died in 1937."

"Then I don't understand."

"We are a very pious family, sir."

"Ah. . . . Is that perhaps why you're wearing your medals back-to-front?"

Wolff stiffened. "These are my mother's medals, sir. She flew a Heinkel with the Condor Legion in Spain. General Franco himself decorated her." He reversed one of the medals. "The Iberian Order of Pluck," he said. "Third Class."

Rimmer saw Maria Limner watching, and he gave her a short, formal smile. "I still think you should be in bed, Wolff," he said. "You've been overdoing it, you know."

Wolff took him aside, and spoke confidentially. "In actual fact, sir, her birthday is not until late September. And she was my stepmother. Nobody else here knows. Only you."

"And you," Rimmer pointed out.

Wolff twisted his face into an expression of uncertainty. "Frankly, sir, I'm not convinced. Things are not always what they seem. For instance, Beth Schumacher has lovely tits, hasn't she?"

Rimmer looked. "Yes, quite admirable."

"I have measured them and they are precisely eighty-eight millimetres in diameter. Now, with only two more eighty-eight millimetre guns I could have captured the strategically vital village of Gavrilovka."

"Well, you didn't," Rimmer said, "So don't worry about it."

"Gavrilovka was strategically vital," Wolff told him, "because it was the only Russian village which General Zeitzler could pronounce. If we couldn't take Gavrilovka, he said, we might as well go home."

Beth Schumacher joined them. "Did I hear my name just now?" she asked.

"Did you?" Rimmer said. "Major Wolff was talking about artillery."

"No I wasn't," Wolff said, "I was talking about your lovely tits." Beth stiffened, but she also almost smiled.

"Dinner is served," Schumacher announced.

"He couldn't pronounce Stalingrad," Wolff said. "He tried awfully hard, but he just couldn't pronounce it." He took Beth's arm and led her in to dinner.

The meal itself was uneventful. Rimmer was ready to send Wolff to his quarters if he became difficult, but Wolff said little except to praise the food: egg mayonnaise; a crown of lamb chops with red cabbage and potato croquettes; and strawberries with cream. Beth liked being praised, and when Commander Hoffman proposed a toast to her the evening was a success as far as she was concerned. The commander was tall, craggy, and amusing without having to work at it. Maria was elegant and provocative without being outrageous. Michael Limner deftly filled any holes in the conversation, and Rimmer

was aware at all times that he was the guest of honour. Schumacher
—in uniform, still—itched and scratched a good deal, but at least he
did it discreetly and didn't knock anything over.

With the brandy came a brisk rattle of rain against the windows.
"Perfect," said Hoffman. "For once the weathermen got it right.
Strong westerly winds, low cloud, broken seas, rain. Just the thing."

"I thought you sailors didn't like gales," Beth suggested boldly.

"We don't, dear lady," said Hoffman, "and neither does that awful
man Eisenhower. He wants a flat calm to go with all his flat-bottomed
boats."

"That reminds me: your cement arrived today," Rimmer told Schumacher. "Only a thousand tons, but it'll keep you going."

"Magnificent! That's the best news I've had this month." Schumacher slapped his thigh, and flinched at the pain. "Now if I could
only get my craftsmen back . . ."

"The Bailiff assures me they will be working tomorrow," Limner
said. "He also guarantees a normal supply of electricity and water and
so on."

Hoffman cocked his head. "Trouble on the island? Gremlins under
the bed?"

"Just a few malcontents," Rimmer said. "You know what these
foreigners are like; one has to shout at them. They don't understand
plain German."

"A thousand tons," Schumacher gloated. "I can start Secondary-
Defence Complex B."

"Colonel Schumacher is the Bunker King of Jersey," Maria told
Hoffman. "He is to bunkers what Don Juan was to orgasms."

Schumacher took out his wallet and tenderly produced a much-
folded piece of paper. "If you mean I have a passion for exploring the
potentials of concrete, Countess, you are right. Not to be shackled by
false modesty, I feel that I am literally building the Third Reich here.
What a privilege!" He handed Hoffman the paper. "This is a photocopy of the Fuehrer's own design for a bunker, executed in 1942. I
have built thirty-seven so far."

"You mean this is an actual photocopy of the Fuehrer's own handi-
work?" Hoffman said. "I don't know quite what to say."

"Those words are his." Schumacher leaned over and pointed. "He
wrote those words himself."

"Two metres eighty centimetres," Hoffman said. "Well! That's
really something, isn't it?"

"Speaking from memory," Count Limner said, "it's slightly less than three metres. About the length of a good cigar less. Have you a good cigar, my dear Schumacher?"

"A thousand apologies, Count!" Schumacher handed round the cigars.

"I'll have one, please," Maria said. Wolff lit it for her. Rimmer watched approvingly.

"I ate a cigar once," Wolff said. "It was during the Panzer attack on Kursk. There are worse things to eat than cigars. Take candles—"

"No thanks," Rimmer declared. Wolff finished his brandy and poured himself another.

"May I ask a purely technical question?" Maria said. "Will this particular portion of the Third Reich last a thousand years?"

"Oh yes," Schumacher said confidently. "In fact my structures will last for tens of thousands of years. They are indestructible."

"Why? Is the Reich going to be at war such a long time?"

"Oh, Maria," Limner sighed.

"No, no, it's a perfectly reasonable question," Rimmer said.

Schumacher was eager to answer. "It's not simply a military matter, Countess. Architecture has a duty to history, too. Take, for instance, the Roman Empire."

"No thanks," Wolff said. Beth gently hushed him.

"What would remain today to testify to the greatness of Rome if there were no great Roman buildings?" Schumacher went on. "The Fuehrer is an artist, he sees the need for an architectural heritage which will inspire the conscience of Germans centuries from now. When I build, I am speaking to posterity. Where someone else might see just a bunker on a hillside, I see a Germanic giant pressed against the soil, tense, poised, balanced, dynamic, eternal."

"Slightly chipped?" Hoffman suggested. "When the Allies start bombarding, your architectural heritage is liable to get knocked about a bit."

"Ah! Now that's where the Theory of Ruin Value comes in. Reichsminister Speer has developed this on the Fuehrer's orders. Modern buildings are no good as ruins; they just look squalid. By contrast the Colosseum of Rome looks superb."

"I hear Rome's fallen," Wolff said. "Sloppy workmanship. Bloody Italians."

"By applying Speer's theories to my designs," Schumacher persisted, "I can ensure that each structure decays properly."

"Bless my soul," Limner said.

"It's what we architects call 'creative dilapidation,' " Schumacher added.

"There you are," Rimmer told Maria. "Satisfied?"

"I don't know," she said. "I still have this mental picture of Adolf Hitler designing bunkers in 1942."

"Why not? He fought in the trenches in the last war, he understands the needs of the infantry."

"On a point of fact," Limner said, "he didn't exactly fight; he ran; he was a regimental runner. I'm sure he ran extremely bravely, because he was twice decorated; but there is a difference. That's all."

"I ran once," Wolff said. "I ran like bloody hell. They didn't catch me. No fear." ·

"But in 1942 there were all sorts of terrible things going on," Maria said. "North Africa, El Alamein, Russia, the U-boat war. If I were Head of State, Supreme Commander of the Armed Forces *and* Commander-in-Chief of the Army, I don't think I'd have time to design bunkers. Would I?"

"It's really an excellent bunker," Schumacher protested. "All the angles are calculated perfectly."

"I know what you mean," Hoffman told Maria. "Somehow one doesn't see Churchill designing landing-craft, or Roosevelt designing bombers, or Stalin designing tanks."

Rimmer felt that the conversation was in danger of becoming despondent. He stood up and cleared his throat. "What matters is results," he said, "and we are fortunate to have a Fuehrer who knows that wars are won with weapons. Thanks to his genius, we have a few trump cards up our sleeves."

"Such as?" Maria said.

"Well now . . ." Rimmer strolled to the fireplace and propped one glossy boot on the red-leather bench. "Most of them are top secret, of course, but I think I can hint at a few little surprises guaranteed to raise the eyebrows of the foe. The army has a nasty little device called the Beetle."

"Hardly a secret weapon, though," Limner said. "I remember reading about it in *The Illustrated London News*. Radio-controlled miniature tank, isn't it? About so big." He spread his arms.

"Quite right," Rimmer said. "The Beetle was merely a prototype for a much larger weapon, called Hog. This is a regular tank, carrying a load of explosives. The driver gets out, steers it by remote control to the target, drops the explosive load, steers it back to him, and bang! Another direct hit. It's a nippy little beast, the Hog. It'll do thirty kilometres an hour over a good surface."

"*The Illustrated London News* said thirty-five," Wolff remarked.

"The Hog was just the start, of course," Rimmer added. "No doubt other models have superseded it by now."

"Is that all?" Maria asked.

"I think I can tell you about our new tank-buster. It's been blooded against the Russians with great success. Basically, it's the good old Junkers 87 divebomber with a brace of thirty-seven millimetre cannon tucked under the wings. It really packs the most tremendous wallop."

"Fundamentally it's still the Stuka, though," Hoffman said thoughtfully.

"The best ground-support aircraft we've ever had."

"Mmm. Pity it's not a bit quicker. We lost an awful lot over England in 1940. Still," he added cheerfully, "I expect the Luftwaffe has got that all worked out by now. Fighter cover, or something."

"What with?" Maria asked.

"With what," Limner said automatically; glumly.

"Have you heard of jet-propulsion?" Rimmer asked her.

"No."

"You will soon. It's a brilliant new way to make aircraft fly without propellors, and German scientists discovered it. Willy Messerschmitt has built a squadron of these jet fighters already. They climb like rockets and they're faster than the enemy's fastest plane. You watch: they'll be absolute murder."

"Swallow," Wolff said. Everybody looked at him. "Just remembered," he explained.

"Is that it?" Limner asked. "Or is there more to come?"

"Name of the plane. It's called the Swallow. Read it in the London *Times.*"

"Ahah!" Maria said. "And are they impressed by it?"

"That was a deliberate leak," Rimmer announced. "Part of our psychological warfare to unnerve the enemy."

Hoffman stretched his long legs and gave Beth something to admire. "Hooray for the Luftwaffe," he said. "I don't suppose they could tie four of these Swallows together with a bit of string and give the navy a decent long-range reconnaissance plane, could they? It might help the poor old U-boat skipper to find what he's looking for. There's rather a lot of the Atlantic out there, you know, and it's all full of foul weather and terribly wet water."

"I suppose the rain does that," Maria said.

"Never stops. There isn't a dry patch to be found. Frightful."

His sombreness disturbed Beth, who said, "Still, they can always get away from it, can't they? Go down, I mean?" She made a neat, submerging gesture.

Hoffman squeezed her hand. "Dear lady," he said, "the way the damp rises from that ocean floor is positively chilling." He shivered so convincingly that Beth gave a sympathetic little shudder too.

Rimmer straddled a chair and leaned on the top. "Sailors are worse than farmers for grumbling," he said. "Wait till they see the new U-boat. Maybe that'll make the sun shine on the Atlantic."

Hoffman grunted, and tugged his tunic straight. "General," he said, "with all due respect, I don't think we ought to—"

"Fiddlesticks." Rimmer smiled at Maria, and she saw again how the mere possession of power gave certain men an extra lustre. "If the Fuehrer were here now, d'you think he wouldn't tell the Countess, just as he told me last week?"

Limner thought, *You and ninety-nine others.*

Hoffman looked away; he had made his objection. "The trouble with U-boats," Rimmer said, "is their speed under water. Even with *Schnorkels* they can only do about six knots. Now, thanks to a bit of good old-fashioned German genius, we've got a new U-boat, the Type Twenty-one, which is more than three times as fast as the ordinary boats. Correct, Commander?"

"So it seems," Hoffman agreed.

"In the words of the Fuehrer, it's the underwater equivalent of the Swallow. Nearly nineteen knots when submerged! For goodness' sake, that's more than some escort vessels! Type Twenty-one is going to be a killer; it'll go through convoys like a shark in a goldfish-pond."

"I won't deny that I look forward to seeing one," Hoffman said.

"One?" Maria queried. "Isn't it ready yet?"

"Virtually," Rimmer said. "In fact we're on the verge of a whole host of surprises. The Commander here would like to have a four-engined aircraft; well, so would a lot of Luftwaffe pilots. The Fuehrer, however, has his own ways of skinning a cat. Very shortly, ladies and gentlemen, you will see London being bombed night and day, seven days a week, *without the use of a single aircraft.*" Rimmer got up and strolled around the table, to let that sink in. "And then we shall see what that gangster Churchill has to say, supposing he's still alive to say anything."

There was a thoughtful silence.

"Do you think they might ever make peace?" Limner asked.

"Oh yes, eventually. Churchill won't, because he knows damn well we'll hang him for his crimes. I hope we do it in the middle of Hamburg, that's all. There are five thousand children buried in those ruins."

"That's nothing," Wolff said. "We used to kill five thousand kids a day, in the Ukraine." He took out his sword and felt the edge. "We cut their little throats for them; they didn't like that one tiny bit. Most unpopular, it was. Still, they didn't bleed much. Catch 'em young, that's the secret. What?" He smiled his tense glittering smile at Schumacher.

"Pay no attention," Rimmer said wearily. "He's lost control, he doesn't know what he's saying."

"Pay no attention," Wolff said, turning his glittering smile on Rimmer. "He's lost control, he doesn't know what he's saying."

"Really now, look here, Wolff," Schumacher said, rising. He had remembered that he was the host. "This won't do, you know. I think you'd better call it a night, don't you?" He took Wolff's arm and tried to get him to stand. "Just put that thing away where it belongs and we'll—"

Wolff slashed at Schumacher with the sword and struck him in the upper arm. The blade was not sharp but the blow was hard: it cut the cloth and broke the skin. Beth screamed. Schumacher staggered back, gaping. Rimmer seized Wolff's chair, tipped him out, and kicked the sword from his grasp. Then he emptied the water-jug over him.

Wolff lay on his back, hooting with laughter. His hair was sodden and his eyes were closed, and he was helpless with mirth. Schumacher felt his arm and discovered blood on his fingers. He howled with pain and kicked Wolff in the stomach. Rimmer turned and punched Schumacher in the chest so hard that Schumacher fell backwards onto his rump with a crash that made the candles jump. "How dare you kick an officer of field rank!" Rimmer rasped. "How dare you attack my Adjutant! You're nothing but a damned tradesman! Get out of here. Go on, get out!"

Schumacher got up and hurried from the room.

"Well, that was fun," Maria said.

"We ought to be toddling off, dear," Limner suggested.

Rimmer was flexing his fist and wincing. "I must have hit his blasted corsets," he said.

"What about the Major?" Limner asked. "Would you like us to drop him off, or . . .?"

Beth was helping Wolff to his feet. "I shall look after Major Wolff," she said firmly. "You may all go. I hope you enjoyed your meal."

"Well," Limner said, "That seems to take care of everything. Except the other casualty."

"He'll be all right," Hoffman said. "It was just a little cut." He kissed Beth's hand, but she was unimpressed and eager for them to leave.

Outside, the rain had stopped but the night was black and gusty. Maria decided to walk home and Rimmer offered to escort her. Limner drove Hoffman to his hotel.

Upstairs, Major Wolff was lying on the bed and Beth was drying his hair, when Schumacher came in. "What the hell is going on now?" he blustered.

"Go away, Felix," Beth ordered. "Go away and stay away." She pushed him out and locked the door.

"Poor old King of the Bunkers," Wolff said.

"He doesn't need me," Beth said. "In fact he doesn't need anybody. But you do, don't you? I've seen it in your eyes before, and tonight I could see it all the time. Poor bastard, I kept thinking. Poor, poor bastard." She brushed his hair back from his eyes.

"Beth," Wolff said, and put his arms partly around her. "Beth Schumacher. Two of the nicest people in the world." He began laughing again.

"You really enjoy your work," Maria Limner said. They were walking along the rain-soaked Esplanade, while Rimmer's limousine prowled fifty yards ahead of them: advance warning for any sentries or patrols to stub their cigarettes and look vigilant. "I was watching your face when you were talking about secret weapons. You really like being a soldier."

"Well, it's a great privilege to serve the Fuehrer," Rimmer said.

"Oh, horseshit. Perhaps not quite horseshit: sheepshit. It's a great privilege to be a missionary in a leper colony, but nobody does it unless he finds it satisfying, does he?"

"That's a circular argument, Maria. Why did I get promoted?

Because I was good. Why was I good? Because I found the life so rewarding. Which comes first, the reward or the promotion?"

They walked in silence for a while. The town was blacked-out, silent, deserted. A cold sea-mist blew across the Esplanade and lost itself inland.

"You, on the other hand, do not enjoy your life," Rimmer said.

"Did you see that in my face?"

"No, no; you hide it well. You have an attractive face, Maria, you've trained it to look calm and interested. But I can sense anger as well as any man in Europe. Four years spent tracking down saboteurs—it teaches you a thing or two! You're angry, aren't you? I don't know why. Do you know why?"

"For God's sake, does there have to be a reason?" She looked away. "Yes, I suppose there does. . . . It's not Michael's fault, anyway, and it's nothing to do with his accident. I'm lucky, really, living comfortably on such a beautiful island, in the middle of a long, horrible war. But that makes it worse, because it's all such an enormous waste. Waste of money, waste of time, waste of *people.* It's like doing a very expensive play in a completely empty theatre. So what? Who cares?"

"If you looked up and saw enemy parachutes falling, I think you would care."

"You want them to come, don't you?"

"Oh, I'm not impatient. But I'm not reluctant, either."

"Suppose you lose."

"Yes, exactly. Suppose I do lose? What's so terrible about that?"

"Well, it would be the end of you."

Rimmer laughed. "It amuses me when civilians try to understand war. They always miss the obvious. The great thing about a battle is the result. Invariably it's a clear-cut decision, one way or the other. Us against them, slam-bang-wallop, and when the smoke clears and the dust settles and the sweat dries, one of us has lost. And that's beautiful for the other! Beautiful. No ragged edges, no long-winded dreary arguments, no piddling arbitrations or concessions or grey-faced compromises. Just a result, a decision, a sharp, clean end. Good. Now we go forward to the next battle."

"So Poland was beautiful?"

"Yes, Poland was very beautiful. That hard, strong, clean thrust to the heart: superb. France was even lovelier, because the Panzer breakthrough was so fast. Our tanks went storming along the roads absolutely flat out, day after day. Greece was best of all. Greece was exquisite. We took Greece in less than a week, just by splitting the Greek and the British armies like two halves of a ripe fig. Now that was sheer artistry. I can still taste the perfection of Greece, the way other people might remember a great painting or a splendid piano concerto. . . . I'm sorry, I mustn't bore you. Let's talk of something else."

"There is nothing else," she said. "That's what's wrong with the world. And when you bore me I shall let you know without invitation."

"Oh dear." Rimmer bowed his head. "Snubbed again."

"You asked for it. What makes me despair about soldiers is their bloody cocksureness."

"Well, I've never had any complaints," Rimmer murmured.

"Yes. Exactly. There you are. Making war or making love, it's one and the same to you."

Rimmer laughed again. "Oh no. At least, I certainly hope not. There are no losers between you and me. We're both winners. Aren't we?" He glanced at his watch. "We have time to put it to the test, if you like."

"But it's the same sort of simpleminded success, isn't it? You don't think any further, you never ask yourself *Why? What's the point?*"

Her forcefulness took Rimmer aback. "Well . . . Let's not forget the circumstances, Maria. Neither of us is a free agent and—"

"Never mind us. What about the war? Why are you fighting? What's the point?"

He sighed. "Once a war's been declared, that question is redundant. When the civilians make a mess of things the simpleminded soldiers have to step in and impose a solution, and that solution is final. Not a romantic explanation, but . . ." He gestured: such is life.

"A final solution?"

"Yes. Ah, you're thinking of the Jews, aren't you? That's a political matter. I'm talking about military affairs."

"What are you going to do tomorrow? If this phantom saboteur isn't found?"

"Proceed. Go forward. Take action."

"You'll shoot hostages?"

"Yes, of course. Every tenth name."

"Even if it's a child?"

Rimmer let the question hang in the air. Then he said carefully, "I don't imagine that the Americans in their Flying Fortresses or the Englishmen in their Lancasters stop to wonder if every tenth bomb kills a German child."

"That's chance, not choice. They're not aiming at children."

Again Rimmer laughed. "Oh, Maria, Maria. You're not really in this war at all, are you? D'you think they care who they bomb? Ask the Swiss. Ask them about the little Swiss town of Schaffhausen. Last month two formations of American Liberators bombed it flat in broad daylight. Killed thirty-seven Swiss civilians and injured sixty. You see, they can't even get their bombs in the right *country*." He shook his head in amusement and amazement. "You really mustn't be so emotional."

They stopped outside his hotel. Rimmer slapped his gloves against his leg. "Shall we? he asked.

"I think not," Maria said stonily. "You really mustn't be so emotional."

Rimmer snuffled, uncertain whether or not to laugh.

"You snigger at me again," she said, "and I'll kick you in the balls."

High overhead an air-raid siren began to wail. "Look out," he said. "Here comes the Swiss Air Force."

Count Limner dropped Commander Hoffman at his hotel and drove home. He found Captain Paulus waiting in the lobby.

"Too late," Limner said, walking past. "Shop's shut. Come back in the morning." He made for the stairs.

"No," Paulus said.

Limner looked back. "Paulus, you are a little toad," he said, "and it's time all good little toads were tucked up under their wet stones. You're not a good little toad, you're a rotten little toad, so hop it and find yourself a rotten little wet stone. With any luck you might provide breakfast for a hungry snake, but it would have to be pretty damned ravenous. And now good night."

"Oh no," Paulus said. He took out his sunglasses and carefully fitted them onto his head.

Limner gently kicked at his stick with his good foot, making it swing in his hand. "If you're here to tell me you've arrested another greengrocer's assistant," he began.

"Oh dear no," Paulus said. "I have come here to discuss a matter of the very highest importance."

"Then it must be completely over your head." Limner turned to the stairs again. "I suppose you'd better come up. Just when we've had the carpets cleaned, too. . . ."

Paulus closed the door of the Limners' suite and leaned against it. "You, Count, have been interfering in the work of the Gestapo," he said. "You must stop that at once."

"D'you mean Langley?"

"Renouf, too, but yes: the case of Langley is more important. While we have been working to eradicate sabotage, you have been constantly intervening with the Fortress Commandant, trying to protect Langley, and so damaging our achievement and threatening the security of the island. This must stop."

Limner yawned and took off his coat. "You've arrested the wrong man on evidence that wouldn't stun a flea. It's as simple as that."

"No, it's not." Paulus stepped forward and removed his sunglasses. His expression was earnest. "Unless you cease interfering in the work of the Gestapo, Count," he said, "I shall inform Berlin that your wife is enjoying illicit sexual intercourse with the Fortress Commandant, and that, of course, will mean the speedy departure of all three of you. I'm sure you know how strongly the Fuehrer feels about these matters."

Limner stood quite still and stared at Paulus. For a moment the only sound was Limner's breathing: heavy and slow, like a man under anaesthetic. "I hope you've got more evidence than a pair of somebody's old boots," he said.

"Oh yes," Paulus said. "Photographs. I brought them with me. I thought you might like to sleep on them, so to speak."

Five minutes later, when Maria Limner came in, Paulus got to his feet. "Oh, hullo," she said.

"The Captain is just leaving," her husband declared.

"Goodness, I'm tired," she said.

"That's not surprising," murmured Paulus. He nodded to Limner. "I shall expect your decision in the morning, then."

Because of delays in unloading, the *Schleswig-Holstein* was fifteen minutes late sailing from St. Helier. She cleared the harbour light at twenty-three minutes past ten and put on all speed. Barring accidents, the captain hoped to make at least nine knots, which meant he would reach St. Malo on the Brittany coast at about three-thirty in the morning, well before daylight. The wind was fresh and gusting. The clouds were low, about six hundred feet, and thick enough to blot out the moon. Occasional rain squalls soaked the ship. For 1944 it was good sailing weather.

The ship was crowded with servicemen going on leave. The escort who was taking Jack Greg to France had found a space for them below, but Greg resented being surrounded by happy, singing Germans and he told his escort to take him back on deck. The man refused. Greg then discreetly poked his fingers down his throat until he began to vomit. The escort changed his mind.

The ship was completely blacked out, so there was nothing to look at except the shifting blur of whitecaps. It was cold and boring. After five minutes the escort told Greg that he was going to the lavatory. He handcuffed Greg to the rails and disappeared. He did not come back.

Martin Lang was one of the lucky ones. He had found a good seat, and he was dozing with his head pressed against his pack and his legs braced against a stanchion to counter the roll and shudder of the ship. On one side of him, four sailors played bridge; on the other side, a sergeant-cook was patiently murdering Strauss on an accordion. Lang was half-thinking, half-dreaming about Nancy Buchanan. It was ironic, the way the war had brought them together and yet it kept pulling them apart. They had met in a civilian hospital: a German Army doctor came to perform an operation and Lang was his assistant. Nancy was working in one of the wards and she asked Lang to help her move a patient, not realizing that he was German. After that they managed to meet often, but never often enough.

In some ways it was worse for Nancy, because any Jersey girl who became friendly with a German was asking for trouble: "Jerrybags" was the Islanders' label. But she was in love with him as much as he was with her, and there was no way they could alter that. Surely the war must end soon; perhaps in only a few months, even weeks; then they could be together always. Bloody stupid war. If he could, he would sign a total surrender right now, provided they let him keep Nancy. Was that callous, he wondered? Was absolute love making him callous? It was all beyond understanding; you just had to trust your feelings and go ahead. He slid his fingers inside his tunic and made sure the Deutschmarks and the diamond were safe. The time was 10:53 p.m.

Five miles to the north, the air-raid sirens were sounding. The wind, and the rumbling of her engines, overcame any faint wail which might have reached the *Schleswig-Holstein*, not that the captain could have done anything if he had heard the warning. At 10:55 a formation of three RAF Coastal Command Beaufighters, flying at two hundred feet in line abreast, swept in from the west. Their airborne radar picked up the ship at a range of three miles. They altered course, closing at 330 miles an hour; one mile every eleven seconds. When they were two miles away the ship's captain first heard the throaty roar of their engines and tried to place the sound. Thirteen seconds later he stopped guessing: the central Beaufighter switched on the searchlight installed in its nose and lit the *Schleswig-Holstein* with a soft, wavering radiance. The beam narrowed and intensified as the aircraft lost height and raced closer. At a distance of two hundred yards it released its torpedo and the searchlight died.

The three Beaufighters stormed overhead in a raucous bellow that ripped the night. The captain, dazzled, had not seen the splash of the torpedo but he knew it must be coming and already the ship's rudder was locked hard to starboard. The ship heeled, forcing Martin Lang to grab at his bench, so he was already tensed when the torpedo struck. Its warhead exploded thirty feet away from him, shattering a bulkhead into flying fragments, including a jagged hunk of steel which chopped a double-fistful of flesh from his right thigh. It cut the femoral artery and he bled to death where he lay.

Jack Greg cheered the Beaufighters as they flew overhead. He cheered the torpedo when it struck. Nobody heard him and nobody paid him any attention. The *Schleswig-Holstein* sank rapidly, going down first by the starboard side. Greg was manacled to the rails on the port side, and he strained and hauled against the handcuffs until his wrists were gouged and bloody. The ship keeled over more and more until the deck was nearly vertical and Greg was hanging by his hands. Passengers and crew were scrambling and shouting all around, but they could save neither him nor themselves. At 10:58 the *Schleswig-Holstein* went down. She took one hundred and sixty-three men with her.

MONDAY

37

Came the dawn, and it was still raining.

General Rimmer breakfasted at seven. The weather pleased him, and he was not surprised to find another *Northview:4* on top of the signals waiting beside his rolls and coffee. The report of the loss of the *Schleswig-Holstein* dented his pleasure, but it could have been worse; at least she had delivered the cement. No officers had been on board and the only cargo was tomatoes and mail. It could have been worse.

At seven-thirty his car arrived and he drove with a motorcycle escort to the Military Cemetery at Mont l'Abbé. On the way he wondered about the curious behaviour of Maria Limner. She had been her usual charming self during dinner; and then suddenly she turned spiky. Odd. Time of the month, maybe.

As they neared the cemetery the roadside became lined with civilians, both men and women. Rimmer wiped the mist from the window and looked more closely. Many were carrying wreaths. "What's all this?" he demanded.

"Don't know, sir," the driver said.

The crowd outside the cemetery was several hundred strong. They completely outnumbered the soldiers drawn up by the gates. Three coffins rested on wooden trestles, each coffin draped with a swastika flag. The wet flags clung to the smooth wood.

Rimmer got out of his car. There was no sound apart from the patter of rain and an occasional cough. A sergeant shouted, and the burial party stamped to attention, less than perfectly. Rimmer made short work of inspecting them (even so he found an unbuttoned epaulette). The officer in charge marched to the head of the formation, while beside the graves a military band, its instruments fluttering with black ribbon, began to play a slow march.

Rimmer saw Count Limner and went across.

"I take it this is a massive spontaneous demonstration of civilian grief over our recent tragic losses," he said.

"No."

"No. So what in the name of Joseph Goebbels is going on?"

"They're here for the funeral of that American airman who was washed up yesterday," Limner said.

"Oh-ho." Rimmer studied the crowd and recognized a few faces: Renouf, de Wilde, Beatty. "And who authorized this?"

"It's standard practice, General. We buried twenty-nine men of the British Navy last November, all with full military honours and a firing party. They don't go in the same part of the cemetery as our dead, if that's what's worrying you." Limner pointed to a corner. "That's their bit, over there."

"But why now?"

Limner shrugged. "Your men provide the pallbearers. It makes sense to use one squad for both burials."

"You think so? This looks more like an uprising than a burial."

"Oh, the Bailiff is here, there won't be any trouble." Limner took a couple of paces and looked down the road. "Extraordinary. There must be a thousand of them, and yet there was no announcement. We didn't even fix the time until yesterday evening. Amazing."

The cemetery had been opened, and the pallbearers were slow-marching carefully up the wide, gravelled path. Already the rain had washed the sharp creases from their grey serge uniforms, leaving the tunics wrinkled and the trousers baggy.

There came a clop of horses and a grinding of coachwheels, and the crowd stood bareheaded for a horse-drawn hearse. The coffin was draped with a Union Jack. "I hope you don't object," Limner said "They couldn't find an American flag, and there wasn't time to make one. All those stars."

"The only thing I object to is everything. What comes next? 'Land of Hope and Glory'? 'Yankee Doodle Dandy'? Let's get it over with All those damn wreaths are giving me hay-fever." Rimmer strode into the cemetery.

The funeral service was short and sombre. Two military chaplains shared the ritual of committing the bodies to the earth. General Rimmer spoke a few forgettable words, honouring (he said) this gallant sacrifice; he mentioned Private Keller by name. The soldiers hunched their shoulders to keep the rain from running down their

necks. Meanwhile de Wilde and Canon Renouf, with a dozen repre-
sentatives of the crowd, were in a corner of the graveyard burying
their faceless airman. The rest of the mourners pressed against the
cemetery gates and watched in silence.

The firing-party pointed their barrels at the heavy sky and the
volleys rippled out in a stuttering crash; the troops' gunnery was no
better than their drill. The bandmaster raised his baton, and the
soldiers filled their lungs. Down came the baton.

> *Deutschland, Deutschland über Alles!*
> *Uber Alles in der Welt. . . .*

Rimmer glanced at the crowd and was surprised to see that several
of them were singing. He turned his head in order to listen better.
There was definitely some singing going on, quite a lot in fact. They
were singing more slowly than the soldiers, but the tune was unmis-
takeably the same.

Half-way through the verse, the rest of the crowd had picked up
the song and their thousand voices overwhelmed the anthem. When
the soldiers finished, the islanders were just approaching the climax,
and their music filled the air:

> *On the Rock of Ages founded,*
> *What can shake thy sure repose?*
> *With salvation's walls surrounded,*
> *Thou may'st smile at all thy foes!*

Rimmer met de Wilde, Beatty, and Renouf on the way out.

"Splendid old hymn, that one," boomed Renouf. "I'm so glad you
chose it."

"Next time we'll sing the Anvil Chorus," Rimmer said.

"I particularly like the last verse," Renouf remarked. " 'Fading is
the worldling's pleasure, All his boasted pomp and show.' Grand
stuff."

"I'm sure the guests of honour enjoyed it too," Rimmer said.

"General, I'd like you to know that we take no pleasure in occasions
like this," de Wilde said. He glared at Renouf, who looked back in
wide-eyed wonder.

Rimmer watched the burial party march out to the beat of a single
drum. "Oh well," he said, "we must take death as it comes, just as
we take life as it comes. I am a professional optimist. One must hope
for the best. Otherwise nothing useful would ever be accomplished."

"Does that explain your country's actions on September the third, 1939?" Renouf asked.

"Why, what did we do?"

"You invaded Poland."

Beatty said, "Canon, there is a time and a place—"

"Oh no we didn't," Rimmer interrupted.

"History differs," Renouf said stiffly.

"History is wrong. The invasion of Poland was ordered for Oh-four-thirty hours on August the twenty-sixth 1939. Those orders were cancelled at the last minute—too late to stop all our forward assault units. Part of the Forty-Sixth Infantry Division attacked without support and got shot to bits. So you see we invaded Poland a good seven days before the so-called invasion of Poland. I know; I was there. And the Poles knew too, because they were there."

"By all reports," Renouf boomed, "great numbers of them are not there any more."

"The partisans were troublesome," Rimmer said. "We removed them. If necessary we'll do the same thing here."

"You Germans do seem to spend an awful lot of your time in Poland," Renouf said. "Is it such an attractive place?"

"Hideous. Frightful."

"Then if I were you I'd leave," Renouf said; and left.

Rimmer turned to the Bailiff. "Have you found your saboteurs yet?" he asked.

"Nothing has changed since yesterday."

"Then the gravediggers will soon be busy again."

The three men stood for a moment in the steady drizzle.

"Just as a matter of interest," Beatty said, "why didn't Poland kick up a fuss when you attacked on August twenty-sixth?"

"Oh, the Poles weren't at all worried," Rimmer told him. "They actually thought they were going to win." He raised a finger to summon his car. "They had great faith in their cavalry, I believe."

Nancy Buchanan had only one dress: a sleeveless frock of cornflower blue made out of some old linen curtains, which she saved for special occasions. She was wearing it at breakfast when Kramer came down. In half an hour, so she promised herself, she would find a quiet corner in the conservatory and open the letter which Martin had given her just before he left. Martin wrote good letters; they made her laugh at the start and lust in the middle and smile at the end. Well worth waiting for. Well worth the blue dress. Nancy smiled in anticipation.

"Hi," Kramer said. He had woken up convinced that he could live without her, that she wasn't worth it; but as soon as he saw that smile he began to have doubts. Okay, so she fooled around, she broke the rules. All the same she was a young goddess. They didn't make rules for people like Nancy Buchanan. She was one of a kind, exceptional. He looked hungrily at her face, at her smile. How could you go to war with someone like that?

"I hope you like porridge," she said. "Because that's all there is."

"Tell you what," said Kramer, deadpan, "I'll settle for some porridge. But if you want to know the truth what I'd really like is porridge. On the other hand, a plate of porridge would sure hit the spot."

"Well," she said, "that's just as well, isn't it?" She ladled some out.

"Don't rush me." He took the bowl. "Listen, you couldn't rustle up a mess of porridge, could you?"

She actually laughed at that. Kramer felt a thrill of pride, but he kept his deadpan expression. Experience was a great teacher.

"Put some of this on it," she said.

He sniffed the black, treacly substance. "Uncle Dudley struck oil at last, huh?"

"It's sugar-beet syrup. We make it ourselves. It takes hours and hours and hours just stewing the sugar beet and making sure it doesn't burn or boil over. Martin helped me make this lot; he's an expert."

"Yeah, sure." Kramer spooned some on his porridge. "I bet Martin's got the golden touch, all right."

"He can be so funny," she said.

"Uh-huh." The stuff didn't taste bad; like burnt molasses. Kramer took more.

"Would you like to know what he said about you?"

Kramer gave her a steely glance, and spilt syrup on his thumb. "Wait while I get my lawyer on the phone," he said.

"He said you were very unusual. He said you had the brains of a great hand-surgeon."

Kramer licked his thumb. "I don't get it," he said.

Nancy tried to keep a straight face, and failed. "I'm sorry, it just makes me laugh," she said, and laughed freely. "I'm not sure what it means either, but it's funny, so it must be true."

"Listen, I could tell you a thing or two about *him*," Kramer growled.

"Really? What?"

He looked at her. It was raining outside and yet she was sunny. Part of him hungered for a showdown, and another part enjoyed the sunshine too much. "The guy's not perfect," he said. "I mean, he's no goddam angel, is he?"

"I suppose not. But to me he's perfect."

"Maybe you haven't had a chance to compare."

"Why? Because all our young men went off to England in 1940?" She shrugged. "But I've met lots of other young Germans, good-looking ones too, and Martin's worth all of them put together."

"You didn't tell me he was a German." Kramer felt angry, cheated of his showdown.

"What difference does it make?" She wasn't even scornful.

"That's the craziest question I ever heard in my life," he said.

"You don't really know him. If you lived here for a year, you'd know what a marvellous person—"

Kramer shoved his porridge aside and pounded his fists on the table. "Why in everlasting hell do we have to go on talking about him?" he cried. "Why don't we talk about *us*, for Pete's sake?"

"Us?"

"Sure, us, you and me, we two. *Us.*" Kramer ground out the words, bitterly, savagely. "Okay, so this dumb kraut has hot pants for you. So what? Does that make him Jesus H. Christ? What about me? I may not be Flash Gordon, but for crying out loud I am at least a goddam American! We're supposed to be on the same side, you and me! Is it asking too much for you to give me the lousy time of day, once in a while?"

The outburst left him red-faced and trembling. Nancy was both startled and puzzled.

"D'you mean . . . I don't quite understand. D'you mean you want to . . . to take Martin's place while he's away?"

"For Christ's sake, I'm not gonna play second fiddle to any crummy Nazi! Jesus, Nancy, I love you, I loved you ever since I saw you standing out there on that dumb road, waving your crazy Red Cross bag! I love you more than I ever loved anyone! Now you just gotta love me back, honey. That's all there is to it." He was pleading for his life with the desperate, cockeyed logic of the infatuated. "If I love you, you *gotta* love me. Can't you see?"

Nancy sat and stared, searching for a way to tell the patient that his sickness was incurable.

Uncle Dudley pottered in. "Nice drop of rain," he said. "Just what my lupins need."

"Yeah," Kramer growled. "Sure."

"I expect the farmers will be glad of it, too."

"Happy as clams," Kramer muttered. "Laughing their little socks off."

"Jolly bad luck on Hampshire, though, if it's like this over there. They thought they had Middlesex on the ropes."

"Screwed again," Kramer said. "Some days you just can't depend on anything."

The telephone rang, in the hall. "That'll be the hospital, for me," Nancy said. She hurried out, glad of the excuse.

Kramer sat hunched in misery. He made shapes in his porridge and watched them fade and disappear. *How can she be like that?* He spooned up some syrup and ate it. *Cruddy kraut crap.*

Uncle Dudley finished inspecting some potted geraniums on the windowsill and blew his nose. From the corner of his eye he saw Kramer. "Hullo," he said. "I'm Nancy's Uncle Dudley. You must be Michael."

"No, I'm Joe Louis," Kramer said. "George Washington couldn't come. He's playing tennis with Betty Grable."

The old man nodded amiably. "Well, I expect you're more interested in cricket anyway," he said.

"Shoulda seen me at the World Championships," Kramer said morosely. "I killed three umpires and a hot-dog man."

Uncle Dudley looked at him uncertainly. Nancy came in and sat down. Kramer refused to look at her and Uncle Dudley's mind was elsewhere.

"Hey, they tell me you fought in the last war," Kramer said. "That right?"

"Shut up," Nancy whispered.

"Oh, I did my bit, you know," Uncle Dudley said. "Shocking weather most of the time. Worse than this."

"You know all about the goddam krauts, then. The only good Hun is a dead Hun. Right?"

Nancy made a sound that was heavier than a groan, more painful than a sob. She held her hands pressed in her lap and bent her head until the hair almost hid her face. She was weeping uncontrollably. "My dear!" Uncle Dudley said. "My poor dear girl, what's . . . what's . . ."

Nancy raised her head. Her teeth were bared and her eyes were anguished. She was straining for breath. "It's Martin," she gasped. "Martin. . . ."

"Oh Christ, no," Kramer said. He was stunned, shocked, appalled. He felt like a murderer.

"Who?" Uncle Dudley asked.

"The kraut," Kramer told him harshly. Uncle Dudley blinked foolishly, still not understanding. "The kraut, the Jerry, the guy who brought the jam and biscuits!" Kramer cried.

Nancy turned and hit him in the face, hard, with her fist, and split his lip. Kramer nearly fell off his chair.

"I say, look here, steady on!" Uncle Dudley exclaimed.

By the time Kramer got to his feet, Nancy had gone from the room. Moments later they saw her running down the drive. "Goodness gracious me," Uncle Dudley said. Kramer said nothing. Just at that moment he would have done anything, said anything, given anything, to bring Martin back to life.

"No news," de Wilde said when Labuschagne came in.

The banker took off his coat and hat and hung them on the back of a chair. The linoleum was wet with criss-crossing footprints. Beatty stared out of a window, the Bailiff sat at a table and looked at a telephone, and the whole place smelled of damp and despair. Labuschagne sensed the exhaustion of defeat and busily rubbed his hands together: anything to break this gloom. "We've still got, what, three hours?"

Nobody answered. Labuschagne glanced across at Beatty and saw that the flesh around his eyes was strained and haggard, as if he had spent too long searching for something in a bad light. "You've heard about the boat, I suppose," he said gently. Beatty blinked once. "Poor Greg," Labuschagne whispered. "What atrocious luck."

"I don't suppose it's done General Rimmer's temper any good," said de Wilde.

"I shouldn't have asked that lad to go," Beatty muttered. "He wouldn't have gone if I hadn't asked him."

"That won't wash," Labuschagne declared firmly. "You really cannot blame yourself for a thing like this."

"He didn't want to go on leave. He was happy here."

The Bailiff shook his head. "I can't understand what they think they're up to. They couldn't possibly mistake her for a warship. I mean, do they want to starve us all, or what?"

"Bloody RAF," Beatty growled. "Bunch of cowboys."

"Well, it's done and it can't be undone." Labuschagne walked briskly around the room. "Now, assuming we do find this American airman in time, what happens then?"

"We hand him over to Rimmer, of course," de Wilde said.

"They may shoot him."

"That's true."

"Use your brains, Dick," Beatty said angrily. "They're going to shoot someone, whatever happens."

"I appreciate that. But if we hand over an Allied airman, it could be interpreted as collaboration. Perhaps even treason."

De Wilde looked up. "What do you suggest we do?"

Labuschagne thought it over. "All right. . . . Now supposing we don't find him. This business of selecting the hostages. It's a horrible thing, but should we leave it all to the Germans? Perhaps if we were to provide the lists we could at least save the children."

"No." The Bailiff stood up. His eyes were filmed with red and his hands trembled, but his voice was firm. "We cannot condone or assist any illegal action. We must insist on the rule of law. It's all we have. I have refused to provide lists from which hostages can be chosen because it is utterly and totally wrong. We must protest and protest and protest."

"Yes, of course you're right," Labuschagne murmured.

Beatty cleared his throat. "I don't want to sound melodramatic," he said, "but is there any merit in offering ourselves as hostages on behalf of the rest of the island? Speaking for myself . . . I'm quite ready to go . . . if it'll do any good."

They looked at de Wilde and were surprised by the desperation in his eyes and his voice. "By God, so am I, Henry," he said. "I'm more than ready to go; damn it all, I can't resign, so what else is there? But the truth is it wouldn't do any blasted good. They'd shoot us first and then work their way through their hostages and the island would end up with no bloody protection at all."

Beatty turned back to the window. "We could do with a miracle," he said.

At nine-fifteen Count Limner surprised General Rimmer by arriving at his quarters and requesting a meeting.

"My dear Count," Rimmer said. "Come in, come in. Will you have coffee? I feel as if we have only just said good-bye. Has something happened?"

"Yes and no. There's a matter I'd like to discuss which couldn't be mentioned in all that crowd by the cemetery."

"Of course. Security, and so on. I quite understand."

Limner hesitated. "Perhaps 'confidentiality' is a better word. First, may I ask: do you intend to go ahead with the execution of civilian hostages?"

"Yes, of course. Unless the Bailiff can produce his local murderers I have no alternative. You saw the results for yourself, this morning."

"Yes . . . I want to be absolutely clear about this, General. You intend to select civilians at random and have them shot. Is that correct?"

Rimmer leaned back and thought. "No, I wouldn't have thought so. I'm selecting every tenth name, in alphabetical order, and that's hardly a random choice. Incidentally, the Bailiff has refused to supply a nominal roll, so my men are compiling one now."

"Nevertheless, what you intend to do amounts to the indiscriminate killing of innocent civilians. Is *that* correct?"

Rimmer shook his head. "Far from it. All the indiscriminate killing has been done by these saboteurs. I, on the other hand, am discriminating very carefully. Only women and children will be shot. No essential workers. The smooth running of the island will continue."

"I see. One final question: is this killing an act of reprisal?"

"I expect it to be an act of persuasion."

Limner took a sheet of paper from his pocket and placed it on the desk. "That is my official protest, as Civil Administrator. You'll see that I quote the terms of the Hague Convention and paragraph eight of the Agreement by which we occupied these islands in 1940. 'In case of peaceful surrender, the lives, property, and liberty of peaceful inhabitants are solemnly guaranteed.' "

Rimmer did not look at the letter. "Peaceful inhabitants?" he scoffed. "They're worse than the Poles. At least the Poles didn't have the gall to recite the Hague Convention whenever they garrotted a sentry."

"If you go ahead with the executions," Limner insisted, "you will renege on promises made by a German officer, and you will bring grave dishonour to the German people."

"Fine," Rimmer said. "Is that what you came to tell me?"

"No, that's just the beginning. Unless you agree to cancel the executions I shall telephone your superior officer at once and tell him what is planned."

"Rommel?" cried Rimmer. "He's got half of Europe to defend! D'you think he cares how many civilians I shoot? He'll tell you to go and soak your head."

"No, not Rommel," Limner said. "Rommel's commander: Field Marshal von Rundstedt. In Paris."

"And you'll get even less thanks from him. He'll refer it to Rommel, and Rommel will—"

"No, he won't."

Rimmer stared. Limner was actually angry. He was hiding it well but it showed in his voice.

"There are two reasons why von Rundstedt will take action," Limner said. "One is that he and I happen to be cousins." Rimmer snorted. "Very distant cousins, but enough to make him listen. The other reason is that I shall tell him that you have been copulating with my wife."

During those last few words Rimmer had felt it coming and he managed to keep his face under control. "My dear Count," he said patiently, "you really must not pay attention to garrison gossip."

"This isn't gossip. Maria herself told me all about it. If necessary, she'll tell von Rundstedt, too. If I may say so, you don't emerge from the affair with honour. It sounds casual, carnal, and squalid. I don't know how well you are acquainted with von Rundstedt, but he is an old-fashioned soldier. Honour still means a great deal to him. He'll sack you in five minutes."

"And the Fuehrer will reinstate me in ten. He *is* the C-in-C of the Army, remember?"

Limner relaxed and gave a crooked smile. "You don't deny it, then?"

"No, no." Rimmer felt a curious mixture of pride and guilt: the guilt was not towards Limner but towards von Rundstedt who, he knew, would do just as Limner had said. "Did you expect me to?"

"Not really, but . . . Well, women have been known to say and do some strange things. . . . Well then: may I use your telephone?"

"Why? You'll merely create a completely unnecessary scandal, and I shall still be here."

"If that happens I shall kill you."

For once Rimmer was alarmed: the man meant it. "Good heavens, Count. You really do value your wife's honour."

"Not at all," Limner said. "I don't value her honour in the slightest. But I value my own very highly. Now: may I use your telephone?"

Rimmer opened his mouth but he had no words to speak. He was trapped. Whatever he said would condemn or betray him. Panic, amazement, and anger competed within him: surely this situation was impossible; he was the Fortress Commandant, wasn't he? He must speak, yet he was deeply afraid of what he might say; he was teetering on the brink of disaster. Before he could say anything the telephone rang. He picked it up. "Rimmer," he said.

"Captain Paulus, sir. I'm at the airfield, and I thought you'd like to know that Field Marshal Rommel has just landed."

"For God's sake!" Rimmer cried. "What's he doing here? Why didn't anyone tell me he was coming?"

"Apparently he wanted it to be a surprise," Paulus said.

38

Kramer's lip bled both inside and out, and would not stop bleeding. Nancy Buchanan had punched it against his teeth and the teeth had made the cuts. He cupped cold water in his hands and sloshed it over his mouth. The damaged lip stung furiously and blood dribbled down his fingers. One of his teeth ached. He sucked his lip and swallowed. It tasted salty. Kramer decided it was time to get the hell out of this house of pain.

Halfway down the stairs he met Uncle Dudley coming up. "Hi," he muttered, but the old man held him by the arm.

"Nancy seems a little out of sorts this morning," he said. "I wonder, would you mind awfully just picking up my copy of *The Times* at the tobacconist's?" He wasn't going to let go of that arm.

"She got it already," Kramer said. "I know where it is."

He turned and ran upstairs. *House was full of maniacs.* He flung open the chest and scrabbled through the folded newspapers, found a June copy and ran out.

Uncle Dudley was polishing his glasses. Kramer thrust the newspaper into his arms and kept on running. "I say!" Uncle Dudley called. Kramer opened the front door and looked back. "Thanks most awfully," Uncle Dudley said. "Have a good time, won't you?" He hugged the newspaper as if it were a teddy bear.

The rain had slackened, and the wind was tugging the grey sky into trailing, ragged clouds. Kramer headed for the truck, stopped, hesitated, changed his mind. Maybe she was waiting out there, lying in the driveway perhaps, helpless with grief, washed by the chill rain, sprawled in the pitiless mud, desperate for aid. Maybe she twisted her ankle. Or maybe she ran off to grab the first German patrol she saw. God alone knew what the hell was happening on this crazy island.

He went down the driveway in long, stealthy strides, eyes flickering from side to side. Nobody jumped out at him. He reached the end and prowled around the corner and walked into a German sentry.

"Nicht so schnell!" the man said. He held Kramer by the arm.

"Sweet Jesus," Kramer whispered. Now he was in trouble. They'd stick him up against that wall.

"Was meinen Sie zu tun?" the sentry asked.

"Suss-suss-suss . . ." Kramer stammered. He was trying to say "surrender" but his mouth wouldn't work properly.

"Sie können ja nicht durch hier gehen," the sentry told him. *"Papiere zeigen."* He put out his hand.

Kramer gaped. This was the end. The cold breeze made him shudder, his swollen lip felt as big as a car tire, and his shoulders were trembling with fright.

The soldier smiled, and Kramer saw a pitying look in his eyes. The man thought he was feebleminded. Kramer gaped even more. He let his head slump to one side and he concentrated on drooling. He tried to make his eyes go blank, and he did a little gibbering. "Ga-ga-ga-ga," he said. His mouth overflowed and he drooled spectacularly.

"Na ja, ein Dummkopf," the sentry said. He led Kramer back to the drive and gave him a gentle push.

The howl of a siren came drifting down the road. The sentry hurried back to his position and snapped to attention. Kramer, still drooling, peered around the corner and saw a magnificent open-topped Mercedes-Benz, flanked by motorcyclists, cruising towards him. As it swept past he gaped at the tanned, lean, alert face of the man in the back.

There was no mistaking that face. He'd seen it too often in newspapers, magazines, newsreels. It had to be the Desert Fox, the hero of the Afrika Korps, the hottest German general of the whole damn war. It had to be Rommel.

Kramer stood for a long moment, while the siren swooped and faded and the sentry marched off, his boots clacking unhurriedly on the road. He sucked at his saliva and spat it out. So that was Rommel.

How close had he been, at the closest? Twenty feet? Fifteen? Close enough for someone to toss a grenade and so change the whole entire course of this war, anyway. What would Eisenhower have given for that chance? How many divisions? How many squadrons of B-24s? Take out Rommel and you take out their Montgomery, their Patton and their de Gaulle all rolled into one. What a chance missed. . . .

Kramer turned and walked back towards the house. He wondered what Rommel was doing on Jersey, and immediately answered his own stupid question: it was for the invasion, obviously; he'd come to check up on the defences; what else? So would he stay long? Long enough for someone to get real close and kill him? Kramer let the fantasy grow in his mind: the open-top Mercedes magnifying steadily as it approached . . . a clean, firm swing of the arm sending the sputtering dynamite curling through the air . . . perfect, onrushing inevitability as the target met its destiny in a shattering flash. . . .

Yeah, well, it was a nice dream. He abandoned the fantasy as he came in sight of the truck. Imagine driving around the island in this back-firing old heap, asking every Jerry sentry where Field Marshal Rommel was. Even if he found him again, there would be a security screen three blocks' deep all around. Forget it, Kramer. Go find another place to park your butt, before sweet Nancy comes roaring back with a pickaxe handle to part your hair.

He swung up into the cab. There wasn't a whole lot of choice about where to go next. It had to be Canon Renouf's place or nowhere.

General Rimmer's staff finally located Colonel Schumacher. After looking all over the island they traced him to the military hospital, and had him brought to the telephone.

"Get here immediately," Rimmer ordered. "Rommel's arrived."

"What? Field Marshal Rommel?"

"Who d'you think? Rommel the Fishmonger? Get here, now. What the devil are you doing in that nursing-home, anyway?"

"It's my rash, General. They're doing tests. I'm allergic to my uniform and the rash—"

"Listen, Schumacher, get inside that uniform and rush your rash over here *at once.*"

"But it's bleeding, sir."

"So's my heart!" Rimmer crashed the phone down. "Where's Rommel now?" he demanded.

"Last report," Wolff said, "placed his car on the road into St. Helier, and going well."

"Five minutes away. . . . All right, what can we lay on for him? Mock-invasion exercise? Firepower demonstration? Tactical mobility? Come on, we've got to do *something*."

"I'm still trying to get the regimental commanders together, sir," Wolff said.

Rimmer clenched his teeth, pumping his jaw-muscles. "Tell them to lay on some action," he ordered. "Plenty of noise and smoke and people charging about, you know the kind of war Rommel likes—bags of dash and gusto and counter-attacking from the flank. Coloured flares! Motorcyclists! Bazookas! Show him we're on our toes!"

"Yes, sir. Whereabouts d'you want this action?"

Rimmer grabbed his hat and gloves. "How the hell should I know? Wherever we end up. They'll just have to keep chasing us." He kicked a chair out of the way. "Action, Wolff! Rommel hasn't come here to pick the flowers!" Rimmer bounded out of the room, leading with his powerful jaw.

By the time she reached St. Peter's church, Nancy had cried herself out. She was wet and weary and everything she saw was a total waste of time. The world was an elaborate, pointless, stupid, ugly joke. She saw people working, going from here to there, talking, and she hated them for their dull stupidity. How could anyone go on as if anything mattered? To carry on behaving normally was a kind of madness. It made her feel sick.

The church was empty. She sat on the floor, and then lay back. The tiles were hard and cold, which was right. The world should be flat and dead, because its life had been killed. The telephone bell had killed the life of the world with one clear, cold ring. You picked up the telephone and Martin was dead and that was that. It was so easy, that was the wrongness of it. Martin had so much life that death shouldn't be so easy. *Oh God*, she prayed, arms outstretched, staring up at the faded gilding on the hammerbeams, *take me now, please take me now*!

Canon Renouf came out of the organ loft and saw her lying there. He waited and watched for a moment, then came down and walked over.

"It's Nancy Buchanan, isn't it?" he said. She didn't speak, didn't move. He sat in a pew and put his feet up. "I've just been up in the

organ loft. The Bailiff told me we had dry rot. Absolute nonsense, you
know. Extraordinary ideas some people have."

She clenched her fists until the veins and sinews stood out from
wrist to armpit.

"I did find the odd bat," he said. "How do you feel about bats?
Some people can't stand them, I don't know why, they couldn't be
more harmless. I mean to say, bats have as much right to live in that
loft as I have."

"I don't want to live," Nancy said.

"Isn't that strange? I've been getting that feeling regularly lately,"
Renouf said. "I put it down to all these tedious turnips, but I may be
wrong. Tell me what's happened, Nancy."

Ten minutes later, Nancy still lay stretched out on the cold floor,
but her fists had unclenched and one leg was slightly bent.

"I'm sure I remember seeing him," said Canon Renouf. "A most
attractive lad. Not handsome but attractive. And easy to know, by the
look of him. No false barriers. I often thought I should stop and have
a chat, and now you say it's too late. The chance has gone for ever.
That's very hard to believe, isn't it?"

"I don't believe it," Nancy said. "Martin's not dead. He'll come
back. It's all a stupid mistake."

"I know exactly what you mean, and the terrible thing is you're
partway right, Nancy. When my father died I kept seeing him come
around the corner. Or sometimes he was standing on the other side
of the road. That went on for . . . oh . . . weeks afterwards. It was
always somebody else, of course."

"Somebody else?" Nancy said wearily. "There isn't somebody else.
Can't be. There's nobody on earth like Martin. Nobody."

Renouf looked up as a sparrow flew in through the open door and
perched on a hanging lamp. "You are forbidden to misbehave in
here," he warned the bird sternly. Nancy moved her head to look at
it, and Renouf saw the faraway, deluded look in her golden eyes. "I'm
afraid it's true that there is nobody on earth like Martin," he said,
"because there were no survivors from that ship. None at all."

She began to cry again and he did not stop her. The sparrow took
fright and hid itself in the roof, where Nancy's sobs echoed and
confused each other.

"I wish I could explain what has happened," Renouf said. "Death
is a terrible mystery, isn't it? At times it seems almost impossible. Like

miracles." He took a handful of cassock and polished his shoes. "I mean, I have great difficulty trying to explain miracles, and I've known a few. Very few, fortunately. Life would be intolerable if God kept interfering."

"What God?" she said, sniffing. "There's nobody up there."

"Well, I'm certainly not going to attempt to prove it," Renouf replied evenly.

Nancy gently hammered her heels on the tiles. "And if there is anybody up there, he's a stupid fool," she said.

"What baffles me, at times, is exactly what He thinks He's doing," Renouf remarked. "No sooner did the Russians get the Germans on the run, after Stalingrad, than von Manstein turned round and recaptured Kharkov. Not for long, I know, but it seemed such a terrible waste. Puzzling, isn't it? You'd think that once He'd got it going right He'd just keep it going right."

"I don't care about any of it," she said. "They can all kill each other now. I don't care if we all die."

Renouf turned and looked at her. "If you're planning not to continue living I may be able to help you," he said. For the first time she looked directly at him. "I've had a lot of experience of various ways of dying," he went on. "It goes with the job, you know. I can see that you're wet, and shivering, and tired, and fed up, and if you go on lying on that cold floor, eventually you may well get pneumonia."

"Good," she muttered.

"Or you may not. You might not get so much as a cold in the head. Even pneumonia isn't guaranteed fatal. I've known dozens of people who recovered; scores, in fact."

Nancy hunched her shoulders. "Who cares?" she said feebly.

"Well, I do, for one. If you're going to stay down there until you catch pneumonia you'll be in severe danger of getting trampled to death by my congregation next Sunday, and then I shall have to clean up the mess, so that's not on." Renouf put his hands under her shoulders and helped her up. She sat in a pew and rubbed her bare arms. Renouf took off his cassock and wrapped it around her. "You wouldn't enjoy being trampled to death," he said. "It's horribly noisy."

The kettle hissed softly.

"I was saving this stuff for the invasion," Canon Renouf said. "Only now I'm not so sure. I mean to say: celebrating one's liberation from fascist tyranny by making a pot of tea seems rather insufferably British. Even if it is real tea." He weighed the packet in his hand. "What d'you think?"

"Don't know," Nancy said. They were in the vicarage kitchen; the fire was blazing; she was wearing an old pair of ski-ing trousers and a cricket sweater with the sleeves doubled back to the elbows. "It's your tea," she said.

"Yes . . . I have this foolish desire to get my picture all over the front page of the *Daily Express,* offering a real cup of tea to General Montgomery."

"He might not come," she said. "It might be that other chap."

"Who? Eisenhower?" Renouf looked at her with concern. "I say, d'you really think so?" He squeezed the packet. "That could be very tricky. You know what Americans are like: it's all coffee and sarsaparilla and stuff. Eisenhower may not even *drink* tea. Even if he does, he probably can't appreciate a really good leaf. . . . I've had this since 1940. It's Orange Pekoe." He showed her the label.

"You could sell that for five pounds," Nancy said. She yawned enormously.

"I'll tell you what: we'll toss for it." Renouf found a shilling in a drawer. "Heads we open it now, tails we save it for the liberation."

The coin came down tails. "I never heard so much rubbish in all my life," Renouf said, tearing the package open. "Smell that!" He waved the tea under her nose.

"You'll be sorry when Montgomery gets here," she told him.

"Never!" He paused with the packet in one hand and a spoon in the other. "D'you know, I've forgotten how to do this. How much should I use?"

"Give it to me," Nancy said.

"Ah! Good idea. I'll get the cups, I'm very good at that. And if Montgomery ever does turn up here demanding tea, I'll send him around to you."

"Yes, do." She picked up the kettle. "You can stop talking, if you want. I'm all right now."

"Thank God!" Renouf said fervently.

Earl Kramer turned the key. No luck. He dragged out the choke and tried again. The starter answered, rustily, and soon lost interest. He stamped on the accelerator a couple of times and turned the key again. The starter churned away with a kind of sullen monotony. It was clearly losing strength.

He found the starting handle and got down. He stabbed around in the bottom of the radiator until the handle seemed to slot into something, and he gave it a strong, two-handed turn.

It was like shifting Grant's Tomb.

After five minutes Kramer had blistered palms and the engine hadn't so much as coughed. "Jesus wept," he said. He flung up the hood and looked inside. Everything was a filthy black, caked and coated with grease and grime. Rain pattered against his back. He thought, briefly, of abandoning the truck and walking to the vicarage, but an obstinate, American-bred addiction prevailed: he wanted the power, he wanted the freedom to be able to go places. The goddam truck *must* start.

Uncle Dudley had found a comfortable corner of the conservatory from which to watch this stranger monkeying around with a lorry.

Nothing as exciting as this had happened within sight of the house for years. Uncle Dudley got the opera glasses properly focused and studied Kramer with interest, especially his hair, which was unusually red; although there was a chap visiting Nancy only yesterday whose hair was almost as red. What was his name? Michael. Or Malcolm, perhaps. No, on the whole, Uncle Dudley thought it more likely to have been Michael.

He watched Kramer take out the plug terminals and the insulators. He watched him dry the insulator cap. At one point it occurred to Uncle Dudley to go out and ask him if he'd like a cup of tea, but then he noticed that it was raining, and by the time the rain had eased he had forgotten all about it. Meanwhile he watched Kramer make several attempts to crank the engine. None of this monkeying about seemed to do the slightest bit of good.

Eventually Kramer gave one of the wheels an almighty kick, which seemed promising, but then he just stood in the drizzle with his hands on his hips. Uncle Dudley got bored.

He put down the opera glasses and discovered *The Times* in his lap. He had forgotten to look at the cricket scores. Goodness gracious, Warwickshire versus Leicestershire, first day; how on earth could he forget that? He fumbled eagerly until he found the sports pages. Racing at Ascot.

That couldn't be right.

He searched all over the sports pages. No cricket, except for a couple of school matches. Not a hint of cricket.

Something was very wrong, and obviously it must be put right; you couldn't let people mess about with the county cricket championship like this. Uncle Dudley frowned and took a good grip of *The Times* and concentrated what was left of his mind on getting to the bottom of it all.

The goddam battery was flat.

Everything in the engine that might conceivably have got damp had been dried. The tank was half-full, so that wasn't the problem. If the plugs had been dirty they were hospital-clean now. On the other hand, Kramer had to admit he'd been working that starter-motor pretty hard, and so there couldn't be a whole lot of juice left in the battery. What a bastard!

He climbed down from the cab. The rain had almost stopped, and muddy rivulets were running down the driveway. Kramer stooped to take a closer look. No doubt about it. The driveway was on a slight slope.

That was terrific news, except the truck was parked at the top of the turning circle, *across* the slope. Kramer released the hand-brake and got his shoulder up against the tail and heaved. His boots sprayed gravel and the truck went nowhere. He found a shovel and jammed the blade under one of the rear wheels and tried to lever it forward. The blade bent. A blackbird on a fence cocked its tail and laid a splashy white dropping. He threw the shovel at it and missed by a length and a half.

Kramer glared at the dripping truck. If he could only move it six feet, it would roll for a hundred yards. There had to be a way! The damn thing was made to go. That's why they put a wheel in each corner.

Something about the wheels interested him. They were heavy and old-fashioned, with stubby spokes angling out from the hub. Now if he could only hitch something on there and *twist.* . . .

Kramer searched all around the house and inside a garden shed, hoping to find some kind of lever. Nothing. He looked in the back of the truck. Nothing. He looked under the seats in the cab and found a crowbar.

The splayed end hooked over one of the spokes on the rear left wheel and the bar pressed against the globular boss which stuck out of the hub. Kramer wrapped both hands around the free end and heaved. The wheel turned. It turned nine inches. Kramer felt triumph send strength surging back to his muscles, and he shifted the crowbar to a new spoke and heaved again. This time he gained a foot.

He'd shifted the truck about four feet when it began creeping forward on its own momentum. Kramer dropped the crowbar, ran to the cab, and jerked up the hand-brake. He sucked his filthy blisters while he got his breath back. Then he climbed inside and let her roll.

Uncle Dudley had finally spotted the trouble—they'd given Nancy the wrong copy of *The Times*. This was last week's paper. He went toddling out in his carpet slippers to ask the redheaded young man if he'd mind awfully just looking in at the tobacconist's and getting them to change it, when the lorry began to roll away.

Uncle Dudley shouted and ran, but he was too weak and too slow. The lorry gained speed down the driveway and left him standing with one foot in a puddle. He saw it jolt as Kramer pulled his foot off the clutch, heard it cough and bang as the engine fired, and watched it roar triumphantly away, manufacturing rich black smoke.

Uncle Dudley felt deeply disappointed. He looked at his wretched, misconceived newspaper and for the first time he saw the headlines. RAPID FLOW OF TROOPS THROUGH DUNKIRK. There was a photograph of dunes and smoke. He turned the page. 1,000 BOMBS DROPPED IN FIRST PARIS AIR RAID. But this was appalling. Why hadn't anybody told him about this? Something must be done, at once. Uncle Dudley toddled resolutely down the drive, carrying *The Times* for 1 June 1940.

The sentry saw Uncle Dudley coming long before Uncle Dudley saw the sentry standing there.

He was guarding a stack of crates; he didn't know why; the sergeant simply told him to stand there and guard them, which seemed like a waste of time, as usual, because each crate weighed a bloody ton and anyway who wanted sixteen crates of hose-pipe nozzles? He leaned against them and watched Uncle Dudley approach.

The old man's style of walking amused him. Uncle Dudley kept his knees and elbows turned outwards and moved in a rolling, bow-legged gait which made him lean forward, and the result was a gentle trot.

Uncle Dudley made walking along a flat road look like tottering down a hill.

Uncle Dudley was unaware of the sentry until he got within ten yards of him. "Hullo!" he said.

"*Guten Tag,*" the sentry said amiably.

Uncle Dudley stopped and stared. He went closer, and the uniform, the coal-scuttle helmet, the rifle, the dirty boots, the grinning Hun face, all came frighteningly into focus. *God help us*, he thought, *the blackguards aren't in France, they're here!*

He rushed at the sentry and tried to strike him. The sentry easily fended him off and backed away, telling him to cut it out and behave himself. He was half-laughing, it was all so absurd and unexpected. Uncle Dudley grabbed his rifle and tried to wrestle it away. The sentry twisted the rifle and broke his grip. "Come on now, you'll hurt yourself, you old fool!" he said.

Uncle Dudley stood gasping for breath. His face was patched with purple and a great roaring filled his ears. His brain had quit; blind instinct drove him to lash out with his foot. By sheer bad luck he kicked the sentry in the crotch.

The sentry staggered back, open-mouthed with shock. Blind instinct made him lash out with his rifle. The butt smacked against Uncle Dudley's head, and the old man collapsed as if God had let go of the strings.

39

By 1944 Erwin Rommel had had a long war.

He had fought over much of Europe and most of North Africa, often with startling success. He was one of the few German commanders who had actually done battle with the British and the Americans and therefore he knew what he was talking about.

In the summer of 1940 Rommel led one of the tank attacks which knifed through the Ardennes and struck deep into the heart of France. In the spring of 1941 Hitler sent him to Tripoli, with orders to help the Italians hold Libya and perhaps even do something about Cyrenaica, which the British led by General O'Connor had just captured. Rommel ignored his supposed superiors in the Italian High Command. He attacked with great dash, retook Cyrenaica, advanced five hundred miles in two weeks, captured General O'Connor and much booty, and threatened all of Egypt, the Suez Canal, and the oil-fields of the Middle East.

Then began the see-saw war.

Rommel beat off one counter-attack, struggled against a second— during which he himself went raiding behind enemy lines and nearly got captured—and had to retreat. By Christmas 1941 he was back where he started. A month later he launched a surprise assault and won back two-thirds of his losses. He was so confident of taking Egypt that Mussolini came over to Libya with a white horse on which to enter Cairo. By midsummer Rommel was two hundred miles inside Egypt, and in Cairo the British Ambassador had a special train waiting, with steam up, to evacuate himself and his staff to Palestine.

El Alamein was only sixty miles from Alexandria, but it marked the limit of Rommel's success. He had outrun his supplies and his men were living on what they could capture. El Alamein was a bottleneck, protected by a great sea of soft sand. Rommel battered the defences and failed to break them. In September, desperately sick with dysentery and jaundice, he flew to Germany. In October Montgomery's Eighth Army attacked the Afrika Korps and Rommel had to return. He fought a rearguard campaign all the way across Cyrenaica. By Christmas 1942 he was once again back where he started—and now Allied forces had landed in Tunisia.

Rommel pulled his troops back another thousand miles. South of Tunis he smashed an enormously stronger Allied army, but he couldn't do it twice. In March 1943 he left Africa for good.

When Mussolini was deposed, Rommel took command of northern Italy. Then Hitler appointed him Inspector of Coastal Defences. Rommel made such a scathing report on the state of the Atlantic Wall that Hitler appointed him C-in-C of the "Fighting Area": the eight-hundred-mile coastal strip running from Holland to the Bay of Biscay. Somewhere along that shore the Allies had to invade. Rommel had to stop them. It was a lot to ask, but Rommel had done the impossible before. He had also disobeyed Hitler's orders before, which was something few German generals could say.

Now he led a party of officers over a hill and tramped down a path which wound across a bramble-covered slope. They splashed through puddles where the rain had not yet soaked into the baked ground.

"A far cry from North Africa, sir," Rimmer said. Rommel nodded.

Evidently he didn't want to talk about North Africa. Rimmer cast around for other subjects. "Have you seen the Fuehrer lately, sir?" he asked.

Rommel grunted and nodded.

"How did he seem to you?"

Rommel sucked his teeth, and thought. "Not well," he said at last.

They walked in silence until Schumacher came hurrying forward. He ran awkwardly, with his knees wide apart, as if the ground were icy. "Here is the best place, sir!" he called.

They stopped. "You see that farmhouse, sir," Rimmer said. It was a granite-grey single-storey building, about a hundred yards away. A vine of honeysuckle grew around the door and shook in the wind. The house had a one-room wing with a lot of ivy on it. A streamer of wood smoke fled from the chimney. Half a dozen hens wandered outside a fenced-off vegetable garden. "That's where we're having coffee," Rimmer said.

Schumacher signalled by swinging his arm in an arc. He groaned and clutched his armpit but nobody noticed. The entire farmhouse was beginning to rotate, as smoothly and silently as a swing-bridge.

Rimmer glanced at Rommel, whose eyes were wide. "A total weight of sixty tons, sir," he said, "of which the battery weighs forty-eight."

As the building turned, so it steadily brought into view a gun barrel the size of a small factory-chimney, which was being raised from the horizontal. When the house had completed a quarter-turn it stopped. The barrel continued soundlessly angling upwards and then it, too, stopped.

"Where on earth did you get that?" Rommel asked.

"It's a twelve-inch battleship gun, sir," Rimmer said. "Captured from the French. It throws a half-ton shell up to thirty-seven miles. We've got four like this one."

The gun fired and the earth shook beneath their feet. Thunder rolled over them, a roaring avalanche of noise which crashed into the hillside and rebounded with diminishing fury. The barrel exhaled flame and a gush of black smoke. The hens panicked, and the farmhouse shuddered as it soaked up the recoil.

"Far too good for the French, isn't it, sir?" Rimmer said. "Wagner, not Debussy."

"Do they make good coffee, too?" Rommel asked. Everyone laughed. For a living legend, Rommel was a very decent sort.

Rimmer let Schumacher show the Field Marshal around the underground chambers which serviced the battery: the shell room with its overhead rails leading to the loading chamber, the range-and-control apparatus, central-heating equipment, washrooms, gun-crew accommodation, engine room. Schumacher rapped the walls around the gun itself. "This armour-plating," he said, "was brought from the Maginot Line."

Coffee was served in the messroom. Rimmer spread a map on the table and pointed out the locations of the other batteries: white stars for army, blue stars for navy, green stars for anti-aircraft. The map was thickly starred. "Altogether we have forty-two heavy-calibre guns," he said.

"How many of the heavy flak batteries are eighty-eight millimetre?" Rommel asked.

"Nearly all, sir, I'm happy to say."

Rommel sipped his coffee. Schumacher leaned over and put his finger on the map. "Here, here, and here we're building secondary defensive lines as well, sir," he said. He was sweating more than ever, and his finger left small damp marks.

"Show me," Rommel ordered. He stood up, and smiled at the mess corporal. "Thanks for the sump-oil," he said. "We could have done with a million gallons of that in Bengazi."

The mess corporal was paralysed with pride. It was the greatest moment of his life.

Canon Renouf stood on his doorstep and breathed deeply. "Nothing like a good lungful of fog," he said. "People are very uncharitable about this sort of weather. After all, there's really no such thing as bad weather. Just different kinds of good weather."

"Irish sunshine, that's what this is," Nancy said. She climbed onto his bicycle.

"Irish sunshine, I must remember that," he called. "I can use that." She waved good-bye and wobbled onto the road.

The rain had eased until it was little more than an occasional spatter, and the wind was behind her. She turned onto a bridle-path, a short-cut home. Renouf's tall bicycle gave her a new view over the hedges, a fresh and different view of a landscape which she had thought was old and boring. She felt as she had felt years ago when leaving hospital after having had her tonsils out: tired, bruised, surprised to see the world again, eager, thoughtful, washed-out; having hated the suffering but relieved that the worst was over. Was that callous? she wondered. Martin was dead and she was enjoying the pleasure of riding downhill on a bicycle. Was that selfish? But Martin would have enjoyed it, too, and not enjoying it couldn't bring him back. It was stupid and dishonest to pretend you were miserable when you were not. There would never be another Martin, but that didn't mean it was wrong to ride home on a bicycle.

A few minutes later she turned into the drive and stood on the pedals to get up the slope. Outside the front door were two figures, one sprawling, one kneeling. Nancy recognized a neighbour, a farmer named Marchant. She grabbed the brakes. The bicycle skidded on the wet gravel and stopped broadside-on. She let it fall, and ran.

Marchant raised his arm to check her. "He's hurt, it's bad, be careful," he warned. He showed her the damage: a bloodsoaked dent behind the ear. Around it the grey hairs had dried in dark, spiky clusters like pointed petals. Nancy fingered back an eyelid, but as soon as she let go it drifted shut. She searched for a pulse and found a limping flicker. His face looked as if it had been cast in clay.

"I suppose he fell," she said.

"Not him. He got into a fight with a sentry. I came by just after it happened, nearly didn't recognize him; I thought he went to England with all the rest. It is your uncle, isn't it?"

"Let's get him inside." Now that the first shock was over she was beginning to feel bitterly angry at all this cruelty. Why was she being persecuted? Because she had accepted Martin's death? Or because she had taken his love? Or what?

"The door's locked," Marchant said. "I was just wondering whether to bust it open. . . .Me and the sentry carried him here. From what I can make out he just walked up to the Jerry and took a swing at him. No reason at all."

They put Uncle Dudley on a couch. Nancy telephoned a doctor. While they were waiting, she and Marchant got the old man's clothes off. She found a crumpled copy of *The Times* sticking out of a pocket.

"He must've dropped that," Marchant said. "It was lying in the road so I shoved it in his pocket."

Nancy saw the photograph: smoke rising behind dunes. She looked at the date. "Oh my God," she said, "this is wrong, this is all wrong."

"I honestly don't think it was the Jerry's fault," Marchant said. "He was just standing there."

Count Limner's driver came into the Central Police Station with a message for the Bailiff: the Count would appreciate the courtesy of a few words with him, now, in private. In the street. The driver had brought a large umbrella.

"Why won't he come in here?" Labuschagne asked.

"Ashamed," Beatty said. They were all dull with fatigue yet restless with anger too. The minutes to midday were rushing past but the morning seemed endless. There was nothing to say and silence was unbearable.

De Wilde went out with the driver.

"There's something you ought to know," Limner said. "It's semi-secret, but not for long. Rommel's here."

"Good heavens! Where?"

"Everywhere. He's doing a tour of inspection. I don't need to tell you how disastrous any further outbreak of trouble would be, now more than ever."

"Of course." De Wilde hunched his shoulders and frowned at his own rain-spotted reflection in the limousine. The image was stretched and twisted, which was how he felt. "Could this make any difference to General Rimmer's plans?" he asked.

"I wish I knew."

De Wilde grunted. "You don't sound as if you got much sleep last night either. . . . All right, Count, I'll do what I can to prevent any demonstrations or shouting or whatnot, but more important than that . . . Look, I want to see Rommel."

Limner stared. "What on earth for?"

"I've got to talk to him. I'm sure if he knew what's been going on here—Oh, hell and blast and damnation, I don't know what I want to tell him, Count, but . . . *I must see him.* It's our last chance. Maybe I can . . . I can show him . . . I don't know . . . the military disadvantages of shooting hostages, or something."

Limner shook his head. "That's a pretty desperate gamble. What if he disagrees? Rommel's a hard man. You might do more harm than good."

"I don't care," the Bailiff said. "I'm ready for a desperate gamble."

Suddenly Limner smiled. "Good for you," he said. "This is the time for risk. Dare nothing, win nothing, right? I'll take you to Rommel but we must go quickly. I too have urgent business, you see."

De Wilde hurried indoors to tell the others where he was going, and found Beatty talking excitedly on the telephone. Labuschagne was leaning over him, listening. "Limner's taking me—" de Wilde began, but Beatty waved him down.

"Right, good, fine, don't let him go," he said, and hung up. "Renouf's got Kramer," he announced.

De Wilde stood quite motionless for a moment, stretching his tired mind to take in this new development. "That was Renouf calling?" he asked.

"Yes, yes. He said he'd heard we were looking for the American airman and guess what, the chap's just turned up."

"Well, well, well . . ." De Wilde took a short walk around the room. "So has Rommel, you know. That's right: the Field Marshal. It's been a busy morning, hasn't it? Rommel's going around the island right now and Limner's agreed to take me to him, so perhaps there's still one last small chance for sanity. Especially if I turn up leading young Kramer by the hand."

"You mean you're determined to hand him over?" Labuschagne asked unhappily.

"Yes. But—in uniform." The Bailiff opened a cupboard and took out a brown-paper parcel. "He'll be a captain in the Royal Jersey Militia. This is his surrender suit."

"Ten to one Rimmer has him shot on the spot," Beatty said. He caught de Wilde's eye and looked away. "No, I haven't any better ideas," he muttered.

Limner agreed to drive de Wilde to Canon Renouf's house and tactfully refrained from asking why the Bailiff had suddenly changed his plans; he made it clear, however, that he could not wait at the vicarage. As the car carried him in smooth and quiet luxury through the cold, grey morning, de Wilde found himself wondering whether he really was travelling towards a confrontation with the legendary Field Marshal Rommel; whether he was really strong enough to make such a meeting succeed; and if not, whether he could return and go on living while his friends of a lifetime were being shot all around, at hourly intervals.

"Rommel's coming here makes it look as if invasion is really imminent, doesn't it?" Limner remarked.

"Perhaps." The Bailiff could not think of anything beyond the coming noon.

"Have you ever thought that you might not survive the invasion?" Limner asked. "I'm not trying to sound ghoulish, but a certain number of noncombatants are likely to die in the fighting, and you or I might well be one."

"There are no noncombatants in this war," de Wilde said. "I used to think there were but I was wrong. Have you worked out yet why it is that I have never attempted to stop the Islanders from helping Colonel Schumacher build his fortress?"

"No," Limner said. "And I've often wondered."

"All right, I'll tell you. It's because this is the best way—in fact it's the only way—that we can help the Allies win the war. The more steel and concrete and guns and mines your people bring here, the less they have to be used on the mainland. The more you pay my Islanders to build fortifications *here,* the less you have left to spend on fortifications over *there.* So anybody who wants to help bring down Hitler doesn't need to perform any acts of sabotage; quite the contrary, he just needs to sign on with the Organisation Todt and get paid for doing his bit to plaster Jersey with yet more arms and armour. The best thing we can do for the Allies is work as hard as possible for the Germans."

"All of which assumes," said Limner, "that the island will not in fact be a target for invasion."

"Right."

Limner thought it over, and eventually smiled. "If you turn out to be correct, Bailiff, the last few years will turn out to have been a huge and expensive joke."

De Wilde grunted. "General Rimmer told me he was most impressed with the absence of sabotage here," he said. "What he didn't know was that the whole history of this occupation has been one long act of resistance."

They reached St. Peter's vicarage. Jack Greg's lorry was parked at the side. "I can wait for just a moment," Limner said, "but no more."

"Then you'd better go on. Tell me where I can find Rommel and I'll meet you there."

"He is being shown the defences along the north coast. By now . . ." Limner checked his watch ". . . he should be about midway. That's all I know, and I can't be sure—" He broke off: a man was calling. Canon Renouf came striding from the house, waving something. A book.

"Ah, Count!" he cried. "What luck. Tell me, is it true that this fellow Rommel is here? On the island? One hears so many rumours."

"It is true," Limner said.

"What luck. . . . I expect you'll meet him, won't you? Tell me: is

he in fact your best general? Absolutely top?" Limner shrugged. "I
don't want him unless he's indisputably the best," Renouf explained.
He gave Limner his autograph book. "Unrivalled excellence, that's
my aim. Charles Lindbergh, Albert Einstein, Somerset Maugham.
. . . Could you very kindly ask this fellow Rommel . . ."

The Bailiff took the autograph book from Limner's hands, picked
up his brown-paper parcel, and got out. "I hope to see you soon," he
said. Limner nodded soberly. The car drove off.

"You are doing altogether too much interfering in other people's
affairs, Bailiff," Renouf said angrily. "I advise you to start behaving
in a much less arrogant fashion. Evidently long association with the
Germans has not improved your manners."

"Just take me to Kramer," de Wilde said, speaking slowly and
clearly, "and then go and boil your head."

Renouf, stiff with disapproval, led him into the vicarage.

Earl Kramer was in the sitting-room, sprawled in an armchair
and staring at the faded pattern of the wallpaper. Since he arrived
Renouf had left him alone, and the events of the past few days had
begun to catch up. Brooding upon them, he was overtaken by a deep
and numbing depression, until he felt so wretched that he actually
cried a little. Everything was a waste. Ever since he crawled ashore
and killed that sentry he had been ricocheting about this island,
risking his life, suffering pain, fighting, destroying, hiding, starving,
running. . . . For what? Nothing made any difference and nobody
cared. Nobody helped, except Greg, and now Renouf said Greg was
dead. Drowned.

I should have drowned too, Kramer thought. *What goddam good
am I to anybody here? They don't want to be helped, they want to be
left alone. Nancy couldn't care less if I was dead. If she doesn't want
me, then what the hell is there to live for?*

He felt a sudden pang of nostalgia for the air war. Oh, to escape
from this drab little room and get back up there in the vast, clean blue
with a whole fleet of bombers around and ahead and behind, all
rippling gently up and down as they churned through the air currents
and the prop-wash, all roaring that deep-throated gutsy roar that still
growled in your head three hours after landing. . . . A man could fight
up there. It wasn't all so goddam mixed-up and complicated that you
ended up staring at the wallpaper in case you said the wrong word
and offended someone.

The Bailiff came in and stood for a moment looking down at him.

"You've led us a merry bloody dance, haven't you?" he said harshly. He threw the brown-paper parcel at Kramer. It landed on his chest and made him jump. "Get inside that uniform. You're going to surrender."

Kramer tore open a corner of the parcel and exposed red cloth with tarnished brass buttons. "You think I'm gonna wear this?" he asked weakly.

"I don't give a damn whether you wear it or not! Either way you're going to get in that lorry and drive us both to where I tell you and then surrender yourself to the German Fortress Commandant."

"You think I'm out of my mind?"

"Yes." The Bailiff grabbed him by the shoulder and dragged him to his feet. "Listen: you've succeeded in making the Germans so mad that in one hour from now they're going to start shooting my Islanders." The years of self-control, of reason and legality and patience, abruptly came to an end and exhausted themselves. Rage overwhelmed him: he struck Kramer in the face. Kramer struck back, a blow to the chest. The two men stumbled apart and stood panting and hating. De Wilde turned away with a jerky gesture of impatience. "Come on!" he barked, and strode out.

Kramer stood, the torn parcel dangling from his fingers, and listened to the Bailiff's angry footsteps fading away.

Shooting Islanders. Executing hostages. Reprisals. There was no way anyone could argue about that. So this was the end of the road. What a waste, what a lousy goddam waste! He threw the parcel through the door and followed the Bailiff, kicking the parcel ahead of him.

40

The North Coastal Road ran along the heights which guarded Jersey's north shore. For most of its length it overlooked cliffs of towering granite, and a glance at the sea boiling endlessly against a litter of fallen rock hundreds of feet below was enough to reassure any defender. At one point, however, the cliffs were split so that jutting headlands created the tiny harbour of St. Simon's Bay. This could be reached by a steep lane which came zigzagging down from the Coastal Road.

The cars carrying Field Marshal Rommel and his party snaked

cautiously down this lane and drove onto the quay. Rommel got out
and looked up at the wet and windy heights. Rimmer, Schumacher,
and a dozen staff officers joined him, their greatcoats flapping.

"There's a command bunker hidden underneath the crest, sir,"
Rimmer said, aiming his baton at it. "It's linked with those three
satellite bunkers. What you can't see from here—at least I hope not
—are all the infantry strongpoints and machine-gun posts. They're
camouflaged, of course. We've built about a dozen in this sector."

"Thirteen," Schumacher corrected. "Sir." He was feverishly hot;
the doctors had smeared antiseptic ointment all over his body and
now the ointment was melting. Whenever he moved, his flesh slid
unpleasantly inside his uniform. Yet he might never get another
chance to show off his bunkers to the Field Marshal. If only he didn't
feel so hot and wet. . . .

"Colonel Schumacher actually designed the defences, sir," Rimmer
said.

"And this pattern is typical?" Rommel asked.

"Yes indeed, sir." Rimmer was encouraged by the flicker of amazement which crossed the Field Marshal's face.

"Of course the vulnerable sectors are much more heavily protected," Schumacher added.

Rommel's eyebrows gave a little jump. "I'll take your word for
that," he said. He spoke quietly, the voice of a man who knows that
everyone is listening. "How many men have you here?"

"We're under-strength, sir," Rimmer told him. "The establishment
is one infantry division, but we're down to about twenty-six thousand
including naval and Luftwaffe units."

"Mmm." Rommel saw a pebble and neatly sidefooted it. The officers watched closely as it skittered over the edge of the quay.

"I think we can take care of the enemy, whether he comes by air
or by sea, or both," Rimmer said. Wolff came up and murmured
something to him. "In fact, if you don't mind waiting a couple of
minutes, sir," Rimmer said, "we can lay on an anti-invasion exercise
right here and now. I think you'll be impressed by our firepower."

Rommel nodded, absently. "If I won't, who will?" he said. Some
of the officers chuckled uncertainly, but Rimmer thought he noticed
a certain wryness in Rommel's voice. Which was strange.

Earl Kramer, wearing a scarlet tunic and dark blue trousers, drove
de Wilde up St. Peter's valley and across the flat uplands of the island

to the junction with the North Coastal Road. The windscreen-wipers were old and loose and they flapped across the streaky glass. The cab smelled of hot rubber and overworked oil. Neither man spoke.

As they cruised along the Coastal Road, more and more German military traffic appeared until they found themselves part of a slow-moving stream of trucks and halftracks and self-propelled guns. The Bailiff sat on the edge of his seat and searched anxiously for some clue to Rommel's whereabouts. A patchy sea-mist came and went like a halfhearted conspiracy. The traffic kept inexplicably slowing and stopping, and de Wilde felt his temper shortening to the brink of fury. Kramer changed the gears and stamped on the pedals and worked the steering with all the stoicism of a long-term prisoner.

De Wilde's problem was solved for him when a German checkpoint appeared ahead. It was at a crossroads clogged with traffic, but as soon as a military policeman recognized the Bailiff's identity card he ordered Kramer to pull onto the grass verge and drive past the other vehicles. Standing on the jolting runningboard and blasting scrambling soldiers out of the way with vigorous blasts of his whistle, the policeman directed Kramer to turn down a side road. "St. Simon's Bay," de Wilde shouted. "Is this where Count Limner is?" The policeman nodded and jumped off.

The lane was steep and twisting and lined on both sides with troops, all armed, all hurrying, many carrying radio packs, bazookas, ammunition boxes, mortars. As Kramer eased the truck around a succession of hairpin bends he saw more troops taking up positions on the hillside. "Hey!" he said suddenly. "You think maybe they know something we don't know?"

"What are you talking about?" de Wilde snapped. The road seemed endless.

"Invasion, dummy!" Kramer snapped back. "These bums aren't busting a gut just to watch the tide come in, are they?"

"Invasion? In broad daylight?" The Bailiff snorted scornfully, and massive resentment tied another knot inside Kramer. An unforgiving silence returned. He spun the wheel again, and again the polished tires squealed as they lost and won their grip while, down below, the grey granite quays of St. Simon's harbour swung into view. Suddenly there were no troops to be seen.

"Stop here," de Wilde ordered. Count Limner was waiting beside his car. Kramer used the gears, the foot-brake and the hand-brake and managed to halt the shuddering truck with six feet to spare. The

Bailiff got out and Kramer searched the sea and the sky. Tattered waves, torn clouds, a blurred horizon. No sign of craft or aircraft. The sonofabitch Bailiff was right. Kramer gunned the engine and glared at him.

Limner shared his streaming umbrella. "Rommel is down at the harbour, in that group," he said. "Please wait here while I go and have a word with him." He glanced at the lorry. "You have brought someone with you?"

De Wilde nodded impatiently. "He's either an ace or a joker, I don't know which."

"Oh." Limner gave him a worried stare. "You realize of course that I am putting my head on the block here. If anything goes wrong—"

"Damn it, Count, too much has gone wrong already and God knows how much more disaster is on its way, so let's—"

"Yes, yes, all right, I'm going."

De Wilde went back to the lorry and climbed into the cab. He pointed ahead. "You see all those German officers down there?" he told Kramer. "If everything's all right, you and I are going to drive down and you're going to surrender to them."

Kramer watched the big black car speed away. He put his head out of the window and blinked against the flickering rain. The figures down there had formed a loose semicircle around a man whose cap gleamed with gold. Kramer stretched out an arm, shut one eye and sighted his thumb against the man. The thumb obliterated him and several others. If only it was as easy as that. He dropped his arm and suddenly understood what was happening below. "Hey, that's Rommel!" he cried.

The Bailiff said nothing. Kramer stuck his head out again and looked harder. Fifty yards away and a hundred feet below, the man in the gold-peaked cap pointed to his right, and all the heads turned. Kramer pulled his head in and sucked rain from his upper lip. "Yeah, it's Rommel all right," he said. "What in hell's name is he doing down there?"

"That needn't concern you," de Wilde said coldly. "Your task now is to surrender yourself to their Fortress Commandant and tell him that you, and you alone, were responsible for the recent killings and explosions."

"Thanks a million." Kramer saw Limner's car pulling up near the officers. "Why don't you just shoot me now and go tell him yourself?" Bitterness pressed his words flat and hard.

"By surrendering in uniform you become entitled to the rights of a prisoner-of-war. Therefore—"

"*This* uniform? You think they're gonna believe I came ashore looking like . . . like Prince Valiant?"

"It's worked before, and in any case we have no choice." De Wilde's gaze was fixed on Count Limner, waiting for a signal. "Now shut up."

Kramer leaned back and swallowed. He felt slightly sick. There was nothing to stop him getting out and running, except that he was tired of running and there was no escape from this half-assed island. Even if he got away from their bony, gloomy Bailiff he couldn't escape the chilling fact of enemy reprisals, of islanders facing execution while he ran free. Yet to surrender, to walk up to some lousy kraut and say *I give up*, wearing this crappy old mothballed fancy-dress joke-suit: that thought made him turn away and shut his eyes in despair.

"All right, let's go," de Wilde said sharply. Kramer opened his eyes and saw Limner's blurred shape waving his umbrella from side to side.

"Get out," Kramer ordered.

The Bailiff stared in surprise. "You can't go down there alone. I have to explain—"

"Just get out." Inside Kramer a young and frightened voice was asking, *Have you gone absolutely crazy?* "This has nothing to do with you," he said. "Nothing."

"Oh, hasn't it?" de Wilde scoffed. "On the contrary, it's got—"

"Go on, beat it, leave!" Kramer demanded. He shoved de Wilde's shoulder, and the Bailiff saw that there were tears in the American's eyes.

"My dear chap, you must realize you'll stand a far better chance if—"

"Chance? I got no chance. Now beat it, you dumb old fool, before I break your goddam neck!"

A hot flood of exasperation boiled up inside de Wilde. "Is that all you can ever think of?" he roared. "Killing, killing, killing? For God's sake, drive!"

Kramer looked across at de Wilde's furious, trembling face and knew that he could not bring himself to attack the Bailiff. "Okay then," he muttered. "So stay." He dragged the toolbox from under the seat and balanced it on his knees. The lid creaked open. At least a dozen sticks of dynamite lay inside. De Wilde leaned over to look and Kramer rammed the heel of his hand against the Bailiff's chest as if he were slamming a heavy door. De Wilde was thrown into the corner of the cab with such force that his head clipped the roof. For a few seconds his ears sang to a high-pitched tone and his eyes saw a wavering, hazy world. Then the sharp smell of sulphur made his nose twitch, and he saw that Kramer was striking matches inside the toolbox. He watched him shut the lid and slide the box beneath his seat.

"Now then," Kramer said. His voice was soft and level, his manner almost tranquil. He pointed ahead. "I'm going to barrel this truck down this hill and deliver it personally to Mr. Rommel and friends. The fuses are burning and there's enough stuff underneath me even for a near-miss. See . . . if I've got to go, then I might as well do some good on the way. *Now* will you get out?"

De Wilde couldn't move. "You kill Rommel," he said, appalled, "and they'll kill us all."

Kramer shrugged. "Maybe I'll save a few hundred thousand lives too. . . . Okay, dad. Hang on." He released the hand-brake and tramped the accelerator to the floor. The truck dithered as its rear wheels spun, and then it jumped at the hill. Rommel's party had begun to stroll along the quay. The engine howled and Kramer changed gear just as de Wilde flung himself across the cab, his shoulder thudding into Kramer's side. Kramer was caught off-balance; he lurched against his door and scrabbled at it for support; but this was the broken door and it swung out like a sail. Kramer fell through space, arms windmilling, a flying shambles, and hit the ground hard, rump-first. He rolled helplessly into a shallow ditch and lay sobbing with pain.

The lorry was halfway down the slope when de Wilde got his hands on the wheel, and he knew that it was moving too fast to be stopped. He slammed his palm against the horn button. Its cracked blare seemed to magnify as the quay rushed towards him. He screwed up his face, spun the wheel all the way, and uttered a weak cry of terror as the truck went completely out of control, its nose iceskating, its tail swinging wide. His eyes were clenched shut when it charged up the bank and slammed through a low wall. The impact jolted his arms and threw him forward. He opened his eyes and saw a steep and broken hillside falling to a stretch of beach. The truck sprang at it, bouncing from rock to rock. His foot was stabbing at the brake. The futility of this angered him. He switched his foot to the accelerator and stamped, making the engine bellow. The end hurtled upwards, and de Wilde was aware of only one feeling: relief. Total, final, utter relief.

The blare of the horn, screaming of tires, crunch of metal on stone, made the German officers turn and look up. They saw the lorry above them swerve, skid, and smash through the guard-wall as if it were a pile of children's bricks. They watched it curl over the edge, take the plunging hillside at a rush, and wreck itself savagely on a scattering of lumpy boulders.

"Spectacular," Rommel observed.

Then it blew up.

The blast was like a sudden hot gale, and when he had regained his feet he had to dodge the lighter bits of debris still tumbling from the sky. Somebody dusted off his cap and returned it to him. A great deal of Are-you-all-right-ing was going on all around.

"Well, Rimmer," he said, "now that you have gained our attention, what is it you want to tell us?"

They all laughed, some very loudly, except Rimmer. Rimmer stopped brushing himself down and realized that Rommel was of course quite seriously waiting for an answer. For an explanation. He looked from the Field Marshal to the smoking twisted wreckage and then to the waiting faces of the other officers. He was helpless. He had no answer, except sabotage, and that was far worse than no answer. *Oh God*, he prayed . . . and did not even know what to pray for; when Major Wolff coughed. Rimmer turned to him like a bad actor searching for prompt.

"Our new anti-invasion device, sir," Wolff said. "I should have mentioned beforehand that it was due to be demonstrated."

"Yes, you certainly should," Rimmer said warmly. "Nevertheless . . . the demonstration was . . . impressive."

"Remote-controlled, sir," Wolff told Rommel "Virtually unstoppable. Very nasty."

Rommel looked at him sideways. "Use less baking-powder next time," he said.

"And here comes the rest of the exercise," Rimmer announced with relief as a green flare arched across the sky. They all settled down to enjoy plenty of noise and smoke and people charging about with bags of dash and gusto; while half a mile away Earl Kramer threw his tunic behind a bush and limped inland, ignored in all the confusion of

manoeuvres; and the mutilated body of Daniel de Wilde lay face-
down in a rock-pool, ignored by everyone.

While the non-battle raged, Count Limner tapped Rimmer on the
shoulder and took him aside.

"I have a telephone call booked to von Rundstedt at noon," he said.

"Bully for you. Who was in that bloody truck? He nearly killed us
all." Rimmer glanced back nervously at Rommel.

"I want to know what I can tell von Rundstedt."

"Go to hell."

"That's no answer."

"Tell him I told you to go to hell."

As Rimmer rejoined the Field Marshal he felt the back of his neck
prickle. Suppose the silly bastard had a pistol in his pocket now. Was
he crazy enough to try to satisfy his damned honour right here? Lord
Almighty, why couldn't people behave *reasonably*?

The echoes of the last thunderflash faded and died, and the mock-
invasion was mock-repelled. "There's one other thing you might like
to see before lunch, sir," Rimmer said. "It's a hospital. Not far away."

Rommel nodded. He was looking very thoughtful.

They entered a long white corridor. "Carry on, Schumacher," Rimmer said.

"Well, sir, we turned the first sod in July 1942. No time has been
wasted: night and day, seven days a week, work goes on. . . . To your
left, sir, is the mortuary; beyond that, the fuel store, which leads to
the central heating system. We're aiming for a capacity of five hundred beds."

Rommel grunted.

"I expect you've noticed the comfortable atmosphere, sir," Schumacher said. Several officers breathed deeply and looked around at the
atmosphere. "The entire hospital is air-conditioned. . . ." He blinked
at the sweat in his eyes.

"Yes," Rommel said, and stopped. Everyone stopped.

Schumacher blinked again. "Over there are more wards, dispen-
sary, operating theatre, telephone exchange, and commandant's headquarters."

"Tell me," Rommel said. "Why was it necessary to build this
hospital underground?"

Rimmer shrugged. "It's obviously much safer, sir."

"And a hundred times more expensive."

Schumacher said: "The Fuehrer decided, sir. By putting the hospital underground we don't spoil the natural beauty of the island, which is eventually to be a holiday resort for German workers."

"I knew there had to be a reason."

"It's part of the Strength Through Joy programme, sir."

"I remember it well," Rommel said. He slapped the corridor wall. "Tunnelling this lot out must have taken much strength and given little joy."

"We've excavated fifteen thousand tons of rock so far, sir," Schumacher said. He felt faint and had to lean against the wall for a moment.

Rommel turned, and they all turned.

They emerged into fresh, grey daylight, with a spattering of rain. Schumacher shivered; he was too hot and too cold at the same moment; his uniform felt like tight, wet, rusty armour. He wished desperately that Rommel would commend his work, just say a few words of praise and encouragement, and then go. . . .

"Now, sir," Rimmer said cheerfully. "We've got a spot of lunch laid on at my headquarters. And, of course, we're all hoping you can find time to say a few words."

Rommel saw another loose pebble and sent it skittering down the road. "What about?" he asked.

Rimmer spread his hands. "I leave that to you, sir."

"All right. Here are some observations to consider while you have your meal. First, this island is a strategic disaster, second, it's a military blunder, and third, your presence is a total waste of time. Fourth, fifth, and sixth I expect you to work out for yourselves."

Schumacher looked as if he had just witnessed a multiple murder. Rimmer's head was thrust forward, staring, like a handsome gargoyle.

"I take it this is some kind of war-game, sir," he said.

"I don't play games," Rommel told him.

Rimmer nodded a couple of times. "I see," he murmured.

"Do you?" said Rommel. "Good. That didn't take long."

Rimmer lurched as Schumacher grabbed at his arm and, in a series of jerks, slid to the ground. Schumacher's eyes were bulging and his mouth was blowing bubbles.

"Put him in his underground hospital," Rommel said. "I suppose it deserves one patient."

There was little conversation in the back of the staff car. Rommel had nothing to say, and Rimmer had plenty to think about.

Halfway between the Underground Hospital and his headquarters, Rimmer ordered the driver to stop. He apologized to the Field Marshal, hurried into the guardroom of an army post, and telephoned Captain Paulus. The time was ten minutes to twelve.

"Cancel all the executions," Rimmer told him. "Have you got that? Don't shoot anybody until further orders. And pass the word to Limner's office."

"Yes, sir." Paulus waited. "Has something happened?"

"Yes. No. God knows," Rimmer said. He hung up.

Paulus dropped the telephone as if it were a dirty handkerchief. "The old fool's got cold feet again," he told Zimmerman.

Rimmer hurried back to the car. "Sorry about that, sir," he said. "Just a little local difficulty. Right, driver."

41

Lunch proceeded quietly and cautiously. About twenty officers were seated at a long table, with the Field Marshal and the General facing each other in the middle. After Rommel's remarks nobody knew what to talk about. Conversation flagged, until there was more silence than speech.

Rimmer decided to give a lead.

"The prospects for our new secret weapon seem good, don't they, sir?" he said. "I mean the flying bomb, of course."

Rommel finished chewing his food, swallowed unhurriedly, and picked his teeth with his tongue. "Everyone seems to think it'll win the war for us," he said. He drank a little water. "How big a bomb-load do you suppose a pilotless plane could carry?"

They all looked at the sole Luftwaffe officer present. "At least one ton," the man said.

"What is the bomb-load of an American Flying Fortress?" Rommel asked.

"Three tons, sir."

"Nine out of ten Flying Fortresses survive each mission. How many flying bombs can be used twice?"

"That's true, sir, but surely nearly all of them will get through.

Isn't there a good chance we'll devastate London?"

Rommel forked a small potato. "How many flying bombs would that take?" He chewed the potato while the Luftwaffe officer thought hard. "Fifty thousand?" Rommel suggested.

"Give or take a few, yes, sir."

Rommel nodded, and there was a stir of interest. He finished his potato. "The enemy bombers have already dropped fifty thousand tons of bombs on Berlin," he said. "Have they won the war?"

The interest turned to gloom. General Rimmer grew impatient: if Rommel was driving at something, let him get on and say it. "I'm sure we'd all be interested to know what you expect the next phase of the war to be, sir," he said briskly.

Rommel cut up his cold ham. "The enemy will try to invade. If we don't immediately repel them, we shall lose."

"Personally I have no doubt that we shall repel them," Rimmer said.

"You won't," Rommel told him flatly. "They're not coming here."

Rimmer tried to smile. "Sir, the Fuehrer himself—"

"The enemy is not coming here, General. Why do you think he abandoned these islands in 1940 without a shot being fired? This place is militarily useless. It's also economically wasteful and strategically about as much value as the hole in your backside."

Rimmer's food had stopped going down. "Sir, I cannot believe—" he began.

"Look here," Rommel said, and he leaned forward to make Rimmer look at him. "Do you believe that the enemy will be so stupid as to attack these islands simply because we have been so stupid as to defend them?"

"No, sir," Rimmer muttered huskily.

"And can you tell me any other reason why they should come here?"

Rimmer unfolded a handkerchief and mopped his face and neck. Rommel ate some ham. Nobody else was eating.

"Neither can they," he said. "As I told you before, this place is a blunder and you are all a waste. I intend to shift every fighting man and every weapon out of here and put them where they can do some harm."

"And where exactly is that, sir?" Rimmer asked.

"Normandy," Rommel said.

The luncheon table had been cleared. Rommel sat on it, leaning over a mass of charts and maps. Rimmer and a secretary stood nearby. From time to time aides hurried in with more documents. Rommel was in his shirt-sleeves and he was finishing a ham sandwich made from the remains of his lunch.

"Guns, guns, guns," he said. "I've lost the damn gun-map again."

Rimmer saw it and tugged it out. Rommel's blunt fingers thudded against the starred artillery positions. "I want these, and these, and these. . . . All those. . . . This lot. And this. I don't suppose you can shift those battleship guns?"

"For God's sake, sir. It took a year and a half to install them." Rimmer felt like a bankrupt, watching the receiver strip his home.

"Well, I'll take all your eighty-eight-millimetre flak batteries, anyway. I need them for tank-destroyers. D'you know how many heavy guns I have on the Cherbourg coast? One battery! *One!* Now then . . . What's this?"

"Just a chart, sir. . . ." Rimmer tried to take it but Rommel tightened his grip.

"Reinforced concrete. Does that really represent half a million cubic metres?"

"Slightly less, sir."

Rommel slowly doubled the chart until the cardboard cracked, and fanned himself with it. "Half a million cubic metres. . . . And over there, four out of five infantry strongpoints aren't even bombproof. Why? Because they couldn't get the cement and the steel." He threw the ruined chart across the room. "How much cement and steel can you give me?"

"There's a thousand tons of cement down at the docks," Rimmer said bleakly. "They've just finished unloading."

"Start them reloading. Steel?"

Rimmer spread his fingers and examined his empty hands. "You might as well take the armour-plating from the gun emplacements, sir, don't you think?"

"Certainly. And I want your mines, all of them." Rommel unrolled a map of the mine-fields. "Looks like about a hundred thousand."

"One hundred and fourteen thousand, I understand."

"Dig 'em up and send 'em over." Rommel slid off the table. "You get the idea. Keep a few men to do the work and ship the rest to Normandy, fast, today, tomorrow, this week."

"I shall need a new title, sir," Rimmer said. He was tasting the gall of disgrace without even having had the opportunity of failure. "I can scarcely go on calling myself 'Fortress Commandant.'"

"Well, that's no great loss, is it?" Rommel put on his tunic. "Who wants to live in a fortress anyway? Don't worry, I have plans for you, too." He checked his watch. "You've got five minutes to give orders and boot backsides, then we're off to the airfield. There's a divisional commanders' conference in Britanny, tonight. That's for you."

"And for you, sir?"

Rommel shook his head. "I'm flying to Berchtesgaden to see The Man. He's still convinced Eisenhower's going to take the short route. If I change his mind we can still . . ." He shrugged.

They both looked out of the window. It was raining again. "Keep it up, God," Rommel urged.

At the airfield there were ten minutes to spare while the engines were run up. Rimmer decided to telephone the meteorological office in Paris and get the weather picture for the next twenty-four hours.

While he was away, Major Wolff came up to Rommel and saluted. "Hello, sir," he said.

"D'you know, I *thought* I recognized you," Rommel said. "It's Max Wolff, isn't it? You've changed a lot. Didn't I hear that you'd gone mad?"

"Only part time, sir."

"Well, you always were a bit dotty, weren't you? I seem to remember the Ardennes in 1940: you got left behind by your Panzer column for some dotty reason—"

"I went for a pee," Wolff said.

"Right! And you caught a train instead, a French train, and met the column seventy miles ahead."

"*And* I had lunch on the train," Wolff said proudly. "*Coq au vin* with some nice Brie and a half-bottle of Côte du Rhone, twenty-two francs."

Rommel patted him on the shoulder. "You're wasted here. Maybe I can get you posted to my staff. How dotty are you really?"

Wolff rocked his head from side to side. "It comes and goes, sir. Loud noises set me off. Actually, I'm a bit mad today, I think."

"Not as mad as some. D'you know where von Rundstedt keeps the armoured divisions? Deep inland. We'll never get them up to the coast in time. The bridges are down and the railways are smashed to pieces.

You can plot the damage on a map and see where it points: Normandy. If I could just get one armoured division into that area. . . ."

"I don't care, you know," Wolff said. "It sounds terrible, but I
really don't care."

"Well, I can understand that," said Rommel.

"I mean, we're not going to win, are we, sir? We can't beat Russia
and the British Empire *and* the United States of America, can we?"

Rommel put his hands on his hips and exercised his back-muscles.
"One man thinks we can," he said.

"He's such a bad loser, that's his trouble," Wolff remarked. "He's
never forgiven his grandmother for getting knocked up by a Jew. . . .
Frankly, sir, I wonder why you go on, but then I'm a bit mad."

"I'll tell you why," Rommel said. "If by some miracle we beat off
this invasion they won't try again this year, and then anything's
possible. It might even allow time for some kind of political settle-
ment. I don't know."

General Rimmer joined them. "No change," he said. "Storm conditions expected to continue tomorrow. What on earth are you doing
here, Wolff?"

"Came to see Colonel Schumacher, sir."

"Schumacher's in hospital, you fool."

"I know, sir, but I don't like hospitals."

On the way to the aircraft, Rimmer said, "It's not his fault, you
know. I'm told he had a rough time at Stalingrad."

"More than rough," Rommel said. "The Russians were on the
point of overrunning the unit on his flank, so poor old Wolff had to
call down artillery fire on friend and foe alike."

"Yes, I've heard of that sort of predicament, sir," Rimmer said.
"Did he save the position?"

"Oh yes, the barrage did the trick. It also blew Wolff's younger
brother to bits. He happened to be serving with that unit."

"Good heavens. One of those freaks of coincidence."

"That's one way of looking at it." Rommel went up the aircraft
steps. "Understandably, Wolff took it rather more personally."

TUESDAY AND AFTER

42

The German meteorologists in Paris were wrong. The rain and wind that buffeted Rommel's aircraft marked the end of the storm. Out in the Atlantic a patch of calm weather was moving towards the English Channel. It arrived during the night, when the invasion fleet had already sailed.

The first troops waded up the Normandy beaches just before dawn. It was Tuesday, the sixth of June 1944. Rommel was asleep at Berchtesgaden, seven hundred miles away. During a long and exhausting conference he had almost convinced Hitler that the landings would be in Normandy and not at Calais; but Hitler had refused to release any of the troops massed at Calais or to move the armoured divisions closer to the Normandy coast. The idea of strengthening one general at the expense of the others always disturbed Hitler. He preferred to see power dispersed. It made him feel safer.

General Rimmer was asleep in Rennes, seventy-five flying miles from Jersey and at least a hundred miles by road from the scene of the invasion. He was awakened at four-thirty and went straight into a conference with the other commanders. Reports were confused and sometimes contradictory, and the conference broke up after five minutes; everybody wanted to get back where he belonged. There was no news at all from the Channel Islands.

Rimmer took the first car he saw and drove to the airfield. There was only one aircraft left, and it was burning. A flight of rocket-firing Typhoons jumped out of nowhere, strafed the field six ways at once, and vanished. Rimmer climbed out of a trench to find his car on its back.

He took another car and headed north for St. Malo. It was the nearest port, only fifty miles away. Two hours later St. Malo was still forty miles away. On every road, bridges were down or blocked. Rimmer made detour after detour. He got lost in straggling lanes which ended in farmyards. He almost ran out of petrol, reached a garage, went inside to get some food while they filled his tank, and came out to find all his tires flat. He ran back inside, pistol in hand, but the garage was deserted. It took him twenty minutes to pump up the tires.

Three miles north of the garage he took a sharp bend and hit a large tree which had been felled across the road. The front axle was smashed and he broke his nose on the steering wheel. Dripping blood, he walked back to a crossroads and got a lift with a column of armoured personnel-carriers, heading for Normandy. Rimmer abandoned St. Malo. A five-hour sea journey was too long, anyway.

By midafternoon half the column had been destroyed by air strikes and Rimmer's breeches stank from the mud of many different ditches. They reached St. Lô, forty miles from the coast, and found it full of smoke and casualties. Rimmer went to 7th Army HQ. Nobody knew what was happening in the Channel Islands. No aircraft were available. What was the situation at the Front? "Go outside and listen, sir," said an intelligence officer. "Then you'll be more up-to-date than we are."

Rimmer went outside and took a motorcycle. From the northwest to the northeast, gunfire rumbled and the sky was stained with smoke. He kicked the machine into life and aimed for Carteret, a small port only twenty miles from Jersey, or failing that, Cherbourg, where he might even get a seaplane.

The farther north he went, the worse conditions became. Almost every bridge was blown, and he was often forced to ride through fields in order to get around burning vehicles. The repeated detours pushed him off-course. At five-thirty he rode into the town of Carentan, already half in ruins, and heard the stutter of machine-gun fire.

By now Rimmer was very tired. His eyes hurt from the cold rush of air and his backside was stiff and bruised; his nose ached and he couldn't breathe through it. He turned the motorcycle around and headed out of town.

Two miles into the countryside he was stopped by a roadblock. A dozen infantrymen were dug in but there was no firing.

"American paratroops, sir," the lieutenant said. "About a hundred yards ahead."

Rimmer took his field-glasses. He saw no sign of the enemy. "How long have they been there?" he asked.

"All day, sir. I'm waiting for dark so we can get closer."

Rimmer borrowed a submachine-gun and sprayed the enemy area. There was no response. "Ten to one they're out of ammunition," he said.

"I don't think so, sir."

"I'll do the thinking from now on, son. Come on, we'll outflank the bastards."

Rimmer divided the unit in half and sent each half wide to the flanks. He led the attack himself and proved that the paratroops were not out of ammunition. Their first burst of fire put six bullets through his chest and killed five other men. The lieutenant was shot in the leg but he was able to call off the attack while there were still enough survivors to carry him to safety.

On the morning after D-day, Admiral Blamberg flew into Jersey as Rimmer's successor.

His first act was to assemble all senior officers and tell them that, whatever might happen on the mainland, this particular fortress of the Reich would hold out to the last man and the last bullet. If necessary, he said, they would hold out till doomsday. The troops' rations were far too high and must be cut immediately. The civilians had been having a comfortable time; that too must stop.

His second act was to send for Count Limner and the new Bailiff, Dr. Beatty. Again he emphasized his unshakable determination never to give in, and he assured them that the slightest opposition would be treated as sabotage and instantly suppressed.

His third act was to issue an Order of the Day. It read:

I have only one aim: to hold out until final victory. I believe in the mission of our Fuehrer and of our people. I shall serve them with immutable loyalty. Heil our beloved Fuehrer.

"That's charming," Beatty remarked when he read it.

"He's actually worse than Rimmer," Labuschagne said. "Rimmer was a thug but at least he was a fairly intelligent thug. This chap's merely a fanatic."

There was a gloomy silence.

"So Dan was right after all," Beatty sighed. "The war's gone and passed us by. It looks as if I might be Bailiff for quite a time yet. It's an impossible job, you know; I've found that out already." He waved a weary arm at the rest of the island. "If you do nothing, you've given up; if you do something, you must be collaborating. You'd be amazed how distant some of my friends have suddenly become. I wish to goodness I knew how Dan made such a go of it. I really do."

Labuschagne cocked his head as the gentle rumble of gunfire reached them. "Every time I hear that sound, I realize it means some poor devil is getting blown to Kingdom Come," he said. "We all wanted it here, didn't we? We wanted a Glorious Liberation, with Allied paratroops and tanks and dead Germans everywhere. God Almighty, what an awful shambles that would have been!"

"That reminds me," Beatty said. "Has our American friend said anything yet?"

"Nothing. Not a word. He's been totally silent ever since he gave himself up."

Earl Kramer was locked in the vaults beneath Labuschagne's bank. He had walked to St. Helier, walked into Labuschagne's office, and shut the door behind him. He shook his head to all questions and he gave no explanations. He simply listened carefully to everything that was said, and gave it a lot of thought. Or he gave something a lot of thought. Labuschagne, watching the American's face, realized that he looked five years older.

Beatty had come and examined Kramer. There was a deep cut on the side of his head which took two stitches, and a lot of bruising and abrasions on his hips and shoulders. He took the doctor's treatment stoically, almost absently, and put on his clothes again. When Beatty questioned him he listened and thought and said nothing. It was not that he ignored the questions; on the contrary he paid courteous attention to them, and the mental effort which they produced was obvious from his tense, slightly frowning expression. When Beatty got tired of waiting for an answer and asked something different, Kramer blinked and straightened as if he were still working on the previous question. Finally Beatty grew impatient.

"You know that Dan is dead, of course," he said.

Kramer stood absolutely still. His arms were folded and his eyes were focused on a point just above and behind Beatty's head.

"You know how it happened," Beatty declared. "How did it happen?"

Kramer stood there for a full minute, his head nodding slightly, the crease on his smooth, clean brow tightening as his brain got to work. The two men watched and waited, and again Labuschagne recognized the hard imprint of adulthood on Kramer's face; yet some of the buoyancy of youth was still there too. He was trying; he really wanted to explain; but first he had to understand. He had to make it all add up to something. He looked at his hands. The barbed-wire scratches were beginning to heal.

"What's the matter?" Beatty asked sharply.

Kramer looked at him, and as the silence lengthened the question seemed to expand and inflate until it involved the whole island, all Europe, America, everywhere: not just what was the matter with Kramer but what was the matter with a world at war? Kramer's silence became a form of answer. It reflected attention back to the question, and understanding the question came before finding the answer.

"All right," Beatty said. "I mean it's not all right, it's all bloody wrong." Kramer chewed his lip and nodded, and said nothing.

Since Rommel's visit, Michael and Maria Limner had not exchanged more than a dozen words. They took their meals separately and slept separately. He had plenty of work to occupy him, but she was very bored. The weather was too bad for riding, and in any case riding would have suggested a normal way of life. Maria Limner didn't feel normal. She felt like a shop-girl who has confessed to stealing from the till and is waiting for the sack.

She knew that Michael would never talk about Rimmer. That was part of the trouble: Michael couldn't understand how she could give herself to a man like that, a Party loyalist, a partisan-hunter, a man who enjoyed listening to *Die Meistersinger* merely because he had been told that Hitler enjoyed listening to it.

What Michael didn't realize was that she hadn't given; she had taken. Why? Maria walked around the apartment and wondered about Karl Rimmer. Really, he had been nothing but a jumped-up peasant: all instinct, no taste. Show him a stained-glass window and he'd put his boot through it. Part of Maria Limner—a growing part —wanted to ride through Europe, bareback and naked except for a pair of Cossack boots, kicking out every stained-glass window she could find. Rimmer had given her a taste of that pleasure, a taste of the pleasure of war. The trouble with the Channel Islands was that they combined the discomfort of war with the boredom of peace. If you're going to have a war, make the most of it. When else will they give out medals for burning cities?

Michael came in at midday.

"You know the executions are off?" he asked.

"They were off yesterday," she said.

"No, they were only postponed. Now they're cancelled for good. Paulus is no fool. He knows the invasion is odds-on to succeed; damn it all, they're fifteen miles inland already. He doesn't want to be hanged for atrocities when all this is over, especially now that—" Limner was about to say *Now that Rimmer isn't alive to take responsibility*. He poured himself a drink instead.

"I'm surprised Admiral Blamberg agreed," Maria said. She wanted a drink but she wasn't going to ask for one.

"Oh, Helldorf and I cooked up a story that satisfied him," Michael said. "All the trouble was caused by fugitive Russian slave-labourers: they killed the sentry, and so on. For all we know we may be right, or partly right. Helldorf found some evidence." Limner finished his drink. "Poor old Dum-Dum."

Maria felt slightly ill. "What about Dum-Dum?" she asked.

"Helldorf found a cave in the cliffs on the north shore," Limner said. "It was obviously a hide-out. He waited inside and nearly caught a couple of slave-labourers, but they ran like the devil and went straight into a mine-field, so that was the end of them."

"And where was the dog?" she asked.

"Its head was in the back of the cave. Helldorf showed it to Blamberg on a plate, literally on a plate. That's what convinced him. So, no shootings."

Maria went to a window. The weather was quiet but grey. "Poor Dum-Dum," she said.

"I don't give a damn about Dum-Dum," Limner said. "But I still find it very hard to believe that Daniel de Wilde is dead. That hurts. It really hurts."

She turned and looked at him, and he looked at her. She wanted to ask, *Well, what now?* She wanted to be able to apologize, so that he could forgive her. The trouble was, she wasn't sorry for what she had done, only annoyed that it had all gone wrong; and he could never forgive her.

"Well, I have to get back to work," he said.

Major Wolff visited Colonel Schumacher in the Underground Hospital. He found him lying naked on a rubber sheet, packed in bags of ice. His body was coated with a shiny film of sweat, diluted with blood.

"Hullo, Schumacher," he said. "How are you?"

"Awful."

"Yes, you look awful. Like veal. I'm not fond of veal, it reminds me of those children in the Ukraine. Look, I've brought you your slide-rule."

Schumacher took it in his slippery hands. "Why? Why have you brought this?"

"Oh, Beth said you'd want it. Beth says you sleep with it under your pillow. She sends her love, by the way. No she doesn't: she sends her best wishes."

"Every time they bring the fever down, the bleeding starts up again," Schumacher complained. "Every time they stop the bleeding, the fever comes back. It's really awful."

Wolff looked at the temperature chart. "Just like the Tyrol," he said. "You wouldn't get me up there. Frankly, I don't know what you see in it, Schumacher. Is it the view, or what?"

Schumacher's eyes were slightly crossed. He was breathing shallowly, and he held the slide-rule to his breast like a crucifix. "Rommel saw it all, anyway, didn't he?" he said. "D'you think he might tell the Fuehrer? All I really need is six thousand tons of cement. . . . "

"Don't give it another thought, old chap," Wolff said.

Schumacher raised his head and uncrossed his eyes. "You mean it's coming?" he asked. "You mean I've got it?"

"I mean it's gone," Wolff announced. "I mean you've had it."

Schumacher stared. "What . . . " he began. "How . . . "

"Eisenhower sent a postcard. He says he's not coming here this year, he's taking his holidays in Normandy instead." Wolff took an ice-cube from one of the bags and sucked it. "If you want my opinion, Schumacher, this place simply isn't fashionable any more."

Schumacher let his head fall back. He looked at the ceiling, blankly. "Then what have I been doing here all this time?" he whispered. "Where's the point in it all?"

"Don't ask me," Wolff said. "General Zeitzler had it last, and you know what he's like for losing things."

"It can't all be for nothing," Schumacher said. "It's just not possible. It can't all be a waste. Can it?"

"He lost Stalingrad, after all." Wolff spread his hands. "Great big place like that. I said to him: 'You must have put it down somewhere.' He didn't like that, I can tell you."

"I might as well die," Schumacher whispered.

"They don't like the truth," Wolff said, his cheek bulging with ice-cube. "It doesn't suit their game."

The *Hyacinth* came past the headland and headed north-west, away from the island. It was a dull, misty afternoon and the soldier sitting amidships felt deeply unhappy. The news of the Normandy landings had depressed everyone; then this idiot Blamberg arrives and cuts the rations; and to cap it all, guard-duty on this stinking, rolling old tub.

He saw the patch of broken water ahead. He felt ill already. "Not good," he told one of the fishermen. "Bad water!"

"Ah, but wait till you see the fish," the man assured him. "Admiral Blamberg is going to love you. *Gross Fisch! Beaucoup de gross Fisch!*"

The *Hyacinth* started her jerky lurch and slither, jolting and sliding, slapping and butting. The soldier felt his stomach rebel and didn't try to fight it. He lay with his head over the side and let his body punish him. He could hear the fishermen whistling. He closed his eyes and tried to close his ears.

The fisherman on the tiller kicked aside a tarpaulin. Earl Kramer stood up and hung on to the side. He saw the body of the soldier, limp except for its convulsing back, and he swallowed uneasily. The fisherman nudged him. Together they lifted a yellow rubber dinghy and carefully lowered it into the water. The fisherman hung on to the rope handles while Kramer climbed in; then he gave the dinghy a powerful shove.

The chop sent the dinghy turning and bouncing. Kramer sat in the middle like a passenger on a fairground ride. Every few seconds he caught a glimpse of the *Hyacinth,* and each time it was farther away. Blurred and featureless to the south he saw the Island of Jersey.

Eventually he drifted clear of the broken water. A steady breeze was blowing up the Channel, carrying him towards the crowded sea-lanes off Normandy. Jersey faded and lost itself in the hazy horizon.

Mary Betteridge took the new towels which Major Schwarz had sent her, tore them into narrow strips, and—singing to herself all the while—knotted the strips into a rope. She was trying to hang herself from a hook in the kitchen ceiling when her husband heard the noise and came to see what was happening. He took the towel-rope from her and put her in an armchair while he wondered what in God's name he was going to do now. He was brushing the tears from his eyes when he heard a ripping and snapping of fabric and saw that she was destroying the upholstered arms of her chair, using her torn and bleeding fingernails. Betteridge tied her wrists together, sat her in the cart, and drove her to Canon Renouf's place. Renouf gave them hot sweet tea to drink and made some telephone calls, as a result of which Mary was taken to the mental ward of a nursing home. She refused to eat, and she died there after five weeks. Betteridge buried his wife and went back to his farm. Apart from Mary, it was all he knew. And people needed food.

Uncle Dudley, on the other hand, recovered. He was weak and his memory was worse than ever, but there was no brain damage and his body worked well enough. However, he needed constant nursing, and as soon as he could be moved he was put in hospital. "Got hit by a cricket-ball," he told the man in the next bed. "I was just going to hook the blighter for six, too. You interested in cricket?"

Nancy locked up the house and moved to St. Helier. There was plenty of work for her, and occasionally she was surprised to find that she could not remember at all clearly what Martin Lang had looked like. But at other times he was as real, and as tormentingly unattainable, as the sun; and when that happened his absence became a greater presence than that of any living thing. Then she felt the torment of grief, and she withdrew from the less real world so that she could be alone with her wonderful, smiling, cruel ghost.

Field Marshal Erwin Rommel was seriously injured when his car was strafed by Allied aircraft on 17 July 1944. He was involved in the unsuccessful bomb plot against Hitler on 20 July, and to protect his family he committed suicide on 14 October 1944.

Jersey was peacefully liberated on VE-day, 8 May 1945, without having taken any active part in the war at all.